stitches & snake oil

A Cozy Fantasy

Tales from the Broken Claw
Book Six

don jones

donjones.com

contents

Urwald
Darkename
Darkestore Forrest
North Pointe Common Towne
Gray Foal Pass
The Mistral Mountains
Strongfast
Lake Evendim
Celestrum
Elyndam
Smallhaven
Scintas
Demonbane Range
Westhold
Lake Midton
Holderdown
Skyrean Reige
Stormport
Magefell
Kithwellen
Lake Trenton
Salten Sea
Flameheight Range
Trenton
The Mountedives
Dunereach
Shorehaven
Highseas
Farreach
The Forbidden Continent
Bright Islands
Amber Sea
N

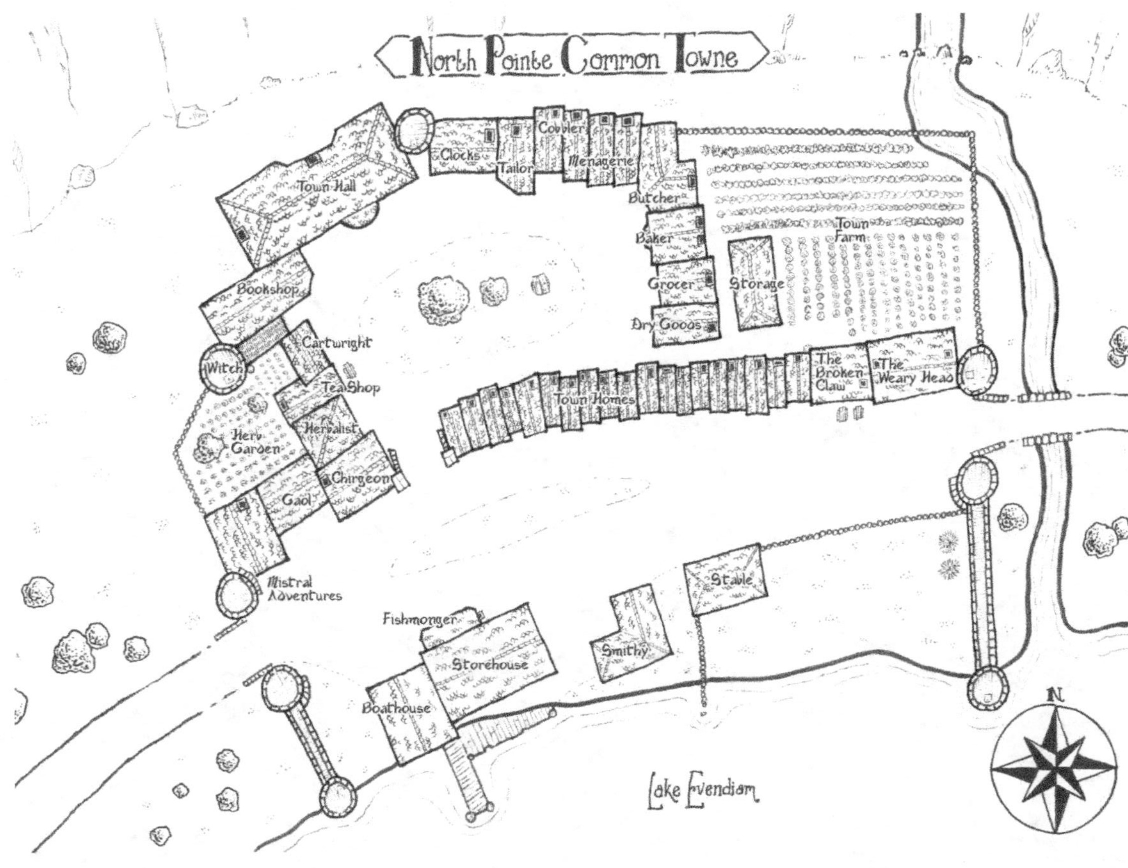

North Pointe Common Towne
Witch
Herb Garden
Gaol
Herbalist
Chirgeon
Tea Shop
Cartwright
Bookshop
Town Hall
Mistral Adventures
Boathouse
Fishmonger
Storehouse
Smithy
Stable
Lake Evendiam
Clocks
Tailor
Cobbler
Menagerie
Butcher
Baker
Grocer
Dry Goods
Town Homes
Storage
Town Farm
The Broken Claw
The Weary Head
N

one

. . .

DAWN ARRIVED as a smudge of milky blue along the attic beams, and nothing more. The room's chill announced it long before the light. Prudence Simonsdotter lay for a count of ten after waking, as was her habit, listening for the world to remind her of its own existence. Today, she caught the faintest hoot from the watch-owl that roosted behind the bakery, then the persistent tickle of north wind at the seams of the window. The bed beside her own was silent, but for the delicate scratch of a child's exhalation.

She propped herself on her elbow and surveyed the room. Its dimensions were not generous, yet she kept the space rigidly divided: the far wall with its tiny hearth, the rug and two beds, the chipped basin on its stand. Everything stood as she had arranged it the previous evening, down to the neatness of the folded blanket at the foot of Bryant's bed.

Bryant himself slept in the shape of a question mark, knees tucked against his chest, fists under his cheek. Four years old, yet by all logic of the outside world, he should have grown at least a sennight for each one spent in North Pointe. Prudence had seen it herself, the way time oozed and congealed in this town, slowing some, speeding others to their end. But Bryant had remained as he was since the day she arrived: flaxen-haired, sallow-cheeked, still round in the joints like bread dough not yet risen. She allowed herself a minute—no more—to watch him, to press the sight of his smallness into memory, and to give thanks that, here at least, children could linger.

She slid from bed and braced for the icy floorboards. The first motion of her day was always to light the timekeeping candle, a squat column marked with hand-drawn lines for each candlemark. The match struck, flame trembling in the half-dark; Prudence shielded it with her palm and touched it to the wick. Pale light splashed across the shelf, the basin, the dress hung from a nail.

Bryant stirred, releasing a sigh. He did not open his eyes.

Prudence padded to the hearth and coaxed yesterday's embers to life with a twist of kindling. She ladled water from the bucket, measured oats, set them to boil. She moved with the economy of one who had been doing everything alone for a long time, who thought of silence as a comfort rather than a want. This was not entirely true—she had grown up in a houseful of voices, women and brothers and the stern oversight of a father—but it suited her, now.

When the porridge began to simmer, she washed her face at the basin, wrung her hands dry on the towel, and retrieved her dress. It was black today, although she sometimes relented and wore the coarse brown one when it was warmer outside. Either way, the cut was severe, and stitched so precisely that the seams ran like rules on a ledger. She stepped into it, buttoning the front from hem to throat, and bound her pale hair beneath the tight cloth cap. She never looked at herself in the sliver of mirror that hung by the door. She had no need to.

Only then did she allow herself to wake Bryant. "Rise, child," she said, voice just above a whisper.

He opened his eyes, blue as glacier melt, and stared back at her. Bryant was not a talker. In his four years he had learned only a handful of words, and even those he parcelled out with miserly care. He rolled onto his back, blinking, and did not sit up.

Prudence knelt by his bed and swept her palm along his hair. "Time for morning." She knew better than to coax or plead, so she simply gathered him, blanket and all, and bore him to the hearth. He tolerated this in silence, snuggling into the blanket's warmth while he watched the flame lick at the bottom of the cookpot.

They ate porridge with a spoon each, Prudence dipping hers into honey before each bite and Bryant following suit, always in imitation. The window held a rectangle of pale, featureless light. She estimated it to be nearly the first bell, and felt a pinch of pride at her accuracy. The tailorshop below would need opening soon, and she preferred to have all evidence of domesticity scrubbed from their quarters before customers began to arrive.

Bryant finished first, then sat with his hands in his lap. He gazed not at his mother but at the dance of steam above his bowl.

"You may play until I finish the dishes," Prudence said. "Softly."

He nodded, and walked on bare feet to the battered box of wooden blocks. Prudence listened to the soft clack and shuffle as she rinsed the bowls, her movements brisk. She wiped the table, dried the dishes, and set them in their places. Each gesture contained a secret tally, a satisfaction in order.

She dried her hands and joined Bryant on the rug. He was assembling towers, the blocks stacked with surprising precision, each layer squared off before the next was added. When the structure toppled, he started again, betraying no frustration. He never reached for her; instead, when he wished for company, he sat as close to her skirt as possible without touching it.

After a few minutes, Prudence checked the candle and noted that nearly a full mark had burned away. She packed the blocks away and helped Bryant into his day-clothes: a smock of undyed linen, patched at both elbows, with woolen trousers beneath. His feet were always cold, but he refused shoes unless forced. She applied a dab of balm to his lips, which chapped easily, and let him squirm away while she donned her own apron and rolled down her sleeves. There was a comfort in these rituals, but also a discipline, as if strict adherence to form might prevent the day from mutating into something dangerous or unknown.

At last, she stood by the narrow staircase that led down to the shop. Bryant stood beside her, hands at his sides, alert. She placed her hand on his head, briefly, then opened the door and started down. Bryant followed, quiet as breath.

For all her strictness, Prudence felt something loosen in her chest every time she descended those stairs and found that the world below had not fallen to ruin in the time since she last saw it. For today, at least, she and Bryant were as safe as anyone could be.

———

The fourth bell struck just as Prudence drew back the bolt on the door. The sound carried through the cold morning in a slow, even toll— never a peal, never an invitation, but rather a warning that the town and its shopkeepers should now, if they pleased, make themselves available to the world.

She lifted Bryant in one arm and carried him down the steep stairs, feeling the familiar pull in her shoulder, the ache that never entirely left. The landing was unheated; her breath bloomed in faint puffs. She set Bryant down at the foot of the steps and watched as he padded, blanket and all, to his designated place by the window. There, she had arranged a square of old quilt for him, with a battered tin of colored chalks and the wooden blocks. He took his seat without a word.

Prudence made her first round of the shop, as she did every morning. She opened the inner shutters, one by one, and let in the uncertain light. The interior remained mostly dim; no matter how many candles she burned, no matter how much sunlight struck the glass, the air inside seemed to cling to a muted sort of twilight, heavy with the smell of lanolin and old paper.

The shop was, in some ways, a madness. She had inherited it, after a fashion. There had been a tailor before her, but from the tales told by her fellow townsfolk, he had kept a very different business than her— one cluttered and cozy and chaotic and exciting. When she'd arrived, everything had been neat as a pin the moment she opened the door. Still, she had never gotten used to its proportions, or to the sheer excess of its contents. Shelves lined every wall, stacked with fabrics that no market in the world should have been able to provide. Chests and boxes overflowed with laces, ribbons, and buttons of all imaginable kinds. The bolts of cloth alone—arrayed in rows along the back wall—seemed the bounty of a dozen vanished cities: silks as red as arterial blood, as blue as the sky above the southern sea, green damasks patterned with gold-leafed vines and black brocades shot through with threads that caught and toyed with the light. Here and there, a pattern in peacock feather or lion's mane, or a delicate embroidery so fine it looked painted. On first entering, a customer might imagine she had stumbled into a kind of treasure vault, or a sorcerer's library, and some were bold enough to say so.

Prudence permitted herself a moment to admire the arrangement before she began the day's work. She did not allow herself to use any of the finer fabrics, unless expressly commissioned and paid in advance; she had learned, through the currency of hard experience, that gaudy things brought only trouble. It was enough for her to take pride in her discipline: her own garments, and those she made for Bryant, were fashioned solely from the most sober of wools and linens, dyed in earth tones, cut for utility and modesty. Color, here, was a forbidden fruit.

She unshuttered the front window and dusted the sill, then set about preparing her tools. The worktable occupied the middle of the floor, a broad plank polished by decades of labor. She laid out her best shears—scissors with the weight and sharpness of a surgeon's blade— then her pin cushion, her basket of threads, her brass-rimmed tape measure. Each was placed with care, each with a purpose.

Bryant watched her, silent as ever. He had stacked his blocks into a tiny wall and was now demolishing it methodically, one piece at a time. Prudence felt his gaze like the warmth of a hand on her sleeve; she smiled, very slightly, and gave him a nod of approval.

Next came the ritual of selecting the fabric for the day's work. She approached the shelves and ran her fingers along the bolts, feeling their textures: the raw itch of hemp, the softness of washed cotton, the slub and resistance of tweed. Each one called up a memory—a customer, a purpose, a story—and some, more rarely, a longing.

Today's first order was a traveler's cloak, commissioned by a widow from two towns to the east on the road. The note she had left was precise: "Brown, nothing fancy, to fit a woman of broad shoulder, lined for warmth, pockets large enough for bread and cheese." Prudence reached for the brown wool, but before she could grasp it her hand drifted—against her will, it seemed—to a bolt of emerald green. The color was so vibrant it almost hummed. She allowed her fingers to rest upon it for a heartbeat, then another. She could picture it made up into a cloak, lined in grey, perhaps a trim in black velvet at the hood. It would be beautiful, and it would not last.

She closed her eyes, withdrew her hand, and reached for the brown. It was coarse, practical, and wholly without appeal. She measured out the required length, cut it cleanly, and set it on the table.

For a moment, she stood with her hands braced on the edge of the table, breathing slowly. The urge to create something lovely had always been a temptation, and always, she had denied it. Even as a child, she had been made to understand that plainness was a shield; her mother's warnings had not been metaphors, but instructions for survival.

She threaded her needle, knotted the end, and began the work. The rhythm of her stitching was calming, each pass of the needle a reassurance. She worked quickly, and with a precision that bordered on mechanical. Once the first hem was finished, she pressed it flat with her iron, then began to shape the cloak.

A customer's shadow passed the front window, paused, and continued. Prudence glanced at Bryant. He looked up at her, blue eyes unblinking, and she nodded again. "Good," she said, very softly, unsure whether she meant it for him or herself.

She worked until the fifth bell, by which time the body of the cloak was nearly complete. She pressed the seams once more and hung the piece on a form by the window. It looked shapeless and dull, exactly as the note had requested.

There would be others, she knew—orders that begged for color, for texture, for the transformation of body and spirit that only fine clothing could give. She wondered, not for the first time, whether she would one day give in to the longing and pay the price. But for today, at least, she had done what was required.

She cleaned the table, swept the trimmings into her palm, and dropped them in the fire. Then she wiped her hands, retied her apron, and turned to see Bryant, who had built a perfect square from his blocks, then set a blue chalk at its center. He looked up at her, and in that moment she decided that plainness, while a poor shield, was sometimes a blessing.

The sixth bell would bring the day's first customer, and Prudence was ready for them.

———

That bell had barely died away when the day's first customer arrived. He opened the door with more force than strictly necessary, setting the little bell above it rattling in its bracket. Prudence looked up from her table and took in the shape of him: a traveler, that much was obvious, with boots caked in the mud of three or four counties, and a cloak so rent across the back that the lining hung out like a tongue.

He glanced about, not just at the goods but at the air itself, as if seeking a sign that he belonged. His hair was untrimmed, beard uneven, eyes as alert and wary as a fox's. He paused by the threshold, one hand pressed to the tear in his cloak, and waited for her to speak.

"Welcome," Prudence said. She inclined her head, neither warm nor cold, and gestured with her scissors to the rack of completed garments by the door.

The man nodded, and stepped inside. The scent of outdoors—smoke, river, sweat—clung to him. He moved as though he half-expected the floor to betray him, or for something to leap out from behind the piles of fabric. He ran a hand along the brown cloak on the form by the window, then frowned at his own in comparison.

"I need it mended," he said, holding the damaged section out to her as if she might be able to fix it by glance alone.

Prudence stood, wiped her hands on her apron, and examined the cloak. She ran her finger along the tear, noted the quality of the cloth (poor, but not hopeless), and the filth worked into the hem. She caught the man's gaze, and he gave a sheepish smile.

"I slept in the ditch last night," he explained. "Long story."

"All stories are long," she said, and took the cloak from him. "Is there a name for the order?"

He hesitated, shifting on his feet. "Only if it must be. I'm not local."

"No-one is, and no matter." She set the cloak on the table and reached for her repair kit. "Price is two coppers, three if you want it before the tenth bell."

He whistled, low, then shrugged. "Sooner is better. I have to meet someone upcountry by nightfall."

"Very well." She gestured to the bench by the stove, but the man remained standing, hands buried in his pockets.

The silence pressed in, thick and unyielding. Prudence threaded her needle and began the mend, each pass of the needle swift and sure. She took care to match the tension of the original stitching, to reinforce the fabric without making the repair visible from the front. Her hands worked faster than her mind; within minutes she had closed the wound, anchored the ends, and trimmed the thread. She held the cloak up to the light, inspected her work, and nodded once.

The man watched with open curiosity. After a minute, he ventured, "Don't see many tailors work so quiet. Not even a song?"

Prudence shook her head. "Singing is not required."

He chuckled, though it sounded nervous. "Where I'm from, shops are… louder. Even the cobbler never shuts up. Here, it's like walking into a church." He laughed again, louder this time, but the sound evaporated as soon as he met her eyes.

She handed him the cloak. "Try it. Make sure the fit is right."

He slipped it on. The repair, though invisible to most, must have made itself felt, for his posture straightened and his smile widened. He flexed his shoulders, testing the seam.

"Good as new," he pronounced, and paid her three coppers without argument.

Prudence counted the coins, dropped them into the tin, and jotted a quick note in her ledger. There was no need; the townsfolk charged each either for neither goods nor services, and everyone's income was pooled toward those expenses for which they could not themselves provide. But habits died hard, and her father's unyielding exactitude with the family ledger was never out of mind.

The man hovered, uncertain.

"You have need of anything else?" she prompted.

He glanced around the shop, eyes lingering on a bolt of deep blue. "What's that one called?" he asked, pointing.

"Indigo suiting. Not for sale. Custom orders only."

He nodded, scratched his chin. "Someday, maybe. When I'm less likely to get it ruined." He looked at Bryant, who had not moved from his post by the window, and then back to Prudence. "You run this place yourself?"

"I do," she said.

He seemed about to ask something further, then thought better of it. "Thank you," he said, with unexpected sincerity, and left, the bell clattering behind him.

Prudence stood a moment, collecting her thoughts. She hung the repair kit back on its hook, swept the trimmings into her palm, and added them to the small fire under the stove. She looked at the next item in her work queue—a set of work clothes, requested by Cole for his own slowly-growing children—and felt a flicker of satisfaction at the day's beginning.

She smoothed her skirt, checked on Bryant (who had begun a new arrangement with his blocks, blue chalk at the center), and resumed her work. The silence of the shop, so oppressive to some, felt to her like the first exhale after morning prayer. There was much to do, and a whole day left to do it.

She threaded her needle, and began again.

two

. . .

THE FIRST LIGHT of the sennight's second day struggled to find a foothold inside the tailor's shop, and Prudence preferred it that way. There was enough illumination to work by—thin, cold daylight filtered through the window, supplemented by the uneven burn of a stubby beeswax candle perched at the edge of her worktable—but the shadows absorbed any excess, making the corners seem farther away than they truly were. The hush suited her, as did the routine of labor.

Her hands, ringless and pale, hovered over the spread of brown wool. She was sewing a travel cloak: unadorned, tightly woven, and stitched to outlast any likely owner. This was the most common order she received, aside from mending, and after so many iterations, she knew every seam by heart. The fabric yielded beneath her needle in a way that was deeply satisfying—a soft but distinct give, each pass of the thread drawing the raw edges together, erasing the memory of their original division.

The only sounds were the muted clack of her thimble against the needle, and the low, even breathing of Bryant, who sat cross-legged by the window and moved his wooden blocks in precise, measured incre-ments. He'd already built a rampart and was now arranging small piles of blue chalk within it, as if preparing for a siege. He did not speak, nor did he sing or hum as other children might; he simply existed, quiet and intent, as much a fixture of the shop as any spool of thread or pair of shears.

Prudence worked quickly, not because she felt any urgency, but because it was the rhythm that best soothed her nerves. She had nearly finished the left shoulder when the silence fractured.

"Miracles bottled, destinies found—only here!" The voice rang out from beyond the walls, just outside the shop on the town green, loud enough to carry through stone and wood with ease. It was a voice neither masculine nor feminine, exactly, but pitched to appeal to all at once: honeyed, assured, as if the speaker were accustomed to being obeyed.

The effect on Prudence was immediate and absolute. Her hand jerked, and the needle slipped, drawing a stinging line across the webbing between her thumb and forefinger. A bead of blood welled up, dark against her skin. For a heartbeat she could do nothing but stare, paralyzed by a blend of recognition and dread. The wound itself was trivial, yet she felt herself tipping, like a chair about to fall backward, into memory.

She clamped her hand shut, squeezing out a second drop of blood onto the coarse brown fabric. The stain was small, barely more than a dot, but its presence was intolerable. Prudence laid the garment flat, pressing her palm to the table to steady herself. The wood was cool and unyielding, and she tried to imagine her panic sinking down through her bones, into the table, into the floor.

The voice outside had not finished. "Come see the fates! A future on the tongue, a fortune in your hands!" Laughter—his own, or perhaps conjured from the air—followed.

Prudence's breath came quick, each inhalation loud in her ears. She closed her eyes and counted silently, the way her mother had taught her long ago, when she was still a child who woke up screaming. One, two, three. Her knuckles whitened against the wood. Four, five, six. The needle clattered onto the table, rolling until it hit the lip of the pin cushion and stilled.

She looked at Bryant. He had paused his siege, but was not

watching her. His focus remained on the blocks, as if the world outside was no more real than the woolen battlements he constructed.

She tried to rise from her chair, but her knees refused. Instead, she forced herself to look down at her hands, at the neat crescent of blood, at the trembling fingers that would not be still. It had been six years—six entire years, by any honest calendar—since she last heard that voice. She would have known it among a thousand others. The words were different, but the cadence was the same, and the promises no less empty.

Her thoughts threatened to spiral, so she gripped the edge of the table and willed herself to observe. She watched the trembling recede to a fine, barely perceptible quiver. She saw the little stain darken as it dried, then begin to feather outward into the wool, capillary by capillary.

Outside, the voice paused, as if listening for a response, then resumed: "Only this day! Only this bell!" Another round of laughter, this time punctuated by the clatter of glass vials.

She remembered, then, with sickening clarity, the first time she had heard that voice. The memory came unbidden, as sharp as a knife drawn from cold water. Holderdown, the village of her youth. The marketplace, crowded with women in dark aprons, men in hats pulled low against the sun. She had stood in the dust, newborn Bryant swaddled to her chest, and watched as the stranger set up his stand, unrolling a patchwork of bottles and jars that caught the light in dazzling array.

She remembered the crowd's laughter, the way the voice pulled them closer, the way it turned suspicion into delight. She remembered her own curiosity, a faint echo of hope that perhaps something—anything—could make the ache of absence less constant.

And she remembered what happened next, but she could not allow herself to dwell on it. Not now. Not with Bryant so near, and the town so small.

Her heart pounded, each beat an insult to her sense of control. She reached for the nearest cloth scrap, wrapped it tightly around her hand, and pressed. She knew what she must do, but it required standing, and she was not ready for that. Instead, she counted again, slow and measured, until her pulse fell back to something like normal.

Bryant, sensing perhaps that something was amiss, turned his head and regarded her with solemn blue eyes. He did not speak, but the question was there, suspended in the air between them.

She forced a smile—her lips pulling tight rather than curving—and shook her head, just enough to assure him that all was as it should be. He blinked, then returned to his arrangement of blocks.

The fabric under her hand was still damp, but the bleeding had stopped. She straightened her cap, wiped the table clean with a practiced swipe, and gathered the scattered tools into their tray. She rose, legs stiff, and reached for the wool cloak. The stain, though minuscule, seemed to radiate heat. She folded the garment, set it aside, and made a silent promise to replace the entire panel before the customer's return.

Outside, the voice launched into another appeal. "Free demonstration at the half bell! Taste the future, shape your fate!"

She could hear, beneath the bravado, the measured steps of someone laying out their traps with the precision of a chessmaster. She could also hear, faint and reluctant, the beginnings of a response—shuffled footsteps, the creak of a door, a child's gasp. The townsfolk were gathering, as they always did for the arrival of anything new.

Prudence closed her eyes and let the sound wash over her. She imagined the salesman's wagon: the painted wheels, the weathered wood, the plume of blue smoke from whatever heating device he used to keep his tinctures warm. She pictured the man himself—tall, thin, with a mouth that never seemed to close, and eyes that glinted like fish scales in the sunlight. She tried to recall whether he had worn a hat the last time, and realized, with a twist of discomfort, that she could not.

She pressed her lips together and considered her options. She could close the shop for the morning, claim a sudden illness, and keep Bryant close. She could stay, and hope the day passed without incident. Or she could confront the threat head-on, as her mother would have done, and banish it before it took root.

She did not know which she would choose, but for now, she stood perfectly still, watching the world beyond the window as if it might suddenly dissolve.

Bryant looked up at her, silent and expectant. Prudence nodded, very slightly, and returned to her seat. She threaded the needle, wiped away the last of the blood with a fresh scrap, and began again.

Outside, the voice rolled on, promising everything, and nothing at all.

———

It was Holderdown, the last morning. The autumn light was flat and gray, puddling in the muddy ruts between the church and the row of stone houses. Prudence stood near the threshold of the meetinghouse, Bryant swaddled so tightly he looked more bundle than boy, his breath dampening the fabric against her chest. She wore widow's black, the color that marked her as unfit for celebration, for remarrying, for even the mildest gesture of hope. She could feel the other women's pitying eyes on her, though none met her gaze directly. Their murmurs slipped through the cracks in the church door like smoke.

He came toward her from the far end of the green, boots glossy, coat even glossier. A trail of laughter followed him—his own, mostly, but others too, drawn in by the force of his performance. The wagon behind him was a riot of color: banners, bottles, silks, even the wheels painted in alternating red and yellow. In Holderdown, color was considered suspect, but here it worked as intended, the neighbors' eyes snagging on it, unable to look away.

She watched as he performed for the elders, uncorking bottles and fanning out cards in his fingers. He talked in circles, dazzling them with words that sounded learned but revealed nothing. He offered them a taste of "the cordial," an amber liquid that smelled of cloves and honey, and the menfolk accepted it with theatrical skepticism, then pronounced it warming, a fine thing for the long winter. He drew them in, until they stood around him in a loose circle, their suspicion temporarily replaced by hunger for novelty.

When he approached her, the air changed. His smile sharpened, became a thing of precision rather than excess. "Good morning, madam," he said, bowing at just the right angle to show deference, but not so much as to invite ridicule. "May I have a word?" The villagers pressed in, eager for what would happen next.

Prudence kept her hands on Bryant, as if the child might otherwise float away. She nodded, once.

He held up a blue-glass bottle, shaped like a tear. "I could not help but notice your sorrow," he said, in a voice pitched for sympathy. "Holderdown is a fine community, but sometimes its remedies are—how shall I say—stale. This," he said, swirling the contents, "is a tincture for courage. A drop in the morning, and one in the evening. Not more. I call it 'Resolute.'"

The word hung in the air, gaudy as a street performer's cape.

From behind her, a neighbor's voice: "It wouldn't hurt you to try."

Another: "Nothing else has worked."

A third, softer: "He's a good man. He could do for you."

Prudence felt the old reflexes—the ones drilled into her by years of catechism and maternal oversight—rise to the surface. Don't refuse a kindness. Don't call attention to yourself. Don't let them see you break.

She nodded again, but did not reach for the bottle. "I have no money," she said, truthfully.

He grinned, wider now, but not unfriendly. "A drop for a drop," he said, and leaned in, lowering his voice. "When you're ready, there's a place for you in my wagon. A real place, not just some parlor trick. I know what it's like to be alone among so many friends." He looked at the child, then back at her. "I won't press you. But you should think it over."

He stepped back, letting the offer linger. The onlookers nodded, a ripple of relief passing among them. The strange had been neutralized, the deviant domesticated.

The church bell tolled, and the crowd began to flow toward the meetinghouse, the air filling with the sound of boots on wet earth. The salesman returned to his wagon, where he arranged his bottles into neat rows, each one gleaming in the reluctant daylight.

Prudence entered the church, sitting in the last row. She did not pray. Instead, she counted the marks until it was proper to stand again, to walk home, to tuck Bryant into his cot and boil water for their dinner.

The day passed in ordinary misery: a neighbor brought soup, another left a loaf at her door. At twilight, she ventured outside to fetch water, and saw him again. The salesman had drawn his wagon to the edge of the village, away from prying eyes. He stood on the running board, peering at her with a look that was neither invitation nor threat, but something in between.

That night, she did not sleep. She held Bryant in her lap until he drifted off, then sat awake, watching the slow arc of the moon through the attic window. Every sound—every creak of the house, every gust against the shutters—became a prelude to disaster. She remembered, with a kind of clinical detachment, the way the man's eyes flicked to her child and then back to her, as if assessing a pair of horses before a trade.

She thought of her mother, who had survived three husbands and buried each with more composure than sorrow. She thought of her father, dead of a fever, and how little the village had changed for his absence.

By morning, Prudence had decided. She rose before the bell, packed what she could into a canvas sack, and bound Bryant to her with a length of plain cloth. She left the cottage without closing the door behind her.

The road was dark and empty. No one watched her go.

She walked for a while, until the bottle-bright colors of the salesman's wagon faded from memory, until her legs ached and her throat burned from the cold. When Bryant woke, he did not cry. He pressed his face into her shoulder and went back to sleep.

She did not stop until the sun rose and the roofs of Holderdown disappeared behind a stand of poplar trees.

Only then did Prudence allow herself to breathe.

———

The memory's grip loosened slowly, as if her body needed a full candlemark to believe it was no longer caught in Holderdown's orbit.

She blinked twice, focusing on the now. The low flame of the work-table's candle, the faint hiss of Bryant's breath as he leaned into his towers, the silver thread of pain at her thumb where the needle had bitten her—these small realities led her back.

Prudence set aside her sewing with the reverence of someone handling a broken relic. She pressed the folded cloak flat and aligned her tools in a row, smallest to largest. Only then did she smooth her skirt, straighten the tight black cap over her hair, and walk to the door at the back of the shop. She laid her palm against the wood, feeling the trembling there, and told herself: I am not that girl anymore.

Outside, the town green shone with dew. The grass was wet enough that it soaked her hem as she crossed, but she barely felt it through the layers of petticoat and wool. The morning was still cold, the air sharp in her nose, but it was not Holderdown's chill. The sky here, though gray, was vast and unbounded, and the houses stood farther apart, as if even the architecture had more room to breathe.

She skirted the edge of the green and angled herself toward the east road gate. The green's curve hid her from the bulk of the trade road's traffic, but the sound of the salesman's voice floated easily above the stone walls.

"Step right up, step right in—find your calling! I guarantee satisfaction, or you get double your disappointment back!" He paused for laughter, and to her surprise, a few voices complied.

Prudence stopped short of the gate, hiding herself behind the heavy timber post that marked the division between town proper and the open road. She peered around it, careful not to be seen.

The salesman's wagon was exactly as she remembered: a gaudy beast, its body lacquered and striped, the wheels painted in alternating colors that drew the eye and then refused to let it go. There were banners, but the wind had curled them into snakes, so they writhed in the chill air. The table he'd set up was already lined with bottles and flasks, their contents flashing green, amber, and ruby in the uncertain sun. Beside the table, two folding chairs faced each other like opponents in a contest.

And there he was. Cornelius "Coin-Hand" Scaleswind. He wore a waistcoat so bright it hurt to look at, patterned with a species of check unknown to normal tailors. His top hat was battered but bore a fresh feather, and his mustache—thin and oiled—arched over his upper lip in a perfect tilde. His shoes, so polished they reflected the sky, clicked against the plank whenever he shifted his weight.

He worked the crowd with effortless authority. If he saw her, he gave no sign. Instead, he performed: sweeping up a vial, uncorking it with a flourish, then wafting the aroma toward his intended mark—a young man in a forester's jerkin, who seemed both transfixed and skeptical. The salesman offered a taste on a wooden spoon, and the man took it, then looked surprised at the sweetness.

A second mark, an older woman from the baker's, sidled closer. Scaleswind noticed and slid her a small tin, telling her to "sample at your leisure—no charge!" She laughed, pleased by the attention.

Each movement was calculated, every gesture designed to draw others in. Prudence watched him orchestrate his audience, never losing track of the next potential buyer, never missing a trick.

A third voice called out—this one belonging to the stable hand, whose task was to water the morning's guest horses. "What's in the blue bottle, Coin-Hand?" he shouted.

Scaleswind spun the bottle on his palm and caught it at eye level. "A rare cordial from the Southern Isles—imbues clarity, burns off morning sloth, and provides the fortitude to survive a whole sennight of hard labor." He winked. "I could use some myself, if I hadn't built up an immunity in my travels."

The stable hand laughed, and even the old watchman at the gate snorted with genuine amusement.

Prudence pressed her back to the post, breath slow, heart steady. She had feared that seeing him again would undo her, would turn her into a stammering child who wanted only to vanish. Instead, it produced the opposite: a clarity, sharp and almost welcome, that cut through her usual hesitance.

She did not hate the man, she realized. He was only doing what he had always done—selling lies to people who secretly desired to be deceived. What she hated was her own vulnerability, the knowledge that it would always be easy for someone like him to exploit people like her. Her cheeks burned at the memory of Holderdown's elders nodding, approving, certain they were arranging her salvation. The truth was that she had almost believed it, for a time.

She peeked again. Scaleswind was still at his post, but the crowd had grown. The menagerie owner had come out, as had one of the kits from the bakery, her apron dusted with flour. Two travelers, one with a longbow strapped to his back, had joined the audience, listening with the faint smirks of men who expected to be entertained but not surprised.

Scaleswind began a new pitch. He held up a box of tiny glass vials, blue as glacial melt. "Destiny in a drop," he said, voice carrying like a bell. "Not for the faint of heart. One drop will bring you to the crossroads of your own life. All you have to do is choose." He let the words hang, then looked each person in the eye, as if assessing which of them might dare.

The crowd leaned forward, hungry for the story if not the product.

The salesman removed a vial, popped the wax seal, and sipped it. He closed his eyes, swayed, and let out a sigh that bordered on the obscene. "I see myself, standing in a distant city, surrounded by coins and jewels and friends I haven't met yet. I see adventure, romance, a tavern with my name above the door." He smiled, inviting them all to picture their own reward.

A murmur of interest passed through the crowd, and three hands went up at once. He sold the first vial to the bowman, who paid in silver without bargaining.

Prudence shook her head, not out of pity but of contempt for the ease with which people sought out the extraordinary, even at their own expense. She turned away from the spectacle, facing the green, the low wall, and the safety of her own shop. She had to return soon; Bryant was resourceful, but she preferred not to leave him unsupervised for long.

She started back, her skirt brushing the wet grass. Her mind raced, but it was not fear that drove her anymore. It was the awareness of how quickly the world could tilt, how the presence of a single man could threaten to collapse years of discipline. But North Pointe was not Holderdown. The people here were wary, but not cruel. They would not force her hand.

Prudence crossed the green and paused at the shop door, hand on the latch. She glanced behind her, half-expecting to see the salesman striding after her, arms wide in greeting. But he remained at the road gate, surrounded by his audience, the ringmaster in his proper ring.

Inside, Bryant had not moved. He looked up as she entered, and she saw the question in his eyes. She knelt beside him, brushing the hair from his forehead. "No one comes in unless I say so," she whispered.

Bryant nodded, small and grave.

She rose, straightened her cap, and set herself behind the work-table. She drew the stained cloak toward her, retrieved the needle, and resumed the seam where she'd left off. This time, her hands did not tremble.

Outside, the voice persisted, but it was only a voice, nothing more.

Prudence worked until the bell tolled, the steady rhythm of her needle a promise to herself that she would never run again.

three

. . .

BY THE TIME the salesman's voice faded from earshot, the world inside Prudence felt slick with sweat. She decided to finish the last seam of the cloak—two stitches too long, an error she would not tolerate any other day—and set it aside. Then she rose, pressed her hands flat to the worktable to steady herself, and gathered Bryant into the crook of her arm. He offered no resistance, though his eyes registered surprise; he was not used to being whisked from the shop midmorning.

She did not bother with cloak or bonnet. The walk across the green was brief, and the tea shop promised warmth and privacy, or at least the illusion of them. Prudence paused just once, glancing back at the shop window. The glass reflected only a pale oval of sky, washed blank by the sun.

Inside, the air was instantly richer: a tide of thyme, mint, and lemon balm overtopped the faintest trace of woodsmoke. The warmth seeped through her dress, prickling the skin beneath. Most mornings, she took the leftmost table, near the hearth, but today she found it already occupied. Jen, the constable, was planted there, boots apart and arms crossed, as if the chair might tip her out if she slackened her vigilance.

Jen looked up, her gaze flicking from Prudence to Bryant and back again. She raised one weathered hand in salute, then resumed glaring at the fire.

Galhani, proprietress of both the tea shop and herbalist's, appeared from behind the counter at that moment. If her gnomish height put her eye-level with Prudence's hip, it never seemed to put her at a disadvantage; her briskness made her seem to occupy more space than she did. She wore her usual apron, embroidered with tiny herbs, and today her silver-white hair was arranged in a crown of braids.

"Morning, Pru! Morning, dear Bryant." Her voice was a clear, high melody. "You look half-frozen. Come sit by the oven and I'll get you something to thaw your bones."

Prudence hesitated, but Galhani was already pulling a chair for Bryant and bustling to fetch a second cup for Prudence. The tea shop was quiet—only two other patrons, both locals, neither likely to bother them. Still, Prudence felt every set of eyes in the room, even the ones that were not turned toward her.

She settled Bryant at the table, then sat opposite Jen, who regarded her with a mix of curiosity and grim satisfaction.

"Surprised you got out at all," Jen said, without preamble. Her voice was gravel rubbed against steel, but not unkind. "Thought for sure you'd barricade yourself in there until the wind changed."

Prudence managed a small nod. She watched as Bryant tucked his feet up on the chair, drawing himself as compact as possible.

Galhani appeared again, balancing a tray with two mugs and a tin of sweet biscuits. "Here you go, loves," she said, setting everything down with a practiced flourish. She poured the tea—pale green, fragrant—and set the mug before Prudence, then did the same for Jen.

Prudence took the cup but did not sip. She let the heat radiate into her palms.

Jen, by contrast, gulped hers, barely wincing at the temperature. "Can you believe it?" she said, to no one in particular. "Not even two seasons since the last wagon vendor, and now here's another, with twice the brass and none of the sense."

Galhani slid into the remaining chair, folding her hands in her lap.

"He isn't bothering anyone, is he? Just hawking potions and stories, like they always do."

Jen snorted. "Always starts that way. Then it's some wager, or a stunt, or worse. I chased the last one halfway down the west road after he tried to pass off a love tonic as wine." She splayed her hands, palms up, as if offering the story as proof. "If it's not love, it's luck, or magic, or something else to part fools from their coin."

Prudence stared into her tea, saying nothing. She could feel Jen's scrutiny, like the press of a thumb against a bruise.

"He called himself Cornelius last time, didn't he?" Galhani asked.

Jen shook her head. "No, this one's got a different title. Cornelius 'Coin-Hand,' he says. As if the coin comes to him by right." She made a face. "Couldn't even run him out. The charter says—"

"All are welcome so long as they come in peace, stay in peace, and leave in peace," Galhani recited, grinning.

"Exactly," said Jen, sourly. "Peace, my arse. He sets up inside the gate like he owns it." Jen's mouth tightened. "If it weren't for that clause, I'd have bundled him into a sack and dropped him in the creek."

Galhani patted Jen's hand. "You're just cranky because nobody's challenged you in sennights. Why not let the man have his fun? He'll move on in a day or two."

"Because he's trouble." Jen's boot tapped a slow, arrhythmic tattoo against the chair leg. "And you know it." She lowered her voice, just a notch. "We have enough oddities in town already. The last thing we need is a carnival act drawing attention."

Galhani shrugged. "If he bothers you so much, buy a tonic and wish him away."

Jen's laugh was a single bark. "Only thing I want is a tonic to let me thump him without breaking the peace."

Bryant, silent all this time, had slipped a biscuit from the tin and was now eating it with infinite care, as if it might crumble to dust if handled too quickly.

The conversation lapsed into a comfortable, if tense, silence. Prudence drank her tea, letting the warmth melt some of the stiffness from her jaw. Across the table, Jen watched her with the detached interest of a cat awaiting a mouse's next move.

Eventually, Jen spoke again. "You're not usually one for the tea shop, Pru."

Prudence considered her words, then replied, "Today is not usual."

That seemed to satisfy Jen, who nodded. "You should be careful. That sort of man sniffs out weakness."

"I am not weak," Prudence said, more sharply than intended.

Jen raised an eyebrow, but did not argue. "Didn't say you were."

Galhani intervened, lightening the tone. "No one here is. Not after what we've all survived."

For a moment, no one spoke. Bryant looked at Prudence, then at Jen, then back at the biscuit.

Jen drained her mug, slammed it onto the table, and let out a breath. "If he bothers you, just say the word. I'll find a way to make him less comfortable." She smirked. "Maybe give him a tour of the old jail cell."

Prudence doubted the man would fear a jail cell, but she appreciated the offer, in its way. She nodded again, slowly.

Galhani poured her a second cup, her smile softening. "There, that's better. It's not so bad, Pru. North Pointe isn't like Holderdown. People come and go, but nobody owns you. Not here."

The words landed, but Prudence could not bring herself to accept them. Not yet.

She finished her first cup, set it aside, and squared her shoulders.

She did not speak right away. Even with the words shaped and sharpened, they did not wish to leave her. Prudence's gaze dropped to the table, where she watched her own fingers spiral and unspiral on the rim of her cup. She willed her tongue to move.

The effort showed. Even Jen, who could not be accused of subtlety, seemed to sense it. "Say what you mean, Pru. We're listening."

Prudence took a breath. "He's not a stranger to me," she said, voice barely above a murmur.

Jen's brow furrowed, her irritation giving way to a flicker of concern. "You know him?"

Prudence nodded. "From Holderdown. My… my former home."

She paused, then added, "He came through often. Selling. Trading. Always with the same promises."

Bryant, who had been stacking the empty tea cups, looked up at her with perfect, intent stillness.

Jen leaned forward, arms on the table. "Did he ever try anything?"

She hesitated. It was not a story she'd told, not in any complete sense, to anyone. The details of her exit from Holderdown were known, in outline, but not in depth.

"He proposed," said Prudence, and immediately hated how the word sounded—too clean, too simple, nothing like the reality of it.

Galhani's eyebrows shot up, and she clapped a hand over her mouth. "Oh, dear." Her sympathy was not performative; it spilled over and filled the room.

"He made a contract offer," Prudence clarified, though the difference was academic. "Said it would solve everyone's problems. The elders encouraged me to consider." She did not say forced, though that was closer to the truth.

Jen shook her head, as if to dislodge a bad taste. "Bastard."

"I refused." Prudence's hands went tighter around the cup. "He left that winter, but said he'd be back." She looked up, meeting Jen's eyes for the first time. "He always comes back." She swallowed lightly. "I left instead."

There was a silence. Bryant reached for her hand and squeezed two of her fingers together, then let go.

Galhani broke the tension with a rustle of skirts as she leapt down from her chair. "No wonder you're rattled," she said. "That kind of man never knows when to leave well enough alone." She began rummaging behind the counter, the clink of jars and spoons filling the air.

Jen looked ready to bite nails. "Do you think he'll try to contact you?"

Prudence shrugged. "He may not even remember me."

"Doubtful." Jen's voice was flat, no-nonsense. "Men like that never forget a grudge. Or a mark."

The door to the tea shop swung open with a high-pitched squeal. The bell above it jangled, announcing a new arrival. Leota Harbinger stepped through, black dress trailing over the threshold, her movements graceful but cautious, as if she glided rather than walked.

"Am I interrupting a funeral, or is this just the usual morning lamentations?" Leota asked, voice a dry whisper.

"Neither," said Galhani, now busy at the counter. "We're bolstering the walls, is all."

Leota drifted to the table and took a seat beside Jen. She nodded to Prudence, then to Bryant, who responded with a small, solemn wave.

Jen filled Leota in with a single, clipped sentence: "Vendor outside. Bad history. Prudence's bad history."

Leota's lips quirked. "Is it the one with the dreadful mustache?"

"Mustache," said Prudence, and surprised herself by nearly laughing.

Leota turned her gaze on Prudence, dark eyes unblinking. "He's a pest, but a manageable one."

Galhani returned to the table, setting a new cup before Prudence. The tea was a deeper green, with tiny shreds of something blue floating atop it.

"For your nerves," Galhani said, and patted Prudence's wrist.

Prudence accepted the cup, though she doubted even Galhani's best brew could unknot what years had bound.

"Do you want me to deal with him?" Jen asked. Her hand absently circled the heavy bracelet at her wrist, a chunk of metal thick enough to serve as a weapon.

"You can't," said Prudence, softly. "The town won't allow it." The rules—the contract—still held.

Leota smiled, sly and sharp. "Rules are for those who cannot read between the lines." She turned to Bryant, who had been watching her intently. "Don't you agree?"

Bryant considered, then nodded, solemn as a priest.

"I can keep him away from you," Leota said to Prudence. "It's nothing at all. I'll just have a word."

Galhani nodded, her braid bobbing. "And if he steps one toe inside my shop, I'll put something in his tea that'll have him running for the nearest ditch."

Jen, too, joined in. "I'll watch him like a hawk. He won't get within a mile of your place without me knowing."

The certainty of their support—immediate, unreserved—was more jarring than the threat itself. Prudence felt her eyes sting. She drank from the new cup, letting its heat fill her mouth.

"Thank you," she said, the words thick.

Leota nodded, as if accepting a contract of her own. "We look after each other here," she said. "Even the quiet ones."

Jen made a harrumphing sound, but her face was set, resolute.

Bryant reached again for Prudence's hand. This time, she squeezed back.

The rest of the tea cooled, but no one seemed to mind.

———

When the shop's other patrons finally trickled out, Prudence took advantage of the hush to voice her last, rawest fear. She spoke it into her teacup, barely loud enough for anyone but Bryant to hear.

"If I have to hide here, I can't work. I can't contribute." The admission came with a sting of shame. "I'll be a burden. I don't want that."

Galhani blinked, then cackled in delight. "A burden? Prudence, you have done more for this town in a year than I have in a lifetime. Half the childrem in North Pointe wear your coats, and the other half wish they did." She reached across and squeezed Prudence's hand. "We can handle one slippery salesman."

Leota, who'd been tracing patterns on the table with a single elegant finger, spoke next. "If you're a burden, we should all be so lucky. And don't tell me you're leaving—I'd sooner hex the road itself than see you go."

Jen just snorted. "You think any of us would last a sennight in this place without someone to mend our clothes, or sew our wounds when Dexter's overwhelmed? We take care of our own. That includes you, and Bryant too."

The clarity of their conviction startled Prudence. She'd expected argument, persuasion, maybe gentle chiding. Instead, their answers were immediate, elemental. It was not a question to them.

She wiped her eyes with the back of her sleeve, embarrassed at her own emotion.

Jen pushed back from the table. "You've had enough excitement for one morning. I'll walk you home."

Prudence tried to protest, but Jen waved her down. "It's not a suggestion. That man's got eyes like a bird of prey. If he's smart, he'll steer clear, but I'd rather he know he's being watched."

Galhani boxed up a handful of biscuits, wrapped them in waxed paper, and handed them to Bryant with a wink. "For bravery," she whispered, loud enough for everyone to hear.

Leota promised to "stop by in the evening, just to check on things," and somehow the threat in her voice sounded like comfort.

Prudence gathered Bryant, and together with Jen, stepped into the cold morning. The wind had picked up, scouring the green and tugging at loose threads on their clothing.

They walked in silence for a time. Bryant trotted alongside, munching his biscuit with small, methodical bites.

Jen waited until they were almost to the shop before she spoke. "You brought him with you, this time. You don't always."

Prudence nodded, suddenly defensive. "He's safe alone. He knows not to answer the door."

Jen grunted. "That ends now. This town is a family, Pru. You and Bryant are part of it, like or not. I know you're strong enough to stand on your own, but starting now, I'll not allow it. When you need help, you're to ask for it, and if you don't, you'll receive it anyway. Clear?"

Prudence was so stunned, she missed the stoop and stumbled, nearly tripping over the threshold. Jen caught her by the elbow, steady as a fence post, and set her back on her feet.

"Thank you," Prudence said, her voice tight.

Jen softened, just a little. "Don't thank me yet. Wait till you see how annoying I can get."

They reached the shop door. Bryant ran ahead, eager to be home.

Jen paused, glancing over her shoulder at the empty street. "Don't worry about the salesman. He's loud, but he's got no claws."

"Is that official?" Prudence managed a shaky smile.

Jen flashed a rare grin. "As official as it gets."

With a final, companionable nod, Jen departed, her boots thumping away into the chill.

Inside, the shop was exactly as Prudence had left it: neat, silent, familiar. Bryant was already stacking blocks on the rug, humming to himself, as if the day's drama had never happened.

She watched him for a long moment, then crossed to the window and looked out. Across the green, she could just make out the gaudy blur of the salesman's wagon, banners snapping in the wind.

For the first time in memory, Prudence felt less afraid of what the future might bring.

She turned from the window, and set about the business of living.

———

The warming afternoon found her at the kitchen table, a thin line of lamplight falling across the scrubbed boards. Bryant was curled in her lap, head nestled against her shoulder, his hair smelling of soap and woodsmoke.

The shop was still dim, the street beyond gone silent. Prudence cradled her tea—her third or fourth cup of the day, she'd lost count—and let its warmth gather in her chest.

She could still feel the ghosts of Holderdown at her back. Even now, the urge to flee remained, coiled beneath her ribs, a snake that never slept. Prudence remembered the night she left: how her heart had thundered, how every step away from the village felt like a crime. She'd told herself she'd never run again, and meant it, but fear had a way of coming due in installments.

She sipped her tea, and found she did not tremble.

Bryant shifted, muttered in his sleep, and pressed closer. Prudence's hand traced slow circles along his spine, a motion she'd learned soothed them both.

She tried to picture what might happen if the salesman forced her out—if he pressed and prodded and conjured up the old terrors. In her mind's eye, she saw herself walking the open road again, child on her back, no destination but away. But then Jen's words—sharp, unyielding—echoed over the imagined scene:

This town is a family, Pru. You and Bryant are part of it, like or not.

It was a kind of spell, she realized. A magic stronger than the rules that bound the constable's hands, or the charm of a salesman's tongue. It was the spell of being seen, and not merely tolerated.

Prudence set down her cup. In Holderdown, even kin could not be trusted to care for their own, not when reputation or suspicion was at stake. Here, among strangers, she'd found a different order.

She let her eyes drift over the room—her room, now, and Bryant's too. The certainty of that brought an ache sharper than fear. She was not alone. The world would not end if she reached out for help. The worst thing that could happen, she realized, was that someone might actually answer.

Prudence drew Bryant close, breathing in the fragile, living weight of him. Tomorrow, she would open the shop at the usual bell. She would sew, and mend, and make her small contribution to the world that had claimed her. She would wait for the salesman to pass, as all things did.

And if he did not, she would not run. She would stay.

She would trust that, this time, she would not have to face the future alone.

four

· · ·

THE AFTERNOON FOUND Prudence at her worktable, needle in hand, the silence in the shop held taut as a drawn thread. The light had turned honeyed and slant, finding new angles through the wavy glass panes and layering the bolts of cloth in subdued stripes of gold. Bryant played in the corner, as always, orchestrating an uneven progress of block towers: building them, knocking them down, gathering the blocks in a circle as though keeping them safe from something invisible. The clatter and soft thunk of wood were the only sounds—until the sharp rap of knuckles at the door.

Prudence tensed, the thimble on her finger pausing mid-stitch. Bryant stilled, his head cocked toward the sound. She set the fabric down, folded her hands neatly over it, and tried to slow the prickling crawl at the base of her skull. The knock came again, followed by the familiar rasp of Jen's voice.

"Open up, Pru. It's only me."

She crossed the shop with two strides, unlocking the door and pulling it open half a hand's width. Jen stood on the threshold, shoulders filling the space. Her graying hair was tied back tight, the lines around her eyes deeper than ever, but her posture carried the same unyielding command as always.

"Good afternoon," said Prudence, keeping her voice neutral.

"Good enough," Jen replied, stepping inside before the invitation could be rescinded. She shut the door with a solid thud, then turned, surveying the room as if taking stock of a crime scene. Her eyes flicked once to Bryant, then back to Prudence. She wasted no time.

"Word's out," Jen said. "Half the town heard about the vendor's history with you. Didn't think it'd get round so fast, but—" She shrugged, one-shouldered, as though dismissing the inevitable.

Prudence waited, hands twisting together. She could feel the heat rising in her face. She'd lived her whole life ducking notice, and now she was the main course in the town's rumor mill.

"Listen," Jen continued, voice dropping to a register barely above a whisper. "I can't put the man out. Charter's clear—so long as he's not breaking the peace, he gets to pitch his wares like anyone else. Even if I'd rather stuff him in a sack and post him to the nearest swamp." She gave Prudence a pointed look, as if daring her to suggest otherwise.

"I understand," Prudence said, looking past Jen's shoulder to the wall of fabric beyond.

"But just because I can't run him off," Jen pressed on, "doesn't mean you need to see his face. Or hear his damn voice." She reached into her coat and withdrew a folded slip of paper. "The plan is this. For as long as the man's in town, nobody expects you to step out. If you need something—groceries, letters, even just a walk—you send word to me or Galhani. Someone'll take care of it." She dropped the note on the table, where it landed with a dry slap. "People signed their names. Made it official."

Prudence stared at the slip. The signatures crowded the bottom in various hands: some sharp, some blunted by years of labor, one or two in elegant script that looked almost like embroidery. Her eye caught the bold strokes of Galhani's name, the looping flourish of Leota's, even a smudge she guessed belonged to Dardrad the butcher.

"I don't want to be a problem," she managed.

Jen snorted, a sound halfway between laughter and disgust. "You're not the problem. Man like that, with his history—he's the problem. Everyone knows it. Town's had enough of being pushed around by folk with louder mouths and looser morals." She stepped closer, dropping her voice again. "They just want you to know you're not alone. You hear me?"

Prudence nodded, staring fixedly at a spot on the counter. Her thumb spun the thimble on her finger, again and again, until she realized Jen was watching the movement with a half-smile.

"Don't be ashamed," Jen said, her tone softening. "Most people would have left a dozen times by now. But you stayed. You built a life." She glanced over at Bryant, who was lining his blocks into an arrow. "That's what people respect. Not how loud you yell, but how steady you keep."

Prudence could think of nothing to say, so she offered a small, formal curtsy instead—absurd, really, in her own shop, but the gesture came from an old layer of habit. Jen shook her head, almost laughing.

"Right, then." The constable squared her shoulders, all business once more. "If the man tries anything, even just a word out of turn, you tell me. Or Galhani. Or Dardrad—hell, even Bartram, he's got the ears of half the square." She pointed to the paper. "The whole town's got your back, whether you want it or not."

"I'm grateful," Prudence said, her eyes still on the counter, voice barely above the sound of Bryant's blocks clacking together.

Jen reached out, hesitated a moment, then patted Prudence's shoulder. The touch was brief, but not unkind.

"I know you are," she said. "But you don't have to carry all of it yourself." She turned to leave, then paused in the doorway. "Oh, and one other thing—Makota's bringing a delivery by later. Says you're overdue for a proper treat. Don't argue."

With that, she left, boots making a dull percussion on the threshold and then receding down the stoop. The door shut with its habitual groan, and the shop returned to its old stillness.

Prudence stood in place for a long minute, the weight of the town's attention settling on her like a new and unfamiliar garment. Bryant looked up, catching her eye, and smiled—just a brief, shy thing, but it did more to thaw her than all of Jen's blunt affection.

She moved back to her worktable, gathered up the fabric she'd abandoned, and set about the next row of stitches. Her hands were steadier than she expected. She let the rhythm of the work guide her, and when she glanced up at Bryant—still playing, still safe—she found the afternoon light was softer than before, and the air a little less cold.

She managed nearly half a sleeve before the door creaked open again—no knock this time, just the abrupt rattle of the handle, followed by a flood of brisk footsteps. Prudence looked up to see Dardrad Pebbleblade entering first, laden with a bundle of brown-wrapped parcels cradled against his barrel chest. His beard was full of sawdust and what looked suspiciously like flour. Behind him came Alred Grasswalker, the Plains Elf, his arms occupied by twin baskets brimming with root vegetables and cured grains. Bringing up the rear was Makota, the Felis baker, who balanced a long loaf of bread atop her head and cradled a second, larger basket in the crook of her tail.

"Delivery for the tailor!" Dardrad boomed, his voice echoing off the ceiling with the force of a tradesman used to shouting over hammers. "Special order, straight from the green. Stand back, lad!" This last was aimed at Bryant, who had scrambled to his feet at the commotion and now hovered uncertainly near the end of the rug.

The butcher set his parcels down on the worktable, sending a tremor through the pile of fabric. Alred, more measured, arranged his baskets on the edge of the counter, each motion gentle and precise. "Cole's got another harvest in, so he sent me instead." The vegetables —some of which Prudence could not name, their hues tending toward ochre and slate—were set in order of size, the grains tucked in small cotton sacks that cinched shut with a twist of twine.

Makota sashayed up behind them, flicking crumbs from her paws before laying her basket atop the others. She peered around the room, whiskers twitching, then fixed her golden eyes on Bryant.

"I brought sweetling things," she said, voice a warm trill. "And a treat for the little man, if his mother says it's all right."

Bryant glanced at Prudence, face brightening at the prospect. Prudence hesitated, then nodded once. The Felis baker produced a small, round roll from her apron, dusted with powdered sugar, and handed it to Bryant, who clutched it with both hands and retreated to his corner as if afraid it might vanish.

Makota laughed softly, the sound somewhere between a purr and a human giggle. "He's clever," she said to no one in particular.

Dardrad, having freed himself of parcels, set about unwrapping the packages with a practiced flick of his pocketknife. "Cured highelk, peppered pork, two kinds of sausage," he recited. "Some for now, some for later. Store the smoked stuff in a dry place, it'll keep till next frost." He shoved the parcels toward Prudence, who managed to catch one before it toppled from the pile.

Alred, meanwhile, was arranging the baskets in a precise line. "You'll need a hand with these upstairs," he said, his voice a soft glide. "Can't have you making two dozen trips, not with the child to mind."

Makota nodded her agreement, tail curling in affirmation. "We're not going until it's all put away. That's the rule."

Prudence opened her mouth to protest, then closed it again. It would do no good to argue with the three of them, not when their collective stubbornness outmatched any resistance she could offer. Instead, she gathered herself, straightened the apron she wore over her dress, and nodded toward the staircase at the back of the shop.

Dardrad took the lead, picking up the heavy basket as if it were a bundle of feathers. Alred followed, balancing two smaller baskets against each hip. Makota padded silently behind, loaf still poised on her head. Bryant trailed after them, biting into his roll with deliberate, careful teeth.

They ascended the stairs in single file, the rhythm of their footfalls oddly comforting. Prudence brought up the rear, fingers trailing the worn banister, her thoughts swirling in a mix of gratitude and discomfort.

At the top of the stairs, the air was noticeably warmer. The apartment was modest: a single large room, with a narrow cot for herself and a trundle for Bryant, a battered oak table, and a shelf lined with jars of preserves. The hearth was cold, but the sunlight slanting through the dormer window made up for it, painting the space in clean, white lines.

Dardrad placed his parcel on the table and immediately began unpacking. "Where do you want it all?" he grunted.

Prudence hesitated. "Anywhere," she said. "There's room in the pantry, or—"

The butcher ignored her, opening the cupboard above the counter and stacking the meats inside with geometric precision. "If you keep them here, they won't tempt the mice," he pronounced, and Prudence realized she would not be allowed to rearrange them later, not without risking his offense.

Alred set his baskets on the table, then methodically decanted the grains into glass jars, each labeled in his elegant, slanted script. He moved quietly, careful not to disturb the fragile truce of the household, and when he finished he bowed his head slightly in Prudence's direction.

Makota swept the loaf from her head with a flourish, landing it on the table with a soft thump. She then set about laying out a linen cloth and arranging an array of pastries and buns, each one perfectly shaped and lightly glazed. She glanced at Bryant, who was already licking sugar from his fingers, and smiled. "Eat slow," she said. "Some of these might show you a glimpse of tomorrow."

Prudence frowned, uncertain whether the baker was teasing or serious, but Makota's eyes twinkled in the afternoon light.

The three set about tidying the room, sweeping up stray crumbs, adjusting the level of the rug, even straightening the chairs around the table. It was a whirlwind of efficiency, and Prudence found herself sidelined, watching as they transformed her apartment from a place of survival into something almost welcoming.

When at last they were finished, Dardrad clapped his hands together and announced, "That's a job done." He looked at Prudence, his face severe but not unkind. "You let me know if you need anything else."

Alred smiled, a brief but genuine expression. "We'll send the children round tomorrow, if you're low on anything."

Makota wiped her hands on her apron and fixed Prudence with a long, appraising look. "You don't have to say thank you," she said, "but it helps if you do."

Prudence opened her mouth, and this time the words came easily.

"Thank you," she said, and meant it. The three nodded in unison, then filed back down the stairs, their footsteps softening as they descended.

Bryant, now dusted head to toe with sugar, looked up at her and grinned. She gathered him in her arms and sat at the table, letting the warmth of the bread and the sudden fullness of her shelves seep into her bones.

The sun had shifted by the time she returned to the shop, casting the space in a deep, even blue. The air was tinged with the scent of smoked meat and baking bread, and for the first time in years, Prudence felt not just safe, but cared for.

She moved behind the counter, where the deliveries had left a small chaos of twine, paper, and stray vegetables. She swept the scraps into the bin, lined up the bolts of cloth, and set about the slow, deliberate process of restoring order. It was work she could do in the dark, and often had, but tonight she allowed herself the luxury of a candle.

As she stitched, her mind wandered to the faces of those who had come for her: Jen, Dardrad, Alred, Makota, even Galhani with her quick wit and bottomless tea. She wondered, not for the first time, what it was that bound them all together in this strange, out-of-the-way place. It was not just necessity; it was something warmer, something almost like loyalty.

She watched the needle move in and out of the cloth, the thread closing tiny wounds with each careful pass. She wondered if that was what it felt like, to let others help. To trust that the world would not collapse just because you accepted a kindness.

Bryant, now drowsy from his feast, curled up on the rug, his face serene in sleep. Prudence worked on, the small noises of the night replacing the chaos of the afternoon.

She let herself believe, just for the span of a few stitches, that things might turn out all right. That the future, glimpsed through the lens of a bakery treat, might hold more than fear.

And in the quiet blue of evening, she almost smiled.

———

It was well past the evening bell when Bartram Lastmaker breezed through the shop's door, the cheerful clatter of the bell above punctuating his arrival. He carried with him the faint tang of lamp oil and shoe polish, his boots leaving a trail of clean, damp prints on the threshold. Bryant looked up from where he'd been constructing a fortress out of empty thread spools and immediately scampered to Bartram's side, accepting a gentle hair-ruffle and a quick, whispered joke that made him beam.

Bartram's presence always changed the air. Even Prudence, whose guard was rarely down, felt the temperature of the room tilt a degree warmer. He spread his arms as if presenting himself for inspection.

"Evening, Mistress Simonsdotter!" he called, voice a soft boom. "I trust the world's not ended yet, though I half-expected to see the tailor's shop in flames, what with all the excitement on the green."

"It has not ended," Prudence replied, allowing herself the smallest of smiles. "Though I do expect to see it try again tomorrow."

Bartram laughed, a round, pleasant sound. He leaned against the counter, hands resting on his ample hips. "You've had visitors, I hear. Quite the day for company, eh?"

She nodded, glancing at Bryant, who had returned to stacking his spools—this time with a focus so fierce it looked as if he meant to keep the walls up through force of will alone.

Bartram sobered a fraction, then lowered his voice. "I didn't come just to gossip, though you know I'm fond of it. I thought, perhaps, you'd like a little intelligence on our new neighbor."

Prudence's fingers, which had gone back to their slow, repetitive sewing, paused over the hem she was finishing. "You mean the salesman."

Bartram's mouth twitched. "The very one. I thought I'd offer my services—as a spy, if you will." He leaned closer, his tone conspiratorial. "I can take a stroll past his wagon, maybe even get a look at what he's hawking. Pretend I'm in the market for something invigorating, and see what else he lets slip."

Prudence considered, then nodded once. "If you think it's safe."

Bartram rolled his eyes, mock affronted. "Safe? Please, the man's an amateur. I've haggled with worse in the back alleys of Cherum." He lowered his voice again, softer now. "But it's good to be careful. You're not wrong there."

He seemed ready to move on, but his eye caught on the fabric in Prudence's lap. "What's that?" he asked, reaching out, but stopping short until she nodded permission. He lifted the sleeve between his fingers, feeling the texture.

"Work jerkin," Prudence said. "For Darby. He grows out of them twice a year, at least."

Bartram grinned. "Fine work. Sturdy, like all your things. You mind if I show you something?" He fished into his own pocket and pulled out a scrap of cured leather, already punched through at the ends with neat, uniform holes. "Same stitching, different medium. See?" He held the two pieces side by side, drawing a line along the seams.

Prudence looked, and saw: the tiny, even stitches—nearly identical, despite the difference in tools and purpose.

Bartram smiled. "Kindred spirits, you and I. Always making things to carry people from one place to another." He set the leather down gently, then straightened, satisfied.

He seemed about to speak further, but caught himself. He looked at Bryant, who was now arranging the spools in careful concentric circles. "It's a good thing, you know. Teaching a child to build. It lasts longer than people expect."

Prudence didn't trust herself to answer, so she simply inclined her head.

Bartram's expression grew serious. "You know, if you ever need an extra set of hands—or just someone to talk shop with—my door's open."

This time, Prudence's smile came easier. "Thank you," she said. "You're a good neighbor, Bartram."

He looked genuinely pleased by this. "Right, then. I'll make my rounds and report back if I hear anything." He made to leave, then paused, hand on the doorframe.

"Don't let the day get to you," he said, softer. "The town stands with you. Even the ones who don't say it loud."

And with a final wave, he stepped into the dusk, letting the door close gently behind him.

Prudence stood in the hush that followed, watching the way the lamplight played on the wood and glass. Bryant was yawning now, eyelids drooping in time with the slowing cadence of his play.

She crossed to the worktable, running her hands across the grain, then over the bolts of cloth, the jars of buttons and pins, the scraps and spools and carefully hoarded notions. Each item had its place, each served a purpose.

For the first time in years, she felt less like an exile and more like a fixture—one of many hands holding the town together. She would never say as much, not aloud. But as she watched Bryant curl up and drift into sleep, she understood that some things, once mended, could hold stronger than they did before.

She gathered the jerkin and thread, and set to work.

five

· · ·

MORNING'S CHILL HAD SOFTENED, but the light that crept across Prudence's worktable remained thin and nervous. It hovered just above the surface of the plain brown jerkin she was mending—a children's size, destined for some neighbor's boy with arms that outpaced his sleeves every sennight—the town's magic apparently having decided to speed him through his teenage years and directly into young adulthood. Her hands moved steadily, the rhythm of the needle in and out as regular as her own pulse, but both were too fast for comfort. She felt a tremor in her right hand, though she was careful not to show it, even to the silence.

Bryant was already awake, stacking wooden blocks in the narrow patch of sunlight near the stove. He was content to exist in her periphery, as he always did, but today Prudence felt herself attuned to even the smallest changes in sound—the thump of a block, the faint sizzle from the kettle, the exaggerated click of each second as it fell away. Every so often, she glanced up from her work, scanning the window for a shadow or a movement beyond the glass.

It was on one of these scans that she saw Galhani's unmistakable silhouette, small and quick, darting across the green with a parcel hugged tight to her chest. The gnome's stride was purposeful, her braided hair streaming behind like a battle standard. Prudence set her work aside, smoothing the cloth before the bell above the door even had a chance to sound.

"Delivery!" Galhani announced as she entered, the word rising clear and sharp above the usual hush. "Specialty blend, with extra honey for courage." She climbed the stepstool by the counter, set down the parcel—a tin cup wrapped in a handkerchief—and surveyed the shop with a seasoned merchant's eye.

Prudence nodded her thanks, but her gaze trailed to the window again, unwilling to let her guard down.

Galhani followed the look. "He's still at the east gate," she said, the syllables clipped with irritation. "But he'll not come in, not today. There's too many of us being… inhospitable." She grinned.

Prudence picked up the cup, which steamed against the cold of her fingers. She brought it to her lips, not to drink, but to let the heat calm the stutter of her hands.

Galhani leaned forward, lowering her voice. "Do you want to hear about the wagon? Or should I save it for later?"

Prudence hesitated, then nodded. "Now is fine."

The gnome grinned, a flash of white in her round face. "It's a real eyesore, I'll tell you that. Painted in stripes, banners all over. Says 'Destiny in a Bottle' and 'Fate, Yours for the Taking.'" She rolled her eyes, then mimed the flourish of a curtain. "He's got little glass vials in every color, set out on velvet—blue, green, something like gold, and even one that looks almost black." She wrinkled her nose. "Like anyone wants to drink black."

Bryant looked up from his blocks, curious. Prudence touched his shoulder, reassuring him with a brush of her palm, then turned her attention back to Galhani.

"He's got a whole crowd," Galhani continued, "mostly the travelers who've stopped overnight. Saw a group of those young adventurers—three girls and two boys, all with their packs and not an ounce of sense between them. He's selling them colored water at five silver a vial." She snorted. "Robbery, but they love it."

Prudence stared into the tea, watching the swirl of honey dissolve.

"Did he... did he mention my name?" The question came out small, and she hated the sound of it.

Galhani shook her head, braid whipping. "Not once. It's all about the product with him. 'Change your fate,' 'skip the hard work and get right to the end.' That sort of thing. I stayed near the edge for a bell, just to be sure." She leaned in, conspiratorial. "He's clever, but not subtle. I don't think he's here for you. And why would he even know you're here?"

Prudence tried to believe it, but found herself gripping the cup too tight. She eased her fingers, set the cup down, and tried to smooth her features.

Galhani must have noticed. "If he tries anything, Jen will be on him before he's done with the first lie." She winked. "You know how she is."

Prudence forced a smile, then looked again toward the window. She could see two travelers now, ambling toward the gate with bright bottles sticking from their packs like trophies. The sight made her teeth ache.

Galhani followed her gaze, then patted Prudence's forearm with a brisk, no-nonsense touch. "You're safe here, Pru. This place—" She gestured to the shelves, the crowded bolts of fabric, the whole tiny world Prudence had built. "No one's going to take it from you. Not while we're all watching."

Bryant had abandoned his blocks to climb onto her lap, his weight a small anchor against the jitter in her chest. Prudence rested her chin atop his hair, breathing in the familiar scent of woodsmoke and soap.

Galhani, sensing the change in mood, shifted tactics. She raised her voice, putting on an exaggerated version of the salesman's pitch. "'One drop and you'll be the man you always knew you could be!'" She shook her head. "What rubbish. I'd sooner buy a tonic from the old sheep herder who lives out past the mill." She mimed a swallow and made a face. "Probably get a better result, too."

Prudence almost laughed. The sound hovered just behind her lips, but she let it go unspoken.

Galhani finished her report with a flourish. "Anyway. If you want a look at him, he's got his show running until at least the next bell. I can stand outside and keep watch if you'd rather not have him see you, but—" She shrugged. "I doubt he's interested in old business."

Prudence shook her head. "Thank you. I have work." She stroked Bryant's back, steady and slow.

Galhani made a satisfied hum, then slid from the stepstool. She paused at the door, looking back. "If you need anything, send the boy. Or just wave from the window. I'll come running." She thumped her fist over her heart—her usual goodbye—then left, the bell chiming behind her.

The shop settled back into its habitual silence. Prudence finished her tea in three steady swallows, then gathered the jerkin and her tools. She set Bryant on the stool beside her, handing him a bit of twine to untangle. She let the rhythm of the needle calm her, but every time a voice rose outside, she glanced toward the door, half expecting it to burst open.

The candlemarks crept by, slow and uneven. Travelers came and went along the green, some pausing to peer into her window before moving on. More than once, Prudence caught sight of a bottle, bright in the sunlight, clutched in a hopeful hand or tucked into the strap of a knapsack. She could not decide if the sight was more ridiculous or terrifying.

Each time, she bent closer to her work, determined to outlast the day.

By dusk, the shop was filled with the faint glow of candlelight and the richer aroma of Galhani's tea, long since cold but still sweet on the air. Prudence set aside her needle, stretched her cramped fingers, and took stock of the day's labor. Three jerkin repairs, one dress hemmed, and a length of linen measured for a new order. Not the most productive day, but not the worst, either.

She gathered Bryant, who had dozed off on the stool, and lifted him to her hip. She locked the shop door, double-checked the latch, and swept the windows with her eyes, scanning for any trace of the salesman or his customers. The green was empty, except for the last fugitive streaks of sunset.

Prudence exhaled, slow and deliberate, then climbed the stairs to their small apartment. She tucked Bryant into his cot, then sat by the window, watching as the town's lanterns blinked on, one by one.

Below, the world kept moving: footsteps on the stone walk, a distant burst of laughter, the metallic whine of a wagon axle in need of grease. Each sound was a promise that tomorrow would come, and that she and Bryant would meet it, the same as ever.

She allowed herself a single moment of peace, then rose and set about preparing for the next day, determined that nothing—not even fate in a bottle—would disrupt the simple, necessary work of living.

———

Evening inched closer, and with it the chill that always found the soft places in Prudence's resolve. She tidied the shop, checked the lock, and set a small meal for Bryant—half a heel of bread and a wedge of sharp cheese, which he picked apart with patient curiosity. She let the boy eat at the worktable while she swept the shop's floor, using the work to distract herself from the crawling sense of anticipation she could not quite banish.

The distraction lasted only as long as it took for Jen to fill the shop's doorway, her presence as subtle as a thunderhead. She carried a wax-paper parcel in one hand and a look of battered amusement in the other.

"Makota's new, I think you'll like it," Jen announced, waving the parcel. "Even brought extra for the boy." She stepped inside without waiting for an invitation, her boots loud against the floorboards.

Prudence set the broom aside and gestured for Jen to use the counter. "Thank you." Her voice was thick with humble appreciation.

Jen unwrapped the bread—still faintly warm, dark-crusted and streaked with something sweet in the swirl—and tore off a piece, which she handed to Bryant before Prudence could intervene. The boy took it solemnly, eyes darting from the constable to his mother, then back again.

"Good appetite," Jen said, grinning. "Sign of a healthy child." She leaned against the counter, arms folded, and watched as Prudence portioned the loaf, arranging it on a plate with deliberate care.

For a few moments, there was only the sound of eating, the soft crackle of the time candle, and the hush that seemed to gather in corners at this time.

It was Jen who broke the silence. "Had a word with your favorite vendor, out by the east gate." Her tone was light, but Prudence could hear the underlying tension, like a wire pulled too tight.

"Did you," Prudence replied, her voice carefully measured.

Jen's mouth twitched. "Told him I'd be watching. Even used my 'official' voice. Didn't slow him down a tick." She cocked her head, mimicking the salesman's oily tone: "'Why, officer, I'm just a humble purveyor of dreams! Is it wrong to sell hope?'" She rolled her eyes, then returned to her own voice. "Offered me a sample, too. I nearly took it, just to see if it'd shut him up."

Prudence's fingers tightened on the plate. She made a sound that might have been a laugh, if she'd let it.

Jen grinned wider. "He's a persistent little snake, I'll give him that." She stole another piece of bread and chewed thoughtfully. "But he'll not enjoy much hospitality here. Sam's only serving him warm ale, and even then only in the chipped mug. Minnie flat-out refused him a room at the inn. And Warren—" She let out a low chuckle. "Warren's made it his business to lurk at the gate with me, just in case the fellow gets ideas about wandering."

Prudence set the plate down, arranging the slices so the cut faces alternated directions. She nodded, then spoke softly. "Is he making many sales?"

Jen shrugged, but there was a heaviness in it. "Steady business, from what I see. Travelers are the worst—always looking for the easy fix. But even a few townsfolk have tried his stuff. Nobody you know, and no one's come to harm, but..." She let the sentence hang.

Prudence stared at the table, her knuckles white on the edge.

"Worst part is," Jen continued, lowering her voice, "I saw a woman yesterday—one of the outlanders—who'd been asking after Elspeth. Had maps, supplies, the works. She was set on finding her. Then she spent ten minutes with the salesman and walked away with a bottle of 'Wisdom Distilled.' Never even tried the climb."

The news struck harder than Prudence expected. She felt her shoulders tighten, her fingers clamp around the workbench so fiercely that the tips went numb. It was as if the salesman had robbed the world of a small, honest struggle, and left only the shell behind.

Jen must have seen the reaction. She reached across the counter, resting her hand on Prudence's for a moment. "He's not going to break this place," Jen said. "Not while any of us are around."

Prudence nodded, but it took her a moment to find her voice. "Thank you. For watching."

Jen squeezed her fingers, then released them. "Don't mention it." She straightened, already halfway back to the door. "I'll be at the gate for another bell, just to see if he tries anything clever. If you hear or see anything strange, let me know."

"I will," Prudence promised.

Jen's hand was on the latch when she paused. "You're doing fine, Pru. Even if you don't always believe it." Then, with a nod to Bryant, she slipped out, her shadow dissolving into the deeper blue of evening.

Prudence stood at the counter for a long minute, the stillness of the shop settling around her like a weighted blanket. She forced her hands to unclench, then gathered up the bread and brought it to the tiny kitchen, where she stored the remainder in a tin.

Bryant finished his piece, wiped his hands on his smock, and looked at her expectantly. She gathered him into her arms and pressed her cheek to the crown of his head, breathing in the comfort of him.

She returned to her sewing, but her thoughts were slower, more troubled. The salesman had found a new way to cheat the world, and though he hadn't targeted her directly, the injury was the same.

She stitched in silence, the rhythm a poor substitute for peace, but better than letting the fear win.

———

The bell above the shop door rang in the next afternoon's first task: a young man, tall but not yet filled out, with sandy hair and a face so open it bordered on foolish. He stepped inside with the caution of someone unused to commerce, pausing just past the threshold to scrape mud from his boots and eye the racks of fabric as if half-expecting them to snap at him.

Prudence assessed him the way she did every customer—posture, hands, the set of his shoulders, the anxiety in his eyes. He was farm stock, likely, or from one of the inland towns that skirted the old foothills. He wore a tunic so threadbare it was translucent in places, and carried a pack bulging with poorly packed belongings.

He hesitated at the counter, wringing his hands. "Is this the tailor's?" he asked, though the evidence was all around him.

"It is," Prudence answered, keeping her voice level.

He approached, every movement careful, as if trying not to bruise the air. "They said—well, the constable said—you do repairs, and also new commissions?"

"I do," she said.

He exhaled in relief, then dug into his pack. He produced a vest, the seams split and the fabric spotted with sap and something darker, which she guessed to be berry juice. "Can you make me one like this?" he asked. "But, um, stronger? I'm going on a journey."

Prudence took the vest, turned it over in her hands, examined the construction. The original maker had used decent material but careless stitches. She nodded. "I can. When do you need it?"

He looked away, then back at her, earnestness blazing. "Tomorrow, if possible. I'm leaving at dawn."

She weighed the commission, then set the vest on the table. "It will be ready," she said. "Six coppers."

The boy beamed. "Thank you. Truly." He hesitated, then looked around the shop, as if gathering courage. "Can I—do you mind if I tell you why I need it? Or is that strange?"

Prudence found herself saying, "Go on," before she even realized it.

He blushed, but pressed on. "I'm going to win her back. My love, I mean." He stood straighter, as though he'd rehearsed the speech. "She's beautiful, the prettiest in her village. Smart, too, though not everyone sees it. I was going to bring her a meadow's worth of airblooms—" Here, his eyes grew distant, almost dewy. "You know them, right? Blue and white, grow only in the highest passes?"

Prudence nodded. She'd seen the flowers once, pressed between the pages of a book, as delicate as breath.

He rushed ahead. "They're said to bring good fortune to couples. If you give them as a gift, you'll always find your way back to each other. I planned to hike up into the Mistrals, but…" He trailed off, the confidence draining. "But there's a shortcut, maybe."

Now he fidgeted, glancing at his hands. "I met a man on the road. Salesman. He said he could help. Had a tonic—'Destiny's True Love,' he called it. Just three silvers." He swallowed, then whispered, "He said I'd never have to climb a mountain or risk a storm, just drink it and everything would come out right."

Prudence listened, a mixture of pity and irritation building in her chest. She looked at the boy—his hopeful face, the hands that couldn't stop moving—and thought of all the people in the world who wanted something as badly as he did. Her gaze drifted to the shelves behind him, where the finer fabrics waited, never touched, as if guarding themselves from disappointment.

For a heartbeat, she let herself imagine making him a suit—white linen, shining blue trim at the cuffs, the sort of finery that would dazzle any girl and shame the flower's fragile beauty. She imagined the girl as well: perhaps not as lovely as he believed, but kind, with a laugh that made even the harshest day worth surviving. She pictured the two of them together, clothed in hope and newness, walking the town's green in the spring sunlight.

She blinked, forcing herself back to the present.

"Best to have a good vest," she said, a touch more sternly than intended. "The Mistrals are cold this time of year, and steep."

He nodded, then looked at her, earnest and uncertain. "You think I should go, then? Not trust the potion?"

Prudence opened her mouth, then closed it. Words failed her, as they often did when advice was needed. She wanted to tell him that shortcuts never led to anything worth having, that pain and risk were the only way to earn something real. She wanted to say that no bottle could give him what he wanted, only effort and stubbornness. But the words stuck.

She shrugged, looking away. "If it's worth doing, it's worth doing right," she managed.

The boy seemed to take this as gospel. "Thank you," he said, bowing slightly. "You're very wise. I'll come back tomorrow for the vest."

He left, the door's bell clattering in his wake, and Prudence let herself exhale. She picked up the old vest, studied the seams again, then set about cutting the new fabric—this time using the heavier wool she kept for the coldest months. As she worked, her mind returned to the boy and his hope, fragile and ridiculous but pure. She hoped he would climb the mountain, and that the girl would be waiting.

But more than that, she hoped the salesman would choke on his own false promise.

She sewed past dusk, and when she finished, she held the vest up to the light, running her fingers over every seam, every edge. It was not beautiful, but it was strong, and she liked to think that would be enough.

———

The boy returned late that night, despite his promise to return the following morning. Her was coatless and shivering. He'd scrubbed his hands and face, and looked, if anything, younger than before. He stepped inside with a nervous energy, gaze flicking from the counter to Bryant—who was now stacking spools into pyramids—and back.

Prudence, having had something of a premonition that the boy would return early, had stayed awake, puttering around the shop and glancing out the window, and was therefore ready when the little bell over the shop door jangled. She offered him the vest. "It's ready."

He took it reverently, then shrugged it on over his thin shirt. The fit was perfect; he grinned, teeth white and crooked. "I've never worn anything so fine," he said, and Prudence nearly laughed. But she looked at the garment, at its utter lack of flourish, and felt, for the first time, a deep disappointment in her own restraint.

He set the copper coins on the counter, then fished in his pack for a small blue bottle. "I got the potion, too," he said. "Felt stupid handing over the coin, but… sometimes it's best to try everything."

Prudence eyed the bottle. It was nothing—a trick of syrup and dye —but the boy clutched it as though it might save his soul.

He noticed her stare and blushed. "I'm staying at the inn tonight. Minnie's putting me in a corner room, says it's the warmest." He hesitated. "Thank you, truly. For this. I'll tell everyone, if I make it back."

Prudence nodded, but as the boy turned to go, her mind conjured a vision of him a year from now—broader, sure of himself, returning to the square in a shirt of fine linen and a jacket stitched in blue, hair combed back, hands uncallused. In the daydream, he was arm in arm with a woman: not the silly, vain girl he'd described, but someone older, with a wry smile and a gaze like a clear sky after rain.

She blinked, the fantasy dissolving. "Good luck," she said, the words sharp as a knife.

The boy smiled, bowed, and left, the bell a brief, cold echo.

Prudence watched him cross the square, the new vest already dusted with a fine haze of twilight. She found herself frowning, then shook her head. Bryant, seeing her mood, abandoned his spools and attached himself to her skirt.

She sent him up the stairs, then followed, moving through the ritual of evening meal with a precision that bordered on frantic. She lit the lamp, cut slices of the dark bread, poured milk into their shared cup. Bryant ate in silence, as always, but she spoke to him in gentle tones, narrating each movement—the buttering of bread, the addition of honey—until her hands stopped shaking.

Afterward, she tucked him into his cot, smoothing the blanket three times before stepping away.

She stood by the window and watched the stars come out, one by one, above the rooftops. In the darkness, the regrets and what-ifs came alive, flickering like the first faint points of light in a new night.

She whispered a silent wish for the boy, then another for herself, and let the dark close around her like a cloak.

———

The morning after, the air in Galhani's tea shop carried the weight of unspoken accusations and the oily tang of strong black tea. Prudence sat in her usual corner, Bryant pressed close to her side, while the townsfolk gathered at the mismatched tables, all eyes fixed on Bartram Lastmaker.

Bartram was in fine form, balancing a steaming mug on one palm and using the other to punctuate his every word. "It was a show, I tell you—like something out of the old markets in the capital." He set down the mug and flexed his hands for effect. "This Cornelius fellow had a whole table lined with bottles, all lined up neat as soldiers. Each one glittered in the morning sun—red, gold, even one that looked like melted emerald." He waggled his eyebrows, drawing a small laugh from Makota, who stood behind the counter arranging a display of biscuits.

Dardrad and his wife occupied the next table over, nodding along as Bartram painted the scene. "He had a crowd, too. Travelers, all—I think our neighbors have finally given up on his shiny promises. He'd pour a measure into a glass, hold it up so the light hit just right, and say, 'Drink your destiny. No mountain, no trial, just the end you want in a single swallow.'" Bartram paused to let that sink in.

Prudence watched him, jaw set, her hands curled around her cup so tightly that the ridges of the porcelain left marks in her skin.

Makota piped up, voice high and sweet. "Did you see him actually drink one?"

Bartram shook his head. "He claimed he already had his fill. Told a story about losing his true love and finding her again after taking his own potion, but…" Bartram snorted. "If I had to guess, he'd never lost anything except his morals."

A few nervous chuckles rippled around the room. Leota, seated beside Prudence and wrapped in a black shawl, fixed Bartram with a look both wry and sharp. "And did anyone actually buy?"

"Of course," Bartram replied. "He never missed a chance." He leaned closer, dropping his voice. "There was one—a young scholar, from the look. He had a pack full of books, proper boots, and a stack of maps rolled up under one arm. I watched him bargain for ten full minutes over the 'Elixir of Enlightenment.' Paid four silver for a half vial, then sat down in the dirt to drink it right there." Bartram shook his head, incredulous.

Dardrad made a harrumph, the sound as thick as beef stock. "Fools and their coin. Shouldn't be allowed."

Leota raised her mug, swirling the contents with slow deliberation. "He's not breaking the rules," she said. "That's why the town magic won't let Jen throw him out."

Bartram looked offended. "He's tricking people. That's a kind of harm."

Leota smiled, but there was little warmth in it. "Only if you believe a lie can wound more than a knife." She set her cup down and looked at Prudence. "It's dangerous, what he's selling. Not the bottle—anyone can see it's just colored syrup—but the promise." She tapped the table, once. "He's offering results with no labor. Destiny without the difficulty. People always want the easy end." She paused, and then her expression tightened. "True magic never comes without a price, and it's far steeper than he's charging."

A heavy silence settled, broken only by Bryant's soft humming and the scrape of Makota's knife on a cutting board.

Prudence stared at the dregs of her tea, jaw working as she tried to shape a response. She could not. Instead, she looked up and said, "He's keeping people from what they're meant to do." Her voice was flat, nearly a whisper, but every ear caught it.

Leota inclined her head, as if to say: exactly.

Bartram, unwilling to let go, insisted, "But what if someone gets hurt? What if the potion does nothing and they get lost, or worse?"

Leota shrugged. "That's not on him. The town sees harm as harm —the rest is just… human nature." She shrugged again, then turned to Prudence. "You can't save them from wanting."

Prudence thought of the boy, marching out in his new vest, clutching the bottle and hoping for a miracle. She thought of herself, years ago, buying into the idea that suffering could be traded for an easier path. She clenched her hands tighter, then let go, forcing her fingers to relax.

Bartram, sensing the mood, finished his tea in a single gulp and excused himself to check on his shop. Dardrad grumbled and followed, leaving the women alone with the aftermath.

Leota waited until the shop emptied, then leaned closer to Prudence. "You did right by him, you know. The boy from yesterday. I saw the vest—best work you've done."

Prudence shook her head. "He took the potion anyway."

Leota smiled, not unkindly. "But he'll remember the vest. When the potion fails, he'll still have something that keeps him warm."

Makota joined them, setting a fresh bun in front of Bryant and tousling his hair. "You can't fix everyone, Pru. Sometimes you just have to feed them and hope they come back."

Prudence nodded, but inside, the ache grew sharper. She wanted to say it was not enough, but the words turned to ash on her tongue.

Leota patted her hand, soft and deliberate. "We watch out for each other. And when he comes back, we'll be here."

Prudence held her gaze, then nodded once, steady as she could.

They finished the tea in silence, the morning sunlight slanting through the window and casting sharp shadows on the table. Outside, the world carried on, full of people buying and selling hope.

Inside, Prudence resolved to hold on to the small, hard things that lasted longer than promises.

———

From the window of her shop, Prudence watched Makota in full persuasion, tail lashing and ears flat, as she tried to intercept a traveler on the green. The young man—barely more than a boy, with a tan that suggested long days on the road—stood at a respectful distance, arms folded over his chest, but his gaze was fixed past Makota's shoulder, toward the distant shimmer of banners at the east road gate.

Prudence couldn't hear the words, but she read the story in posture and gesture: Makota's pointed finger, the circle of her hands as she mimed a bottle, the exasperated flattening of her ears when the traveler shook his head and pressed on. In the end, Makota gave a theatrical shrug and let him go, then lingered a moment, scanning the square, before returning to her bakery with a visible slump.

This was not the first such scene of the day. Prudence had watched a parade of hopefuls—some local, most just passing through—drawn inexorably toward the promise of a shortcut. The morning's rain had left puddles that reflected the colors of the salesman's banners, and every time the light shifted, it made the whole affair look more like a traveling circus than a fraud.

From her vantage, Prudence caught flashes of the new arrivals as they filtered through the town gate: a pair of sisters, hair cropped to the chin and dyed copper; a merchant with the green coat of the southern routes; even, at midday, an old woman with her hair in a white net, walking with the assistance of two carved canes. Each one paused at the wagon, some longer than others, and nearly all departed with a bottle, the glass flashing in the weak sun as they slipped it into a pocket or pack.

Bryant, oblivious to the drama, drew chalk patterns on the worn floorboards, humming tunelessly to himself. Prudence wished for a moment that she could inhabit his world, where the only magic was the satisfaction of drawing a perfect circle, and the future stretched no farther than the next meal.

By evening, the clouds had returned, low and bruised, with wind that pressed at the windows and carried distant laughter from the inn. Prudence turned down the lamps and tidied the day's debris: a patch here, a hem there, and a new apron ordered for one of the servers at the bakery. She was knotting the thread on her final seam when a heavy knock rattled the door.

She opened it to find Dardrad, the butcher, balancing a basket on his hip. The smell of fresh bread and smoked meat chased the wind into the shop.

"Evening, Pru," he said, voice like granite gravel. "Makota sent this —said she owed you from this morning."

Prudence accepted the basket, nodding her thanks. "You saw her on the green?"

Dardrad made a noncommittal grunt. "She's been out there most of the day, trying to warn folk off that fraud at the road gate. No luck. You'd think she was telling them the moon was made of cheese, the way they look at her." He shook his head. "It's getting worse. He's got a new pitch now—claims it's 'essence of mountain wisdom.' Says you don't need to make the trip to Elspeth anymore, just drink up and wait."

Prudence's stomach turned. "They believe it?"

Dardrad's beard split around a scowl. "Most want to. That's all it takes. Once he started hearing folks with plans to seek out the Enchantress, he worked that right into his tale. He's slick, but he's smart." He stepped into the warmth, closing the door behind him. "And the worst part is, the magic of this place isn't doing a damn thing about it."

Prudence met his gaze, then risked the question. "Jen said. Why not?"

Dardrad shrugged, setting the basket on the counter. "It stops fights. Keeps people honest in trade, more or less. But it doesn't stop foolishness. Or the wanting for something that's not yours." He fixed her with a look that was both challenge and warning. "You can't make people do the right thing. Not really. Not even with magic."

Prudence nodded, eyes downcast.

Dardrad pulled a wrapped parcel from the basket and set it in front of Bryant, who greeted it with a wordless clap. "For the little one," Dardrad said, softer now. "Makota made them herself. Sweet, with just a bit of spice."

Bryant smiled, and Prudence offered a genuine thanks, the warmth of the moment briefly banishing her unease.

Dardrad made to go, then paused at the door. "If you need anything, let me know. The rest of us—we're not running off after bottled destiny. We'll still be here."

She nodded, and Dardrad left, the door closing with a reassuring thud.

Night came on, blue and wind-bitten. Prudence finished her chores, then sat by the window with Bryant curled in her lap, watching the east gate. Lanterns danced in the wind, casting wavering circles across the puddled road. Though she could not see the salesman's face, she could hear, faint and persistent, the sound of his voice —never shouting, just a patient drone, steady as the tide.

As the 'marks passed, the voices thinned. Some left with their bottles, others with nothing but the old ache of wanting something impossible. Prudence watched, and waited, and wished for the strength to look away.

At last, the square fell silent. She tucked Bryant into bed, wrapped herself in a blanket, and stood by the window once more.

The lanterns at the east gate burned long into the night, a stubborn, hungry glow.

Prudence closed her eyes and promised herself—again, and again—that she would not give in.

She would hold fast, even as the world outside grew stranger by the day.

six

· · ·

THE EARLY AFTERNOON cast a coppery slant through the tailor shop's window, drawing long parallel lines over the worktable and the bolts of cloth arranged behind it. Dust specks orbited lazily in the beam, never quite settling on anything that mattered. Prudence had always admired that quality in dust, its refusal to obey the logic of gravity or order.

She sat at the table's end, needle in hand, her back rigid as if braced against a blow. The air was sharp with the scent of freshly sheared wool and the ghost of last night's candle. In the corner by the window, Bryant arranged his blocks in quiet columns, so silent Prudence sometimes forgot to check that he was there.

She worked on a jerkin for a farmhand who was passing through—tan, undyed, the only ornament a tidy line of brown thread to reinforce the seams. The fabric, coarse and stubborn, fought her every stitch, but she found comfort in the battle. When the bell above the door clattered its warning, she did not flinch. She simply set the needle down and pressed both hands flat against the wood, waiting for her breath to catch up.

The door swung wide and admitted Bartram in a gust of brisk air and self-confidence. The cobbler's scalp gleamed in the light, the last wisps of hair clinging to the idea of their former glory. His cheeks were dappled with the flush of outdoors, and his arms were loaded with a basket as large as Bryant's entire torso.

"Afternoon, Mistress Simonsdotter!" Bartram's voice filled the space, leaving no room for silence to regroup. He made a show of wiping his boots on the stoop, then stepped inside and shut the door with a careful hand.

"Bartram." Prudence gave a nod, almost a bow. "I wasn't expecting you till the seventh bell."

He grinned and shrugged, setting the basket on the nearest flat surface with a solid, bread-loaf thump. "Finished my orders ahead, and besides, I had a delivery. Makota's best rye, still warm enough to burn your fingers." He lifted the top of the basket to let the aroma spill out, and even Bryant looked up from his blocks, blue eyes rounding.

Prudence inhaled, then looked away quickly, focusing on the unfinished hem in front of her. "You're kind to bring it."

"Not kindness, duty!" Bartram said, spreading his hands in mock protest. "If the tailor collapses from hunger, who will patch my breeches?"

He plucked a chair from beside the worktable and dropped into it, the wood creaking in protest. He leaned forward, arms braced on his knees, and pitched his voice low.

"Didn't just come for the bread, truth be told." He angled his head toward the window, as if the salesman's wagon could be seen from there. "Had myself a stroll past the east gate. Figured a report might be wanted."

Prudence glanced at Bryant, who had gone still and attentive. She folded her hands in her lap, careful to keep them out of sight. "What did you find?"

Bartram scratched the side of his jaw, a gesture that always seemed to accompany the start of a long story. "The man's set up like a king, now. Table out front, banners—blue and gold this time, he must have had different ones. Can't imagine where else he would have gotten them. Brought out a chair for himself, and one for the poor soul being sold to." He shook his head, marveling at the nerve of it. "He'll let you sit, pour you a drop of whatever it is he's hawking, and talk you out of your last coin while you're still busy sniffing the glass."

Prudence pursed her lips, wishing she could claim surprise. "He makes it look like a festival, then."

"Exactly!" Bartram snapped his fingers. "Crowd in the street, travelers gawping, even a dog or two sniffing at the table leg. He's got something for everyone. And a story to match."

Bryant edged closer, now arranging his blocks into a ladder, as if to climb into the conversation.

Prudence let the silence stretch, hoping Bartram would offer his favorite quote without needing to be prompted. He did not disappoint.

"Friendly enough fellow, but he's got that slimy way about him that shady salesmen have anywhere," Bartram declared, leaning back as if giving a formal judgment. "Said he'd be gone in two bells, on to the next town. And I believe him—he's not a lingerer, that sort."

A stiff smile tugged at the corners of Prudence's mouth. She straightened the black cap that always felt a half-size too tight, and shifted in her chair to better face her guest. "Did he ask about anyone? Names, where you're from?"

Bartram shook his head. "Didn't seem to care, as long as I had ears to listen and fingers to hold a glass. Never even asked after the cobbler's shop." He grinned, pleased at having passed as an anonymous mark. "Only wanted to know if I ever felt... stuck, as he put it. Or if I had any dreams left that needed chasing."

Prudence exhaled, slow and careful. "He's good at that," she said, half to herself.

The basket of bread sat between them like an offering, but neither reached for it. The silence grew crowded with the weight of what neither wanted to voice. Finally, Bartram broke it with a question.

"You want me to try again? See if he's asking after you, or just anyone?"

Prudence shook her head, the motion quick and final. "Better not. Someone like that, he'll be clever with faces, even after years. You did well to keep your distance." She picked up the jerkin, ran a finger along the new seam, and tried to pretend the conversation was as ordinary as any other. "Thank you, Bartram."

He waved away the gratitude. "Least I could do, with all you've done for me and mine." His gaze flicked to Bryant, who was now crouched at the base of a chair leg, constructing a bridge of blocks from floor to rung. "And for all of us, really."

For a moment, the room was just the rustle of fabric and the soft tick of Bryant's blocks against the floor. The world outside pressed in at the edges, but inside the walls of Prudence's shop, everything held its place.

Prudence returned to her needlework, but this time she let herself relax, shoulders unknotting by increments. "Did the man say what he planned to do after North Pointe?" she asked, not looking up.

Bartram shrugged. "Said the trade road's always hungry, and there's no shortage of fools with coin and longing. Might swing through Holderdown again, or head west to the lakeside towns. Why?"

Prudence's lips pressed into a thin line. "Just curious."

Bartram watched her work for a moment, then softened his voice. "He's not coming for you, Pru. I'd stake my best boots on it."

She gave a single, almost invisible nod. "Still, thank you for looking."

Bartram reached for the bread, finally, and tore off a chunk. He offered the first piece to Bryant, who took it with both hands and retreated to his circle of blocks, already chewing.

Prudence's shop fell into its familiar rhythm: the hum of activity, the slow turn of sunlight across the floor, and the even quieter satisfaction of danger held at arm's length. The world would bring trouble soon enough, but for now, she allowed herself a moment of peace.

That moment of peace lasted a mere quarter-bell before the front door rattled again, this time with a rhythm that bespoke not commerce, but conspiracy. Prudence had just found her place in the row of stitches when two sets of boots, light and quick, scrabbled at the threshold. The bell above the door sang a bright, hurried note, and through the gap tumbled Senan and Willow, Cole's eldest son and daughter.

They entered as a unit: Senan with a self-assured stride, old enough to feign maturity but not so old as to suppress joy; Willow, younger by a year but already more forceful, swept the room with a gaze that weighed and measured all it saw. Both wore the uniform of country children—patched smocks, the faded memory of color at sleeve and hem, boots crusted with the evidence of serious play. In their hands, they carried an armory of entertainment: a leather ball, a carved hoop, and a handful of brightly painted sticks for some game Prudence could never remember the rules to.

Bartram greeted them with a clap that might have startled a less battle-tested child. "There's the new constable's force! Are you here to arrest us, or just to steal our bread?"

Senan grinned, showing all the gaps in his teeth. "Neither, Mister Lastmaker. We're here for Bryant."

At this, Bryant's head jerked up. He looked from the children to his mother, then back, blue eyes wide and hungry.

Willow advanced a step, chin high. "We have orders," she said, solemnly. "From Jen, and from our father, and even from Galhani. We're supposed to give Bryant the afternoon off." She held up the leather ball as evidence. "He's behind on play."

Prudence felt her throat constrict. "That's very kind," she said, hoping her voice did not betray her.

Willow nodded, businesslike. "We're going to the green. We'll stay where you can see us. And Senan knows not to let anyone talk to strangers."

"I'm not a baby," Senan added, and his glance at Bryant showed he'd accepted the charge.

Bartram was already halfway invested in the plan. "Well, there you have it," he said, turning to Prudence. "A direct order, and a proper chaperone. What say you?"

Prudence folded her hands in her lap, fingers weaving and unweaving as she calculated the risks. She'd let Bryant play with other children before, in brief supervised doses, always at arm's length and never out of sight. But the notion of an unscheduled, unstructured afternoon gnawed at her, a tiny, persistent ache.

Bryant had drifted closer to the newcomers, drawn by the gravitational pull of their excitement. Willow handed him one of the painted sticks, and he turned it over in his hands as if it were some rare artifact. The corners of his mouth twitched in something almost like a smile.

Senan spoke up, voice confident. "We promise we won't go far. Only the green. And Constable Jen is by the town gate."

Bartram leaned in, lowering his voice as if sharing a secret. "It'll do him good, you know. Running with the others. Builds the sort of courage they never teach in schools."

Prudence hesitated, but the evidence before her was overwhelming: Bryant, already halfway to the door, his tiny body vibrating with anticipation; Willow, holding out her hand with the casual authority of someone used to being obeyed; Bartram, beaming with the unshakeable confidence of a man who'd made the right call.

She relented, but not before laying out the terms. "Stay where I can see you, and if you need anything, you come straight back." She tried to sound stern, but even to her own ear the words rang thin.

Willow nodded, her solemnity now edged with triumph. "We will." She took Bryant's hand and, with a leader's certainty, shepherded him out the door. Senan followed, hoisting the ball over his shoulder like a prize. In an instant, they were gone, the only sign of their passing the echo of laughter and the quick patter of feet on stone.

Prudence stood for a moment, watching the void where her son had just been. The shop felt emptier than it should, as if some integral part of its structure had been removed. She sank back into her chair, but did not pick up the needle. Instead, she let her gaze drift to the window, where she could just make out the children tumbling into the grass, a riot of motion and color against the dull afternoon.

Bartram watched her, his expression softer than usual. "You did the right thing," he said.

Prudence answered without turning. "He's not like the others. I worry—" The admission hung in the air, brittle and exposed.

Bartram shrugged, his hands spreading wide. "All children are strange, in one way or another. That's why they need each other. Makes them less likely to grow up cruel."

She was silent, considering the wisdom of this. In Holderdown, difference was a weakness, an excuse for the world to press in and close ranks. Here, it seemed the opposite might be true: the more oddities you collected, the richer the town became.

Bartram watched the children for a moment, then turned back to Prudence. "It's a fine thing, the way he looks at you. Like you hung the moon yourself."

She smiled, this time letting it reach her eyes. "He's a good boy."

Bartram snorted, amused. "He's a miracle, is what he is."

The two of them sat in companionable silence, the world outside humming with the safe chaos of children at play. Every so often, Prudence glanced to the window, checking that Bryant remained within sight. He did, always, his hair a bright flag amid the brown and gray of the others.

In time, the tremor in her hands subsided, and she reached for the needle once more. The work was there, as it always was, waiting for her to return. But this time, she allowed herself to pause between stitches, to look out and watch as her son navigated a world bigger than the one she'd built for him.

When the jerkin was finished, she set it aside and permitted herself a moment to savor the hush. It was not the silence of loneliness, but the lull that follows the letting go of a long-held fear.

Bryant would be back soon, she knew. And when he returned, the shop would be fuller for his absence.

———

The bread basket, once the centerpiece of Bartram's errand, now sat forgotten between the two. Bryant's absence left a mild, but not unpleasant, hush. Through the window, the green was a stage: Bryant, flanked by Senan and Willow, running circuits around the grass, occasionally glancing up to the tailor shop as if to check the anchor still held.

Inside, time flowed differently, slow and thick. Prudence returned to her needlework, hoping the act of sewing would muffle the aftershocks of letting Bryant go unsupervised. But she made little progress. The jerkin before her, so plain and scratchy, looked unfit for any living creature, much less the eager farmhand it was meant to serve.

Bartram, noticing her lack of momentum, busied himself by scanning the shelves that ringed the shop. "I've always wondered," he said, rising from his chair, "how you keep track of so much fabric. There must be a hundred colors in here, and I can't remember half the names for them."

Prudence forced a smile. "Most are never used. The shop itself chooses what appears." She gestured vaguely to the top shelf, where a stack of bolts leaned against one another in an arrangement too artful to be accidental.

Bartram peered up, his brow furrowing. "Is that real velvet?" He pointed to a bolt at the far end, color electric even in the muted winter sun.

Prudence hesitated. The bolt had been there since she first claimed the shop, its texture finer than anything she'd touched in Holderdown. It seemed to shimmer with its own internal light. She'd always avoided it, preferring the drab and utilitarian. Yet now, with Bryant occupied elsewhere, she felt the shield of necessity waver.

She set her needle down, wiped her hands, and crossed to the shelf. On tiptoe, she retrieved the bolt and brought it to the table. The velvet's green was so pure it seemed to pulse. Bartram watched, openly delighted.

"I've never seen anything like that," he said, running a finger along the edge, careful not to crease the nap. "What's it meant for?"

Prudence laid her palm flat on the cloth, feeling the surface as if it might vanish with too much pressure. "Nothing. It's not for anything. No one in town could afford a gown from this, and it would draw too much attention. Travelers passing through are satisfied with studier fabrics." She tried to say it with conviction, but the fabric's radiance made her words seem paltry.

Bartram let out a small, thoughtful hum. "You ever think that's the problem? Folk wear gray and brown so long, they forget there's any other way."

Prudence did not answer. She lifted the bolt, measured a hand's width, then set it back down. "There's comfort in being unnoticed."

"Is there?" Bartram looked at her sidelong. "Seems to me, people just want to be seen for what they are." He slid the bread basket aside and drew his boots up for inspection. "Take these," he said, tapping the leather with pride. "Good sturdy boots, best I ever made. But look close." He turned the toe to the light, where a row of gold thread traced a spiral along the upper. "See? No one needs that little bit. Doesn't make the walking any better. But when folk see it, they remember. They say, 'That's Bartram's work.' And I'm all right with that."

Prudence looked at the boots, then back to the velvet. She touched the selvedge, letting it slip between her thumb and forefinger, slow as a secret. "Where I grew up," she said, "showing off was—dangerous."

Bartram leaned forward. "This isn't Holderdown." He softened the words with a smile. "You're allowed to stand out, if you want."

Prudence shook her head, but she could not stop touching the fabric. "I was taught that function matters. Beauty is for weddings. Fine fabric for funerals, but always in black."

"Why not both?" Bartram said. "Why not a coat that's warm and bright, a shirt that lasts but makes you glad to see it in the morning?" He swept his hands over the table, brushing up imaginary bits of lint. "You could make something no one's ever seen, and folks would be grateful for it."

The old reflex—defensiveness—rose in her throat. She fought it down, then said, more softly than intended, "They'd laugh. Or worse, they'd notice."

Bartram gestured to the shop itself, a riot of pattern and shade. "I'd say you're already noticed. You're the only one who doesn't see it." He lowered his voice. "Prudence, you got out. You built something here. Don't let a fear from another life run the new one."

She looked up, and for a heartbeat, let the words land. Then, as if embarrassed by her own pause, she returned to rolling the velvet. "Maybe for a festival, then. Something for next summer. Or perhaps..." She trailed off.

Bartram finished it for her. "Or perhaps, something for yourself."

She did not answer, but the way she wrapped the cloth was slower, almost reverent.

Bartram sat back, satisfied. He folded his arms and watched her, waiting for the moment to breathe and settle. Then, with the gentleness only someone truly at ease could muster, he said, "Whatever fears you carried from Holderdown have no power over you here in North Pointe."

Prudence traced the green edge one last time, then set the bolt aside, where the sunlight struck it full. It lit the shop with a color so deep, it might have changed the temperature of the air.

She did not reply—not with words, at least. But her hands, so careful and deliberate, betrayed her in the best possible way.

The bell caught them both off guard. Its deep, deliberate clang carried from the town hall, each toll as unhurried and certain as a heartbeat. Bartram finished the last of the bread and brushed his hands together, sending a small cascade of crumbs onto the table. "That's my cue," he said, rising. "If I don't get back soon, the world might end, or at least the boots will."

Prudence helped gather the basket's remnants. She ferried the heel of the loaf to the pantry—such as it was, a single shelf above the washbasin—while Bartram wrapped up the stray pieces in their wax paper. "You know," he said as he worked, "some towns, they have a bell for every quarter-candlemark. Here, it's just the full 'mark. I like that. Makes each bell matter."

"It gives the day a shape," Prudence agreed, tucking the bread behind a jar of pickled greens.

Bartram followed her into the kitchen corner, his eyes still catching on the green velvet every time he passed the table. "What will you do with it?" he asked, his tone light, but not unserious.

Prudence hesitated. "I haven't decided." She wiped her hands on the towel, then straightened the edge of her apron, a nervous habit she'd never shaken.

"Maybe you could make a scarf for Bryant," Bartram mused. "Or for yourself." He smiled, but made no effort to press her further. "It'd look well on either of you."

They returned to the front of the shop, where the sunlight had shifted to catch the completed jerkin, draping it in a gold so forgiving, it almost looked refined. Bartram picked it up, examined the seams, then held it at arm's length. "That's good work," he said, his voice serious. "But imagine it with a collar of that green. Just a touch, nothing showy. What would the boy think of himself then?"

Prudence did not answer, but her gaze lingered on the garment.

Bartram shrugged the jerkin back onto the waiting form and retrieved his own coat from the chair. He turned to the door, paused, then looked back at Prudence. "Don't be a stranger," he said. "I'll be in the square tomorrow, if you're out."

She nodded, but could not think of a reply. Bartram smiled again— so easy, so practiced—and slipped into the dusk, his steps brisk and certain as he crossed the green.

Prudence closed the shop door behind him, sliding the bolt with a satisfying thunk. The world outside had dimmed, but inside, the velvet's hue seemed even brighter, as if the absence of sunlight only condensed its power.

She crossed to the worktable, hand hovering over the fabric. When she picked it up, she let it spill across her forearm, the way the water at the lake sometimes did when she and Bryant would visit the shore. She held it up to the window, watching how the light transformed it from emerald to peacock blue and back again. It was a foolish thing, indulgent, but she let herself enjoy it.

The door rattled before she could return the bolt to its place. Prudence's heart jumped—then she heard the unmistakable laughter of children, and knew it was Bryant and his companions. She opened the door just in time for the three of them to tumble inside, each more flushed and wind-chafed than the last.

Bryant's hair stood at odd angles, and his cheeks glowed with exertion. He trotted straight to Prudence, arms outstretched, and latched onto her skirt with the full gravity of a child returned from a successful campaign.

Senan and Willow, less attached, hovered by the door, looking pleased with themselves. Willow still carried the ball, now dusted in mud. Senan wiped his nose on his sleeve, then surveyed the shop with a merchant's practiced interest.

Prudence bent to brush Bryant's hair back into place. "Did you have fun?" she asked, already knowing the answer.

He nodded, but words were not forthcoming. Instead, he peered up at her, then at the velvet still clutched in her hand. He reached for it, fingers brushing the nap. His eyes widened.

"It's soft," he whispered, testing the word as if it were a spell.

Senan sidled up, curiosity piqued. "What's that for?" he asked.

Prudence considered. "I don't know yet," she admitted.

Willow came closer, peering at the cloth with an appraising eye. "It's the same color as the forest in spring," she said, matter-of-fact. "Maybe even brighter."

Prudence smiled, then let Bryant take a corner of the fabric. He pressed it to his cheek, giggling at the sensation. Willow and Senan both tried, and soon all three were passing it between them, testing its texture with the seriousness children reserve for the truly new.

Prudence watched, something uncoiling in her chest. She thought of Bartram's words, of the way the velvet had drawn every eye in the room, and of the difference between being seen and being noticed.

When the children tired of the game, she reclaimed the bolt and, instead of returning it to the shelf, set it on the worktable. There it caught the last orange rays of evening and shone as if it belonged.

Bryant watched her, blue eyes solemn, then reached out to pat her hand. It was a gesture of comfort, one she'd learned to accept. She let her fingers close around his, and together, they regarded the fabric as if it were a promise.

For the first time, she wondered what it would be like to make something beautiful just because she could.

She left the velvet on the table overnight. By morning, the memory of its color had seeped into every corner of the shop, and Prudence, for once, did not mind at all.

seven

. . .

MORNING AGAIN, and the light slanting through the tailor shop's front window was as weak and brittle as ever. In the fortnight since the salesman's arrival, Prudence had developed a new kind of relationship with dawn—a suspicious one. Each sunrise was a fresh accounting of what the world would demand from her, and every day she weighed it, measured it, and sewed herself into the answers she could afford.

She sat at her worktable, bent over a neat row of children's shirts, her fingers extracting the smallest, most stubborn stitches. She'd developed the habit of over-tightening her own seams, as if more thread would hold the day at bay, but it made the undoing that much harder. Her thimble was cold against her thumb; the raw edge of the cloth pricked the skin where her hands had softened in the winter. She worked by habit, mostly, letting her mind creep into the empty spaces left by repetition.

Bryant was already awake, tucked in the corner by the stove. He was not stacking blocks this morning—he'd lost interest in the towers, said they kept falling even when he was careful. Instead, he arranged a garrison of wooden figurines: two soldiers, a horse with a broken ear, a bird with one wing, and a flat, painted square that claimed to be a "shield" but looked more like a breadboard. Warren had carved the lot, as a bribe to keep Bryant from touching the hammers at the forge. The figures stood in ordered rows, waiting for Bryant's next command.

The shop was cold, and Prudence had not yet lit the second lamp. She preferred it that way. It made the world outside seem farther off, and made the quiet of the morning more absolute.

She was re-threading her needle—silver, still sharp enough to catch the skin if she was careless—when a sound at the door brought her head up. Not the sudden clatter of a customer, but a hesitant, rhythmical tap: three knocks, then a pause, then three more. The code was town-wide, and it meant no danger, only a neighbor.

Prudence set the shirt aside and rose, smoothing her skirt with one hand. She opened the door to a low fog and the equally low figure of Galhani, who stood wrapped in a moss-colored shawl, a steaming mug balanced in both hands.

"Tea delivery," Galhani announced. "Special blend. Two parts morning, one part courage."

She offered the mug up, and Prudence accepted it, the warmth seeping into her palms before the aroma did. The gnome's nose was already pink from the cold, but her eyes were sharp as frost.

"Come in," Prudence said, stepping aside. Galhani entered, untying her shawl as she walked, and made directly for the hearth.

Bryant looked up at her, then at his mother, then back down at the figurines. He arranged them into a tighter line, as if fortifying the soldiers for the arrival of a new general.

Galhani perched herself on the edge of a stool, feet dangling above the floor. "It's brisk out," she said, not as an observation, but as a sort of weather report. "But peaceful. I walked the whole square and saw only four cats, Makota's kits, and the clouds."

Prudence nodded, sipping the tea. It was sweet and smoky, and the heat reached her chest before the taste did.

They sat in silence for a moment. Galhani took in the shop with a single, sweeping glance, her gaze pausing at the piles of folded work and the collection of mending that lined the shelves behind the counter. "Busy morning?"

"Always," Prudence said, then caught herself. "It's better this way."

Galhani made a sympathetic sound, then pulled a folded note from her apron. "I've got the day's report. Jen wanted you to know: she was at the gate before sunrise, and our friend with the bottles did try to come in early. She intercepted him herself—stood right in the center of the arch, hand on Hellsting's, ah, bracelet, and made him wait until the next bell before letting him pass."

Prudence took this in, letting the warmth of the mug offset the chill that the mention of Hellsting brought. "Did he complain?"

"He did," Galhani said, grinning. "But only to the air. I'm told she didn't give him a word back, just glared at him until his mustache wilted."

Prudence almost smiled.

"After that," Galhani continued, "she walked him all the way down the main road, made a show of it. He was so busy acting unbothered that he nearly tripped over his own wagon."

Bryant giggled, the sound as quiet as a mouse in a cupboard.

"Thank you," Prudence said, meaning it. Her shoulders, which had knotted up during the night, loosened a notch.

"Nothing to thank," Galhani said, dismissing the gratitude with a wave. "The town's got your back, as always." She craned her head toward Bryant. "How's our captain this morning?"

Bryant picked up the horse and held it aloft. "They're going to battle," he said, then corrected himself. "But not a real one. Just for practice."

Galhani made a show of widening her eyes. "A practice battle? That's even better. No one gets hurt, and you still get to win."

Bryant grinned and returned to his troops.

Prudence set the mug on the table, then glanced at the window. "Is he still here? The salesman?"

Galhani followed her gaze. "Not even pretending to leave. He's set up at the green now, with twice as many banners. I saw three travelers there already, and he was pouring samples before I turned the corner."

Prudence's hands found the hem of her sleeve and began worrying at a loose thread. "I thought he would have moved on by now."

"He's making too much coin," Galhani said, plainly. "A new crowd every day, and no one to stop him. But Jen says he's not causing trouble, only noise. Not even the town magic will let her chase him out for that."

"Noise is enough," Prudence murmured.

Galhani cocked her head, studying the seamstress. "You should get out today, if you can. There's a lull at the tea shop—no one but me and the plants, and Makota's coming by at the next bell. She's got news."

Prudence hesitated. Her gaze traveled over the unfinished shirts, the baskets of mending, the half-done promises she'd stacked up to keep her hands occupied.

"Just for a little while," Galhani added, reading the answer in Prudence's silence. "Bring the boy. I have biscuits."

Bryant looked up at the mention, but waited for his mother's verdict.

"I will," Prudence said, after a pause. "Thank you, Galhani."

"Good," the gnome said, brightening. "It's no use locking yourself in here. The world's not so dangerous, not with the whole town watching it for you."

She hopped off the stool, retied her shawl, and made for the door. She stopped at the threshold, turned, and smiled—a gesture that took up her whole face.

"See you soon, then," Galhani said.

Prudence nodded.

When the door closed, the room seemed colder for a moment, then settled. Bryant rearranged his soldiers into a defensive ring, muttering to them under his breath.

Prudence returned to her worktable, set the tea beside the shirts, and tried to resume her stitching. But the line she sewed was crooked, the thread uneven. She paused, needle in hand, and stared at the work. It was unlike her to slip. She'd always prided herself on perfect seams, even when the world was bent around her.

She unpicked the stitches, started again, and this time the line was only a little better.

She knew it was not just the salesman. It was the waiting, the not-knowing. The endless hum of voices outside, the certainty that someone, somewhere, would bring her news of him every day.

She finished the shirt, folded it carefully, and set it on the pile.

Bryant was lining up the bird and the horse, making them bow to one another in a strange, polite dance.

She watched him for a moment, then looked past him, out the shop window, where the sun was still struggling to find its courage.

A fortnight, and the world was already starting to fray.

Prudence pressed her hands together, as if she could keep the threads from loosening.

But the worry was still there, running just under the surface, waiting for the next tug.

She rose, tidied the table, and began preparing for the walk to the tea shop.

If there was to be a battle, it would have to wait for after lunch.

———

At the stroke of the next bell, Prudence bundled Bryant in his jacket and set out across the green. The chill was nothing compared to the sharpness she remembered from Holderdown, but it stung the cheeks and made the walk brisk. Bryant's hand was small and hot in hers, and though he kept pace, every few steps he would cast a backward glance toward the shop, as if reassuring himself that the world would stay in order until he returned.

Galhani's tea shop was just off the square, half a block down from the smithy. The sign above the door was newly painted—crimson and gold, with a linework of herbs that danced around the shop's new name: "Galhani's Steeps." The windows fogged with warmth from inside, and the bell above the door chirped a bright greeting as Prudence opened it.

If the tailor shop was all muted earth, the tea shop was an explosion of texture and color. Bunches of dried leaves and flower heads dangled from rafters, their scents twining in the air: chamomile, sweet mint, peppery sprigs that tickled the nose. Sunlight, filtered through lace curtains, spilled across the waxed floor in soft, intricate puddles.

The whole place radiated a warmth that was more than just the oven's glow.

Galhani was waiting, standing on a two-step footstool behind the counter and pouring hot water over a mesh ball of purple-blue petals. She wore a dress the color of overripe plums, with sleeves too long for her arms, and her silver-white hair was tied in a braid that circled her head like a crown.

"Pru! Bryant!" she called. "Right on time, you are."

Bryant released his mother's hand and rushed toward the table nearest the window, where a plate of cookies already awaited him.

Prudence approached the counter, the scents growing more complicated as she drew closer. "You said Makota would join us?"

"She's due any moment. I told her there was a batch of ridge-peach scones, and you know how she is about those."

Galhani poured a cup of tea into a large, human-sized mug, then, standing on tiptoe, slid it across the counter. Prudence caught it with both hands, cradling the warmth.

"Thank you," she said, the phrase feeling like a life preserver.

Bryant, meanwhile, had already set to work dismantling the plate of cookies, selecting each one with a deliberateness that bordered on scientific.

The bell over the door sounded again, this time with a sharp, metallic urgency. Makota slipped through, bringing with her the smell of snow and baking bread. She wore an apron dusted with flour, and her fur was puffed against the cold, giving her a stately, if slightly ruffled, appearance.

"Apologies for the delay," Makota trilled, smoothing her whiskers with both paws. "There was a crisis with a rye loaf, and Kene tried to eat the dough before it even went into the oven. But we're safe now." She dropped onto a chair opposite Bryant and eyed the cookies.

"You said you had news," Galhani prompted, as she set a teacup—gnome-sized—at her own place.

Makota's tail flicked, and her ears angled forward. "Oh, do I ever. But first, introductions." She fixed her gaze on Bryant. "Captain," she said, "you are looking especially well-dressed today."

Bryant beamed and pointed at his shirt. "My mother made it," he announced, then added, after a beat, "and my scarf, too."

Makota smiled, sharp teeth and all. "It's the best scarf in the town, and you wear it like royalty." She glanced at Prudence, lowering her voice. "You should consider doing a line of accessories. Perhaps… some in brighter colors."

Prudence felt her cheeks grow warm. "Thank you," she said, unsure what else to offer.

Makota sipped her tea, then leaned in conspiratorially. "So. The salesman." Her tail whipped behind her, telegraphing the mood. "He came to the bakery today."

Galhani's eyes narrowed. "Did he try to buy you out?"

Makota shrugged, all feigned nonchalance. "He tried. But Jen had warned me, and I was ready." She tapped the table with one paw. "I sold him one—count it, one—small loaf, and a jar of yesterday's jam. No fresh cakes, no honey, nothing with value."

Bryant giggled.

"He tried to charm me," Makota went on, "with compliments about my baking. Asked if I put 'special' herbs in the dough." She rolled her eyes. "I've heard better lines from apprentice bakers. I told him the only magic in my kitchen was what came out of the oven, and that he was lucky to get a loaf at all."

Galhani grinned. "He's never met his match until now."

Makota preened a little, then turned back to Prudence. "He did ask about you. Not directly, but he circled the subject. And not you specifically—just 'the tailor.' Wondered if your work was any good. I told him you were too busy to take on more."

Prudence's hands trembled around the mug. She set it down, fingers spread wide to steady herself. "Thank you," she said, the words barely audible.

Makota's gaze softened. "He won't get near you. Not while we're here."

Galhani poured herself another cup, topping off Prudence's as well. "We've got a whole plan, actually. Dardrad's been taking deliveries to the inn in person, so he can keep an eye on things. Bartram's started a rumor that the salesman is selling hair tonic made from old shoe leather, and I'm pretty sure half the town is passing it on to the road custom."

Makota nodded. "Warren posted Darby at the gate for most of yesterday. If anything odd happened, he was to come straight to Jen."

Bryant, emboldened by the sugar and the warmth, piped up: "Are you talking about the bottle man?"

All three women looked at him.

"Yes," Galhani said, kindly. "But you don't have to worry about him. The grownups have it handled."

Bryant accepted this, and took another cookie.

For a while, they let the conversation drift to other things: the state of the road, the latest delivery from the lake, the way the crows had grown bold and were raiding the seed shop again. Bryant listened, rapt, as Makota's kits—Sora and Kene—appeared from the bakery's back door and delivered a miniature honey cake to his table. The treat was crowned with a single preserved cherry, and Bryant made a ceremony of dividing it into precise halves, so he could share with his mother.

Prudence nibbled the cake, letting the sweetness settle the tremor in her hands. She looked at the three women around the table, all so different from one another, and felt the old ache of not belonging grow smaller, if only for a moment.

After a candlemark, when the sun had shifted a full handspan along the table, Prudence stood and smoothed her skirt.

"I need to get back," she said. "There's a family leaving in the morning, and I promised to have their repairs done before they set out."

Makota stood as well. "I'll walk you partway. I have to check on the rye loaf."

Galhani reached up to squeeze Prudence's arm. "Come back any time. Next time, bring some of that green velvet Bartram is going on about. I want to see it in the light."

Prudence hesitated, then promised she would, and collected Bryant, who was now sugared and sleepy. They stepped out into the street, the chill no worse for all the warmth they carried with them.

Makota walked beside her, silent at first, then said, "He really won't get near you, you know. Jen and Galhani and all the rest—we'll see to it."

Prudence looked at the ground. "I'm not afraid for myself," she said. "It's Bryant. I just want him to grow up where nothing can get at him."

Makota's tail flicked, but she said nothing more.

They reached the corner, and Makota peeled away, waving with one paw. Prudence and Bryant crossed the green together, their shadows long and almost touching.

Inside the shop, the world was exactly as she'd left it. The piles of mending waited, the lamp was cold. Bryant climbed onto his stool and began playing with the wooden horse, galloping it in circles around the edge of the worktable.

Prudence watched him for a moment, then set herself to work. She picked up the half-done shirt, threaded her needle, and began again— this time, the stitches were straight.

———

The afternoon thinned itself out, stretching into dusk with the lazy persistence of winter. By the time Prudence finished the last of her promised repairs and set the mended shirt atop the delivery pile, the sky outside had turned a somber violet. The town green, which in summer held the memory of laughter and sunlight, now brooded under the gray weight of approaching night. It seemed to her that the day's warmth had gone into hiding.

She closed the shop a half-candlemark early. There were no expected visitors, no last-minute orders. Bryant was already yawning, his energy spent on the earlier parade of cookies and wooden horses. Prudence tidied the counter, swept the thread scraps into a neat pile, and then—after a pause—crossed to the window and drew the curtains closed. The fabric was thick, and when it fell, the world outside was shut out completely.

She locked the door and set the bolt, then sat down in her rocking chair, Bryant nestled into her lap. His head lolled sideways, and she stroked his hair with automatic, steady movements. He resisted sleep for a few minutes, but eventually, the regular tick of the wall clock and the gentle movement of the chair did their work.

A sharp rap at the door jolted her.

She held perfectly still, counting the heartbeats in the silence that followed. The knock came again, but softer this time. She eased Bryant into his cot, padded across the room, and peered through the curtain. The square was mostly empty, save for the hunched shape of Darby, Warren's son, who stood at the doorstep with his hands shoved deep into his coat.

Prudence opened the door a crack.

"Evening, Darby," she said, her voice low so as not to wake the child behind her.

He held out a folded note. "From Sam," he announced. His eyes were wide, solemn in a way that belonged to someone far older.

Prudence took the note. "You want to come in for a minute?" she asked.

Darby shook his head. "I have to get back. Pa's fixing the bellows again, and Ma says if I'm late, he'll send me down the vent with no dinner."

Prudence smiled, but it was only for show. "Tell your parents hello from me."

"Will do," Darby said, and then hesitated. "Sam said to make sure you read it right away."

"I will," Prudence promised.

He turned and trotted off, cutting across the green toward the blacksmith's shop. Prudence closed the door, checked the bolt again, and unfolded the note.

The writing was Sam's: compact, assertive, slanted like it wanted to outpace itself.

He tried the pub tonight. Ordered a round for the whole house, then sat at the window facing the square. I let him, but no one talked to him, not even when he started singing that awful Holderdown song. I left him his cup but made him fetch the next one from the bar.

Warren and I watched him go at closing. He stood outside, looking at your shop for a long time, then walked off toward the west end.

If you want me to do more, send a word. Otherwise, I'll keep the same watch tomorrow.

- S

P.S. If he tries your door, yell and Warren will come running. He's been looking for an excuse.

Prudence read the note twice, then folded it and tucked it into her apron. She closed her eyes, took a deep breath, and tried to picture the scene at the pub: Sam behind the bar, one hand never far from Nailbiter's hilt; the salesman alone, surrounded by the pointed silence of a room that had already made up its mind.

She almost laughed, imagining the salesman's face as he realized his usual tricks would get him nowhere here.

When she opened her eyes, Bryant had already wriggled half-out of his blanket, his hands making lazy circles in the air. Prudence bent and scooped him up, hugging him close. He smelled faintly of honey and woodsmoke.

She carried him to the rocker, then sat with him, holding him as she used to when he was a baby. The darkness outside pressed at the windows, but the room was warm, full of small, good things. For a little while, she just sat, letting the day unravel itself, until a soft knock sounded again at the door.

This time, it was tentative, almost apologetic. Prudence peered through the curtain and saw Darby again, this time looking more sheepish than before.

She opened the door a sliver.

"Forgot," he whispered, "Pa said to give you this." He held out a small package, awkwardly wrapped in brown paper and twine.

She took it, and Darby darted away before she could ask what it was.

Prudence closed the door and set the bundle on the table. She opened it carefully, half-expecting a tool or some odd part from the smithy, but inside was a kerchief—plain linen, hemmed in the manner she'd shown Darby herself, the stitches small and almost invisible.

She felt something tighten in her throat.

When Bryant was finally asleep, she sat by the window, staring at the curtains as if they were a stage and the next act could begin at any moment. She thought of Sam, and Warren, and even little Darby—of all the people in this town who had chosen, deliberately, to make her part of their story.

She set the kerchief in her lap, ran her fingers along the perfect edge, and closed her eyes.

The salesman could wait. For tonight, she was home.

———

Morning began with the sound of rain on the shutters, but by the time Bryant finished his breakfast, the world outside had changed its mind. Fog clung to the cobbles in shreds, the wet grayness making the square seem smaller, more private. Prudence spooned oatmeal into Bryant's bowl, watched him pick at the raisins, and considered her own options.

She'd slept little, her mind looping through the note from Sam, the memory of Darby's kerchief, and the slow, relentless churn of the town's rumor mill. Every so often, she'd think of the salesman—what he wanted, where he'd go next—and the thought would set her jaw. She hated that he was a mystery, even now. She hated the not-knowing.

Bryant finished his bowl and announced, "I want to go to the window."

Prudence lifted him from his chair, set him at the sill, and opened the curtain just a slit. The fog had thinned, but the square remained deserted. No sign of the wagon yet. She looked at the clock, calculated how long before the first travelers would be stirring, and made a decision.

"Stay here, love," she said, pressing Bryant's hand. "I'll be back in a minute." She dressed quickly, wrapped her hair in its tight black cap, and slipped out the side door of the shop, locking it behind her. The Weary Head was half a block away, its rear alley deserted except for a single stray cat searching for a mouse. Prudence skirted the animal, then ducked through the kitchen door.

Minnie, busy preparing breakfast in the inn's tiny kitchen, nodded gently as Prudence passed by the open door. The inn's front room was empty at this time of day, although the prior evening's tenants would soon be down. She quickly crossed the room to the front window, which overlooked the trade road just inside the east gate. She'd imagined doing this for more than a fortnight now, and her heart hammered and her hands trembled as she drew the curtains open a spare inch.

From this vantage, she could see the east road and the patch of mud where the salesman always parked his wagon. At first, nothing. Then, as the fog continued to break, the outlines of the wagon's wheels appeared, bright as circus paint. A few moments later, the salesman himself emerged, cloak flapping, hands full of glass bottles that shimmered even in the thin sun.

He set up with practiced efficiency: a folding table, a clutch of paper banners, and a row of vials in every color of the rainbow. He arranged them with a showman's precision, wiping each bottle with a white cloth before setting it just so. The sign went up last—blue letters on white: *Destiny Potion, 2 Silvers.* Beneath, in smaller script: *Guaranteed to Change Your Life.*

Prudence watched as the first customers appeared—two travelers, muddy boots and tired faces, clearly just in from the night's journey. The salesman beckoned, spun a tale, poured them each a swallow from a green bottle. They laughed, they paid, and then they were gone.

She kept watching. Through the late morning, the parade of customers never quite stopped: a merchant with a limp, a pair of sisters in matching wool cloaks, a farmer from the outlying lands. Each left with a vial. Most seemed happier for it.

At midday, the square grew busier. Prudence watched as a pair of young men—too old for boys, too young for wisdom— approached the wagon. They wore matching daggers at their belts, the kind sold to adventurers in every trade town on the continent. They circled the wagon, debated in low voices, then at last walked up to the table.

The salesman greeted them with a sweeping bow, uncorked two bottles—one blue, one gold—and offered each a taste. The taller boy hesitated, but the shorter grinned and tossed his back in a single gulp.

"Why climb a mountain when the answer's right here?" he said to his friend, loud enough that Prudence heard it through the glass.

They paid, tucked the bottles into their packs, and walked off toward the west road, arms around each other's shoulders.

By now, the square was noisy with the business of the day. Prudence, her breath fogging the window, saw Knodalon sitting on his usual bench outside the storehouse. The old man looked even older than before, white hair tangled around his ears, chin on his chest. He sat motionless, hands folded, but his eyes followed the salesman's every move.

Prudence stayed another quarter-bell, watching as the merchant packed up for the noon meal, then moved to a new spot on the square —closer to the bakery this time. He seemed to sense where the next wave of customers would be, and he always got there first.

She returned to her shop to find Bryant, arms crossed, waiting for her at the door.

"You said a minute," he said, as if time were a promise.

She knelt to his level, kissed his forehead, and held him close. "I'm sorry," she whispered. "It was important."

He considered this, then nodded, apparently satisfied.

They spent the afternoon together, Bryant playing at her feet while she worked. But the memory of the salesman lingered in her mind— the glint of his bottles, the ease of his lies, the endless hunger of people who just wanted something to believe in.

As dusk fell, Prudence returned to the inn's window, drawn by the pull of routine. The wagon was still there, though the customers had thinned. The salesman counted a heap of coins by lantern light, his shadow stretching long and thin across the cobblestones. Prudence could see Knodalon still at his bench, unmoved by cold or dark, eyes narrow and bright as a winter's star.

She stood there for a long time, watching the salesman gather his things and retreat to his wagon, the colored bottles glinting in the last light.

It was the same every night, but tonight, it felt different.

Tonight, she saw the shape of the battle she was fighting—not with swords or magic, but with the everyday grind of work, and the relentless, simple act of refusing to give up what was hers.

When the square was empty again, she closed the curtain and locked the door. Bryant was already asleep, curled around his pillow. Prudence checked on him, pulled the blanket up, and then, finally, allowed herself a few candlemarks of rest.

She dreamed, that night, of bottles filled with light, and of a mountain that reached all the way to the sky.

———

The day after the dream dawned sharp and cold, the square glinting under a thin film of ice. Prudence woke early, set a pot of water to boil, and spent the first 'mark of daylight in silent company with Bryant, each of them lost in their own thoughts. Bryant watched the new cat, now curled at the window ledge, and Prudence let her gaze drift between the dull orange horizon and the empty spot where the salesman's wagon would soon appear.

She dressed, swept the shop, and stepped outside to fetch in the day's delivery—milk, a loaf from Makota, and a neat bundle of correspondence left by Bartram. The ritual steadied her.

She had just returned from the Weary Head's rear entrance, where she'd spied again on the early stirrings of the square, when the bell above her shop door rang twice in quick succession. Bryant looked up, startled, but relaxed when he saw the familiar shape of Dooley in the threshold.

Dooley stood with both hands in his pockets, face flushed either from the cold or embarrassment—it was always hard to tell. He rocked on his heels, eyes darting everywhere but directly at Prudence.

"Morning," he said, and then: "Do you have a minute?"

Prudence nodded, beckoning him in. "Of course."

He entered, shutting the door behind him with more care than was strictly necessary. A strange, muffled mewling came from under his coat, and for a heartbeat Prudence wondered if he had brought a half-feral kitten or, gods forbid, a wounded crow.

Dooley's hand emerged from his coat holding something much stranger.

It was an owlcat—a tiny, furred creature no bigger than a teacup, with round, solemn eyes, feathery tufts at the tips of its ears, and vestigial wings folded against its sides. It regarded Prudence with an almost comical gravity, then emitted a small, questioning trill.

"I thought," Dooley started, stumbling over the words, "maybe you could use some company that didn't talk back quite so much."

Prudence blinked, unsure if she was meant to accept this as a joke or a serious gift.

He stepped forward and offered her the owlcat, which latched immediately to her shoulder with a delicate but decisive grip. The animal weighed almost nothing, and its body was so warm it seemed to radiate through the fabric of her dress.

"It's a gift," Dooley clarified. "From the menagerie. They don't do well in crowds, and Bryant's always gentle."

Prudence reached up, tentatively, to stroke the creature's back. It preened, then began to purr—an odd, chirring sound that reminded her more of a grasshopper than a housecat.

"Thank you," she said, genuinely surprised by the emotion that crept into her voice.

Bryant crept closer, hands behind his back, eyes wide. The owlcat noticed him, dropped to the floor in a single fluttering bound, and padded over to nuzzle his ankle. Bryant crouched, face lit up, and stroked the animal's head. The owlcat flopped onto its back, demanding belly rubs.

"It likes him," Dooley observed. "I think you're safe now."

Prudence smiled, the first time she'd done so without effort in days.

She set water to boil for tea and motioned Dooley to a seat at the worktable. The owlcat followed Bryant, leaping from lap to lap and never making a sound above a faint, intermittent squeak.

Dooley sipped at the tea, and for a moment they were quiet, watching the boy and the animal tumble together. Then he cleared his throat.

"I've been thinking," he said, "about how hard it must be. With the salesman and all." He fiddled with his cup. "Not just for you, for everyone. But you most of all."

Prudence shrugged. "I'm used to it."

"That's what I mean," Dooley said. "You shouldn't have to be."

He hesitated, then reached into his satchel and pulled out a bundle of clothing: thick, woolen trousers, a patchwork jacket, and a shirt that had once been white but now leaned heavily toward beige. "I was hoping," he began, "if it's not too much trouble—you could fix these up? I used to wear them when I traveled, but haven't for a few seasons, and I thought…"

"I'd be happy to," Prudence interrupted.

Dooley's relief was almost comical. He handed her the bundle, then ran a hand through his hair, looking everywhere but at her face.

"They're not fancy," he said, "but they're sturdy. Thought they might be useful again, what with all the excitement."

Prudence nodded, setting the clothes on her mending pile. "You'll have them back by the end of the sennight."

He seemed about to say something more, but the owlcat had wormed its way onto his lap, and for a moment, the conversation dissolved into cooing and mutual admiration.

When Dooley finally rose to leave, he lingered in the doorway.

"If you need anything," he said, "even just a walk or an extra set of hands—you know where to find me."

Prudence smiled. "Thank you, Dooley. I mean it."

He ducked his head, embarrassed, and slipped into the cold.

Bryant watched the door close, then looked at Prudence. "Can we keep it?" he asked, motioning to the owlcat, which had already curled up in a sunbeam and begun to snore.

"I think so," Prudence replied. "I think it's ours now."

The shop, which for days had felt like a fortress under siege, seemed smaller and warmer for the animal's presence. Prudence looked at the pile of mending, then at Bryant, and for the first time in a while, believed she might finish it all.

The salesman was still out there, and tomorrow would bring the same trials as before.

But tonight, at least, they had each other.

———

Night had fallen with a finality that left no doubt about its intentions. The square outside was a pool of cold shadow, the only movement the occasional shudder of wind that rattled the shutters and sent a flurry of grit skittering down the cobbles.

Prudence sat at her worktable, a single candle guttering in a dish nearby. The flame cast her profile in sharp, shifting relief against the wall. She worked with a bolt of plain brown fabric, folding and unfolding it, measuring its length, then smoothing it flat only to start the process again. Each repetition grew less precise, her hands working faster, the fabric's edges creasing where they shouldn't.

Bryant was asleep upstairs, but the hush of the house was unsettled, like the quiet before a storm. The owlcat perched on the highest shelf, tail wrapped around its feet, eyes huge and unblinking in the candlelight. It watched Prudence with a strange patience, as if it knew that something was wrong and was waiting to see what she would do about it.

At last, Prudence stood, the fabric slumping to the table. She paced the length of the shop, three times back and forth, then stopped at the window. She drew the curtain aside just enough to peer out, her breath fogging the glass. The salesman's wagon was still visible, lantern aglow, a pale shape hunched over his table. For all her vigilance, Prudence could not tell if he was awake or asleep, plotting or simply existing.

She let the curtain fall, then turned and found the owlcat's gaze had not wavered. The animal cocked its head, as if urging her to get on with it.

She returned to the table and sat, pressing her palm to the cool wood. She closed her eyes, counting slow breaths, willing her heartbeat to settle. When she opened them again, she reached for her ledger, flipped to a fresh page, and dipped her pen in ink.

She began to write out the coming days' orders, but her thoughts would not stay in line. The names and dates blurred together, and when she tried to sum the coppers due for the month, her hand slipped and left a dark blot on the page.

She set the pen down. For a long time, she just sat, head bowed, listening to the candle's tiny hiss and the faint, irregular thump of the owlcat shifting on the shelf.

"There must be something more I can do," she whispered to the empty shop.

The words surprised her.

The owlcat chirped, low and insistent. Prudence looked up and found her gaze caught by the shelf above the worktable. There, untouched since she'd arrived in North Pointe, was the row of bolts she'd always considered too fine for the town's needs. Velvets, brocades, and cottons in colors so bright they seemed almost to glow in the half-light: sapphire and gold, crimson and a green so pure it could have been a blade of summer grass.

She stood and crossed to the shelf, running her hands along the fabric. Each felt different—slick, soft, whisper-light, or heavy with promise. She let her eyes linger on the green velvet, remembering how Bartram had praised its color, how Bryant had pressed it to his cheek and laughed.

She looked at the rest, hungry for something she could not name. For a moment, she tried to imagine what she might make, if she could make anything at all.

She sighed, let her hand fall, and returned to the table. The candle had burned low, and the shadows danced larger with every flicker. The owlcat yawned, enormous eyes closing to thin slits, and Prudence felt her own exhaustion settle in.

She gathered her things, swept the ledger shut, and tidied the brown fabric into a careful bundle. The owlcat followed her with its eyes as she climbed the stairs, pausing at the top to look back down at the darkened shop.

For the first time in sennights, Prudence wondered if the future could be changed—not by potions or lies, but by the slow, steady work of making something new.

She closed the door behind her, and the house fell silent once again.

eight

. . .

THE MORNING HAD COME thin and watery, the sort of light that only barely qualified as day and seemed to hold back the world outside. Prudence felt the difference on her skin as she settled at the workbench: a prickle less sharp than candleflame, a chill persistent in her knuckles. The town square beyond the frost-clung window was quiet—too early for the first post, too late for the scavenger cats, a hush perfect for the kind of work that demanded everything and nothing from the mind.

On the floor, Bryant had arrayed his wooden figures in a looping procession, circling a painted shield as if paying their respects. The boy had grown quieter in the last few days, his play more focused, the game inside his head something Prudence could only guess at. Once, she might have interrupted to ask about it, but now she watched from the corner of her eye, letting his small rituals run their course. She wondered if all children became less legible to their parents as they aged, or if hers was a special case.

Her own rituals were unchanged: a shallow basin of clean water for her hands, a waxed sheet to protect the bench from frayed edges and ink, the neat alignment of pins and shears along the rightmost reach of her arm. This morning, the task was a jerkin for Dooley. The one he'd brought her as a template was beyond salvaging—a decade old, threadbare as a moth's wing, the collar near to rotting off, the cuffs notched with repair upon repair. She had not said so aloud, but Dooley had understood; the animal was best put down, he'd said, and better a new one than a resurrection.

The fabric she'd chosen was a brown so unremarkable it might have been mistaken for raw wool, though it was a finer weave—light, hard-wearing, stubborn under the needle. She'd made the pattern from memory, drawing the lines on the reverse in black graphite, each mark a promise to herself that this time, at least, there would be no mistakes.

She stitched, and as she stitched, her eyes found the shelves on the far wall—heavy with folded cloth, their colors sorted by a system that had seemed sensible once but now struck her as oppressive. The lower shelves held the everyday hues: slate, tan, gray, the palette of a country that knew the value of not standing out. Higher up, less practical and more precious, the bolts shaded from dull rose to a startling deep blue, a handful of reds and greens with nap like the surface of water at midnight. She rarely touched those. No one asked for them. She was not even sure if she wanted anyone to.

Yet, some mornings, she caught herself glancing at the upper reaches, half-ashamed, as if the fabric itself had grown eyes and would judge her if she dared disturb their slumber.

She finished a row of stitches and set down her needle, flexing her fingers to work out the ache. The thread, despite being labeled "invisible," stood out in tiny pips along the seam, a testament to her mood. She frowned and picked at the thread with the tip of her nail, then looked away.

Bryant, sensing the pause, glanced up. "Is it almost done?" he asked, voice just above a whisper.

"Nearly," Prudence said, trying to sound as if she believed it.

He nodded, returning his focus to the circle of soldiers. One toppled, and he righted it, whispering something to the figurine that sounded suspiciously like an apology.

She resumed work, her hands moving on their own, the muscle memory so strong she need not think about it—could, in fact, think about anything but the task at hand. And so, as she stitched, her mind wandered to Bartram's words: Why not a coat that's warm and bright, a shirt that lasts but makes you glad to see it in the morning? He'd spoken as if the two—function and beauty—were not only compatible, but inseparable.

It had rankled her, even as it stuck. She'd been raised to distrust pretty things, to think of them as traps or signs of pride. Her mother's dresses had all been black, even in the high summer, and her father's only indulgence had been a single silver cuff-link, promptly lost to the pawnman the first winter the crops failed. Even after leaving Holderdown, Prudence found herself gravitating to the ugly and the strong, as if expecting the world to test every inch of her with the same mercilessness it had in the old country.

Still, Bartram was not wrong. Even here, people noticed small flourishes: a flash of blue thread at a hem, a scallop to a collar, a hidden lining in a pattern only the wearer would see. She knew this—had, in fact, made her own secret deviations from time to time—but never on commission. Never where it might matter.

She finished the jerkin's outer body and turned it inside out to check her work. The seams were straight and the shoulders neat, but there was no pleasure in the examination. The thing was solid, unyielding, and had the personality of a boiled potato.

Prudence pinched the fabric, feeling its grain with her thumb. It would outlast two of Dooley, maybe more. But the color looked funereal, and the shape was so severe that she could not picture anyone wearing it without feeling trapped inside. She sighed, set the garment down, and for a long moment simply stared at it.

In the hush, Bryant rose from his game and came to her side. He pressed his cheek against her arm, then pointed to the jerkin. "It looks sad," he said.

She laughed, but it sounded bitter to her own ears. "It's supposed to look strong," she said, softer than before.

He shrugged, and returned to his soldiers.

She picked up the next piece: a length of the same brown, already cut and marked for the matching trousers. She did not want to work on them. She wanted to set them aside, to reach for the blue velvet on the top shelf and run her fingers through the nap, to imagine for just one moment what it would feel like to craft something purely for joy.

Instead, she threaded her needle and began again, each stitch a small act of resistance.

The morning's first commission behind her, Prudence turned to the next, her needle slipping through the crisp, undyed muslin with a speed that made the minutes blur. She had always believed in the power of routine, the way it could tie down unruly thoughts, but today the effort backfired; her mind, freed by the automatic rhythm of her hands, wandered with a will of its own.

At first she tried to focus on the customer's request—a shift for the herbalist, loose-cut for ease of movement, reinforced at the shoulder seams where Galhani liked to keep her tiny glass vials tucked out of sight—but the task soon faded into the background hum, and memory filled the space.

She saw herself in Holderdown, much younger, her hair not yet tamed into the severe cap she wore now, hands raw from scrubbing the communal laundry. The only warmth in that life came from Master Thatcher, the carpenter who shared the alley behind her childhood home. He was older than anyone she knew, his beard the color of smoke and his teeth mostly gone, but he had a laugh like the sound of knocking two stout logs together—surprising, full-bodied, and real.

It was Thatcher who taught her to whittle. His hands were hard and broad, veins ropey, his nails perpetually rimmed in sawdust. He had the patience to sit with a silent girl on a back stoop, the patience to show her how to brace the wood against her thumb, to let the blade do the work, to accept the occasional nick and not make a fuss. In that world, kindness was always secret; he called her "apprentice" in the alley but "girl" in public, and never looked away when the other men spat at the sight of her belly swelling with Bryant.

He gave her scraps: walnut, cherry, maple so light it seemed to float. With these, Prudence learned the language of grain and knot, the trick of finding a form inside what others saw as waste. After Bryant was born, Thatcher brought her offcuts shaped into horses, birds, and once a rabbit so perfectly round that it made her laugh—aloud, for the first time since her father's burial.

The memory lingered: his hand, twice the size of hers, covering her own as she fumbled the knife through a tight curve; his murmured correction, barely more than a breath on her ear; the subtle way he placed his boot to brace the bench for her, as if by accident. At town gatherings, he never let her stand alone at the edge of the crowd, always found some excuse to drift near and ask, quietly, if she needed a rest or a drink or a way out.

He died in the winter after Bryant's birth, and she never found a friend in Holderdown again.

A soft thunk from the floor brought her out of the memory. Bryant, his soldiers now in disarray, was staring up at her, his eyes gone wide. At her side, the owlcat had leapt onto the table, tail lashing, ears angled with concern. Prudence blinked and looked down. Blood welled at the tip of her left forefinger, a bright bead that trembled before falling onto the muslin in a perfect, damning circle.

Bryant scurried to the table's edge. "Are you hurt?" he asked, voice almost steady.

"It's nothing," she said, already pressing the tip to her tongue to stop the bleeding. "Just lost in thought."

The owlcat, emboldened, crossed to her arm and pressed its small, feathery head against the wound, then chirped—a sound both soothing and urgent. Prudence laughed, then winced; the puncture stung.

Bryant climbed onto the bench beside her and peered at the drop of blood on the fabric. He looked up, meeting her gaze. "Does it hurt?"

"Only for a second," she said, meaning it.

He nodded, and settled in next to her, his head warm against her side.

She remembered, suddenly, a winter day when Master Thatcher, shaking with fever, had handed her a box of splinters and said, "Every little thing can be mended, if you give it time." He'd been talking about the staircase in his cottage, but the words stuck.

In North Pointe, it was Bartram who filled that space. She hadn't realized it until now. The way he lingered after a delivery, the casual, gentle way he explained his tools to Bryant, the habit he had of checking on her even when he had nothing to gain. He'd never taken her aside to teach, but everything about his manner said he was hoping she would ask. Maybe she should.

She pressed a fresh kerchief to her finger and let the pain ebb. The owlcat trilled, and Bryant mimicked the sound, giggling. She smiled, for real this time, and wrapped her free arm around both of them, holding them close.

The sun had risen a little higher, warming the glass of the window and sending a thin shaft of gold across the shop's floor. She closed her eyes and let the memories settle, mixing the old with the new, until the differences no longer hurt so much.

———

The shop bell chimed with an authority that made both Prudence and Bryant look up. Into the hush strode Dardrad Pebbleblade, boots dusted with the granular crust of a morning's walk, basket slung over one shoulder and beard trailing a faint scent of pine. He moved like he owned the floor, every step efficient and sure, but when Bryant let out a whoop and dashed to the threshold, Dardrad stopped short and set the basket down, meeting the boy at eye level.

"Well, if it isn't North Pointe's smallest watchman," the dwarf rumbled. "Stand tall, lad."

Bryant squared his shoulders, only a little cowed by the deepness of the voice. Dardrad extended one massive paw and, with more care than his size suggested, ruffled the boy's hair.

"Better," he pronounced, and gave Bryant a gentle tap on the chin.

Prudence stood, smoothing her skirt, and approached with deliberate calm. In Holderdown, she would never have let Bryant so much as greet a dwarf—her mother's warnings too vivid in memory—but here, the rules were different, or perhaps dissolving. She felt the old fear in her spine, a residual prickle, but forced herself to step forward anyway.

"Master Pebbleblade," she said.

"Morning, Simonsdotter," Dardrad replied. His face was as immobile as a door lintel, but his eyes flicked with interest.

He straightened, lifting the basket onto the worktable with a grunt.

"Dalossalda says I've got to eat more green," he said, peeling back the cloth. "But she can't stop me from sharing a bit of the good stuff."

Inside the basket, nested in cool leaves, were several cuts of Highelk—marbled, rich, wrapped with a care that spoke of pride in the work. Prudence could smell the faint iron of blood, the musk of fresh-cut meat. She tried to summon her childhood distaste, but all she felt was the hollow in her own stomach.

"For you and the boy," Dardrad said, sliding the basket toward her. "Thought he could use some meat on his bones."

"That's—" Prudence stammered, caught off guard by the gift. "Thank you."

He shrugged, like it was nothing.

She gestured to the mess of sewing at her station. "You caught me in the middle of a commission."

Dardrad grunted. "Saw your lamp burning late last night. New customer?"

"Old one," she replied. "Dooley's jacket gave up the ghost. I'm making him a new set. And a few shirts for Galhani."

Dardrad picked up the unfinished jerkin, holding it to the light. "Good weight," he said, running a thumb along the seam. "But—" He pinched the shoulder, testing it. "This would give way if the wearer fell, say, off a wagon or into a fence."

Prudence bristled at first, but then curiosity won out. "You think so?"

He nodded. "Here." He pulled a length of rawhide cord from his pocket, then gestured for a needle. Prudence handed him one, and he used it to whip-stitch a tiny patch along the inside shoulder, demonstrating as he spoke. "Stitch it double. Use a cross pattern—like so. Holds better against a sideways pull."

She watched, fascinated despite herself. His fingers, despite their size, were nimble; he'd probably stitched up wounds as well as hides.

"You worked as a tailor, before?" she ventured.

Dardrad snorted. "Butchers have to sew, too. And my people—" He paused, as if weighing how much to say. "We live underground. Everything is built to last. No shame in learning from the best." He handed the jacket back, now reinforced. "Try that. You'll see."

She traced the new seam with a finger. "I will."

Bryant, meanwhile, had climbed onto a stool to peer into the basket. "What kind of meat is it?" he asked.

Dardrad grinned, the effect startling and not unkind. "Highelk. Ran wild in the Mistral, until it met an axe. You want to hear the story?"

Bryant nodded, wide-eyed.

Dardrad launched into a brief, dramatic account: the dawn, the white mist, the herd ghosting along the ridge, the single old bull that tried to turn and fight. Prudence listened, more charmed than she wanted to admit, as Dardrad described the precision needed to bring down such a beast, and the respect owed to its life.

"Nothing goes to waste," he finished. "We eat, we use the hide, even the antlers for tools."

Bryant ran his hand along the basket, as if he might find a remnant of the animal's story in the shape of the meat. "Will it make me strong?" he asked.

"Strong as you want to be," Dardrad said. "But eat slow. Too much, and you'll feel it in your belly come night."

Prudence caught the faintest flicker of pride in the boy's eyes.

As the talk turned to food, the conversation relaxed. Dardrad asked about her other projects—did she do cloaks, could she repair mail, what was the best way to fix a tear in heavy wool—and Prudence answered, at first by rote, then with more ease as the discussion deepened. She found herself telling him about Bartram's idea for a new coat lining, and even asked Dardrad's opinion on different types of thread.

"There's no point in mending a thing if it won't hold," Dardrad said. "But there's no pride in wearing rags, either. Even in the mines, my father would bring home a shirt stitched with blue at the collar. 'Shows you have a family,' he said. 'Shows you belong somewhere.'"

Prudence thought about the bolts of cloth on the high shelf. She imagined Dardrad, underground, in a shirt with blue piping, surrounded by others who looked and dressed the same. She imagined what it would be like, to know at a glance that you belonged.

"Did you make your own?" she asked.

He looked surprised. "My mother did. All of us. She was—" He paused, then shrugged. "Better than me, at the fine work. But I learned enough."

"I wish I'd been taught," Prudence said, more honest than she meant to be.

Dardrad met her gaze. "You teach yourself, it looks like."

They stood in companionable silence, the only sound the soft breathing of Bryant and the fainter snuffle of the owlcat, which had curled up on the windowsill to nap in a patch of sun.

Dardrad reached for the basket, then seemed to reconsider. Instead, he squared his shoulders, as if preparing for a new fight.

"If you have nothing on, tomorrow, come to the shop at the first bell. Dalossalda wants to try a new recipe—says it needs a proper taste-tester. And I could use help keeping her from burning the cheese again."

Prudence blinked, caught off guard. "Are you sure?"

He grunted. "You patched Darby's hand, after he caught it in the door. Never charged us, even for the bandage. It's the least I can do."

"I'd like that," she said, and found she meant it.

Bryant looked up, thrilled. "Can we bring the owlcat?"

Dardrad grinned, wide and white. "If you can keep it from eating my supplies."

He gathered his basket, wrapped the cloth tight, and turned for the door. Before leaving, he paused, his voice softer. "If you want the recipe for that blue piping, I can find it. Mother's old pattern book is in a trunk somewhere."

"I'd like that, too," Prudence said, the words unfamiliar but not unwelcome.

The bell jingled as he left. Prudence stood in the shaft of morning light, the basket of meat still warm in her hands, and watched Bryant bounce with anticipation.

The room felt less empty than before, and the bolts of colored cloth above seemed, for once, to glow in the new sun.

———

The noon bell rang in the square, shivering through the window glass and into the seams of Prudence's skull. She set the last stitch in the traveling cloak, then bit off the thread and tucked the loose end under with a flick. The cloak joined its matching shirt and trousers—a set so plain and featureless it could have been intended for a shadow or a ghost. She arranged them on the mannequin near the door, per custom, but found herself studying the ensemble as if it might reveal a secret.

She waited for the satisfaction that always followed a job well done. It did not come.

Instead, she remembered Dardrad's words: even in the mines, my father would bring home a shirt stitched with blue at the collar. Shows you belong somewhere. Prudence touched the shoulder of the cloak, ran her hand down the sleeve. What did this say about its future owner, she wondered? That they wished to be invisible, or merely that they could not imagine wanting more?

She slumped into her chair and let her gaze drift around the shop. The air had warmed with the sun, bright enough now to catch on the faces of the spools, the polished heads of the scissors, the smooth curve of Bryant's cheek as he slept on the pallet in the corner, one hand knotted around a bit of soft cloth.

The rest of the space was hers alone, and she felt the weight of it.

She looked to the high shelves. There they waited: bolts of cloth in the shades of fever dreams and distant holidays, each one a challenge to her discipline. The blues—some as deep as the lake at dusk, others the color of old bruises, still others so sharp they seemed to hum with their own light. The burgundies, rich and secretive, a touch of defiance in every fold. The greens, forest-dark and threaded through with golden pinpricks, as if the sun itself had been unraveled and woven in.

Her hand trembled, and she stood before she could talk herself out of it. She reached for the nearest—ruby velvet, heavy and plush—and drew it down into her arms. The cloth pooled there, richer than blood, smooth as the skin behind Bryant's ear. She let it slide over her hand, then against her cheek. It was almost alive.

She pressed her palm to it, harder than necessary, and felt a pang that she could not name.

She glanced back at the mannequin, at the somber row of recent commissions lined up by the door. How long had she been making the same thing over and over, the same flat brown, the same dampened gray? They were sturdy and perfect, but not meant to last in memory. No one would remember the girl who made them, nor would she remember herself in the act.

The velvet called to her, an old hunger unstarved. She thought of the dress her mother never allowed her to wear, of the scarf Master Thatcher had once let her finish, the blue thread so bright it made her ache. She wondered if Bryant would remember her only as a woman who kept to her own corner, who said no when it was easiest, who never made a single thing that might bring joy just for the doing.

She pressed the velvet to her lips, then folded it again, her hands lingering on the weight and the promise. She set it back on the shelf, gently, as if it were a sleeping animal.

She returned to the workbench. Her shoulders were stiff; her throat felt thick. She took up her scissors and stared at them for a long moment, weighing their heft in her palm, the blades shining in the hard noon light.

All around her, the shop was silent except for the soft, even breath of Bryant's nap, the only pulse she needed.

The scissors caught the sun and, just for a moment, shone brighter than any jewel.

Prudence took a breath, and another, and did not cut.

Yet.

nine

. . .

THE DECISION, once made, set Prudence's nerves jangling. She finished tidying the shop in an uneasy quiet, every motion practiced but off-kilter, her hands dropping pins and misaligning the shears. Bryant chattered at the window while the owlcat trailed him from table to step to curtain rod, never straying far from his warmth. Outside, the clouds had thickened, and a wind from the lake pushed wet air into the town's hollows.

The meeting, called by Sam and sanctioned by Jen, was to be held at the Broken Claw—the only venue in North Pointe more reliable than the Town Hall. It was tradition, Sam had said, that real decisions were made where there was drink and light, not in the cold echo of civic duty. Prudence doubted whether she belonged at either, but attendance was both expected and, after the day she'd had, necessary.

She wrapped Bryant in his coat and scarf, pulled her own black cap snug, and left the shop behind with a final check of the lock. The owlcat, newly bold in the dusk, perched on Bryant's shoulder as if ready to captain him through any squall. Together they navigated the greasy cobbles, the mud in the square growing more adhesive as the cold set in, until they reached the back steps of the pub.

Ahead, the green was a dull smear, the lamps at the inn flickering yellow and blue behind rain-streaked glass. A knot of children, older than Bryant but happy to claim him for the evening, clustered near the stables and let loose periodic shrieks as they played some hybrid of chase and climbing contest along the fence. Prudence, after a pause, let Bryant drift to the edge of the group, though she kept his scarf in view at all times. The owlcat, unperturbed, watched the other children with grave suspicion and made a show of sharpening its claws on Bryant's sleeve.

The rear entrance to the Broken Claw stood at the far corner of the square, under a roof overhang that dripped steadily onto the plank stoop. She slipped through the door and into the narrow hall that connected the pub to the inn. She paused, peeking out past the bar top toward the main entrance. It was here that Prudence saw Warren, his silhouette unmistakable even in low light. He leaned against the door-post, arms folded, white hair a wild halo in the glow from the inside. He was dressed in his second-best shirt, the buttons straining at the chest, and he tapped one foot with a rhythm that matched the nervous percussion inside Prudence's own body.

She inhaled sharply as she caught sight of the salesman standing opposite Warren, posture combative but face pasted with a smile that was more muscle than meaning. The man wore the same lurid waistcoat as the day before, his hat now tucked under his arm in a gesture of respect—or surrender, depending on the eye. Warren said nothing, only stretched to his full height and let the light catch the green of his skin, the dented edge of his jaw, and the ivory expanse of his one tusk. The salesman's smile slipped. He took a half-step back, opened his mouth, and then seemed to think better of it.

"Private meeting tonight," Warren rumbled.

The salesman nodded silently and backed away into the dark street.

"Hrmph," Warren muttered.

Prudence, uncertain, moved out of the back hall and behind the bar, weighing whether to retreat or wait out the performance. The choice was made for her as Warren caught her eye, offered a nod, and moved his body to further fill the front doorway.

"Evening, Mistress Simonsdotter," he said, voice pitched low. The effect was meant to be casual, but the words rumbled like distant thunder.

"Evening, Warren," she replied, and could not help the way her voice shrank in his shadow.

The ogre smiled, this time the closed-mouth smile that he used when he wasn't trying to be frightening, and stepped into the pub, pulling the heavy wooden door closed behind him.

Inside, the Claw was at capacity. The air held the usual scents—smoke, barley, old cheese, the faint but not unpleasant edge of human sweat—but tonight it glimmered with an undercurrent of urgency. The usual tables were crowded into a misshapen horseshoe around the main hearth, where Sam presided with a mug in one hand and the other draped casually over the back of her chair. Jen was there, too, her hair coiled tight, eyes shining with a readiness for whatever fight might present itself. Galhani perched on a stool near the fire, cup of tea balanced on one knee, while Makota occupied the high shelf behind the bar, trading jokes with Sam and pawing a plate of twisted breadsticks.

Prudence scanned the room and found a place near the rear wall, as far as possible from both the main door and the commotion around the bar. She unspooled her shawl, draped it over the back of the chair, and took a moment to adjust the cap that always seemed to want to creep up her scalp. From this vantage she could see the whole room: the glow on the faces, the easy violence of laughter, the cracks in the ceiling where the last winter's freeze had split the plaster. She kept her hands in her lap, clasped so tight the blood threatened to drain out.

Jen, always alert, spotted her and offered a nod of recognition. Prudence nodded back, then dropped her gaze, unwilling to become the topic of conversation. She knew her presence was both expected and, for some, a novelty. Even now, months after her arrival, she felt the heat of attention whenever the town gathered en masse.

Sam ran the meeting as she ran her pub: with a minimum of ceremony and a maximum of effect. She banged her cup on the tabletop and shouted, "Settle in, you lot! We have one matter of import before we get to the usual complaints about Makota's baking and Galhani's experiments." The laughter, though loud, was good-natured, and the accused parties responded in kind—Makota with an exaggerated huff and a flick of her tail, Galhani with a mock-bow so deep her braid swept the floor.

As the room stilled, Sam's voice lost its comic edge. "We're here because, for the first time since two seasons past, we have some strangers in town who won't leave. And with strangers comes strangeness." She let the words hang, then added, "I know most of you can handle yourselves. But it's my duty, and Jen's, to see to it that nobody gets hurt by what they don't understand."

There was a murmur of assent, a shifting of bodies as people leaned in.

Sam continued. "First, the matter of the potion-salesman. He's selling nothing but hope, and the town's protections aren't meant to keep fools from buying hope. That's how it's always been. But some folks are worried he's working an angle, or planning something more."

She looked to Jen, who took up the thread: "He hasn't broken any laws. He's careful that way. But I worry there'll be fights, if these fools realize they've been sold colored water and return to make good on the so-called 'guarantees.'" She swept the room with her eyes, and every gaze found her in return. "So we keep the watch. We pay attention. And if anyone sees something off, they come to me or to Sam or to Warren. Understood?"

The chorus of "Aye" and "Understood" was uneven but sincere.

"We'll serve him as the town requires, and as you've all been doing for nearly two fortnights now. But we'll give him no more than the minimum, yes? And he stays away from the center shops. Especially Pru's."

Prudence felt the tension in her shoulders loosen, but only slightly. She still tracked every shift in the room, every entrance and exit, every look that lingered in her direction. She reminded herself that Bryant was with the children outside, guarded by the sturdy walls and the even sturdier town kids, and that Warren, when not blocking doors, was never far from the action. Still, she did not let herself relax.

Makota, emboldened, stood and announced, "And the bakery's running a contest—best story about a visitor wins a fortnight of pastries. Judging is impartial, but bribes will be accepted." This time, the laughter was genuine, and even Prudence found herself smiling.

The rest of the meeting devolved into the normal ebb and flow: bickering about the next day's custom, updates on the hunting and harvests, a brief but intense debate about whether a proper chicken coop would be useful and where it might go. Prudence let herself drift, the murmur of voices and the rhythm of the hearth lulling her into a rare state of calm. She watched the room, not for danger, but for the ways in which people built safety from small gestures: the refilling of a cup, the sharing of a crust, the leaning in to listen.

After a while, Sam called a break, and the crowd dispersed into smaller, more manageable knots. Prudence found herself joined by Jen, who set her tankard on the table with a weight that made the wood shudder.

"You good?" Jen asked.

Prudence nodded, then shook her head. "It's a lot."

Jen followed her gaze to the door, where Warren now stood alone, arms still folded, eyes scanning the square through the glass. "He's not coming in," Jen said, meaning the salesman.

"I know," Prudence replied, though she did not know it, not truly. "I just… it's hard to shake the feeling he's waiting for something."

Jen considered this. "He is. They always are. But he can't do much while the town's whole. That's why we do this." She gestured to the room—the tables, the crowd, the empty mugs awaiting refills. "A town is just a bunch of people looking after each other, when you get down to it."

Prudence looked at her hands, now unclenched. "I never had that, before."

Jen smiled, the expression softening the steel of her features. "You do now. Even if you don't want it."

Prudence wanted to say thank you, or maybe I'm sorry, or even just I'll try. Instead, she said nothing, and Jen seemed to understand.

The meeting wound down in stages. The children, tired and hungry, filtered inside for scraps of bread and cheese before being shooed back out for the final game of the night. The shopkeepers lingered, sharing news and rumors and the small, essential complaints of people who intended to live long enough to fix them. Prudence joined the line for a cup of tea, accepted it from Sam with a nod, and sipped it while leaning against the wall, the way she'd seen others do.

From her place, she caught sight of the salesman's wagon, lit from within by an unsteady lantern. The man himself sat at the table, alone, arranging and rearranging his bottles with the care of someone afraid they might shatter. He did not look up. The rest of the world carried on as if he were not there.

The final bell rang—Minnie's invention, a sound more soothing than insistent—and people began to gather their things, wrapping up scarves and counting heads before braving the cold again. Jen found Bryant, tucked him under one arm, and delivered him to Prudence with a promise to see them home if needed. Bryant clung to her skirt, eyes wide but clear, the owlcat now nestled in the crook of his arm.

They left through the rear, the night colder than before but less threatening. Prudence walked the cobbles with a steadier gait, Bryant's hand in hers, and the echo of voices from the pub behind her.

She did not look back until she was at her own door, the shop warm and still, the only sound the owlcat's contented chirr and the slow, steady breathing of her son.

She set her shawl on its hook, ran a hand along the edge of the workbench, and let herself rest.

For tonight, it was enough to have survived.

———

The next evening, the Claw was even more crowded, if that was possible. The spell of early spring had broken overnight, and the roads running to the lake were nearly impassable with melt and mud. Most of the travelers had huddled at the inn, but the townsfolk were once again shoulder to shoulder in the pub, grateful for dry wood and something to do besides fret about the weather.

Prudence arrived with Bryant just as the first lamps were being lit, the rain on her cap trickling down the bridge of her nose. She wiped her hands at the threshold, looked around for Jen or Sam, then claimed a quiet spot at the far end of the bar. The owlcat rode Bryant's shoulder as always, earning them both a few awed stares from the newcomers. The animal blinked its wide eyes, unimpressed by the attention.

Inside, the mood was lighter than the night before. Makota had staged a contest for the children—something involving flour, colored stones, and an alarming quantity of jam—and the resultant chaos kept the back rooms busy. Galhani and Dardrad manned the corner table, talking shop in hushed tones, while Bartram entertained a small knot of townsfolk with the story of his latest and most foolish customer.

Prudence had almost managed to relax when the noise thinned, the current of talk stilled by the sight of Dooley in the doorway. He stood for a moment, letting the chill of the evening radiate off his coat, then removed his cap and made his way to the bar. The familiar satchel, patched and battered, hung at his hip. He looked older tonight, though it was impossible to say why.

Sam poured him an ale without asking. Dooley nodded his thanks and set the satchel gently at his feet. He did not drink, only held the tankard in his hands, letting the foam settle. He seemed to be measuring the room, cataloging faces and details, as if memorizing them for a purpose.

When he finally spoke, the volume of his voice was just enough to slice through the crowd. "Friends," he said, and everyone turned to listen. Even Bryant, caught mid-argument with another child over a sticky feather, stopped and looked up.

Dooley glanced once to Sam, who gave him a single, almost imperceptible nod. "I wanted you to hear this from me, before the rumor mill did its work." He cleared his throat. "I'll be leaving North Pointe. Within the sennight, if the roads permit."

A hush moved through the crowd, followed by a ripple of disbelief. Even the travelers, who had no stake in the matter, paused to take in the news. Dardrad's mug froze halfway to his lips; Galhani set her tea down so abruptly it sloshed over her fingers. Bartram only stared, his jaw working as if struggling with a toothache.

Sam was the first to recover. She topped off Dooley's ale, slid it closer. "You sure?" she said, the question more ritual than anything else.

Dooley smiled, the lines around his eyes deepening. "There's a calling," he said. "Word came up from the south—someone's found a colony of the lesser Wisp Rats, near to the southern marshes. Rare as hens' teeth. I've been asked to catalogue and help rehome them before the traders get wind." He hesitated. "It's what I was made to do."

Makota's ears drooped. "You could send someone else," she said, but even as she said it, her voice faded.

Dooley shook his head. "It's my work, not anyone else's. And besides, there are better menagerie keepers in the city than me, but not another who knows the rats like I do." His gaze swept the room. "I'm grateful for this place—more than I can say. But it's time."

For a moment, no one spoke. Prudence felt her own face settle into a rigid mask, her lips pressing together so hard they went numb. She wrapped both hands around her cup and stared at the far wall, refusing to let herself cry over a man she'd spoken to maybe a hundred times, in passing, always about animals or the weather or the cleverness of Bryant's hands.

It was Bartram who broke the silence. "What happens to the shop?" he asked, voice rough.

Jen answered. "Remember how your place was set up perfect when you arrived? As if it had been waiting for you?" Bartram nodded, his eyes widening slightly. "The opposite. All likelihood, the place will be empty as echoes within a candlemark. Waiting for whoever is next. For whatever shopkeeper the town needs next."

Prudence's heart tightened. Another merchant was already in town.

There was a pause, then Galhani, voice barely above a whisper: "It won't be the same."

Dooley's mouth quirked in what might have been a smile, but it never reached his eyes. "Nothing ever is," he said. "That's the nature of things."

Prudence risked a glance at the other shopkeepers. She saw a mixture of sadness and quiet resignation, but also a kind of calculation —a reckoning with the gap that would soon be left, and the inevitability that it would need filling. She remembered what Leota had said, once, about the Icosagon: if even one link in the chain was lost, the whole would be less. Maybe not at first, maybe not even in a way you'd feel, but sooner or later the difference would show.

Knodalon was at his usual table, unmoving except for the slow, deliberate blinking of his eyes. He made no sound, but Prudence saw his hands tighten on the mug, the knuckles pale as marble. For all his oddness, she thought, he had watched over the town longer than anyone else, and maybe took the loss hardest of all.

Dooley finished his ale in two quick swallows, then replaced the tankard on the bar. "I'll stay a couple more days until the weather dries a bit," he said. "If anyone wants to come by the menagerie—say goodbye, or ask a favor, or just have a last look—my door's open."

He glanced at Prudence again, a brief, flickering look that held something more than gratitude but less than hope. She returned it, unsure what to feel.

Jen, who had watched the whole exchange with the fixed patience of a judge, raised her glass and said, "To Dooley. Who follows his path with honor."

The room responded with a soft clink of cups, and a round of "To Dooley," and then, as if by magic, the pub's usual noise returned. The children, indifferent to the drama, resumed their sticky feather wars; the travelers hunched back to their soup and gossip. Only the shopkeepers lingered on the moment, their eyes not quite meeting as they considered what had just shifted under their feet.

Prudence drank the rest of her tea, which had gone cold. She found her hands trembling, and steadied them by folding them under the table. Bryant, sensing her mood, sidled up and leaned against her arm, owlcat and all.

She looked at the boy, the animal, the rough crowd of townsfolk whose world had been changed in a single breath, and wondered how long it would take for the difference to show.

Not long at all, she suspected.

———

The night rolled on, but the news of Dooley's departure hovered in the Claw's beams and rafters like a dense fog that refused to lift. The conversation drifted from gossip to reminiscence, the usual squabbles over bread and barter replaced by quieter talk. Prudence nursed her tea and watched the faces of the townsfolk: the way Bartram sat silent, hands folded in front of him; the way Makota, usually a flicker of movement behind the bar, now perched with her chin in her hands, eyes fixed on nothing; the way Galhani, always at ease in a crowd, seemed to grow smaller and smaller with each passing minute, her gaze rarely leaving the small cloth bundle on her lap.

As if on cue, Galhani rose, crossed the room with her usual light step, and stopped beside Dooley. She offered the bundle—a pouch, hand-stitched in the pattern of the southern reeds, cinched with twine the color of willow bark. "For the journey," she said, the words clear but soft. "It's a blend for mornings, when you miss the way the air smells here."

Dooley accepted it with a bow, not of the head but the body, full and unguarded. He pocketed the pouch, then reached out to squeeze Galhani's hand, a gesture more intimate than anything Prudence had ever seen between them.

Makota was next, slipping off her stool and appearing at Dooley's side with a sly, lopsided smile. She offered him a flat, carved piece of wood—a travel token, shaped like the town's green, with the bakery's spire in miniature. "It's for luck," she said. "And to remind you that you owe me three coppers and a story when you return."

Dooley laughed, a real one, and promised he would pay with interest.

The others followed, each in their own way. Dardrad, gruff and unvarnished, handed Dooley a strip of jerky wrapped in butcher's paper, muttering something about "real food" for the road. Even Bartram, who rarely ventured into the emotional, pressed a square of oiled cloth into Dooley's palm, saying only, "To keep your tools dry."

Jen waited until last, then beckoned Dooley outside for a brief, low-voiced conversation that ended with a brisk handshake and a nod. When they returned, Jen's eyes were red around the edges, but her voice was steady. She lifted her tankard, and this time the whole room followed suit, the toast louder and more defiant: "To Dooley, who follows his path with honor."

As the mugs clinked, Prudence felt it: a subtle shift, a prickling along her scalp. The lanterns overhead wavered, their light flickering not with draft or faulty wick but with something else—like a pulse, a heartbeat, a momentary skip. Only she seemed to notice at first, but then Galhani glanced up, and Makota's ears twitched, and even Sam, usually unbothered by the supernatural, looked uneasy for a breath.

Prudence remembered what Leota had said about the Icosagon: that the town's magic was never truly stable, that every soul in the circle mattered, and if you removed just one, the lines would shimmer and lose their edge. She looked at Dooley, then at the faces of those who would remain, and wondered what kind of world they'd wake to in the morning.

By the time the final bell rang, the Claw was down to the regulars and the few travelers too tired or wet to leave. Sam went about the room with a damp cloth, wiping tables that were already clean, her motions more deliberate than usual. Makota swept the floor, tail dragging in a way that betrayed her mood. Bryant, long since asleep, rested on Prudence's lap, owlcat curled atop his feet, both of them dead to the world.

Dooley stood by the fire, hands clasped in front of him, as if awaiting a verdict. One by one, the townsfolk gathered their things and lined up at the door—not to leave, but to see him off. Even Knodalon appeared, shuffling in from the cold, his coat patched with a dozen different colors, his beard newly combed and shining.

Dooley nodded to each of them, spoke a quiet word or shared a private joke, and then stepped into the night. For a moment he lingered on the threshold, framed by the swinging sign of the Claw, the rain painting him in glimmers and streaks. Then he turned, his boots loud on the wet plank, and vanished into the darkness beyond the green.

Prudence carried Bryant to the door and watched as the night swallowed Dooley whole. She stood a long time, thinking of the days to come, of the gap that would be left in the line of shops and in the shape of the town's magic. She wondered if Leota would appear in the morning with an answer, or if there would simply be silence.

She looked across the road, beyond the glow of the pub's lamps, to where the salesman's wagon rested at the edge of the world. He was still there, and would be, until the weather or some sharper force of will drove him on. Prudence shivered, not with cold, but with the knowledge that nothing in her life would ever stay the same for long.

For whatever shopkeeper the town needs next.

She ducked back inside, wrapped Bryant in his coat, and left through the rear. The alley was slick with rain, the air sharp with the scent of wet stone and bread. She crossed to her shop, unlocked the door, and set the boy to bed with the owlcat tucked beside him.

Only then, with the house quiet and the world outside barely more than a rumor, did Prudence allow herself to mourn. She sat at the workbench, the green velvet in her lap, and traced her fingers over its nap again and again. She could not bring herself to cut it, not yet. But she knew, deep down, that soon she would have to.

For whatever shopkeeper the town needs next.

Her soul chilled.

ten

. . .

THE MORNING after the Claw's farewell found North Pointe Common Towne washed and raw, the grass of the green gleaming with the sort of shine that only happens when rain has stripped away every last bit of dust and memory. The town, always so stubbornly itself, seemed a touch less complete. Prudence noticed it at once—how the air had a new clarity, almost surgical, the edges of every sound and shape too keen for comfort. She stepped to her shop door with Bryant in tow, and stood half behind the threshold, watching the stretch of the road and the swathe of green where the last of the puddles clung, catching the sunlight in brief flashes.

A small knot of townsfolk had already gathered at the town gate. Prudence could pick them out easily: Wilem, the cartwright, with his awkward, square-shouldered stance and the new brown cap that didn't quite fit his head; Warren, looming a full head above the rest, arms folded as if to keep his sadness from spilling; Sam, present even this early, her hair still unbraided and her eyes rimmed dark; Makota and Galhani, close together as always, Makota's tail flicking in the damp; and, at the center, Dooley, packing the last of his world into the shallow bed of the small, single-horse cart that Wilem had built.

The cart was new and solid, and the one horse yoked to it seemed to have resigned itself to the journey before it. Dooley's possessions were few, but their careful arrangement gave the impression of a larger life: a battered trunk, a rolled canvas pack, several cages—empty now —and a low wooden crate sealed with three bands of waxed twine. Wilem double-checked the lashings, his mouth pulled into a line of effort. Prudence could see his breath, which surprised her, since she hadn't noticed any cold in her own lungs.

She counted faces again, noticing the absences: Dardrad, probably at the shop already, and Leota, who rarely ventured out this early, and Knodalon, who rarely ventured anywhere. Jen arrived late, hair still damp, and cut across the grass with the stride of someone unafraid to stain her boots. She paused by the cart, offered Dooley a short word and a handshake, then drifted back to Sam's side, where she stood, hands in pockets.

Dooley seemed smaller than usual, even with the morning's light full on him. He wore his usual vest, the buttons mismatched, and a new knit scarf—Galhani's work, by the look of the embroidery— knotted close against his throat. Underneath, he wore the new clothes Prudence had made for him, and she grimaced slightly at how the plain, dark brown fabric contrasted with the emerald grass of the square. She watched him load a small, brass-trimmed box onto the tailgate, then hesitate, turning it this way and that as if looking for a final place to fit it. It was a metaphor for the man, she thought, always searching for the right gap, never quite trusting that any space would hold him for long.

Galhani was the first to step forward. She cradled a basket in both hands, the contents covered by a napkin. "A bit of tea for the journey," she said, voice bright but held at a careful volume. "And some powder for the horse's feet, if she starts to favor the left again."

Dooley took the basket with both hands and bowed, the gesture exaggerated. "Thank you," he said, quiet enough that Prudence barely caught it. "It's more than I expected."

Warren grunted, his usual conversation starter, and thrust out a paw that engulfed Dooley's hand to the wrist. "If you get into trouble out there, you holler," he said. "I've got a friend on the western trail who owes me two good deeds. I'll send word."

Dooley nodded, managed a smile.

Makota offered nothing at first, only a flick of her tail and a smile as sharp as a seam ripper. Then, with a practiced sweep, she produced a paper-wrapped bundle from behind her back. "It's just some biscuits," she said, "but eat them before the third day or they turn into bricks."

Dooley took it, then opened the paper just enough to peer inside. "I'll ration them," he promised.

Sam reached into her vest and withdrew a narrow bottle, the glass clouded with the recent chill. "You're not leaving without one last drink," she said, the words as much command as offer. She passed the bottle to Dooley, who pulled the cork and took a single, measured sip. He coughed, eyes watering, and passed the bottle back to Sam, who wiped the neck with the heel of her hand and finished it in two easy swallows. Prudence thought she saw Jen's mouth twitch in amusement, but the expression vanished as quickly as it came.

At last, Dooley stepped back from the cart and faced the group. He looked as if he meant to say something grand, but the words stalled. He hunched his shoulders, then shrugged. "I wish I could stay longer," he said, voice hoarse, "but the road calls, and I hadn't expected the weather to clear so quickly."

Makota said, "That's a lie. You always know when the rain's done."

Dooley grinned, the lines of his face arranging into something easier. "Well. I hoped it might last a day or two more. Give me an excuse."

Wilem clapped him on the back, a gesture meant for heartiness but landing just shy of brittle. "Take care, then. I'll watch your place until the new tenant comes."

"Don't let it get lonely," Dooley replied.

Jen, who had stayed back from the cluster, stepped forward now. She produced a slim box—wood, with inlaid stars—and pressed it into Dooley's palm. "From the town," she said. "Not official, but you know how it is. Don't open it until you reach the next stop."

He took it, silent, and tucked it into his coat.

At the end, Dooley reached for the canvas pack, drew out two small parcels. "These are for you," he said, holding the first out to Galhani: a tiny, carved owl, the detail so fine it seemed alive. "From one caretaker to another." The second, a feather of impossible blue, he handed to Jen. "I found it near the lake. It seemed like something that ought to be kept safe."

Jen ran a finger along the vane, then nodded, eyes fixed on the feather.

The gathering stilled, each person aware that the moment had reached its natural end. The first bell rang, its note sharp and unadorned in the emptied morning.

Dooley climbed to the driver's seat, the motion practiced but slow. He settled the reins, patted the horse's neck, and looked out at the road beyond the gate. "Don't forget me," he called, the words thin as thread.

"We won't," Warren replied, and for once, Prudence believed it.

Dooley flicked the reins and the cart rolled forward, the horse's hooves making deep, careful sounds against the wet stones. The others watched until he had cleared the green, until even the battered trunk was a mere dark smudge against the horizon.

Then, as one, the knot of townsfolk loosened. Wilem turned back toward the cartwright's with a last, slow glance at the empty road. Warren disappeared up the trade road, probably to check on the forges. Sam and Jen lingered together, their voices low and companionable. Makota and Galhani picked up the pace, heading toward the bakery, arms close but not touching.

Prudence watched it all from her doorway, Bryant at her side, the owlcat pressed into the crook of his arm. She realized she was shivering, though the sun had already burned through the night's chill. She stood there until the green was clear, until the only movement was the shiver of dew in the rising breeze, and the only sound was the slow, measured breathing of her son.

Then, reluctantly, she closed the door, and began her own day.

———

But the sense of absence lingered. Prudence felt it in the way the second bell failed to echo as it usually did, the sound swallowed by the dampness in the air. She felt it in the strange reluctance of the scissors as she tried to cut through cloth that, yesterday, had yielded without question. Even Bryant, who spent most mornings talking to himself or the animals, played in a hush, lining up the wooden figures with the deliberate care of a child afraid they might break.

The absence grew louder as the day wore on. By the time the sun reached its apex, Prudence realized that no one had come by for mending or gossip or even the usual complaints about the weather. She found herself peering through the window at intervals, searching the street for movement, but the only shapes were the occasional traveler or the town's own cats, who seemed to sense the deficit before any of the humans did.

At midday, Galhani stopped by, her cheeks flushed with the effort of walking briskly in the new chill. She carried a fresh loaf and a pair of scones, wrapped in linen.

"I had to bring them," she said, a little out of breath. "Otherwise Makota will eat the lot, and then where will I be?"

Prudence set the bread on the counter and offered Galhani tea, which she accepted with gratitude. They stood together at the workbench, Bryant perched on his stool, owlcat at his elbow, each of them picking at the crust in silence.

When the tea was gone, Galhani turned to the window. "It's quieter, isn't it?"

"Yes," Prudence replied, not sure if she meant the world outside or inside.

Galhani put a hand on her arm, gentle and unhurried. "Change is hard. But it isn't always bad. Sometimes it means the next thing will be better. You remember when Sam came."

"When Nate left," Prudence said softly.

Galhani nodded slowly. "Aye. But still."

Prudence wanted to believe it, but the words caught in her throat. She nodded anyway, and when Galhani left, she felt a little lighter for having heard them.

After lunch, Bryant asked if they could visit the menagerie, and for a moment, Prudence forgot. She told him yes, and even tied his scarf herself, before the truth caught up and stopped her cold.

"It's closed, love," she said, kneeling to his level. "Dooley's gone, remember?"

Bryant frowned, his eyes searching her face. "But the animals are still there."

She shook her head. "They're not. He took them with him. There's nothing left."

Bryant looked down at his boots, then back at her. "But he said we could come by."

Prudence hesitated, then relented. "We'll go," she said, "but just to see, all right?"

He nodded, and together they made the short walk to the edge of the green, where the menagerie stood dark and closed. The windows were shuttered, the sign taken down. Even the bench out front had been carried off, probably to serve as firewood somewhere along the road.

Bryant pressed his nose to the glass, searching for a flicker of movement. The owlcat leapt from his arms to the windowsill and peered inside, as if expecting a friend to appear. The three of them stood like that, silent and unmoving, for a full minute.

At last, Bryant turned away. "It's really gone," he said, the words more question than statement.

"Yes," Prudence answered. "But we remember, don't we?"

He nodded, then reached up to take her hand.

They walked back to the shop, the owlcat darting ahead and then circling back, as if guiding them home.

———

By dusk, the world had settled again, or pretended to. The lamps along the road flickered to life, their glow warm and reassuring. Bryant finished his dinner, then curled up by the stove, the owlcat wrapped around his feet. Prudence swept the floor, wiped down the counter, and checked the lock on the door. She set out the next day's work, then paused, hands flat on the table, her mind as blank as the surface before her.

She wondered who would take Dooley's place. What sort of person the town would draw next, to fill the missing corner of the Icosagon. She wondered what would become of the magic that held everything together, if it could survive for long with an empty shop and a silence at the edge of the green.

She wondered if she, too, could learn to change.

The lamps outside burned late into the night. Prudence sat by the window, watching until the last of them guttered out.

She did not want to sleep, not yet. Not while the world was so quiet, and the loss so newly made.

———

She did not open the shop the next morning, though she stood by the door for nearly a 'mark, hand pressed flat to the wood, before allowing herself to unlatch it and push the pane wide. The cold air bit harder than she remembered; it seemed intent on getting past her skin, curling into every hidden seam. From this vantage, Prudence could see the green as well as the first stretch of the trade road, but she positioned herself carefully, angled so she remained mostly hidden from anyone who might look her way.

Bryant pressed up beside her, one hand holding the owlcat, the other clutching the frayed edge of her apron. He said nothing, only stared at the space Dooley's cart had vanished into, his eyes narrowed as if hoping to spot the man returning for something forgotten.

The world beyond the threshold felt less full. The travelers who drifted through the gate did so in singles and pairs, heads down, as if the absence had unsettled even those who claimed no place here. The early market crowd shuffled with less direction, voices low and hesitant. Prudence noted the change with a kind of clinical detachment, but it burrowed into her anyway.

She closed the door when Bryant began to shiver, but left it unbolted for the first time since the winter freeze. It felt wrong to lock herself in, as though doing so might make the loss permanent. She made breakfast, though neither she nor Bryant ate much, and set about straightening the shop. The routine helped, but only a little.

The quiet inside was different, too. She noticed the absence of the usual tick from the stove pipe, the subtle hum that always seemed to vibrate in the walls. There was a lag to the shop's magic now—a delay between wanting a tool in her hand and finding it there, a faint drag on the thread as she pulled it from the spool. It was not enough to slow the work, but it was enough for her to notice, and to resent.

By midday, the shop had not seen a single visitor. Prudence finished her pending mends, then swept the floor twice over, more from restlessness than necessity. Bryant sprawled in the window seat with the owlcat and watched the green, eyes never quite settling on anything. Every so often, he would lift his head and say, "I thought I heard him," but each time it was only a wagon, or the far-off cry of a gull.

It wasn't until the fourth bell that Prudence realized the town had changed in a way she could never explain to anyone but those who lived here. The bell's ring was subdued, as if the sound had to travel through a thickness before reaching the air. When she peered out the window, she saw that the lamps along the green were already lit, though the sun still rode high. Their glow was feebler than before, pale and uncertain. Even the cats—the flesh-and-blood kind—moved with greater caution, lingering at the edges of the square rather than strutting across the stones.

Prudence ran her hand along the workbench, the surface so familiar she could have mapped it blind. She felt for the electric tingle that usually accompanied her touch, but it was distant now, like the voice of someone calling from the end of a long corridor. It confirmed what she'd feared since dawn: the Icosagon was broken. Nineteen, not twenty, and something vital in the world's weave had gone loose.

Bryant looked up from the window. "Will someone new come?" he asked.

Prudence forced a smile, but it wouldn't quite stick. "Maybe," she said. "Or maybe it will just… feel strange for a while."

He nodded, but she could see the worry in his eyes. He was old enough to sense when magic went awry, even if he didn't have a word for it. She wondered if he would grow up always knowing when the world was off-balance, or if he would learn to ignore it, the way children in Holderdown learned to ignore hunger or cruelty.

She spent the rest of the day pretending at normalcy, mending a ripped cloak that had waited a fortnight for its owner and restocking the thread bins. But with each task, she felt the effort required to maintain the fiction—her own, and the town's.

When evening came, she again left the door unbolted, and let Bryant sleep in the window seat with the owlcat curled over his chest. She sat at the workbench with a lamp, running her fingers over the grain, tracing the lines she'd worn into it over a hundred days of work. With each pass, the bench felt a little more like an artifact and a little less like something alive.

She wondered, as the last of the sunlight drained from the sky, how many towns across the world had experienced this precise fracture—a breaking so subtle, only those who knew what to look for could feel it. She wondered if the new vacancy would draw in someone dangerous, or if it would simply remain empty, a reminder of what had been lost.

And she wondered, most of all, whether she could learn to live with this particular kind of silence.

The lamp flickered, and for a moment Prudence thought it might go out. But it steadied, and she kept her hand on the bench until the world outside was fully dark.

———

The next day, the sky held the color of an old bruise, but the wet grass on the green shone as if it were still dawn. The world felt thin, like a shirt stretched too far, the seams of the town showing in places Prudence had never noticed before. She rose early, a habit from Holderdown that persisted even here, and went about her morning with deliberate caution: sweeping, setting bread, winding the clock. Bryant slept in, curled tight around the owlcat, his breaths coming in short, sharp bursts. She left him wrapped in the quilt, unwilling to disturb a sleep that looked more like hiding.

When she returned to the shop, she found herself staring out the front window, eyes drifting across the square to the storehouse and the bench that faced the trade road. Knodalon was there, but he looked… collapsed. The usual ramrod posture had slouched, his white hair wild and unbrushed, the bulk of his coat shrunken as if he'd been hung to dry and never filled out again. His beard was a mess, a sudden and complete undoing of the careful combing he'd always practiced. She tried to catch his eye, but Knodalon did not glance up or wave as he usually did. He simply hunched, staring at the ground, as if something crucial had cracked inside.

She was still watching when the shop bell tinkled. Galhani stepped in, shoulders dusted with powder-fine flour and a clay mug of tea balanced in her palm.

"Early for you," Prudence said.

Galhani shrugged, setting the mug down on the counter. "It's not a usual day. Makota woke before sunrise, said she had a vision of bread that would rise all the way to the roof. The kits are going wild. Lara's buried herself in the garden work. I thought I'd escape here for a moment."

Prudence poured herself a second cup and sipped, holding the heat on her tongue. She nodded to the window. "Knodalon hasn't moved all morning."

Galhani's eyes sharpened, losing the vague, good-humored blur that always hovered around her. "You think he's sick?"

"I think something's wrong with him. He's not… him. Would you check?" Prudence looked down, embarrassed by her own request. "I can't go near the road."

Galhani cocked her head, considering. "I will. He likes the berry blend best—maybe he'll talk to me if I bring it."

Prudence thanked her, but Galhani just waved it off, already reaching for a basket by the door. "No trouble," she said, then added, "We're all a little off today. Even the bread won't hold its shape." The little gnome turned to go.

"Galhani?"

She turned back and gave Prudence a gentle smile. "Hmm?"

"The empty shop."

"It'll fill in time. They always—"

"The potion salesman."

Galhani frowned. Then, as she realized Prudence's concern, the frown deepened. "It won't be him."

"Has he ever been in the Claw?"

The frown became a scowl. "No. Sam's not had a read on him."

"Then we don't know."

"I won't be him," Galhani said firmly. "We'll ask Leota once she's up."

Prudence hesitated, then relented. "All right."

"All right, then."

When Galhani left, Prudence let herself stand in the silence for a while, listening for the faintest sound of animal or human. There was nothing, not even the creak of the menagerie's old weather vane. She watched as Galhani crossed the green and approached the bench, calling Knodalon's name softly as she went. He looked up, eyes huge and haunted, then seemed to melt into the gnome's presence, nodding once and gesturing her to sit. They spoke for a long time, too quiet to overhear.

The urge to move, to do anything, built in Prudence until she found herself walking to the door, then past it, then all the way to the menagerie. The windows, always streaked with the tracks of curious paws and damp with the funk of caged life, now gleamed so clear she saw her own face reflected back. She tried the door and found it unlocked, the bell overhead silent and unblinking.

Inside, the shop was… gone. Not emptied—erased. There were no cages, no scent of animal or straw or the sawdust that Dooley always kept fresh. The shelves were not only bare but utterly clean, their surfaces smooth as the day the shop was built. The floor was swept, with no trace of fur or dander. Even the memory of noise seemed absent; Prudence stood in the center of the room and listened, but all she could hear was her own breathing, a hollow sound that bounced off the walls and back into her chest.

She walked the length of the room, touched the counter, then the place where Dooley had once kept a glass jar of beetles for the children to look at. There was no mark on the wood, no scent of honey or sugar or the odd, heady perfume of molted skin. The place was colder than she expected, though the sun cut across the floor in perfect, rectangular slabs.

Prudence found herself thinking of Holderdown in winter: the way a room could go from lived-in to abandoned in a single morning, the way the wind would find every crack and force its way inside. She lingered by the door, letting the sensation of absence fill her up. She thought, briefly, that she should say something to the room, a goodbye or a thanks or even a curse. But her mouth went dry. Nothing would come.

She stepped outside and closed the door behind her, expecting it to resist or creak, but it did neither. The latch caught without effort, the echo of her own motion lost to the open air.

Prudence paused on the threshold, hands in her pockets, and looked out across the green. The lamps in the square, even at this early time, had already begun their slow, dim progression toward evening. Bryant was still curled up in the window, watching for something to return. Knodalon and Galhani sat side by side on the bench, their heads close together in a way that was both comforting and sad.

The wind caught her cap, and for a moment, she felt the cold straight through to her bones.

She returned to the shop, then stood for a while in the vestibule, not sure whether to cry or sweep or simply wait. In the end, she did none of these. She walked to the workbench, ran her hands along its surface, and looked out at the town that had become her home.

It was still whole, she told herself, but it was also different now, and so was she.

She could not say whether the next piece to fill the empty shop would be friend or danger, or if the magic would ever feel quite right again.

But she would be here to see.

eleven

. . .

MORNING FOUND Prudence at the tea shop, perched on the edge of a chair that creaked with every subtle adjustment of her weight. Galhani's Steeps was already bright with the reflection of lakewater sunlight, the first of it splintering through the lace at the windows and warming the floorboards with precise, golden patches. The room was fragrant and faintly damp from the overnight air—chamomile and mint rising above the earthier undercurrent of dried ginger and rootstock.

Bunches of dried herbs hung from the ceiling beams, casting a penumbral net over the main table and brushing softly against each other with every draft. The table itself was set with mismatched china, each cup and saucer bearing the dings and scuffs of prior owners, but shined to an honest luster. Prudence's own teacup was a battered white, rimmed with a thin green stripe, and she turned it compulsively, making the stripes circle like a failed attempt at hypnosis.

Galhani, for her part, had already brewed a pot—"strengthening blend," she'd said, with a wink—and now busied herself at the tiny bar, pulling fresh honey from a glass jar and slicing lemon into nearly invisible pieces. She wore a smock with half a dozen pockets, each bulging with some secret or other, and her feet, which couldn't reach the floor, paddled in the air as she stood on her own custom-built footstool.

Bryant sat at a secondary table, nearly lost amid the stacked books and oddment displays, a pastry in one hand and the owlcat dozing at his feet. He glanced over now and again to check on his mother, but she was too tangled in her own nerves to notice.

Prudence pulled at her apron strings, retied them, then let her hands drift to the cup. She lifted it, only to realize her grip was so tight her knuckles had paled. She loosened her grasp, set the cup down, picked up a teaspoon, and stirred without adding anything. The spoon clattered once against the inside of the cup, loud enough to make both Bryant and Galhani look up in tandem.

"Do you want to try the wild mint in this one?" Galhani called. Her voice, as always, was the verbal equivalent of a burst of color—a sound that could wake even the surliest winter morning.

Prudence shook her head, but managed a polite smile. "Just as you made it," she said.

Galhani glided over, cup in hand, and slid into the opposite chair with a small, practiced hop. "It'll be good for you," she promised, as if tea alone could shield against the world's larger woes.

Prudence watched the swirl of steam, then the movement of Galhani's hands as the gnome adjusted the position of the honey pot by a fraction, then the lemon dish. "Did you feel it?" Prudence asked, voice low and unfinished.

Galhani's ears flicked. "The quiet?"

"The thinning," Prudence corrected, hushing the last word.

Galhani's gaze sharpened. "It's not just you. Makota felt it in the bakery—the bread didn't rise at all yesterday, and she blames the change." Galhani's lips pursed, and the lightness in her voice was suddenly absent. "We all feel it."

Prudence's hands started their old habit again, fingers rubbing along the inside seam of her left cuff. "If no one claims the menagerie's space, what happens? Does the magic…" She trailed off, unwilling to say it aloud.

"Does it break?" Galhani offered. "Or does it fade?" She cocked her head. "Hard to say. You know, before that first season with Sam, we never had a full twenty shops. I think we all feel it now because we know what it's like to be… complete. You remember back then."

"I do."

"So it'll get better. Or it'll be like this." The little gnome shrugged. "We'll be fine either way."

They sat in the hush, punctuated only by the soft murmur of Bryant's reading and the infrequent click of the owlcat's claws against the floor.

Prudence hesitated, then looked directly at Galhani. "What if it's him?" Her voice trembled—not a shiver, but the distinct aftershock of something snapped and only partially rejoined. "What if the salesman fills the gap?"

Galhani went perfectly still. Even the perpetual motion of her hands, usually busy with some piece of tea service, ceased. "He's not a keeper. He's not even a real merchant," she said, the words unusually cold. "He peddles nothing—hope, lies, spectacle. That's not the same as what Dooley did."

"But if the Icosagon is just about filling the spot…" Prudence began.

"It's not." Galhani's voice quavered, but with conviction. "It's about what the shop does for the town. About the work. Mapmakers. Menagerie keepers. Potters. Those are all trades that help people on their journeys. That's what we do here." She leaned forward, both hands splayed flat on the table. "That Cornelius could never do Dooley's job. Even if he had the building, the magic wouldn't root. Not really. You remember when we had all those silly shops? One just did shoelaces?"

The ghost of a smile wandered across Prudence's expression. "The one that only sold buckles."

"Exactly. The magic never took root for them. Threw the rest of us for a loop, for certain, but they didn't serve the purpose."

Prudence tried to accept this, but the thought wouldn't settle. "He's drawing people, though. I saw it yesterday. He had a crowd."

"Travelers. Outsiders." Galhani's nose wrinkled, and for a moment, she seemed older than Prudence had ever seen her. "He can't fool the town."

Prudence shook her head. "He could fool the magic."

It was a ridiculous claim, but the effect on Galhani was immediate. Her face, usually an open ledger of every mood and thought, blanked for a single beat, then pulled tight around the eyes. "That's… possible," she said, softer than before.

Prudence's hands slipped, and the spoon she'd been clutching fell to the table, bounced, and rolled under her chair. She did not bend to retrieve it. "If that happens, everything will go wrong. The magic that protects this place—it won't protect us. It'll protect him, or something worse."

Galhani stared at the ceiling, at the bundles of herbs swaying gently in the cross-breeze. "I never wanted to believe that the Icosagon could be corrupted," she said. "But if you're right, maybe it could do more than just thin. It could invert." Her expression darkened. "I thought about it, you know. That season."

"The one with the useless shops."

The herbalist nodded. "I thought it was my fault, what happened that year."

"Galhani—"

"Oh, I know. But… it does make you wonder. With different people here, could the town be… different? Could it… take advantage of people? Fool them, on their quests?"

Prudence, at last, met Galhani's gaze. "I've seen it happen before. Not with magic, but with… people. Back home, it only took one. That was enough to turn the village."

Galhani's smile returned, but it was a shadow of its usual self. "It's like offering a shortcut through a garden when the whole point is to enjoy the flowers," she said. "He's the shortcut. But if people forget why the path is there at all, the whole thing goes to weeds."

Prudence sat with that, hands pressed together to keep them from shaking.

They heard the bell at the front, and for a moment both flinched, the same brief animal startle. It was only Makota, trailing flour and the news that the bakery's contest had ended in disaster. Galhani excused herself to go mediate, her mood as unsettled as Prudence had ever seen it.

Prudence stayed behind, her gaze drifting to the window. The sun had shifted, and the golden squares on the floor now revealed the fine, invisible dust that only ever appeared in good light. She breathed, long and slow, and felt the tea's warmth reach her chest. It helped, just a little.

She thought of Dooley, already miles down the road. She thought of the salesman, and what it would mean for someone like that to become the twenty. The thought made her cold.

She sipped again, and the cup trembled in her hand, but only a little.

———

She was watching the square when Leota appeared, a shadow among the brighter morning. The witch wore black, as always, but it was the density of her presence that made her distinct—a self-contained gravity that drew the eye and then made it question itself. Her dark hair was pulled back into a severe braid, a handful of stray strands refusing to be tamed, and her skin caught the light like new parchment. If Galhani was a flame in a wet room, Leota was a candle burning at the bottom of a well: a quiet defiance of the dark.

Leota paused at the threshold, scanning the room with a quick, telescoping focus. When she saw Prudence, she crossed directly to her table, making no attempt at preamble or pleasantry.

"May I?" Leota asked, a finger already hooked under the back of the empty chair.

Prudence nodded, and Leota sat with careful precision, arranging her skirt so the folds fell perfectly straight. She set her hands on the table, flat and unadorned, and studied Prudence's face for a long, uncomfortable moment.

"You're worried," Leota said. She didn't make it a question.

Prudence tried to laugh, but it scraped the air instead. "It's not hard to see."

Leota flicked her eyes at the cooling teapot, then back. "If I said you were right to worry, would it help or harm?"

Prudence considered. "It would help. I don't like surprises."

Leota nodded, and with a single gesture summoned Lara from behind the counter. "Strongest black, please," she said. Lara hurried to comply, the business of pouring and carrying tea providing a brief, merciful interruption.

Leota waited until the cup was set before her, then sipped it, eyes closed. Prudence watched the ritual, the calm it brought, and envied it.

Leota set the cup down with a deliberate click. "The gap in the Icosagon is a liability, but it's not a catastrophe. Not yet." She tipped her head, as if listening to something inaudible. "The town's magic has survived worse. The process is self-correcting—eventually, someone will fit the role, and the circuit will close."

Prudence's hands stilled. "But if it's the wrong someone?"

Leota smiled, small and closed. "The magic chooses based on alignment. Intent. If someone tries to cheat it—" She let the sentence trail off, lifting her cup for another measured sip. "It won't be pleasant. For anyone."

Prudence glanced at the window, then at her lap. "Do you think it could be him?"

"The salesman?" Leota's tone was almost amused. "He doesn't know what he's dealing with. The town would fight him every step. The real worry is that, in the struggle, something else might break."

They sat for a moment, the tension pooling on the table between them. Galhani, who had returned to her tasks, hovered near the back shelf, fussing over a tray of drying lemon peel.

Leota broke the silence. "You know, when Barnaba left—the mapmaker, two years ago—the imbalance was far more severe, wasn't it? The whole town felt like it was stuck in fog, like we couldn't agree on what shape the world even took."

"I remember."

"This is… less."

Prudence frowned. "But it's still there."

Leota nodded, peering into her cup as if reading the future in the residue. "It's still there. But muted."

"Why?"

Leota was about to reply when Galhani hurried back in. "What a mess," she chuckled. She scurried into the back room and emerged with a tray and, balancing it with both hands, made for the door. "I have to bring Knodalon his morning tea," she announced. "He's tired, I think."

Both women watched as Galhani made her careful way to the old man on the bench outside the storehouse. Knodalon was hunched, beard a tangle, eyes fixed on a point somewhere in the dirt. Galhani set the cup in his hands, spoke a few soft words, then stood with him for a time, the two of them immobile as statues.

Leota's gaze sharpened. "That's interesting," she said, almost to herself.

Prudence looked at her, waiting.

Leota steepled her fingers. "I wonder if he's the reason the break is less than expected."

"Knodalon?"

Leota didn't answer at first, her attention still half-outside. "He's… old, but not in the ordinary way. There's a resilience to him. An endurance." She looked at Prudence, her eyes dark and knowing. "You've noticed he almost never leaves the storehouse bench? Never seems to sleep?"

Prudence nodded. "I thought it was just his way."

"It's a way, all right." Leota allowed herself a slight smile. "Last time the town's balance was off, he was the first to sense it, and the last to speak of it. You remember last season, with all the little gods."

Prudence considered this. "So he's… what? Buffering the loss?"

Leota tilted her head. "Something like that. I think he's trying to absorb the shock."

Prudence stared through the window, watching Galhani and Knodalon. The gnome was animated, talking with her hands, but Knodalon was motionless, tea cup gripped tight.

"We owe him," Prudence said, softly.

Leota shrugged, but it was a gesture of respect. "Maybe. Or maybe he's just doing what he was made to do."

"Is he going to sit there until someone comes to fill the empty shop?" Prudence asked after a moment.

Leota looked at her, her gaze almost kind. "Perhaps. And so perhaps you should hurry."

Prudence snorted indelicately. "I'm not going to run a menagerie."

Leota shook her head. "That's not what I meant."

The conversation, for all its tension, left Prudence steadier than before. There were rules here, even if they were strange. There were limits.

Outside, the wind picked up, stirring the grass on the green and rattling the loose signs. Knodalon didn't move, but his white hair lifted and settled like a banner. Bryant, at the far table, had drifted to sleep, his head pillowed on the folded arms of his shirt.

Prudence glanced down at her own hands. They were still now, folded and certain.

She finished her tea and set the cup aside.

"Thank you," she said, to both women at once.

Lara, still standing in Galhani's place behind the counter, nodded, and Leota allowed herself a thin smile.

"We're here," Leota said. "That's the point."

Leota's eyes drifted to the window, following the arc of Galhani's journey to Knodalon's bench. For a moment, the witch seemed lost in calculation—ticking off internal sums, measuring the shift of sunlight or the weight of silence.

Prudence waited, watching the way Leota's fingertips pressed together in a miniature steeple. In the hush, it became clear that the witch was balancing whether or not to speak her next thought.

"When the Icosagon is whole," Leota said, almost musing, "I can sense the flow of magic between the shops. Not precisely, but enough to know when the current is sluggish, or when it jumps." She smiled, a little sheepishly. "The pub draws the most, always. The Broken Claw has to know every traveler's history and destiny, even if only to pour their next drink. Sam is better at reading fates than she lets on."

Prudence's eyebrows crept upward. "She always claims to be ignorant."

"She claims a lot of things," Leota replied. "But her shop has to drink deep, or the town would lose its place on every map. Warren's forge—" She paused, the memory bringing a faint gleam to her eye. "Every time he has a Dream and works the ore, the surge is enough to make my hair stand on end for days. And Dardrad's meat—" Leota looked directly at Prudence, as if inviting her to share the joke. "Has it ever struck you as odd that some of his cuts are from animals not even native to these mountains?"

Prudence's mind snapped to the memory of a steak, marbled in an impossible blue, and a roast feathered with silvery fat. "I thought he just got creative with the seasoning," she said.

Leota's mouth twitched. "Sometimes he does. But sometimes the meat is not of this place." She sipped her tea, then set it aside. "Every shop has its magic, its appetite. But yours—"

She left the sentence unfinished.

Prudence chewed at her lower lip. "What about mine?"

Leota considered. "Your shop draws only lightly. It never leaves me dizzy, never upsets the circuit, even when you work through the night." She held up a finger, as if to forestall an argument. "This is not a complaint, only an observation."

Prudence's hand drifted to her sleeve, rubbing the edge of the seam as if that gentle friction could summon an answer. She found herself wishing she could just ask outright: *why does my shop draw so little? What do I lack, compared to the others?* But pride, or maybe just habit, clamped her tongue.

Leota must have sensed it. The witch's gaze cut through the veneer of small talk and sat, quietly, in the unoccupied chair between them.

"It's not a criticism," Leota said, voice low. "Tailoring is precise work. Maybe it doesn't require a great current."

"Or maybe," Prudence countered, "I'm just not using it right."

Leota smiled, thin and real. "That's the other possibility."

Prudence considered the idea, letting her thumb circle the worn edge of the cuff. "What if I don't know how?"

"I didn't," Leota replied. "Not when I first came." She stared into her tea, the surface trembling with the memory of her words. "My first month, I nearly set the roof on fire every time I tried to cast. The house had to teach me. The magic here isn't just for using. It's for learning, too."

That settled into Prudence like a pebble at the bottom of a pail, small but certain. "And if I never learn?"

Leota shrugged. "Then you'll do fine, but maybe you'll always feel… unfinished. The town will nudge you, though. It always does."

Prudence's eyes dropped to the hem of Leota's robe, the black fabric pooling in careful folds around the witch's ankles. "Do you ever miss it?" she asked, voice more tentative than she liked. "Color, I mean. Or do you just prefer the dark?"

Leota tilted her head, as if the question had never been posed quite that way. She pinched a bit of fabric between her fingers, then let it drop. "Once, I wore livery so bright it could blind a man. Orange and gold. Crest on the shoulder, badges down the breast. I was a battle mage then." She shrugged, and the memory fell away like dust from her sleeve. "It was armor, in its way. But I outgrew it. Now, I wear black because it matches what's in my heart."

She looked up, searching Prudence's face for reaction. "Do you miss it? The colors, the dressing up?"

Prudence startled, then forced a smile. "I don't know if I ever had it, even as a child. My mother wore black every day, no matter the season. The rules—" She bit off the rest, unwilling to dig into the Holderdown logic that had dictated her whole wardrobe.

Leota's eyes softened, and she nodded as if this made perfect sense. "Then maybe your black is your livery, too. But it's not armor unless you want it to be."

A pause stretched between them, broken only by the quiet click of Bryant turning a page in his book and the deeper hush that signaled Galhani's absence. Prudence wondered if all towns had this—these moments where nothing at all seemed to move, and yet everything meaningful was happening out of sight.

Leota steepled her fingers. "You know, it's a funny thing. Most people who come to North Pointe think they'll start over. But really, the town just waits for you to admit what you are, and then gives you more of it." She gestured with a hand, elegant and deliberate. "You could dress yourself in every bolt of green in the world. It wouldn't matter if you still thought in gray and brown."

Prudence bristled, not at the words but at the precision of their aim. "Maybe I don't want to be what I am," she said, more sharply than intended.

Leota's lips twitched. "Then you'll have to change first. The shop will follow, after."

Prudence felt something hot crawl up her neck—anger, or embarrassment, or both—but it drained away as she looked at Leota's steady gaze. "You make it sound easy."

"I make it sound inevitable," Leota said, and for the first time in their conversation, she looked tired.

The bell at the tea shop's door jingled, and Galhani returned, cheeks flushed from the outside air and eyes shining with relief. She tottered back to her seat and took a grateful gulp of tea, only after setting the empty tray on the counter.

"He's better," she announced. "Not good, but better. He said the tea helped. I'll keep checking on him every bell or so."

Leota nodded, then looked back at Prudence, as if daring her to disagree with the witch's earlier pronouncement.

Prudence, for her part, said nothing, but tucked the advice away, deep as she could. She had the sense that she would need it.

The rest of the morning unspooled with more talk, but the weight of the subject had shifted. Galhani and Leota traded stories about the oddities of their shops—herbal tinctures that refused to settle, a pestle that kept hiding from its bowl, a set of scales that read a different weight every candlemark. Bryant drifted in and out of the conversation, sometimes at his mother's side, sometimes pressed to the window to watch the slow churn of clouds over the green.

Prudence contributed where she could, but mostly, she listened. She heard the subtext in every joke and the small, private fears in every pause. Leota never admitted to weakness, but her stories always circled back to loneliness, to the price of being the only witch in town. Galhani, for all her sparkle, seemed most herself when recounting days spent alone in the garden, hands deep in cold dirt.

It was mid-morning when Leota finally stood, smoothing her dress and collecting her empty cup. She gave Galhani a nod, then turned to Prudence.

"Try it," she said, as if they'd been in the middle of a different conversation. "Just once, when no one's watching. Make something for yourself. You might be surprised."

With that, she swept out into the street, black braid swinging like a punctuation mark behind her.

Prudence watched her go, feeling the tug of the suggestion like a thread knotted somewhere under her ribs.

Galhani lingered, the tea shop quiet now but for the ticking of a wind-up clock and the owlcat's occasional chirr. Bryant had settled into a nap, face buried in his arms and hair ruffled by the static of the shop.

"You know she's right," Galhani said, softly.

Prudence blinked. "About what?"

"About the shop, about you." Galhani's voice was gentle, the usual brightness tempered by caution. "We're all… a little wrong, today. But you could fix it, if you wanted. Maybe not all at once. But in a small way."

Prudence let the words settle. "I wouldn't know where to start."

Galhani shrugged. "No one does, at first."

They lapsed into silence, and for a while Prudence just sat, listening to the tea's faint cooling hiss and the slow, uneven breath of her child. It was peaceful, or would have been, if not for the pressing sense that time was running out for things to go back to the way they had been.

The sun was past its peak when Galhani caught sight of something outside. She leaned forward, peering through the window, and clicked her tongue.

"There's a customer at your door," she said. "Looks like they've brought enough work to last a fortnight."

Prudence followed her gaze. Across the green, a figure in a patched coat waited in the shadow of the tailor's awning, arms piled high with what looked like half the contents of a family's wardrobe—shirts, skirts, a winter cloak trailing a damp edge behind.

Prudence stood, careful not to wake Bryant, and rolled down her sleeves. She thanked Galhani again for the tea, for the company, for the advice she couldn't yet voice aloud. Then, after pausing to tuck a wisp of hair back under her cap, she stepped into the sunlight and began the walk home.

The town had not changed while she'd been away, not in any way visible. The square was quieter than usual, but that was only a trick of the air. The lamps, even in full daylight, seemed to glow just a touch more fiercely, as if in defiance of the thinning that everyone felt but no one would name. Knodalon still sat at his post, chin on chest and hands folded, but when Prudence passed, his head lifted just enough for their eyes to meet.

He winked, or maybe it was just the sun in his face, but she felt the permission in it.

When she reached her shop, the customer straightened, shifting the burden to one arm and extending the other in greeting.

"Morning, mistress tailor," they said, a little breathless. "I was hoping you could help with a small emergency."

Prudence smiled, a real one this time, and beckoned them inside.

The bell over the door rang out—clear, familiar, and just loud enough to remind the world that, whatever else happened, the work would go on.

twelve

. . .

SCENE 1 - from Prudence Simonsdotter's point of view

The bell over the door sang out—sharp, unwavering—and the sound reverberated through the shop long after the customer had closed the door behind them. Prudence straightened from where she'd been inventorying spools and thread, smoothing the wrinkles from her apron as she turned to greet her first commission of the day. The customer—one of the recent travelers, judging by the dust that clung to their boots and the sun-browned edge of their hands—hesitated just inside the threshold, as if waiting for permission to cross from the world of mud and road into this cleaner, quieter space.

Bryant, who had been quietly reconstructing a small siege tower out of stacked buttons and a brass thimble, looked up but didn't speak. He retreated instead to the corner, clutching the owlcat, which blinked once at the new arrival and then resumed its nap in the boy's lap.

Prudence offered the traveler a place at the long bench. "You can set the bundle here," she said, nodding at the worn stack of clothing in their arms.

The customer complied, laying out their burden piece by piece: a pair of patched trousers, a faded shirt with cuffs frayed to gauze, a vest with a drooping hem, and what looked like a summer coat whose lining had surrendered the fight several seasons ago. "Best I can do for a wardrobe, these days," they joked, but the laugh caught on the dryness in their throat.

Prudence examined each item with practiced efficiency, lining them up in order of urgency. "You'd like all of them mended?"

The traveler hesitated, then said, "Anything you can do. The shirt's my favorite, but the coat… well, it gets cold on the road."

She nodded, already noting the repairs in her ledger. "Do you want any changes beyond the patching? New buttons, perhaps, or a different color for the thread?"

The customer shrugged, but their gaze flicked to the high shelf of vibrant bolts—crimson, green, the deep, impossible blue. "Plain's best for me," they said, though their eyes lingered for a moment on the blue before dropping away. "Don't want to stand out."

Prudence felt the words land and settle in her gut, familiar as old stones. She slid the clothing to her side of the table, then reached for the needle case. She could hear Bartram's advice in the back of her head—Why not a touch of color? Why not a shirt that makes you glad to see it in the morning?—and for a moment she almost reached for the blue thread instead of the standard brown.

Bryant, sensing the pause, sidled over with the owlcat draped across his shoulders like a scarf. "Will you fix the holes today?" he asked, voice pitched just above a whisper.

"I'll start," Prudence said, brushing a bit of dust from the shirt's sleeve. She glanced at the customer. "I can have these finished by first bell tomorrow, if you'd like."

The traveler smiled, and the lines around their eyes folded in on themselves. "That's more than fair. Never had a shop keep to a promise that quick." Their voice was rough, the accent a little out-of-place—southern, maybe, or just worn down by travel.

Prudence nodded, then, emboldened by something in their tone, gestured at the trim on the edge of the shelf. "If you ever wanted to, I could add some embellishment. Just a bit of blue or red at the collar, maybe. It's no trouble."

The traveler laughed—really laughed, this time—and shook their head. "Plain clothes for a plain life," they said. "Embellishment would be wasted on me."

But as they said it, their gaze drifted again to the bolts on the wall. This time, they reached out and touched the edge of the blue wool, pinching it between forefinger and thumb as if testing whether it was real.

"Never had occasion for such things," they murmured, more to themselves than to Prudence.

She let the moment hang, then packed the clothes into a neat bundle on her work table. "Tomorrow morning," she promised.

The customer thanked her, then turned to leave.

When the customer was gone, Bryant resumed his game, and the owlcat—now roused—began chasing errant threads along the baseboard. Prudence sat at her workbench, surveying the pile of mending. Her hands hovered for a moment over the vibrant red trim Bartram had once praised, but habit was stronger than curiosity. She reached for the brown thread, threaded her needle, and began again—one straight seam at a time.

Yet, as she worked, she caught herself glancing at the blue wool, measuring the risk of a single stitch of color.

She didn't dare—not yet. But the idea had taken root, and even as her fingers moved through the safe old routine, her mind wandered along the untried paths, wondering what it would mean to make something beautiful for someone who thought they didn't deserve it.

Outside, the town was silent, the world holding its breath between changes. Inside, Prudence stitched and mended, the lines of color waiting quietly for their moment.

———

The next day dawned uneven, a trick of light that started gray but sharpened to a piercing, colorless blue by the time Prudence sat down at her workbench to start on the traveler's repairs. The owlcat had taken up residence in the window box, fluffing itself into a loaf and snoring contentedly while Bryant, freshly washed and combed, sorted colored pins into the foam cushion at her elbow. The morning's calm was fragile, but it held—broken only by the occasional shout from the square or the high, reedy whistle of Sam's barked laughter echoing off the stone.

Prudence finished stitching the new patch onto the trousers, careful to match the warp and weft of the fabric so precisely that the repair would only be visible to someone actively searching for it. She liked that about her work: the way good mending vanished, leaving nothing but function. There was a pride in invisibility. Still, she caught herself more than once glancing at the spools of colored thread lined up like soldiers on the edge of the bench, each hue brighter and less shy than the last.

Bryant, noticing her distraction, said nothing, but she felt his eyes on her, small and sharp. He had inherited her knack for silence, but was growing out of her reluctance to break it. "The patch is perfect," he observed, head cocked.

"Thank you," she said, smoothing the seam. "But it's still just a patch."

He considered this, then returned to the pins, making a point of organizing them by color this time, not size.

By midday, Prudence had finished the shirt as well—reinforcing the frayed cuffs, replacing the collar with a bit of salvaged muslin, darning a thumb-sized hole under the left arm. She lined up the completed pieces at the edge of the table, and for a moment just stared at them, her arms folded in a rare moment of indecision.

That was when Bartram arrived.

The cobbler's approach was heralded by a rapid staccato of boot heels on the cobblestones, followed by the energetic double-tap of his knuckles on the glass. He ducked inside before Prudence could respond, beaming as if the cold outside had only made the warmth within more welcome. His eyes shone, and his round, red cheeks gave him a look of perpetual delight, even when he was at rest.

"Busy as ever, I see!" he announced, setting his satchel down with a flourish. "The whole square is talking about you, you know."

Prudence arched an eyebrow. "About my sewing?"

Bartram shook his head, grinning. "About the way you run a shop so tight you could bounce a copper off the counter. And about your customer from yesterday. Apparently they left the bakery with half a dozen rolls, and nothing but good things to say about the tailor who promised to make them look decent for the first time in ten seasons." His tone was teasing, but his eyes were sharp on her work, measuring the quality before the words even left his mouth.

He peered at the completed shirt and trousers, running his hands along the seams, tugging at the patches with a craftsman's skepticism. "You're too good for us, Simonsdotter. You know that?"

Prudence felt the flush rise up her neck, but she managed to keep her voice steady. "It's just mending, Bartram. Anyone could do it."

"Anyone could, but they don't." Bartram straightened, holding the shirt up against his own slight frame. "You know what this reminds me of? The uniforms I used to see on the road—marchers, guardsmen, even the Southern Queen's own footmen. They were always patched, but it was the kind of patch that said, 'I'm still worth repairing.'"

Prudence shrugged, looking down at her hands. "I'm not making uniforms. Most people don't want to be noticed."

Bartram made a show of sighing, then slid onto the stool opposite hers. "That's true, but it's not the whole of it." He leaned forward, conspiratorial. "Have you seen what the salesman's doing now? He's brought out an entire second trunk of vials—colors I've never seen, some that look like they'd light a fire if you set them too close to the stove. He's drawing crowds, even from folk old enough to know better."

Prudence frowned. "He's a distraction."

"He's a symptom," Bartram countered. "People crave something extra, even if they pretend they don't. Look at the bakery—Makota's added berry glaze to the top buns, and now no one will eat the old ones. Or the pub, where Sam's started serving tea in the evenings for those who don't want strong drink. Change is the only thing that really sticks in people's minds." His tone softened. "You should let yourself try it."

Prudence shook her head, but the argument was a weak one. "It isn't needed."

Bartram leaned back, feigning exasperation. Then he unbuckled his satchel and drew out a pair of boots. They were beautiful—thick-soled, built for walking, the upper a deep brown leather tooled with swirling designs that caught the light in waves. The soles had bright copper rivets, each set in a pattern that resembled the peaks of the distant Mistrals. He set them on the bench between them, as if expecting her to appraise them.

She did. "They're for…?"

"A young man from the hills. Heading to the lake, then south," Bartram said. "He said he just wanted something sturdy, but I thought —why not give him something that will remind him of home when he's days away from it?"

Prudence traced a finger along the tooling. "This must have taken you forever."

"Every stitch worth it. But you see the point? We could make plain boots and plain clothes all day, but sometimes it's the extra bit that carries a memory, or a hope, or even just a joke between the maker and the wearer." He tapped the toe of one boot. "It's the difference between surviving and living, if you ask me."

Prudence considered the line of reasoning, the boots, the way Bryant was now openly listening from his station behind the pins. She glanced at the stack of clothes she'd mended—strong, clean, invisible.

Bartram saw the look and pressed his advantage. "Have you ever wondered what the shop's real gift is?" he asked, the shift in tone unmistakable. "Not the sewing itself. The magic of it."

Prudence hesitated. "I've always thought it was just the fit. How I can make anything suit anyone, even if they're not used to well-fit clothes."

Bartram snorted, but without meanness. "That's your skill, not the shop's gift. The shop wants more from you, I think." He let that hang, then continued, "Have you ever tried making something that wasn't requested? A surprise, or a joke, or even just a whim?"

She shook her head, but not quite as firmly as before. "People don't want surprises."

"Sometimes they do," Bartram said. "And sometimes it's the only way to show you care." He stood, rolling up the shirt and trousers into a neat bundle, then set them in the basket at the end of the bench. "Try it," he urged. "Next time, add a bit of color or a secret stitch. You don't have to tell anyone, if you don't want to. But do it for yourself, if nothing else."

Prudence picked up the boots, turning them over in her hands. The copper rivets shone, each a tiny beacon in the dark. "Maybe I will," she said, uncertain whether it was a promise or just a way to end the conversation.

Bartram laughed, already gathering his satchel. "I'll know," he said. "The whole town will know, eventually. But that's the fun of it."

He winked at Bryant, then paused at the door, his hand on the latch. "And if you ever need blue thread, I have a spool that would match that wool exactly." He tipped his cap, then vanished into the sharp brightness of the afternoon.

The door closed behind him, and the world was briefly muffled. Prudence sat, silent, for a long moment, her hands resting on the boots and her eyes fixed on the row of spools. Bryant didn't speak, but after a moment he slid the pins together so all the colored ones sat in a neat little wedge at the top of the cushion.

Prudence reached for the blue, then the red, then, after a moment's indecision, set both aside and returned to the brown. But as she threaded the needle, she caught herself smiling—small, uncertain, but real. She wondered what it might mean to add a single stripe of color to a cuff, or a patch shaped not like a square, but a leaf, or even a sun.

She let the thought linger, and as she worked, the lines of color seemed less like a risk and more like an invitation.

Outside, the world had not changed. But inside, for the first time in a long while, Prudence let herself imagine that it could.

thirteen

. . .

THE MORNING'S first bell found Prudence already at her workbench, hands idle but heart quickened by the anxious thought that maybe—maybe—she had gone too far. The air in the shop still clung to the night's chill, all light filtered through the high, narrow windows as a pale and cautious gold. Bryant was not yet awake; the owlcat had claimed the warmest patch of sunlight for itself, eyes slitted in pretense of sleep but tracking every shadow with a hunter's patience.

On the far end of the table, neatly folded and ready, sat the customer's mended shirt. Prudence had worked late to finish it, the plain brown of the fabric offset now by cuffs edged with a single, careful band of blue. The blue was not bright—not reckless—but in this shop, where everything else existed in shades of earth or soot, it was a tiny act of rebellion.

Prudence ran her fingers along the edge, feeling the faint rise where the colored thread met the old, worn cloth. A small voice inside insisted she could still pick it out and redo the hem in brown, that it would take hardly a moment, that it would be safer. She ignored it, folding her hands in her lap and waiting for the customer to arrive.

She did not wait long. The bell above the door chimed—twice, as if eager to mark the start of things—and the traveler entered with her boots still damp from the grass outside. In the fresh morning light, they appeared younger than Prudence had first guessed, though road dust and too many nights in borrowed beds made them seem older. This morning they looked brighter, or maybe just more awake; their eyes found Prudence's at once, and for a moment both hesitated, caught in the silence of mutual expectation.

"You said it would be ready by first bell," the customer said, their voice a little rough around the edges but not unkind.

Prudence nodded, gestured to the waiting bundle. "It's all there. Mended, as you asked."

The customer approached, peeling back the brown paper with hands that trembled in the cold or perhaps with nerves. They lifted the shirt, running their thumbs along the sleeves, stopping when they saw the edge of blue at the cuff.

A long pause.

Prudence steeled herself, ready for an accusation—too flashy, too showy, a waste of good thread—but the words did not come. Instead, the customer pinched the cuff between forefinger and thumb, rubbing it as if unsure whether it was real. Their lips pressed together, then softened.

"Didn't expect that," they said. "The blue."

Prudence swallowed. "I can unpick it, if you'd prefer. Brown is more—"

"No," the customer said, quick and almost breathless. They held the sleeve up, letting the blue catch the weak morning sun. "It's... unexpected. But I like it."

For a moment, Prudence forgot to breathe.

The customer tried on the shirt, working their arm through the sleeve with practiced efficiency. The cuff settled at their wrist, and the line of blue made her hand look stronger, more certain. They flexed her fingers, then grinned—not the polite twitch from the day before, but a full, surprised smile.

"Won't hurt, I guess," they said. "Bit of color in the morning."

They packed the shirt back into her bundle, then reached into their purse and pulled out a silver. The coin gleamed with the faint promise of more, and they rolled it across the workbench with a snap of their thumb. "That's fair for the lot?"

Prudence nodded, took the coin with a steadiness she did not feel. "If you like, I can do the rest the same. Or leave them plain."

The customer shrugged, their eyes lingering on the repaired shirt. "No reason to match. I'm headed north after this—might be bad luck to stand out too much." They bundled up the rest of her things, but before leaving, they said, "There's a birthday at home when I get back. Maybe I'll wear it for that. Make a story of it."

They left with a cheery wave, the bell's chime a little lighter now, as if the metal itself understood it had witnessed a small, private victory.

Prudence watched them go, arms folded against her chest, the coin still warm in her palm. She stood there for a while, letting the last echo of the bell settle in the rafters, before allowing herself the luxury of a smile.

When Bryant padded down the stairs, hair wild and eyes half-closed, Prudence met him with a ruffled hug, the sort that did not need words to communicate its origin. The owlcat blinked at them both, unimpressed.

Prudence set the next order on the table and drew a single, deep breath. For the first time in a long while, she felt the day might hold something beyond routine.

The blue at the wrist was a reminder, subtle but insistent, that she could be more than she had planned.

And for now, that was enough.

———

By the time the second bell called out over the square, Prudence had finished her tea and set about the day's main work. The customer's silver sat on the corner of her workbench, a small, shining testament that the new day would be much like the last. She laid out the remaining commissions in a careful fan: a gardener's apron in raw linen, a set of sturdy winter breeches for Darby, a child's cloak that had arrived half-destroyed and smelling faintly of fish. Each item was practical, undemanding—work that required no artistry, only patience and a steady hand.

Bryant had claimed a spot by the hearth, a battered box of wooden blocks balanced in his lap. He built a tower with solemn focus, pausing every so often to measure it against the window's light or the height of his own arm. When the owlcat batted a block from the structure, Bryant merely set it back in place, as if he'd expected the challenge all along.

Prudence's needle found its familiar rhythm, passing through cloth with a gentle thock that built its own kind of hush. For a while, she lost herself in it—measuring, pinning, stitching, snipping, and setting each finished edge aside in perfect order. But today, the rhythm did not wholly settle. Each time she reached for a fresh length of thread, her gaze was drawn up, inexorably, to the shelves above.

They'd always been there, the bolts of fabric either left over from the shop's previous owner or provided through the shop's magic— bright colors stacked in high, untouched rows, a silent temptation. On mornings like this, when the light came in sharp and unfiltered, the fabrics seemed to glow from within: a green so deep it conjured the promise of summer grass, a red that hovered between berry and fire, gold with the sheen of honey combed straight from the hive. In the center, a roll of blue velvet—blue like a bruise, or like the candle-mark before sunrise—waited, its nap so dense it looked almost liquid.

She'd tried once to reorganize the shelf, move the colors to the very back where they wouldn't tempt her, but it had made no difference. The blue always found a way to the front, and the gold and green crept along behind, eager to be seen. It was as if the shop itself was insistent on their presence, refusing to let them go unnoticed.

Prudence cut a patch for the child's cloak, her eyes fixed on the dull brown cloth. She traced a shape that would cover the tear, her mind drifting to the possibility of something more—maybe a patch in the shape of a leaf, or edged with a glimmer of gold. But she set the fancy aside, squared the patch, and basted it in place. When she reached for thread, her fingers paused over a spool of sapphire before moving, with a conscious effort, to the brown.

The moment lingered. She shook it off, snipped the thread, and reached for the next commission.

The air in the shop felt different this morning. Usually by now the room was warmed by the sun and the work; the hum of industry, even in solitude, gave everything a pleasant weight. But today the space felt light, as if the walls had thinned and the floor floated an inch above its own stones. The hush was not restful but watchful, as if the world were waiting for her to make a mistake.

She pricked her finger on the next seam. The bead of blood welled up, bright and insistent. Prudence pressed it to her tongue, scowling at her own inattention.

Bryant, sensing the shift in mood, looked up. "Are you hurt?"

She shook her head, tongue already numb to the copper tang. "Just careless."

Bryant considered this, then stood, carrying his unfinished tower to the table. "Maybe it wants a roof," he said, placing it beside her work. "Maybe that's what it's waiting for."

Prudence smiled, despite herself. "Maybe so."

She tore a scrap from the cloak's lining and draped it over the blocks, forming a makeshift roof. The tower wobbled, then held. Bryant beamed, pleased with the collaboration, and returned to his post by the stove.

She glanced at the shelves again. The blue velvet was lit with a shaft of sun, its color deeper now, more insistent.

Her hand went to the back of her neck, massaging the stiff line where her cap pressed against her skin. The black cap was a constant, and she'd long ago taught herself to adjust it whenever she felt out of sorts—a small gesture of control over the day's shape. She did it now, tucking the short hairs behind her ear, then pulling the cap down so it shaded her eyes from the bright onslaught above.

She stitched a row on the apron, then another on the breeches, but the feeling persisted. Each time her hands drifted near the colors, she caught herself, pulled back, and forced her mind to the task at hand. She tried counting the stitches, a trick she'd learned as a child to keep herself steady, but today the numbers slipped away from her, dissolving into memory or static.

She remembered, with sudden clarity, the summer when her mother had allowed her a single ribbon—a blue one, almost as bright as the velvet now watching from the shelf. She'd worn it hidden, beneath her collar, a secret joy that lasted until her father discovered it and cut it free with the same knife he used to clean fish. Even then, she had not cried, only pressed the memory of the blue into a place behind her ribs where no one else could touch it.

That was the lesson she'd carried into adulthood: joy was best kept hidden, safe from the world's indifference or, worse, its scorn. Yet here she was, thirty years old and still tormented by a length of blue thread.

She finished the apron, folded it, and set it atop the growing pile. Her hands shook, faintly, as she reached for the next project. She pressed them flat to the table, willing the tremor to pass.

From the window, she could see the edge of the green and the first arrivals at the bakery, faces she knew but never greeted. The sky was clear now, the sun climbing with slow determination. She took a breath, steadying herself, then returned to the work.

But the balance was off, and she knew it.

Even the owlcat seemed to notice. It leapt onto the bench beside her, curling its tail around its paws and blinking up at the shelves with a look of disdain. Prudence scratched behind its ear, and the animal closed its eyes, purring with the mechanical regularity of a clock.

She tried to match that steadiness, but the sense of disruption had rooted itself deep. Every time she reached for the brown thread, her hand brushed the colors first, as if they had grown longer overnight, their magic seeping into the wood and air.

She finished the breeches, then the cloak. At noon, she set aside her tools and made lunch for Bryant—a crust of bread, a slice of cheese, the smallest apple in the basket. She watched him eat, his face turned toward the light, his movements unhurried and sure. The child was a study in contradiction: as careful as she was, but also prone to small, feral joys. He had named the owlcat "Moss," and insisted that it was the smartest animal in the town.

Prudence poured herself a cup of tea, watching the steam rise in thin, fraying lines. She sipped, letting the heat dull the ache in her throat.

When she returned to the bench, she found the blue ribbon had fallen from the shelf, landing squarely in the center of her work area. She stared at it, then at the shelves above—neatly ordered, nothing amiss, no sign of how it had come loose.

She picked up the ribbon, rolled it tight, and set it aside. For the next 'mark, she worked in silence, refusing to let her attention wander. But every time she glanced at the pile of finished mending, the blue ribbon winked at her, a secret waiting for its chance.

The day stretched on. The bell outside rang again, marking the time. Prudence finished the last hem, then set her hands in her lap and let herself breathe.

The shop was quiet, the air still bright with color, the promise of something different just beneath the surface.

She wondered, for the first time, whether she wanted to resist it at all.

She might have stitched until dusk, or until her hands failed, had not the next interruption arrived in the form of Galhani and her inexhaustible pot of tea.

The gnome made her entrance with typical disregard for decorum, pushing the door open with her hip and ushering in a flood of crisp midday light. In her arms was a basket, draped with a linen that steamed faintly from within. "I brought fortifications," she announced, as if tea were a weapon to be wielded. "Smells like the whole square could use it."

Prudence set aside her work and cleared the end of the bench. Bryant, who'd migrated to the floor with his tower, paused in construction and watched with undisguised interest as Galhani produced two cups—one the battered white with green rim, the other a dainty thing with a hairline crack spidering across its glaze.

Galhani poured for Prudence first, then for herself, then crouched at eye level with Bryant. "For you, young man, a bonus—strawberry tart from Makota's very own oven." She held it out on a napkin, and Bryant accepted with the gravity of a judge presiding over a court.

Prudence sipped, letting the heat fill her chest, then glanced at the workbench. "News?" she prompted.

Galhani's eyes sparkled. "Where to begin? The trade road's gone mad with travelers, every wagon heavier than the last. The stable's overrun with horses and one very cross ox, and the bakery sold out before third bell." She paused, rolling the cup between her palms. "But the best news is this: your friend at the end of the road is doing a brisk business. Three more turned away from the mountain path this morning—decided they'd rather buy colored water than face the old pass."

Prudence made a noise in her throat. "He's been here almost a moon."

"At least," Galhani agreed. "Sam says the potions taste like vinegar and look like pond scum, but they all keep coming. Not a single one's made it to Elspeth's. Even Tyran says his business is down—with nobody heading into the mountains, there's not much call for the gear he sells. One woman had the audacity to proclaim one of those vial, false potions a better buy than a proper enchanted sword!" She shook her head. "I imagine his shop doesn't know what to do with itself, people not wanting their adventure."

Bryant, mouth sticky with tart, piped up. "Why don't they want adventure?"

Galhani grinned, showing teeth. "Maybe the adventure is not in them," she said. Then, looking at Prudence, "Or maybe someone told them it's easier to buy destiny than earn it."

Prudence set her cup down harder than she meant to. "If people could just buy their way out of trouble, there'd be no need for shops like mine. Or yours, for that matter."

Galhani shrugged, but her smile was tight. "You could look at it the other way, you know. Maybe they're only buying a bit of courage, so they can take the first step."

"Or maybe they want to skip the step entirely," Prudence countered. "They want the result, not the work."

A beat of silence. Bryant, sensing the tension, scuttled to the far end of the bench and resumed building, this time with the tart perched atop the highest block.

Galhani sipped her tea and let her gaze travel over the shop, taking in the neat lines of the bench, the piles of unremarkable brown and gray, the way the colored fabrics hovered in their high domain, almost luminous in the noon sun.

"You know," she said, "your shop is different today."

Prudence blinked. "How?"

"It's… brighter." Galhani let the word hang, then nodded toward the shelf. "That blue one moved."

Prudence followed her eyes, and saw that it was true. The velvet, once a third of the way down, now sat right at the top, visible to anyone entering the shop.

"I never touched it," she said, but the admission felt defensive, even to herself.

Galhani made a noncommittal sound. "Shops do as they like. Sometimes ours is noisy, sometimes the herbs grow in wild shapes. It's all the same magic, really." She peered into her cup, then back up. "I think it's trying to tell you something."

"Or maybe I need to tidy more often."

Galhani set her cup aside, hands folded on the table. "If you ever wanted to try something, you could. There's no rule that says you have to stay plain forever."

Prudence stared at the work in her lap—a patch, a seam, the same brown thread. She wanted to argue, to say that some people needed plainness the way others needed air or food, that there was safety in it, but the words would not come. Instead, she tightened her grip on the needle, driving it through the cloth so firmly it left a dent on her thumb.

Galhani watched, expression softening. "You're not the only one feeling it, you know. Since Dooley left, the whole square is off. Like a bell missing its chime."

Prudence nodded, and the silence between them became companionable again. They drank their tea, watched Bryant build and rebuild, and said little more.

When the bell over the door chimed again, Galhani stood, brushed off her skirt, and gathered her things. "I'll bring more tart next time. Tell Makota to save you a slice?"

Prudence smiled, the effort easier than expected. "Thank you."

Galhani left, the shop settling into stillness behind her. Prudence set her cup aside and looked again at the shelf, the velvet, the colors. They were closer now, somehow, crowding the edge of the ordinary.

She finished her mending, each stitch tight, as if it might hold the world together a little longer.

But she knew it would not last.

———

The afternoon stretched long and thin, the sun slanting in at just the right angle to highlight the dust and the way it drifted, lazy, through the air. Prudence left the shop in Bryant's care—he was content to watch the owlcat and the empty street—and climbed the narrow stairs to the living quarters above.

Their rooms were plain, as all her spaces tended to be, but the upstairs was softer for lack of scrutiny: the rugs a little more worn, the curtains faded to a washed-out lavender, the bed piled with a mismatched set of quilts, each one the product of a different season's end. Prudence liked it best in the moments before dusk, when the world was quiet and the rules of the day did not press so hard.

Today, though, she could not settle. She'd promised Bryant she would teach him to tie a proper knot—one that would hold a bundle through a wagon's worst jostling, or secure a package against any wind. They sat cross-legged on the floor, the end of a frayed rope held between them, but every time she tried to show the proper loop or twist, her fingers lost the shape, and her mind drifted back to the blue ribbon, to the way it had landed on the bench, to the way she could not bring herself to throw it out.

Bryant watched her with the unblinking patience of a child who knew the lesson mattered more to the teacher than the pupil.

"Like this, Mama?" he asked, tying a loose knot and holding it up for inspection.

Prudence nodded, forcing a smile. "Yes. That's… close. Here, let me—" She reached for the rope, but her hands fumbled, and she let it drop to the floor.

Bryant scooted closer, tugging at her sleeve until she looked at him. "Are you tired?"

"A little," Prudence admitted. "I think my mind is wandering today."

Bryant considered this, then padded off to the tiny kitchen nook and returned with a wooden spoon. "This will help," he said. "You can use it to show the knot."

Prudence took the spoon, ran her fingers over the smooth handle, and tried to focus. "Thank you, love." She managed two loops, then stopped, lost in the act of winding and unwinding.

Bryant, undeterred, fetched a small toy horse from the shelf. "The horse needs a harness," he explained, offering it up. "You can show me on this."

Prudence tied a length of string around the horse's middle, but the result was unsatisfying. She stared at the toy, the way the blue of its painted eyes caught the light, and felt a hollow open in her chest.

Bryant watched her, then hopped to his feet and rummaged in the small chest by the window. After a moment, he emerged victorious, holding aloft a scrap of fabric—a wild, ungovernable yellow, the color so shocking against the grayness of the room that it seemed to pulse with its own heat.

"Moss was playing with it," Bryant said, by way of explanation. "Do you want it?"

Prudence took the fabric in both hands. It was soft, finer than anything she usually worked with, and she recognized it at once as a remnant from the old shop stock. She pressed it to her palm, feeling how light it was, how insistent.

She meant to say something to Bryant, to explain why this piece of color was different, but instead she folded it, carefully, and tucked it into the top drawer of the dresser. She closed the drawer with a click, then sat back on her heels and pulled Bryant into her lap.

"Thank you," she said, her voice smaller than intended.

Bryant curled into her, content. The rope, the spoon, the horse—all forgotten for now.

For a while, they sat together, and the sun moved across the floor, and the quiet grew less oppressive.

The sixth bell rang out, low and even, and Prudence roused herself. She straightened her dress, adjusted her cap, and lifted Bryant to his feet. "Time to open up," she said, and together they went down the stairs, the memory of the yellow fabric humming in the closed drawer above.

The day was not over, but she felt it gathering itself, readying for something she could not name.

———

By the time dusk found its way through the windows, painting the shop in slow, slanted bands, Prudence stood at her bench and stared at the jerkin she'd spent the better part of a day completing. It was perfect, by every measure she'd ever been taught: seams even and tight, the collar crisp, the pockets squared with ruthless precision. It would stand up to rain, to years of wear, to the careless hands of a dozen different owners. It would be invisible—practically designed to vanish into the world's background.

And that was what made her hate it.

She picked up the jerkin, ran her fingers along the shoulders, then laid it flat again. The fabric was stiff, unyielding. She wondered, briefly, if it would ever soften, or if it was doomed to remain forever on the outside of comfort.

A flicker of color caught her eye. There, beside the scissors, lay a ribbon—blue as lake water under cloud, and as unexpected as a new tooth in the mouth of an old dog. She did not recall leaving it there. For a moment, she considered the possibility that Bryant had placed it as a joke, or the owlcat had dragged it from the shelf, but neither explanation satisfied. The ribbon had appeared, as so many things did in this shop, precisely where it needed to be.

Prudence picked it up, feeling the weight of the velvet against her thumb. It was a nice piece, the edges sharp and true, the surface smooth as breath. She held it to the jerkin's collar, letting it drape just so, and in the dimming light, the effect was astonishing: the whole garment seemed to wake up, the brown suddenly richer, the shape somehow less severe. She imagined the blue as a line along the cuff, or a small band at the hem, and for a moment she allowed herself to see it finished, worn by someone who would notice, and appreciate, the difference.

But then the familiar hesitation set in. Her hand hovered, indecisive, for three heartbeats, then four. With a small, frustrated sigh, she set the ribbon aside, folded it neatly, and placed it at the far edge of the bench.

Her fingers drummed against the wood. She flexed them, shook them out, then pressed her palms flat and stared at the jerkin again. It was fine. It was good. It was enough.

Except that it wasn't, and she knew it.

She slumped, just a little, shoulders sagging under the invisible weight. The owlcat, sensing her mood, leapt onto the bench and curled around her elbow. It blinked up at her, eyes luminous in the half-light, and chirred a low, questioning note.

"I know," Prudence said. "I know."

She reached for the jerkin, preparing to hang it on the waiting form, but the bell over the door chimed—once, then again. The sound was crisp, perfectly timed to the turning of the day.

She straightened, smoothed her dress, and fixed her cap. She put on her best shopkeeper's smile—the one that was all politeness and no invitation—and turned to greet the new arrival.

The customer was a traveler, as she had guessed, hair wild from the wind and face raw from too many nights on the road. He glanced around the shop, taking in the order and the color, and his gaze lingered, as it always did, on the shelf where the fabrics glowed even in the failing light.

He offered a polite nod, then set his pack on the counter. "I heard you do good work," he said. "Could use a patch, and maybe a bit of reinforcement along the hem."

Prudence nodded, taking the garment—another jerkin, battered and soft from years of use. She spread it out, examining the tear. "I can have it done by tomorrow. Did you want it plain, or...?" She let the question hang, gesturing to the spools of color behind her.

The traveler looked, considered, then shook his head. "Plain's best for me," he said, but the words were slower than before, and his eyes kept drifting to the blue, the red, the impossible gold.

Prudence smiled, took the measure, and promised to have it ready by morning.

As the traveler left, the bell chimed again, softer this time. Prudence watched the door swing closed, then turned back to her workbench.

The blue ribbon lay there, patient.

She picked it up, held it to the light, and wondered—truly wondered—what it would mean to say yes to it, just once.

Then she set it down, smoothed the jerkin's collar, and reached for her needle.

fourteen

. . .

THE BROKEN CLAW was at its most honest just after sundown, when the first round of travelers had found their rest and the townsfolk claimed their tables as if returning to an old, well-made coat. Prudence liked it best in the moments before full dark: the lamps lit and set on every post and rafter, the air smoky with peat and warming ale, the clatter of dice and laughter blending with the low, grounding hum of Sam's voice behind the bar.

Tonight, the place was more crowded than usual, with not just the town's fixed stars but also several orbiting bodies—hangers-on from the trade road, the odd pilgrim seeking a hot meal and a cold drink before vanishing at dawn. Prudence slipped in through the rear, taking her usual place at the corner table nearest the hearth, and angled her chair so she could see both the room and, by squinting, the fogged glass of the front door. Bryant had been dropped with Galhani for the evening; the owlcat was presumably terrorizing the gnome's entire pantry. Prudence felt both lighter and stranger without her son's persistent, silent company.

She wouldn't ordinarily have come, but... *something* pulled her out of the shop. Out of the shop and across the green, down the short alley behind the pub and inn, and in through their shared back door. She felt something akin to restlessness, something like anticipation.

Sam, who tonight was running the Claw as she might a ship at full gale, caught her eye at once and signaled that tea would be coming—a brisk, friendly gesture, no-nonsense but not without warmth. Prudence returned the nod, then tried not to flinch at the crash that came a moment later from the front, where Warren was, as usual, playing the role of bouncer whether needed or not.

The ogre occupied the front entry with the ease of a man who had never fit any room made by human hands. He leaned against the doorframe, the boards creaking beneath his weight, one massive arm folded across his chest, the other resting just above the pommel of a ceremonial—but not at all fake—blacksmith's hammer. His presence served as both a reassurance and a warning: those who belonged here could relax; those who didn't, best try elsewhere. This was the line they'd struck with Cornelius the salesman: he could be served, but he'd take his drink outside, and it would likely be warm. Everyone else was welcome in.

A thin, persistent drizzle streaked the window glass, distorting the faces outside. Every few minutes, a shape would appear—sometimes hopeful, sometimes desperate—and Warren would nod them in or gently.

The real show, however, arrived with Elspeth Riverpine.

She slipped through the door just as Warren was busying himself with the gentle removal of a particularly drunken surveyor. Elspeth's approach was stealthy only in comparison; her presence, once admitted, was impossible to miss. She was not tall, but there was a focus to her—like a length of drawn bow, all force and intent waiting to happen. Prudence's eyes flicked up and down in a professional survey, noting that while her woolen cloak was sodden, the hem was clean. She carried no pack, and her cheeks didn't have the raw flush that other travelers' did. Elspeth hadn't traveled into North Pointe in the common way. Rather, she'd likely appeared out of thin air just outside one of the road gates, and then hurried under the protection of the overhang that ran the length of the trade road shops.

She might play the role of Enchantress of the Mountain, but tonight she was merely Elspeth. Prudence knew—from past overhead conversations—that she used her magic to make herself less conspicuous, even to those who could see or otherwise sense her power. A testament to her veil was the conversation in the pub: it remained exactly as it was. Only the townsfolk seemed to notice her, and as Prudence watched, each of them stood or sat a little straighter. Their eyes twinkled a bit more brightly. They were privy to a secret tonight, and they were pleased to be so.

Warren closed the door behind Elspeth, then gave her a courteous but brief nod before returning to his post, oversized tankard of ale in one huge hand. Elspeth, for her part, scanned the room with the crisp economy of a cartographer, mapping each face and angle before settling—much to Prudence's surprise—on the empty seat across from her. She crossed the floor with none of the hesitation common to strangers in a new pub. Instead, she moved with the deliberate, frictionless motion of someone who has never in her life considered she might not belong. She slid into the bench opposite Prudence, folding her hands on the table in a way that was both patient and expectant.

Sam delivered the tea with a speed usually reserved for emergencies. "Evening, Elspeth," she said, her voice pitched low, but not secret.

"Evening, Sam," Elspeth replied. Her own voice was light, with a trace of music in the vowels, but it struck the air as flint might strike steel—sparks promised, if not delivered. She nodded at the mug, then lifted it, inhaling the scent. "Bit weak tonight?"

Sam looked appalled. "Never for you!"

Elspeth smiled, a quick flash. "Then I blame the rain. Everything tastes thinner on wet days."

Sam's lips twitched, as if to say, "Don't I know it," then left the two women alone.

Prudence sipped her own tea, letting the quiet extend itself. She wondered what would be expected of her. As a rule, she tried to avoid wading into the deeper conversations of North Pointe—hers was a job of mending, not meddling—but it was hard not to feel a certain thrill at being chosen, even accidentally, as the focus of attention for someone like Elspeth.

The older woman broke the silence first. "You're the seamstress, aren't you?"

Prudence nodded. "Prudence. Or Pru, if you like."

"I've seen your work," Elspeth said, glancing down at her own tunic, then at the fine repair of the sleeve. "Best hand I've ever come across, and I've seen a few. Patches that hold through a blizzard, and seams that make a lie of the years." She smiled, softer now. "My grandmother used to say that a town's worth could be measured by the way it held itself together. I think she'd have liked you." She tilted her head like a curious bird. "You're not often in the pub when I visit."

Prudence felt heat creep up her neck. She had no ready answer, so she ducked her head and muttered, "Thank you. And no... not normally."

"And tonight?"

Prudence exhaled more sharply than she'd intended. "The weather. My shop... I needed a break."

"Business is brisk, then?"

Prudence nodded silently.

Elspeth sighed and sipped her tea. "I wish I could say the same. But this past moon I've seen maybe three parties on their quests."

Prudence's eyes widened by a fraction.

"I could understand it perhaps, with the weather, but these storm is new-come. It'll linger, by the way. And it isn't just me."

"Oh?"

Elspeth considered for a moment. When she spoke again, her voice was a bit lower, and it was accompanied by a slight muffling of the rest of the noise in the pub. Prudence's heart skipped a beat as she recognized the tickle of magic—Leota had pulled this trick once or twice, when she wanted to have a conversation but not be overheard. "Nimarith doesn't consider himself a great dispenser of divine favor. But he does believe in providing an opportunity for those who are willing to work for it. Those who deserve it. Who are willing to earn it. Did you know there's a she-orc in one of the passes? She'll kill and consume any who try to pass, but bring her enough fresh meat, and she'll gift you a tooth."

"A tooth?"

"A molar. Orc molars are constantly falling out and growing back. Hardest substance in the world, they say. But they contain a spark of the primal magic that keeps an orc alive. If you can crack it, and if you can hold your intention strongly enough in your mind, that burst of released magic can grant wishes." Elpseth grinned. "Simple wishes, mind. It's an orc, after all."

"I had no idea."

"There's a meadow with magical flowers that can bring fortune or ruin. There's a path—I steer well-clear of this one, believe me—that can carry you off the edge of a cliff, although if you've got the right attitude it'll carry you to the place you most need to be in the world." She chuckled. "Nimarith is creative, if nothing else." But then her expression dimmed. "And of all of them, all the paths he's laid out, less than a half-dozen have seen traffic this season."

"It's the man in the wagon outside," Prudence blurted.

Elspeth frowned. "Wagon?"

"His name is Cornelius. I… we have a history. Of sorts. He came to my village in Holderdown, selling false remedies. Now he sells… he calls them 'destiny potions.'"

Now the Enchantress' eyes narrowed. "'See your future' for a silver, that kind of thing?"

"More. He promises they can bring your destiny to life. He's put people off climbing the mountain, ones who had come here planning to seek you out."

"Ah."

"Can you… would you stop him?"

Elspeth took a deep breath and released it slowly. "Sam," she called, turning toward the bar. "Have you nay of that excellent mist-ale you served me last time?"

"Coming right up." Sam's voice cut through the rest of the pub. Prudence looked up and noticed Dardrad and Jen sitting not far away, subtly keeping an eye on her and Elspeth. The Enchantess remained silent until Sam delivered the frosted mug of ale. "Don't mind me," Sam added as she leaned against the wall, arms crossed, clearly intending to listen in.

"Tell me of your history with the man," Elspeth said gently. "If you can."

Prudence leaned back and closed her eyes for a moment. "You know of Holderdown? Our traditions?"

"I would perhaps term it *their* conditions, child, but yes. Very conservative. Suspicious of outsiders."

"You're putting it gently. But yes. I was with child, with Bryant, when my husband, Nikol, was killed in an accident. My family took well enough care of me until Bryant was born, but…"

"A mother without a husband isn't well-regarded there," Elspeth said, nodding.

"Truth."

"And this seller of potions?"

"He… took a liking to me," Prudence said, flushing a furious red.

"*Ah,*" Elspeth said.

"I don't get it," Sam said.

"The people of Holderdown practice contract marriage," Elspeth said, shaking her head sadly. "And the woman is rarely included in the negotiations. If she was a single mother and a single man offered the right bride-price, they'd marry her off and consider it a win all around."

"That's disgusting," Sam spat.

"…it is in dwarves communities," Dardrad said, his voice going from muffled to clear as Elspeth's magic expanded to include the table he and Jen had occupied. "Difference is, the groom's parents are mainly trying to make sure their son won't get killed when he and his betrothed first meet."

Sam stifled a snort.

"And so what happened, child?" Elspeth asked Prudence.

"I left the same night," she replied. "With Bryant bundled to me and whatever I could carry in a pack."

"Oh, my poor dear."

"I didn't know all that," Sam said quietly. "You keep your past close."

"But now he's here," Prudence murmured. "He's *here.*"

"Has he seen you?"

"Hah!" Jen barked. "Not a chance. We've kept on him. Not that it's made him leave, even with the poorest hospitality we could show without breaking the oath." She cocked her head. "Any chance you *could* do something? Nothing dire. Just make him… move on."

"Hmm. No." Elspeth took barely an eyeblink to consider it.

"No?" Sam asked.

"'A fool and their money are soon parted.' And a dozen other aphorisms. Do you know how many of the parties who start up the mountain make it to my keep?" Everyone shook their heads. "Less than half. Most turn back at the first sign of difficulty. And of those who do make it to my front door, fewer than a quarter manage the tasks I set them."

"So an eighth actually get what they set out for?" Sam asked.

"Roughly. And that's as it's meant to be. Fools looking for love potions or idle riches or any amount of nonsense. Nimarith, as I was telling Prudence earlier, has no patience for them. He'd as soon toss them off the peaks. The most I do, usually, is send them packing, beaten and disappointed. It's only the ones who have a true *need*, who will *work* for it, prevail. So your potion-seller?" She shrugged. "Same basic outcome, with less injury and little risk of losing their lives. It's almost a blessing."

"But the ones—"

"Oh, I'm sure he catches some with true intentions and the will to succeed. But… look, dear, there are always forks in the road we're not meant to take. And if we do take them, the consequences fall to us. Life—and, pity knows, the gods themselves—place plenty of distractions in our way. It's not my place to clear the road."

"So it doesn't bother you?" Prudence said quietly.

"Bother me? It vexes me greatly, young woman!" Heat rose in Elspeth's voice. "If I'd my druthers, I'd pitch him into the lake, wagon and all." Her tone gentled as she continued: "But as the Enchantress? There's nothing I can do. Grant you, I don't *believe* he's one of Nimarith's distractions, but it's not like I have tea with the god every moon-day. The Enchantress' role begins and ends in the keep, not down here with you mortals."

Everyone was quiet for a long moment.

"My concern," Jen said evenly, "is the fallout."

"You mean when sins of the past come home to roost?" Elspeth asked, nodding knowingly.

"I, ah… sure. But the man's been here a full moon and then some, no? At some point, won't these people who purchased 'destiny in a bottle' realize they've been had, and come seeking that 'guarantee' he's always speaking of?"

"True," Elspeth said. "S'why that type tends to move on quickly. Surprised he's stayed this long."

"Not that he couldn't do with a thrashing," Sam started.

"But you know damn well I can't permit it, and the town's magic will make it less likely in the first place."

"Point."

They all fell silent again. The mood in the pub remained convivial, but now it seemed to be floating on a gentle undercurrent of dire anticipation.

"Sam," Prudence said at last, looking down at her empty cup of tea, "do you have anything a little—"

"Coming right up," the old merc said, moving swiftly to the bar. She returned with a tall, narrow glass filled with something that glistened softly in the flickering lamplight. "Starwhisper. It'll take the edge off, but not send you reeling. But go slowly."

"Samantha Godsdotter," Elspeth said with mock rage, "you have been holding out on me."

"You'd put me out of my home, madame," Sam teased back. "That mist-ale is dear enough."

For a while, it was enough to sit in the glow of the hearth and let the talk and laughter roll past. Elspeth's attention, having completed its reconnaissance of Prudence, drifted through the room, her presence dissolving into the broader conversation as if she'd never been discrete at all. The Enchantress's gravity warped the orbits of every table: after a few rounds of drinks, knots of townsfolk sidled closer, their faces flushed by drink or anticipation or both, eager to catch whatever stray legend or rumor might float down from the mountain tonight.

The warmth of the pub pressed in on Prudence, unfamiliar and a little too much—a weight built from the humid tangle of bodies, the haze of old tobacco, the crisp sweet of spilled cider, and the insistent, underlying pulse of togetherness. She realized she'd been holding her cup at her lips for some time without drinking. She set it down and tried to will the tension from her shoulders, listening as the room reacquainted itself with its own noise.

The shift was almost immediate. Dardrad, no longer content to merely eavesdrop, pivoted his bulk from the bar and launched, with calculated indifference, a story about the time he'd nearly lost three of his toes on Elspeth's mountain, only to have them saved by an "emergency application of magic socks and a generous helping of gnome-brewed whiskey." Elspeth countered with a description of Dardrad's heroic, if ultimately futile, attempt to bluff a stone troll using only a leg of ham and a set of poorly-remembered poetry. Laughter rippled outward, catching on the edges of each table so that even the travelers, feigning disinterest, grinned into their cups.

Prudence's gaze roved the space, noting the changes since her last proper visit: new scars in the bar top, the absence of a lamp by the window (replaced, she suspected, after Galhani's most recent experiment in pyrotechnic herbal infusions), the subtle but profound reordering of the mugs and tankards along the back shelf, each now arranged by size, then color, then something only Sam could divine. At the north wall, the old dartboard had been joined by a second, smaller one, presumably to keep up with demand; both were ringed with a tragicomedy of missed throws, the pattern of holes a map of the town's patience.

She let herself enjoy the view: Sam in her element, orchestrating every pour and punchline; Warren, who had migrated inside and now filled a bench with his improbable bulk, cradling a bowl of stew and listening with the deliberate focus of a man who measured the world by its stories; Makota and Cole, who had at some point claimed a corner table and were already halfway through the evening's dessert, the baker's tail flicking in metronomic approval with every bite. Even Jen, whose presence in a room was usually marked by the icy tension of command, seemed at ease here—her posture loose, her laugh unguarded as she traded barbs with the nearest table of regulars.

As the Starwhisper relaxed her, she began to notice the clothing of the people in the pub.

At first, the people seemed cut from the same rough cloth: dark wool and worn duck, heavy skirts and heavy boots, the universal armor of a town that spent half its year fighting the wind and the remainder braced for something worse. But as Prudence's gaze lingered, distinctions emerged. Someone's apprentice, a boy no older than Darby but twice his width, wore suspenders made from two mismatched belts, one of them bright green—a touch of humor, perhaps, or poverty disguised as personality. Jen's uniform was so severe it bordered on the ceremonial, but the sharp creases and brass buttons were offset by a scarf, knotted just loosely enough at the neck to hint at rebellion. Dardrad's tunic was patched at the elbows with a fabric so close to the original it took a tailor's eye to spot, but someone had lined the inside with an orange too jarring to be accidental. Sam this evening wore a vest in such an eye-watering plaid that it served as both signature and warning.

It dawned on Prudence, not for the first time, that most of these people were not so much dressed as self-invented, each piece a small act of autobiography. For years, she'd thought of clothing as a kind of camouflage, a means to disappear—but here, and especially tonight, it was the opposite. Even the town's plainest faces wore their difference with the pride of a banner. She thought again of the blue velvet in her shop: the way it refused to stay hidden, the way it drew the eye no matter how she tried to subdue it. Maybe that was its whole purpose.

The travelers. Prudence watched their clothes with the eye of both critic and voyeur, searching for hints of purpose or place in each unfamiliar silhouette. Most were drab, meant to vanish into the bruised landscape between one market town and the next. She spotted the muddy uniform of a drover, the patched oilcloth of a lake barge hand, a threadbare tunic so closely matching the owner's skin that it might have been grown rather than sewn. These garments strove for invisibility, and for the most part, succeeded.

But here and there, a few broke the pattern.

A woman by the window, jaw sharp as the knife tucked in her boot, wore a coat of faded orange, stitched at the shoulders with bands of intricate pick-stitching. The cuffs had been reinforced, over and over, with patches in the same sunset dye, so that the sleeves flared out like the petals of a flower. Prudence guessed she was a messenger, maybe even a runner in the old tradition, prized for speed and cunning more than brute power. No one with a coat that loud wanted to be missed.

Another stood near the hearth—a young man with a hawk's profile and a fringe of dark hair that fought every attempt at discipline—who wore a shirt three sizes too large, belted at the waist with a strip of green velvet. The effect was slapdash, almost comic, until he raised his arms to gesture and Prudence saw how the wide sleeves hid the quick twitch of his hands. A pickpocket, then. Or something adjacent. She filed the observation away, not out of fear, but with a mingled respect for the ingenuity of it.

A third, nearly invisible in the shadow of Warren's bench, turned out on closer inspection to be a pair: a woman in slate blue with a child on her lap, both of them swaddled in a gaudy checked shawl. What struck Prudence wasn't the colors, but the way the woman had rewoven the hem of her dress with what looked like fishing wire, strong enough to take the drag of a child and a heavy pack both. Each stitch was precise, almost invisible, but the net effect was both sturdy and beautiful. The woman's hands, which never stilled, had a callus at the base of the thumb—netmaker, or maybe a weaver's apprentice fallen on hard times.

The more Prudence looked, the less the room appeared a random spill of bodies, and more a gallery of stories, each told in the language of cloth and cut. She tried to imagine how she herself might appear: the severe black dress, collar tight; the cap, always pulled low; the hands pale against the darkness of her sleeves. Once she would have cringed at the thought, but tonight, with the warmth of the Star-whisper curling in her belly and the echo of Elspeth's words in her ear, she allowed herself a moment of appraisal. Not camouflage, then, but a uniform built from all the years spent keeping still, holding together, refusing to break even when holding on hurt.

She wondered what she might look like in blue.

The idea made her smile.

"—is what I mean!" Elspeth's voice, sharper and louder, snapped for Prudence's attention. "Wouldn't you agree?"

Prudence realized the older woman was on her third mist-ale. She looked down and saw half the Starwhisper still in her own cup, and then looked back up. "I'm sorry, I didn't hear you."

"People," Elspeth said, enunciating more precisely than required, "are hampered by the fact that they barely know who they are, let alone who they *might* be."

Prudence blinked rapidly as something in her stomach seemed to curl and uncurl in quick succession.

"People," Elspeth repeated, "need to occasionally try on a new set of clothes. See who it makes of them. Wouldn't you agree?"

Prudence's eyes flew wide. She downed the rest of the Starwhisper, mumbled thanks to Sam, and escaped out the pub's back door.

fifteen

. . .

THE BROKEN CLAW at first bell was nothing like the Claw at night. In the light, the old wood and battered stone showed their flaws without the benefit of shadow, every stain and scrape a record of all the years the world had tried to wear the pub down. The last of the travelers had been hustled out just after dawn; few townsfolk would return before lunch. For now, the only movement came from behind the bar, where Sam polished tankards with the kind of care usually reserved for babies or swords.

Prudence stood in the rear entrance hall, letting her eyes adjust. The Claw's main room smelled of last night's smoke and a day's worth of fresh yeast—Makota's bakery was already running the ovens —and the wet from outside had not yet dried on the rush mats. Sam looked up, caught Prudence's eye, and set the tankard aside.

"You're not often in this early," Sam said, voice low but not unfriendly.

Prudence hesitated on the threshold, feeling for a moment like she might be trespassing, though Sam had called her in more times than she could count. "I wanted to apologize," she said.

Sam waved a hand. "Don't. I get jumpy myself when Elspeth's in one of her moods. Always worried it'll be lightning or hail or something." She grinned and gestured to the bench nearest the fire, its coals just waking for the day. "Come. I'll get you something."

Prudence slipped inside, careful not to track mud, and settled onto the bench. She perched at its edge, hands folded on her lap. "Is it always like that?" she asked, remembering the way the air in the Claw had seemed thinner, the conversation tighter, when Elspeth was in the room.

Sam poured two mugs of tea—strong, black, with just a flicker of cinnamon to cut the bitter—and brought them to the table. "Depends," she said, sitting across from Prudence. "She's human, she gets in a mood. Being alone up in that keep of hers has to play on a should. Sometimes she likes to test the waters when there's an audience." Sam squinted at the window, then back. "How's the boy?"

"Bryant's with Makota for the morning," Prudence said, grateful for the change in topic. "She offered to let him play with the kits. Said he could help harvest catnip from Galhani's herb patch if he behaved." A faint, involuntary smile flickered at the memory of Bryant's eyes when Galhani had handed him the basket, twice as big as his own head.

"He'll be fine," Sam said. "She'd never let harm come to a child, no matter whose it was." She sipped her tea, watching Prudence over the rim. "You look better today."

Prudence nodded, though she wasn't sure it was true. "The quiet helps."

"Until it doesn't," Sam said, and both women lapsed into silence.

It was broken by a sound at the door—a heavy, off-kilter thump, as though someone had missed the last step up from the street. Sam stiffened, but Prudence only watched as the front door creaked open, then slammed hard against the inside wall. The boy—no, man, barely, but already shaped by too many long seasons—stood in the frame, one arm cradling the other, face smeared with mud and something darker. Behind him came a second, taller and more wild, his hair matted and his shirt half torn off at the shoulder. They blinked into the Claw's dimness, eyes darting between the two women, and for a moment neither seemed willing to speak.

Sam set her tea down, voice switching into an older, rougher register. "In or out, lads. You're letting the heat run straight to the baker's."

The taller one shrugged, but it made him wince. "Sorry, ma'am," he said, then guided the first through the door. They both made for the bar, but not the same stool; each leaned away from the other, like magnets refusing to meet.

Prudence could see now that the one with the wounded arm had tied it off with a length of shirt torn from his companion's back. The cloth was red, but not the kind made in a dye-house. The tall one favored his right leg, but made a show of ignoring it, as if to walk normal would reassert something vital.

Sam didn't ask what happened. She fetched the whisky, poured two glasses, and waited. The shorter, wounded one grabbed the drink in his left hand and tipped it back with a speed born of practice. The other sipped slow, eyes never leaving the bar's ancient wood.

"Go on, then," Sam said. "Tell it."

The tall one's jaw flexed. "Is there… are you closed to travelers in the morning?" His voice was hoarse, and the question, meant to be casual, landed flat.

Prudence shook her head. "No one's coming."

"Good," said the tall one. "Didn't want to start trouble. Just needed to get off the street for a minute."

Sam nodded, leaned on the bar. "Name?"

The man hesitated. "It's Lew. This is my brother, Shem."

Shem gave a nod, but the motion nearly doubled him over the bar. He clutched at the glass for support.

Sam waited, the silence drawing itself out.

Lew exhaled, looked at Prudence, then back to Sam. "You heard of the potions, then?"

Sam snorted. "We've heard."

"Yeah. Well. We bought them. Didn't do shit." Lew shook his head, the effort nearly toppling him from the stool. "They said you'd see your destiny. That you'd walk the road to what you were meant for. All it did was… well, it made me throw up."

Shem spoke now, voice barely above a whisper. "We went into the foothills. He thought we'd find the cache."

Lew bared his teeth in something like a grin. "Thought, hell. We were sure. And for a while it worked—every step felt like it was supposed to. Path just... opened for us. Trees got thin, snow was shallow, and the road bent where we needed it. Took us a fortnight, maybe more. We thought nothing of it—plenty of water, the odd game, our rations were holding out. Then—" He looked at his brother, but Shem didn't meet his eyes. "Then we hit the creekbed and lost the trail. Wasn't a trail after that, just rocks and ice. No game. Nothing. Couldn't even find our way back."

Sam let the story spool out. "Go on."

Lew swallowed. "That's where the skraeling found us. Never seen anything like it—" He stopped, then pushed the memory away with a hard shake. "It was fast. It was cold. I tried to run, Shem here tried to pull our friend. But it—" His hand tightened on the glass. "Kanin was dead before we even knew he was gone. The thing just... snapped him up and left us. Didn't even bother to finish the job."

Shem's breath shivered in the space between words. "We walked all night. Couldn't see. Just kept the sound behind us."

Now Prudence spoke, because she had to. "What did you do, when you got back?"

Lew's laugh was hollow. "Came into town, like you do. Thought maybe it was a test. Like the stories say. Maybe the Enchantress herself would meet us. Instead—" He shrugged. "We walked all the way to the square and just sat there. Stared at the sky for a while. Waited for... I don't know. Something. Anything."

Sam was quiet for a long time, then reached across the bar and refilled their glasses. "How long were you gone, altogether?"

Lew nodded. "A moon, I think." He downed the whisky, wiped his mouth with the back of his hand. "We waited half a sennight in a clearing, but nothing changed. The destiny was a lie."

Shem said, "We wanted to break the salesman's wagon. Maybe tip it into the lake."

Lew grinned again, a shadow of mischief in his face. "We tried. But the constable watched us like dogs at a butcher's door."

Sam's face showed nothing. "So you came here."

"Nowhere else to go," Lew said.

Sam looked at Shem's arm. "That needs more than a rag. I'll get Dexter." She moved to the back, leaving the brothers alone with Prudence.

Prudence studied them, her mind mapping each detail. The bandage had soaked through, a dark crust now forming on Shem's knuckles. Lew's eye was nearly closed, purple and swollen, the skin already splitting where the bone beneath wanted out. Both wore the same homespun, the kind found on every farm from here to the lakes, but in worse repair than even the worst hand-me-downs she'd seen since coming north.

She wanted to say something, but the words formed and then shrank away.

Lew broke the quiet first. "You're the tailor," he said.

Prudence nodded.

He looked her up and down, as if taking her measure. "I had a shirt like that, once. From my father. Lost it when we left." He smirked. "You can always lose something, can't you?"

She started to reply, but he waved it off. "Never mind. I just wanted to say—if you see that salesman, tell him it's not safe here for his kind."

Prudence nodded again. She would have promised anything to the boy in that moment.

Shem's head was down, his breath shallow. Lew put a hand on his brother's shoulder, and for a second, the bravado slipped. Lew looked at Prudence again, this time not as a challenge, but as a kind of plea.

Sam came back, Dexter behind her, the chirurgeon's black coat as crisp as if he'd been waiting just outside the whole time. "Let me see," he said in his low, rasping voice, already unwrapping the makeshift bandage. He glanced at Prudence, then at Lew. "He'll live. But you'll need to keep the arm still, or you'll lose the use of it."

Shem nodded, not trusting himself to speak.

Lew stood, awkwardly, then gestured to his brother. "We'll go. Didn't mean to ruin the morning."

Sam shook her head. "You didn't. Stay as long as you want."

They left the bar, moving slow, the air behind them empty and cold.

Dexter lingered, repacking his kit with a care that made it clear he would wait until the brothers were well out of earshot. When the door closed, he set the bag on the counter and looked at Prudence.

"Children," he said. "Every one of them. Taking the easy way out."

Prudence didn't answer, and Dexter didn't wait for one.

Sam poured another round of tea, set the mugs side by side on the bar. "It's going to get worse," she said. "The longer that wagon sits at the edge of town, the more people will try."

Prudence thought of the blue velvet in her shop, the way it always returned to the front, no matter how she tried to hide it.

She wondered if the world really did want what was worst for it.

She sipped the tea, and the taste was sharp and thin on her tongue.

The day outside brightened, but the Claw, for now, stayed dark.

It was several minutes before anyone spoke again. Sam tidied the bar with unnecessary precision, each wiped spot a punctuation to her thoughts. Dexter lingered in the threshold to the back, fingers steepled, gaze unfocused, as if counting the days until something changed. Prudence sipped her tea, letting the bitterness settle her, and watched the way the morning light cut the Claw's gloom into stripes.

The silence broke with the return of Lew and Shem, this time slower, careful, like two dogs who'd been whipped and didn't want to risk another.

Lew kept his eyes down, but Shem looked straight at Sam. "Sorry to barge in," he said, voice softer. "We needed to ask."

Sam set the rag aside. "Ask what?"

Lew's fingers drummed the bar. "About the potion man. The constable. Why won't the town let us—" He swallowed, jaw twitching. "Why's he protected?"

Sam tapped the bar with her knuckle, a sound that would have summoned any of her old mercenary crew to attention. "Not protected, exactly. Just—" She looked up, at the wall above the bar, where a complicated clock hung in pride of place. "We're on a foundation here. A magic, old as anything. In North Pointe, you can't raise your hand against another soul. Not within the line of shops, not on the green, not under a public roof." She smiled, but it was more warning than comfort. "Keeps the peace. But it means even the likes of him can stay, so long as he behaves."

Lew scowled. "He doesn't. Not really. He cheats."

"Cheating's not violence," Sam said, "though I'd grant it's a close cousin."

Shem's arm, re-wrapped by Leota, rested easier now. He flexed his hand, once, twice. "So if we wanted him gone—?"

"Catch him past the gate," Sam said, "and he's yours. Get him outside the line, and the rules don't care what happens." Her eyes were on the clock-like device now—a disc, notched like the face of a sundial but with a single silver sphere that shifted back and forth in half-inch jerks. It hovered near the bottom, trembling. Prudence knew it was how the pub told Sam about patrons' destinies.

Lew followed Sam's gaze. "What is that?"

"Call it a weather vane for fate," Sam said. "If things go wrong for too long, or if the magic gets out of balance, you'll know." She smiled thinly.

Lew watched the disc for a moment, then turned away. "If the town knows he's no good, why not do something?"

"Because it's not for us to judge," Sam replied. "Every shop here, every trade, every life—" She gestured with her hands, as if mapping an invisible circle. "We're here for the travelers, not for ourselves. The town pulls in what it needs, who it needs. Sometimes even the liars and cheats have a part to play." She shrugged. "I don't make the rules."

Shem mulled this, then said, "What about the Enchantress we've heard about? Does she help, or just… watch?"

Dexter, who had been silent, spoke then. "She tests, mostly. The road up is full of her little games and traps. If you want something, she'll make you earn it, or fail in the trying."

Lew gave a bleak little laugh. "Sounds like our farm."

At that, Prudence stirred. "You're from the lowlands?"

"Edge of the southern marsh," Lew said. "Had a field, once. It's mostly brambles now. Mother keeps goats, and Shem here traps or fishes when he can." He hesitated, as if the rest would cost him. "I wanted to be a miller."

Shem made a face. "He's been talking about it since we were kids. Watches every grain wagon, can tell the weight by the sound of the wheels."

Lew colored, but pressed on. "It's a better life. Less mud, more coin. You can learn it, too, if you're willing." He shrugged. "But the guild's closed. Need money to apprentice, and nobody lends to farm boys."

Sam softened, just a shade. "So you went to the mountain, hoping for a shortcut."

Lew nodded. "Heard the Enchantress could grant a wish. Or the god, or whatever's at the top. We figured—" He glanced at his brother, then finished, "—we'd come back with a better deal. Or not come back."

There was a pause, filled by the ticking of the clock and the slow drip of coffee into the pot behind the bar.

Shem spoke into the hush. "The potion man promised we'd see what to do. That if we followed the sign, it would bring us right to our destiny."

"And did it?" Prudence asked, surprising herself with the sharpness of the question.

Lew looked at her, and for the first time she saw something more than bravado or anger: a small, stubborn flicker of hope, bent but not broken. "No. The potion made us bold, but not smarter."

Shem's face was tight. "It killed Kanin."

Lew shook his head, but didn't argue.

Sam folded her arms, a wall behind the bar. "Listen to me. I've seen more schemes come through this place than you've had hot meals. Every single one falls to pieces, unless the people in it know exactly what they want, and what it costs." She pointed at Lew, then Shem. "You want to be a miller? Fine. There's a way to it. Might take longer, might take more work than you ever imagined, but it's there. The mountain won't help if you haven't already helped yourself."

Lew flushed again. "But the potion man—"

"Is a shortcut," Sam finished. "There are no shortcuts in this town." She looked at the indicator on the wall again, watching as the arrow crept ever so slightly upward. "Not for us. Not for you."

Prudence saw, for the first time, the pattern in all these conversations. The townsfolk never offered answers. They offered only the tools to find one.

Shem's voice broke through, shaky but determined. "If you were us, what would you do?"

Sam thought a moment. "You only need a minor miracle. Some coin for tools and to pay your fee. An introduction to someone who can get the guild to admit you, closed or no." She lifted her chin at the window. "That's what the Enchantress does. She doesn't grant wishes. She makes you ready for them."

Lew looked at his hands, the knuckles raw and scraped. "Can't go back home."

"Then you keep moving," Sam said. "It's what all of us did, at one point or another." She glanced at Dexter, who inclined his head in silent agreement.

Lew got up, not with pride, but with the careful dignity of someone who has decided to be upright again. Shem followed, slower but less hunched. They both stood at the bar, the morning light giving their bruises a purplish cast.

Sam set a loaf of bread on the bar, still warm, and broke it in half. "On the house," she said, but Lew shook his head.

"Only if you let us sweep out the ashes," he replied.

Sam looked at him, long and level, then nodded. "Fair."

The brothers went to the hearth, and for a time, there was only the sound of broom on stone and the hush of two lives reassembling themselves.

When the bar was clean, Lew and Shem thanked Sam, thanked Prudence, and vanished into the morning, the bread clutched tight to their chests.

After the door closed, Dexter drifted to the counter, watching the indicator above the bar. "It's moving," he said, almost to himself.

Sam grunted. "They'll do better now."

Prudence said nothing. She understood, finally, that the Claw was not just a place for mending wounds. It was a place for testing whether people could survive the break.

She drank her tea, cold now, and watched the indicator settle, steady and true.

———

Later, as the Claw emptied out and the scent of yeast gave way to the sour linger of ash, Prudence found herself replaying the morning's events—not as a memory, but as a kind of puzzle she was meant to solve.

She remembered the brothers first as shapes in the doorway, battered and stooped. But the more she thought, the more she saw: the stains along their hems, the way Lew's shirt had been patched so many times it was more thread than cloth, the dark, permanent crust under Shem's fingernails, as if the marsh soil had claimed him for its own.

Their clothing had started out plain, but sturdy—a mother's work, perhaps, or a neighbor's. The fabric was the brown of tilled earth, the gray of morning fog. Nothing in it spoke of pride, but everything about it spoke of endurance. Even after the worst of their journey, the seams had held; only the outside had given way to ruin. She imagined their mother, hands chapped from lye, mending in the half-dark after the goats had been milked and the hearth swept clean.

It was the kind of work Prudence had always admired. But now, seeing it in the Claw's unforgiving light, she understood what Sam meant: if you dressed for the life you'd always known, you'd never grow into the one you wanted.

She tried to picture Lew as a miller. The face was there—long, angular, the lines around the mouth ready to set in either authority or laughter. The hair would be cropped shorter, maybe kept under a cap. The arms, used to hefting sacks or repairing a grindstone, would fill out the sleeves of a proper jerkin. She saw him in a shirt of pale linen, an apron over it—not the white of a baker, but something undyed and practical, maybe with a faint blue trim at the collar, just enough to catch the eye. The apron itself would be longer, split for movement, with reinforced ties. At his waist, a pouch for measuring weights, a pocket for the keys to the mill.

Shem she imagined standing just outside the mill, hands on hips, shirt rolled to the elbow. The stains would be flour, not mud. His boots would be the same—he'd never want for better—but the laces would be tidy, and the soles less worn at the heel. There might be a strip of blue at the cuff, if Lew thought to order it. Shem wouldn't ask, but he'd notice.

Prudence tried to picture their faces after a good season— sunburnt, certainly, but with the kind of confidence that comes from doing a thing well, and from having someone recognize it. The bruises would fade. The scars would turn pale and interesting. They'd grow into themselves, she realized, if given the chance.

And the clothes would grow with them.

She blinked, surprised by her own certainty.

For so long, she had worked only to repair: to hide the holes, blend the patches, restore the old order without adding to it. That had been safety. That had been her family's way, the way of everyone in Holderdown, of every place she'd ever called home. But here, in North Pointe, even the world itself seemed to say you had to wear your intentions openly, or else risk being swallowed by the life you'd left behind.

Prudence looked down at her own black dress, the familiar lines and the careful, invisible mending. She tried to imagine herself in color —something green, or gold, or the blue of that velvet that refused to leave her alone. It startled her, the thought, but it didn't seem wrong. She wondered what Bryant would say if he saw her in it, if the whole town would even recognize her.

She set her empty cup on the bench, stood, and went to the window. The road outside was quiet, save for the faint sweep of a broom and the shouts of children on the green. She caught sight of Lew and Shem at the edge of the road, talking in low voices. Lew straightened, and for a moment, Prudence saw it: the silhouette of someone who might one day stand at the head of a mill, or even at the head of a family, and not just because the world had forced him to.

She smiled, just a little, and then let the curtain fall. It was time to go to work.

Back in her shop, Prudence's eyes rose to the top shelves, to all the beautiful bolts of fabric she'd never once unrolled. She pulled down a bolt of blue wool—good wool, not the showy velvet—and ran her hands along the edge. It was soft, but strong. A little like Lew, if she was being honest. Or herself, if she ever allowed it.

She measured a length, then set it aside for later.

That evening, after Bryant had come home, after the supper was cleared and the candles lit, Prudence sat at her workbench and stitched. Her hands remembered every step. They made the old shapes, the old seams. But she found herself adding something new: a stripe at the cuff, a bit of color at the hem, a pattern so faint it would not be noticed unless you knew to look for it.

She thought of Lew, and of Shem, and of every child who'd ever left a farm for a better life. She thought of the Enchantress on her mountain, and the weather vane in the Claw, and all the invisible forces that made a town what it was.

For the first time, Prudence sewed not for the world as it was, but for the one that might be.

The blue thread shone in the lamp-light, bright and sure.

And she let it.

sixteen

. . .

THE MORNING WAS A GLASSY BLUE, so clear it seemed even the wind had been rinsed clean by the night's rain. The clouds had gone, scoured to the horizon, leaving only a sharp, bracing cold and the hard brilliance of the rising sun. Prudence had promised Bryant a walk across the green, and now, with the damp grass not yet pressed flat by foot traffic, they moved hand in hand, each step as deliberate and slow as if they were the ones measuring out the new day.

Bryant's hand was small, his fingers cold even inside her own. He said nothing, but looked everywhere at once—at the bright smear of frost on the bakery's eaves, the black flash of a grackle in the branches above, the way the sun caught the golden paint on the town's sign-board and made it pulse. The Moss trailed behind, silent, its paws darkening with dew at every step. Prudence had set her own pace to match Bryant's, but she realized, as they reached the middle of the green, that she was walking as slowly as he was. Her eyes were on the town gate, and her thoughts ran out ahead, as sharp and ungoverned as the wind.

It was the weather, she told herself, that made everything so exposed this morning. The storm had battered the world down to its bones. Today, the world was soft and light.

A sound reached them—a man's voice, far-off but fluting up the main road like a song. She knew it before she saw him: Cornelius, the salesman, already set up just inside the gate, his pitch bouncing from house to house and back again, the vowels long and insistent. "Not a potion, not a nostrum, but a destiny delivered—direct to you, fine traveler, for a single, shining coin!"

Prudence felt her jaw set and her fingers tighten around Bryant's. He looked up, and though he was still too young to read every tension in her posture, he could always sense when the world was not quite right.

"Are we going to see the man with the bottles?" Bryant asked, his voice so quiet it could have been lost in the grass.

"No," Prudence said, more harshly than she intended. "We're just going to see the sky."

Bryant accepted this, though he kept glancing at her, searching for a sign that the world would return to normal. They walked until the shadow of the old lamppost reached their feet, then Prudence stopped. She could picture Cornelius clearly now: perched atop his wagon like a caricature of himself, his top hat gleaming and his coat fluttering with every grand gesture. He would point and parade, waving glass vials like precious jewels, never noticing that most of the townsfolk gave him as wide a berth as they could.

Prudence felt her own feet root to the spot. She was not going closer. She would not give the man a moment's acknowledgment, not even a glare. Her heart, which had been steady all morning, now thudded so hard she wondered if Bryant could feel it through her hand.

A sudden movement at the bakery's door caught her eye. Two shapes—boys, but grown, at least one of them—emerged into the cold, blinking at the sun as if waking from a long, unhappy dream. She knew them at once. Lew and Shem. The brothers from the bar, the ones who'd nearly died in the hills chasing the salesman's empty promise. The ones who'd come back with nothing but each other and a hunger they could not name.

They paused just outside Makota's door, conferring quietly, their heads bowed and their shoulders so close together they seemed to make a single shadow. Shem's arm was bandaged, thick and clumsy, the linen already spotted with brown. Lew's eye was still swollen half-shut. Their boots were caked with the frozen mud of the trade road, and their shirts—identical in their wear and their color—hung off them like rags on scarecrows.

The sight of them did something to Prudence. She felt it—a shift, a prickling at the base of her skull, as if the world had leaned just a fraction in their direction.

Bryant followed her gaze, then whispered, "They look like they need new clothes."

Prudence nodded, but did not move. She watched as the brothers limped across the green, careful to keep the whole distance between themselves and the salesman's wagon. The moment they were past the sightline, their pace slackened; Shem leaned against his brother, and Lew set a hand on Shem's back, steering him toward the Weary Head Inn. They looked smaller than she remembered them. Smaller and older.

It was the shirts that held her attention. Plain, yes—undyed, unadorned, with the same sad, puckered seams she saw on every shirt from the lowlands. There was a patch at Lew's collar, but it wasn't even a proper patch—just a hasty square, whip-stitched with what looked like fishing line. The cuffs on Shem's sleeves had unraveled; one dangled in a loose, fraying loop. The trousers, once gray, were now a sullen patchwork of dirt and dried blood, with the fabric near the knees so thin she could see the sharp bones beneath.

Prudence felt, for the briefest moment, the weight of the old rules again. Mending was supposed to be invisible. A patch was a defeat, a sign that you couldn't afford new, couldn't earn it. Her mother's voice surfaced, chiding her for every crooked stitch or uneven seam: "If you can't make it look like new, you're just advertising your failure to the whole world."

But that wasn't what she saw on the brothers' backs. She saw proof, instead, of how close they'd come to being erased.

She thought of Bartram's words, their persistence, always a little louder when the shop was quiet. "Why not a touch of color?" "Why not a shirt that makes you glad to see it in the morning?" The ideas had seemed frivolous to her, even dangerous, in the way that all unnecessary things were in Holderdown. But here, on the cold edge of morning, she understood what Bartram meant. It was not just about the beauty. It was about defiance. About the belief that, even if you failed, there was still something worth being seen.

Her mind turned back, unbidden, to her childhood. The blue ribbon. The feeling of it, forbidden and bright, tucked against her skin. The shame when it was found. The finality of its destruction. She remembered how her father had cut it, the way he'd held it up between his fingers, examining it as if to judge whether it was worth burning. She remembered the sick, hungry twist of wanting something so badly, even when she knew it would be taken from her.

She saw the same hunger in Lew and Shem as they hunched their way to the inn. They did not want to be noticed, but they needed to be seen.

Prudence let go of Bryant's hand, her fingers suddenly cold. She imagined, for a second, what the brothers might look like if they had the clothes they needed. Not just patched, but whole. Not just clean, but purposeful. A jacket that fit Lew's broad, uncertain shoulders, with a stripe of blue along the collar, sharp enough to make even the salesman blink. Breeches for Shem with reinforced knees, so the world could not grind him down quite so fast. Boots that would not slip or soak through in the first rain. She saw them in color—real, saturated color—the blue and gold and even a wild red, just a line of it at the hem.

Her breath caught, and she realized she'd stopped seeing the real brothers. In her mind, they were already transformed. She saw them at the head of a mill, like in Lew's impossible dream; saw them walking down the street with their heads up, not because they were proud, but because they'd survived. She saw them as boys, again, shirts clean and sleeves long enough, laughing at some private joke.

The vision was so strong that it stunned her, and for a moment she lost sight of the world entirely.

When the moment passed, Lew and Shem were gone, vanished into the side door of the Weary Head. The inn's sign rocked gently in the wind, but there was no trace of them on the path. The only movement now came from the salesman, whose voice had not let up for a second. He was addressing a new group: three men in surveyor's coats, and a woman with a small child strapped to her back. His arms moved in great circles, the vials flashing in the morning sun.

Prudence felt the old panic rising—a combination of shame and anger, tangled so tightly it was hard to know where one left off and the other began. She did not want to see Cornelius, did not want to be seen by him. But she also did not want to let the brothers vanish, not yet, not with that vision still ringing in her eyes.

She stood, indecisive, at the cross of two paths. One would take her around the green and back to her shop, the other would lead her straight to the inn's back entrance. She hesitated, the cold wind curling under her collar, and looked down at Bryant, who was already watching her with a curiosity far deeper than his years.

"Should we go after them?" Bryant asked, not unkindly.

Prudence almost answered, but the words caught. She looked again at the inn, at the gate, at the bright, bright sky. She did not move, and in the hush, it was as if the whole town was waiting for her to choose.

The decision was made for her.

Jen marched through the town gate with the force of a small avalanche, her boots slapping wet onto the stone and her every step a punctuation of displeasure. She had a way of walking that announced her mood before she even opened her mouth; today, it was clear that whatever patience she'd begun the day with had been spent well before first bell.

She caught sight of Prudence and Bryant, and altered her trajectory by not a whit. "What a goddamn circus," Jen said, arriving in a wedge of cold air. "He's not just selling it now. He's inviting people inside. Like a sideshow. Whole town can hear it."

Bryant shrank back a little, but Prudence put a hand on his shoulder, steadying him. "Does he have customers?" she asked, unable to keep the bitterness from her voice.

Jen barked a laugh. "If you count half that survey team and that porter's cousin, then yes. Otherwise, no, not so much. Sam says he nearly set the wagon on fire this morning. Was lighting his bottles with some kind of flint, made the whole thing smoke up like a pyre." She rolled her eyes, the motion so practiced it looked like a muscle tic. "If I could do anything about it, I would, believe me. But the rules are the rules. Unless he breaks the actual peace, my hands are tied."

Prudence nodded, though her attention was already drifting. Jen noticed, and frowned. "You all right? You look like you've seen a ghost."

Prudence blinked, surprised by the question. "I just… I saw Lew and Shem. They looked—" She hesitated, unwilling to share the full shape of her thoughts. "They looked worse than yesterday. I thought maybe the rest would help, but—"

"Nothing helps after a thing like that," Jen said, not unkindly. "They're alive, at least. Could've been worse."

"They could use some kindness," Prudence said. It came out smaller than she meant.

Jen softened, just a little. "You're a good soul, Pru. Don't let the world squeeze it out of you. As for the salesman—" She jerked her thumb at the wagon, "—I almost let those boys at him this morning. But do you know what happened? I got as far as the bakery porch, and then—pow." She tapped the side of her skull. "It was like the whole world yelled 'No' at me. Couldn't take another step. I saw stars."

Prudence smiled, though the edges of it were raw. "The magic doesn't like violence."

"It doesn't mind a little," Jen said. "A drunken brawl, it'll let go for a moment. But it's got a nose for revenge. That's when it gets nasty." She shook her head, then looked down at Bryant, who was watching the conversation with wide, waiting eyes. "How's the little man today?"

"He's well," Prudence said. "He's growing."

"He'll outpace you by summer," Jen said, smiling. She ruffled Bryant's hair with a practiced hand, then looked back at Prudence. "Sam and I are trying to spread word. Tell people he's a fraud. Not that it's needed, for most, but some want so badly to believe they'll pay even for a pretty lie."

Prudence made a noise of agreement, but her mind was elsewhere, back in the imagined mill, the blue stripe at the collar, the way Lew's arms had filled out the sleeves in her vision.

Jen squinted. "You're not listening."

Prudence startled. "I'm sorry. There's something I need to do."

Jen blinked, thrown. "Now?"

"Now," Prudence said. She took Bryant's hand and started away, not quite running, but close.

Jen stood on the green, watching their retreat. She had known Prudence for years, and had never seen her so abrupt, so distracted. She watched until they'd disappeared around the far side of the square, then set her jaw and turned back to her rounds.

There was more to this day than the usual peace-keeping, she could sense it. She made a note to check in again soon. Just in case.

Prudence and Bryant reached the shop just as the bell on the town clock began its chime, the sound carrying clean and sharp through the winter air. Prudence fumbled with the latch, her hands numb from the cold and the shock of her own intent, then hurried Bryant inside and shut the door firmly behind them.

The shop was cold, but bright—the morning sun cut in through the windows, lighting every dust mote and laying stripes of gold across the workbench. Moss the owlcat hopped up at once to the counter, blinking in surprise at their abrupt entrance, then padded over to Bryant, who plopped down at his usual corner by the pins.

Prudence did not stop to remove her coat or cap. She moved to the tall shelves at the back of the shop, the ones she had always kept in perfect order but never fully explored, and began pulling down bolts of fabric in a frenzy that startled even herself. At first, she reached for the usual: a stout brown twill, a practical gray wool, the kind of cloth that could take a beating and still look tidy at the end of the sennight. But she did not stop there.

Her hands found a deep, lively blue—almost the same as the old ribbon from childhood, but richer, with a subtle sheen she had never noticed before. Next came a bolt of yellow so warm it seemed to hold the summer sun inside its fibers; she pressed her palm against it and felt, truly felt, the heat. There was a red, too, bold and fine, and a strange, almost iridescent green that seemed to change color depending on the angle of light.

Bryant watched her, eyes wide. "Are we making something for a festival?" he asked, but Prudence only shook her head, unable to articulate the answer.

She kept pulling, stacking each new treasure on the long worktable, until it threatened to topple. Then she fetched her favorite scissors and began to cut samples from each, arranging them in careful lines: blue, yellow, red, green, brown, gray, and a soft white that shimmered like water in the lake. She set out the matching threads, too— spools she had bought years ago but never found a reason to use. She laid out a box of brass buttons, the kind Bartram favored for his finest boots. She pulled from the cabinet a strip of heavy leather, perfect for reinforcing the cuffs and elbows, and set it beside a skein of creamy linen cord.

Every choice felt right. Every combination made a kind of sense she had never seen before. It was as if the shop had been waiting for her to make this exact selection, the shelves arranged so that the right colors and textures fell to her hands without effort.

She stopped, finally, and stepped back to survey the haul. It was beautiful—a riot of color and possibility, each piece waiting to be called into purpose. Bryant came over, eyes shining, and touched the blue velvet, then the yellow, then the row of buttons.

"I've never seen you use so many," he said, his voice reverent.

"Neither have I," Prudence replied. She ran her hand along the top of the stack, the fabric smooth and inviting under her fingers. There was no going back now.

She thought of Lew and Shem, hunched and defeated, their dreams shrunk to fit the narrow seams of their shirts. She thought of them in these new clothes, of the way they might walk, the way they might hold their heads. She pictured them in the world she wanted them to have—a world where even the failures got a second chance at beauty.

It was not enough just to mend. It was not enough just to hide the hurt. She had to make something new, something that would tell the world: you can be more than what was handed down to you. You can be worth noticing, even after you've failed.

She took a deep breath, then began to draw the patterns for the brothers' new clothes. Her mind worked ahead of her hands, plotting each seam and dart, imagining the feel of the finished garment against the skin, the look of it in the shifting light. The blue would go at the collar, yes, but also a stripe along the cuff, a secret band inside the lining so even if the rest wore out, the color would remain. The yellow would trim the inside of the pockets, a surprise for the hand. She would use the red sparingly, but where it mattered: a buttonhole, a stitch, a thread winding through the hem.

She drew and cut and arranged, working faster than she ever had, her hands steadier now than in any memory she owned. Bryant sat beside her, offering suggestions—"Maybe a stripe here," "What if you made the elbows stronger?"—and she listened, because it was good advice, and because she liked the sound of his voice in the suddenly bright room.

When everything was measured and matched, Prudence stood back again and let herself smile. She could see it now, the future she wanted—not just for Lew and Shem, but for herself and for Bryant, for the whole town if it could bear it. A future with room for color. A future where no one was ashamed to be seen.

She looked at her hands, at the smudge of blue on her fingertips, at the little half-moon of yellow caught beneath her nail. She had always thought of herself as someone who put the world together, piece by invisible piece, never drawing attention, never asking for thanks. But today, in the full flood of morning light, she saw herself as something else entirely: a maker of things that would last, yes, but also a maker of things that would be noticed, and remembered.

The sun rose higher. The bell rang out again, and Prudence laughed, a sound so clear it startled even herself.

seventeen

. . .

FOR A FEW LONG SECONDS, Prudence could only marvel at her own laughter—bright, foreign, as if borrowed from someone braver. Then the urge to move hit her all at once. She felt the sudden snap of inertia breaking, and she was in motion before her mind could catch up.

The layout of the shop was second nature; every inch of the workbench, every tool, every bolt of fabric had its own place and meaning. Normally, she'd have approached a new project by considering the commission, the customer, and the simplest path to completion. Today, though, the commission was self-imposed, and her own needs had never fit the shop's tidy logic. The usual caution—the weighing, the second-guessing, the endless mental rehearsals—fell away.

She started with the blue. The memory of it, the dream of what it could be, had lingered so long that her hands reached for it with the certainty of muscle memory. It was a heavy wool, rich and dense, the sort of fabric that held its shape no matter how it was folded. She draped it over the end of the bench, then set about cutting two wide swaths: one for each of the brothers, but subtly different in length and width. She could already picture the finished pieces—one cut square and practical, the other with just enough curve to flatter the wearer's shoulders.

Next, she reached for the yellow. It was softer, almost buttery, and it would make a perfect lining or, better yet, a secret accent—something hidden and warm, a gift to the hand that slipped inside a pocket. She measured out two strips, each long enough to trim a collar or edge a cuff, then set them aside with reverent precision.

The red was riskier. Prudence had always avoided it, even in repairs, where a bit of showy thread could turn an invisible patch into a confession. But now, emboldened by the idea of making something truly new, she pulled the bolt down and ran her fingers along its grain. It was finer than the others—a tight weave, but light, with a faint sheen that caught the sun in tiny sparks. She cut a narrow band, then a second, envisioning it as piping, or a stripe, or even a single buttonhole that would draw the eye like a secret.

Bryant watched from his corner, clutching the owlcat in both arms. His eyes darted from the table to his mother and back, tracking the accumulation of color as if it were a game with rules only he could understand. "Are these all for the brothers?" he asked, voice muffled by Moss's fur.

"For now," Prudence said, not looking up. "But there will be enough for more. If we do it right, there will always be enough for more." She smiled to herself at the strangeness of her own words.

She kept moving, the rhythm of her hands so quick it surprised her. She pulled the brown twill and the gray wool next, adding them as an under-layer—a base for the color, a grounding that would let the rest shine without overwhelming. She trimmed pieces for sleeves and backs, then stacked them in neat piles, each group a little army waiting for its orders.

The buttons were next. Prudence had always prided herself on her button collection; she'd inherited half of it from the old shop, and the rest she'd traded for or scavenged from cast-off garments. Most were plain wood or bone, but tucked away in a box at the back of the drawer were three—no, four—brass buttons, each one stamped with a tiny insignia she didn't recognize. She lined them up, then added two more of plain mother-of-pearl. The effect was subtle but deliberate;

each button would serve as a marker of progress, a way to track the brothers' transformation from travelers to apprentices to, maybe one day, men of the trade.

Prudence took a breath, then set to work on the leather. She cut two patches for the elbows, wide enough to take a beating, and another for the knees—"for Shem, who never saw a patch that wasn't a target," she thought, a little ruefully. She also cut a narrow strip, just wide enough to reinforce a belt or a collar. She imagined Lew, older and surer, fastening it around his waist as he measured out flour or checked the weight of a sack, and the thought made her smile again.

She organized the work table as she went, arranging the cut fabrics into three clear sets: one for the journey, sturdy and practical; one for the work itself, more colorful and less afraid to be seen; and a third, reserved for the future she hoped the brothers would one day have. This last set was the boldest—a crisp white linen for shirts, a dash of blue at the collar, and a single length of the yellow to be used as a scarf or kerchief. She stacked these at the very end of the bench, out of Bryant's reach but in full view, as if to make a promise to herself.

Bryant, unable to contain his curiosity, hopped off his chair and padded over. "Why do you need three of everything?" he asked.

Prudence paused, then knelt so that their eyes met. "Sometimes," she said, "you have to prepare for more than just what's needed today. Sometimes you have to plan for what you hope will come, too."

Bryant considered this, then pointed at the blue. "This one is for now?"

"This one is for the road," Prudence replied. "So it's strong, and warm, and won't come apart when they need it most."

"And this one?" He touched the yellow, careful not to wrinkle the strip.

"This is for later. For when things are better, or just different. For when they want to remember today, but not be trapped in it."

Bryant's brow knit in concentration. "And the red?"

She hesitated, unsure how to answer. "That's for courage," she said, finally. "It's just a bit. But sometimes that's all you need."

Bryant nodded, as if this made perfect sense, then wandered back to the window with Moss in tow. The owlcat trilled softly, unimpressed by the colors but deeply invested in the possibility of a nap.

Prudence returned to her work, this time slowing enough to enjoy the feel of each fabric, the sound of the scissors slicing through the weft, the click and clatter of buttons as they fell into place. She remembered her mother's hands, always quick and sure, but never once daring to reach for anything that would stand out. She wondered what her mother would think now—of her daughter, pulling down colors like they were meant for her, ignoring the voices that said no, not you, not ever.

By the time the sun had shifted to the far side of the street, the work table was covered in order: three sets, three destinies, each a little brighter than the last. The room itself felt warmer, as if the fabric had released a memory of summer into the air. Prudence stood back and took it all in, her arms folded, her jaw set. She had done something she'd never dared before, and the certainty of it made her want to laugh again.

For a long while, she simply stood and looked. Then she started on the patterns, tracing the lines with a steady, deliberate hand. The future was uncertain, but the path to it had never been clearer.

Behind her, Bryant hummed a tune under his breath, the owlcat curled at his feet.

For the first time in her life, Prudence Simonsdotter felt as though she was not mending the past, but sewing a way forward—one stitch, one seam, one color at a time.

———

The walk to the bakery took less time than Prudence remembered, though perhaps that was only because her mind kept trying to race ahead of her feet. She and Bryant moved along the hard-packed lane in silence at first, but the morning was far from silent: the caw of birds, the whistle from the cobbler's window, the erratic beat of someone hammering up new roof shingles after the storm. Every sound was brighter, each edge more defined.

Prudence wondered if it was possible to get drunk on nothing but the idea of a good day.

As they reached the bakery, the familiar warmth hit them first—not just the heat from the wood-fired oven, but the thick, sweet air, dough and spice and melting sugar drifting out the door in visible waves. Prudence stepped inside, ducking under the lintel, and found herself met by the sight of Makota's youngest, Kene, streaking flour across the countertop in wide, looping circles. Sora, the elder kit, was standing tiptoe atop a crate, reaching for a sack of salt, while Makota herself worked two batches of dough on the long table with all four hands, never once breaking the rhythm of knead and fold and tuck.

Bryant was through the doorway and into the bakery before Prudence could speak. He made straight for the heap of dough scraps near the end of the table, his hands already outstretched. Kene yowled with delight and pounced, scattering a snowstorm of flour in every direction.

The clamor brought Makota's head up, and her ears perked, the tip of her tail twitching as she grinned at Prudence. "You brought reinforcements?" she called, mock-stern.

"I brought trouble," Prudence replied. "But I'd settle for him not eating all your scraps before midday."

Makota laughed, the sound bubbling out in a purr. "Let him. We'll work it off in kneading." She nodded toward the back. "He's always welcome here."

Sora hopped down from the crate and, without a word, handed Bryant a wooden spoon. The boys eyed each other for a second, then turned in perfect concert to attack a new batch of sticky dough. Kene led, Bryant followed, and within moments the two were deep in some contest only they understood, their arms and faces soon dusted to ghostliness.

Prudence hovered at the door, a habit not easily dropped, watching the kits with an odd sense of vertigo. There had been a time—a year ago, maybe less—when the idea of leaving Bryant in anyone's care, let alone in the company of the Felis baker's children, would have made her skin crawl with worry. Now, standing in the buttery, glowing calm of Makota's domain, she found her worry not gone, but shrunk to a manageable size. It was just part of the world, like the flour that dusted every surface, impossible to sweep out entirely.

Makota must have caught the tension, because she washed her hands and came over, voice lowering. "We'll keep him safe, Prudence. He's better at helping than most grown folk, anyway." Her eyes shone, not just with amusement, but with something like pride. "He always brings ideas I haven't thought of. Like the honey-glaze."

Prudence remembered the honey-glaze. Bryant had, on a dare from Kene, poured half a pot into a cooling pan, and the result had been a hit not just with children, but with most of the town for sennights after.

She smiled, a real one. "He'll be fine," Prudence said, less to Makota than to herself.

"Go," Makota urged, flicking flour from her whiskers. "The little ones will keep each other busy. You've the look of a person with too much on her mind."

Prudence hesitated, but only for a moment. "Thank you," she said. "Truly."

She left as the game reached its crescendo—a thump of dough against the wall, a howl from Kene, and Sora cackling like a mad thing. The sound faded behind her as she stepped out into the crisp air, her own pulse settling to an easy, steady beat.

For the first time since coming north, Prudence realized she did not need to look back.

The walk back to the shop felt different—quicker, lighter, as if she had been relieved of a pack she'd carried her whole life. Her mind leapt ahead to the workbench, the stacks of fabric, the patterns just waiting to be cut and stitched and shaped. The sky above was still the same hard blue, but the light had warmed a little, the edges softened by the smoke curling from every chimney.

She reached the door, paused to brush the dust from her sleeves, and stepped inside.

The shop was silent, the hush of the empty room a perfect counterpoint to the clamor of the bakery. Prudence drew a deep breath, savoring the quiet. She looked over her table, the neatly arranged stacks of fabric and trim, and for the first time, she saw not a daunting task, but a promise—one she finally wanted to keep.

She rolled up her sleeves and got to work.

————

For the next few candlemarks, the shop became both sanctuary and hive, the world outside blurring to nothing while Prudence pieced together the future in tiny, perfect increments. She cut, measured, and trimmed, each seam and edge made with the kind of surety that would have made her mother proud—or perhaps, more accurately, uneasy. She hadn't yet measured the brothers—hadn't even told them they were getting new clothes!—but she could get the basics of the patterns cut out in advance.

The first interruption came just after midday. Darby, face streaked with soot from the forge, arrived with a small bundle wrapped in coarse cloth. "From Bartram and Dad," he said, shoving the bundle onto the counter before Prudence could ask. "He says you'll know what to do." Then he grinned. "Dad made the needles!" The bundle contained three spools of waxed thread and a new set of awl needles, finer and sharper than any Prudence had ever owned. There was no note, but Bartram's mark—a tiny, stamped boot—had been pressed into the wax seal. She smiled and tucked the bundle beside the scissors.

She was just finishing the first pattern when the next visitor arrived. This time it was a deeply annoyed Sam. She stood just inside the door, glowering. "You heard about Cornelius' latest?" she asked, voice low and almost apologetic.

Prudence nodded, keeping her eyes on the line she was tracing. "No."

The bartender leaned closer, lowering her voice further. "He's doing fortunes now. Tells your fate for a copper, but for five silvers, he'll talk to your dead." She shook her head, half in disbelief. "Saw a whole queue of folk waiting. He's got a way with words, I'll grant him."

Prudence made a polite sound, not trusting herself to say anything else. Sam nodded, satisfied, and left as quietly as she'd come.

The afternoon wore on, and the interruptions stacked up. Even Galhani poked her head in, bringing a tart and a quick gossip about Elspeth's last visit. Each new arrival left a ripple of amusement or worry, but none could break the shell of purpose that had closed around Prudence.

When Jen returned, it was not with the usual knock, but with the deliberate, heavy tread of someone on official business.

She stepped inside and closed the door behind her with a decisive click. "He's set up a tent," Jen said, voice flat with effort. "Right inside the gate, just past the marker stone. Says he's holding sessions for the 'grieving and curious alike.'" She crossed her arms, jaw flexing. "I watched three grown men come out of there weeping."

Prudence didn't look up. "Is it hurting anyone?"

Jen exhaled sharply, then paced the length of the shop, boots thudding in time with her irritation. "That's the thing, Pru. It isn't. He's not even cheating them, exactly. They pay, they cry, they leave. Sometimes they feel better, sometimes they don't. But the rules…" She trailed off, then recited in a voice that was not her own, but a perfect imitation of the old mayor: "So long as he comes in peace, stays in peace, and leaves in peace, he can't be turned away."

Prudence let a small smile escape, then reached for the mother-of-pearl buttons. "You could try talking to him."

Jen snorted. "I did. He said he was 'here to heal, not harm.' Offered to speak to my dead grandmother for free." She rolled her eyes so hard it was almost audible. "If he gets any more traction, I'll have to post a watch at the gate."

Prudence stitched a button in place, then snipped the thread. "People want to believe in something."

Jen stopped pacing and stood across the table from Prudence, watching the quick, practiced movements of her hands. "You're not worried?" she asked.

"I'm more worried about what happens when he leaves," Prudence said, matching buttons to thread without looking up. "People will need to fill the space. They always do."

Jen looked at the stacks of fabric, the careful divisions, the bright newness of it all. "You're planning something."

Prudence allowed herself a moment to enjoy the irony. "I am," she said. "But it's nothing that would interest a salesman."

Jen's expression softened, just a little. "I hope you're right."

For a moment, the only sound was the soft tap of the needle against the table. Jen lingered, then looked toward the window, where the last edge of sun burned bright against the pane.

"If he causes trouble, I'll be the first to act," she said, quietly. "But until then… the peace is the peace."

Prudence nodded. "Thank you, Jen."

Jen left as quickly as she'd arrived. The shop settled back into itself, the energy of the day smoothing out into a calm, even buzz.

Prudence glanced at the finished pieces, at the stacks growing taller by the moment, and felt a pride she hadn't known she was allowed to have. The world outside was noisy, always shifting, but here, for a moment, there was order—one she had made, one she could control.

She set aside the finished collar, then turned to the next. With every stitch, the future felt a little more possible.

———

By dusk, the lines on the worktable were as crisp as a map's, and every piece of fabric lay in its proper place: three sets, three fates, each rough-cut and waiting only for their owners. Prudence paused, wiped the damp from her brow, and let her eyes wander over the day's labor. For once, she allowed herself to stand perfectly still and just breathe.

The shop at this time of day had a different kind of silence. Not the hush of an empty room, but a low, steady hum that came from the wood itself, from the quiet tick of the clock, from the grain of the bench worn smooth by decades of hands. She listened to it, willing herself not to worry about what still needed to be done, and instead took the measure of her accomplishment.

There was only one task left: to make sure Lew and Shem received the work.

The plan had taken shape over the course of the afternoon, solidifying with each stitch and seam. At sundown, the brothers would likely pass through the Weary Head's back entrance, looking to avoid both the salesman's pitch and the attention of the square. Prudence knew the pattern—she'd seen it a dozen times in her years here. The battered and the battered-by-life always found the back way, the one that promised less shame and fewer questions.

She wanted to be ready.

She began with the tools. Her best scissors—Warren's gift—were sharpened to a lethal edge and set within easy reach. The needles were lined up by gauge, thinnest to thickest, all threaded and ready, each with a color to match the corresponding cloth. Her old measuring tape was stretched flat on the far edge of the table, the numbers worn but legible, each tick mark a memory. She set out chalk and a ruler, a pincushion, even the little brush for sweeping away threads and dust.

Next came the finishing touches. She sorted the buttons into three bowls: one with the brass, one with the mother-of-pearl, and one with the plain bone. For the ribbons and trims, she took extra care, arranging them in stacks that mirrored the stages she'd imagined for the brothers. The blue velvet was at the front, the gold and yellow tucked behind, and the red—just a whisper of it—coiled neatly in a box, waiting for its moment.

Every time she turned from the bench to fetch something from a shelf or drawer, the thing she needed seemed to be waiting for her, as if the shop itself anticipated her reach. The blue thread she'd been sure was nearly gone appeared full on the spool, and the lining fabric she thought she'd used up last winter unfurled, untouched, from the bottom of the trunk. Even the brass buttons, which she could have sworn were missing one, now numbered an even six, enough for the project and a spare in case of loss.

She did not question it. She let the shop's peculiar will guide her, and the sense of alignment—between her intentions, her hands, and the place itself—made the hair on her arms stand up.

When all was prepared, Prudence stepped back and regarded the array: three piles, each one containing the best she could offer. She imagined the brothers receiving the clothes, imagined the brief shock on their faces as they realized these were not cast-offs or hand-me-downs, but things made for them and only them. She could see Lew struggling to hide his delight; Shem tearing into the package with feral, childlike glee. She wondered if they would understand what she meant by the bands of color, the secret linings, the careful attention to detail. She hoped, fiercely, that they would.

A knock at the door startled her from her reverie. She turned, half-expecting Jen, but instead found the Felis kits, Kene and Sora, their faces a study in exhaustion and triumph. Behind them stood Bryant, hair askew, hands sticky with what looked like equal parts jam and dough.

"We wore him out," Kene announced, voice pitched halfway between pride and apology. "He's been running since lunch."

Bryant blinked sleepily, then reached for his mother's hand without a word. Prudence took it, surprised by the softness of his grip. "Thank you," she said to the kits. "You've done me a great favor."

Sora shrugged, tail flicking. "He's fun. He knows how to cheat at knucklebones, but he taught us anyway."

Kene looked at the stacks of fabric, then at Prudence. "Are you making new clothes?"

"Yes," Prudence said. "For friends."

Kene nodded, as if this explained everything.

The kits disappeared as quickly as they'd arrived, leaving behind a faint scent of sugar and fur. Prudence led Bryant to the bench, settling him in the same spot he'd used that morning. He rested his head on the table, eyes already half-closed.

Prudence glanced at the time-candle. There was still time before sunset. She ran her fingers over the fabric one last time, checking every edge and seam for flaws. She felt her own heartbeat echo in her fingertips.

The knock came again, softer this time, and Prudence realized she had been holding her breath, bone-still, as if expecting something to explode. She exhaled and felt the tremor in her arms as she wiped a smear of lint from her skirt. Bryant, half-asleep on his arm, did not stir.

She moved to the door and cracked it open—not the whole width, just enough to see out. The street was empty except for a low runnel of runoff curving toward the drain. No kits, no Jen, only a strip of golden evening light and the faint, burnt-caramel scent from Makota's bakery. The breeze trailed in, cold and sharp, and for a second Prudence imagined she could hear the thrum of the salesman's pitch from all the way at the town gate. But it was only the wind, and the echo of her own uncertainty.

She closed the door, double-latched it, then turned. Bryant still hadn't moved. His breathing had evened out, slow and sweet as it had been when he was a baby. Moss had found a perch on the windowsill, tail looped neatly around its feet, and seemed to be keeping watch. Prudence took a long look at the shop—the clean table, the neat piles of fabric, the ordered tools—and for the first time in months, she felt at home.

She gathered the three stacks together, checking each for symmetry, and slid them into the broad, shallow basket she used for night projects. It left her hands free—she could carry the whole future up the narrow stairs in one arm, and still have the other to steady Bryant as she led him to supper.

Upstairs, the world shrank to the size of their tiny rooms: the kitchen nook, the low shelf with its mismatched plates, the simple table set for two, candle already guttering in its holder. Prudence set the basket down, then reached for the bread she'd bought that morning, slicing two thick pieces and setting them on the wooden board. She poured the last of the milk into Bryant's cup, and set out a wedge of the cheese Galhani had pressed on her "for growing boys."

Bryant, roused by the clatter, blinked sleepily and rubbed his eyes. "Is it already night?" he asked, voice hoarse.

"Almost," Prudence said. "Eat a little, then we'll wash up and sleep." She slid a plate in front of him and watched as he tore the bread absently, his gaze flitting to the basket, then back to her.

"Those are for the brothers?" he mumbled.

"They are," she said. "But I have to finish them first." She hesitated, then decided it was allowed to say, "I think they'll like them."

Bryant chewed, then nodded and smiled—a real one, all teeth and crumbs and the faintest milk mustache. It filled the room with a warmth the candle could never match.

Prudence ate in silence, savoring the rare luxury of a meal with nothing left to plan.

Tomorrow would be full of color.

eighteen

. . .

THE WEARY HEAD wore the morning like a shawl, its windows fogged with yesterday's breath and its rafters still trembling from the long night of laughter, argument, and song. Before the first bell, the inn was nearly silent. Only the lowest-ranking travelers lingered over cold porridge, staring with blank purpose at the dregs of their cups, and even the common room's hearth had been reduced to the soft, shivering glow of a banked fire. In this hush, Prudence slipped through the kitchen door and into the main room, drawing no more attention than a cat might.

She had timed her arrival with care—before the noise of the square would mask her intent, but late enough that Lew and Shem would be awake and hungry. She scanned the room, then found them exactly where she expected: a table in the far corner, their backs to the wall, their faces haloed by the faint amber light that spilled from the window over the bar.

The brothers did not notice her at first. They leaned close, heads almost touching, hands busy not with breakfast but with the arrangement of small, uneven coins on the table between them. Lew kept his hand cupped protectively around the stack, as if someone might snatch it away at any moment; Shem squinted, tongue caught between his teeth, as he whispered sums too low for even the inn's echo to hear.

Prudence crossed the floor in careful, measured steps, her black dress slicing the warm shadows into sharp lines. She paused only once, when Minnie Trulast caught her eye from behind the bar. Minnie's face split into a broad, approving grin, and she gave an almost imperceptible nod—an offering of solidarity, or perhaps an absolution for whatever rules Prudence was about to break. Trevor, busy stacking pewter mugs, caught his mother's look and matched it with a quick flash of his own, though his gaze followed Prudence with a more open curiosity.

She came to a stop beside the brothers' table. For a moment, she simply stood, letting her presence collect in the air like dust motes caught in a shaft of sunlight. When she spoke, her voice was gentle but flat, stripped of any attempt at disguise.

"You'll never make it up the pass in shirts like that," she said.

Lew startled, almost knocking his pile of coins to the floor. He caught the edge of the table, steadied himself, then looked up at Prudence with a wariness that bordered on alarm. "Ma'am?" he said, his voice hoarse from disuse or bad dreams.

Shem's eyes darted between his brother and the newcomer, then dropped again to the coins. "We're just eating," he muttered, barely loud enough for the table to hear.

Prudence took in the scene—the worn elbows, the frayed collars, the fingers already numbed by cold—and made her decision. She pulled out the nearest chair and sat, planting her hands squarely on the table, the black sleeves of her dress stark against the splintered wood.

"I'm Prudence Simonsdotter," she said. "I'm the seamstress for the town."

The brothers exchanged a look. Shem pressed his lips tight and rolled one of the coins between his fingers; Lew glanced toward the bar, as if checking whether help was nearby, then shrugged and leaned back. "What do you want?" he asked, but the question was honest, not sharp.

"I want you to come with me to my shop," Prudence said. "Now, if possible."

Shem snorted, then coughed to cover it. "We can't pay you," he said.

"I'm not asking for payment."

The table went quiet, save for the coins clinking together as Lew nervously rearranged them. "We're not looking for charity, either," Lew said, softer this time.

"It's not charity." Prudence kept her voice steady, even as she felt the tickle of old shame rising in her chest. "If you're going to reach the Enchantress, you need to look the part. You need to be able to survive the road, and you need to be taken seriously when you get there. Clothes matter." She allowed herself a tiny breath before adding, "They always have."

Shem's eyes, dark and rimmed with exhaustion, flicked up to meet hers. "Why do you care?" he asked, but there was no bitterness in it— just the blunt, resigned curiosity of someone who has stopped expecting sense from the world.

Prudence considered, then decided to give the truth, or as much of it as she could manage before the morning slipped away. "Because I know what it's like to be told you're only worth what you can afford to wear. Because I've just realized how much this matters, although I think I've known for a long time. Because I want to see you come back alive. Because someone needs to make the first move." She held their gaze, daring them to look away.

Lew broke first, a dry laugh escaping his throat. "You're a strange one," he said.

Prudence nodded, accepting the verdict. "So they tell me."

At the bar, Minnie set down her rag and motioned to Trevor, who leaned in to listen. Prudence caught the movement in her periphery but did not turn. Instead, she stood, smoothing her dress, and gestured to the door.

"If you're coming, let's go. The light is best in the morning."

For a few seconds, the brothers just sat, unwilling to move, but unable to refuse. At last, Lew gathered the coins and shoved them into a threadbare pouch. He offered a shrug to Shem, who rolled his eyes but got to his feet, chair scraping the floor with a reluctant screech.

As they made for the door, Minnie's voice called after them. "Prudence!" She waited until Prudence turned, then added with a grin, "Those clothes of yours won't fit much longer, you know."

Prudence felt the flush bloom up her neck. She gave Minnie a look that was half gratitude, half chiding, and then pushed through the door, the brothers close behind.

The street outside was crisp and empty, the sun still low enough to cast long, distorted shadows over the stones. Prudence set off toward the square, not looking back to see if the brothers followed. She knew they would.

She heard their footfalls behind her—hesitant at first, then growing more sure with each step. Lew whispered something to Shem, who snorted, and for a moment the sound of it reminded her of mornings in her own childhood, the way she and her sisters would band together against whatever fresh indignity the day might bring.

She kept her eyes ahead, her jaw set, the memory of Minnie's words lingering in her mind like a dare.

Today, she would make something new. For the brothers, for herself, for whatever future dared to show up next.

She just had to get them through her front door before they lost their nerve.

Prudence's shop was brighter than ever when they arrived, the early sun blazing through both front windows and turning the dust into swirls of gold that danced over every flat surface. It made the whole place seem twice its usual size, and for a moment, even Prudence had to blink at the sudden glare.

She ushered Lew and Shem inside with a stern gesture, then latched the door behind them. The brothers paused at the threshold, uncertain, but then Bryant emerged from his corner and gave a shy wave—half greeting, half warning, as if to say: This is my territory, and things are about to change.

The brothers huddled near the main worktable, shifting from foot to foot, their eyes darting between the walls of fabric and the battered wooden form in the middle of the room. Prudence set about her business with no preamble.

"All right," she said, rolling up her sleeves and reaching for the tape. "Stand straight. Arms out."

Lew obeyed, but only just. His shoulders tensed, and his cheeks flushed in the bright, unmerciful light. Prudence measured him in quick, practiced loops—shoulder to shoulder, wrist to elbow, neck to hem—each reading accompanied by a low murmur as she penciled the numbers into a little pad. Shem watched with an air of resigned awe, jaw tight as Prudence pinched the tape just above his bicep.

When Lew's measurements were finished, Prudence gestured for Shem to take his place. Shem did, but not before making a face at his brother, who snorted and shook his head as if to say, "We're in it now." The whole scene had the air of a livestock inspection, but Prudence's hands were gentle, and her focus so intense that even Shem's usual mischief faded into stillness.

As she worked, Bryant watched from his patch of floor, wooden blocks forgotten at his feet. His eyes tracked every move, every flick of the tape, every scribble in the notebook. He was quiet, more so than usual, and Prudence found herself glancing his way between measurements, as if to reassure herself that he was still breathing.

Once both brothers had been cataloged, Prudence set the tape aside and swept her arm toward the shelves. "There's more fabric here than you'll find in all of Holderdown," she said. "But not much of it gets used." She moved to the racks, pulling down bolts in quick succession, laying them out in layers along the table. "We're going to change that."

Lew and Shem said nothing. Their eyes followed the unfolding display: heavy gray wool, bright blue corduroy, a brown so rich it made their old shirts look like burlap by comparison. There were even a few lengths of deep gold and scarlet, so saturated they seemed to hum in the sunlight. The brothers' mouths opened, then closed; Shem reached for the blue, then caught himself and drew his hand back.

Prudence noticed. "You like that one?" she asked, nodding at the velvet stripe.

Shem shrugged, suddenly shy. "Never seen a color like that on a shirt," he said.

"That's because most people are afraid to stand out," Prudence replied. "But you're not most people, are you?" She paused, then added, "You're going up the mountain. You're going to survive it, and then you're going to come back and build something better than what you left."

Lew barked a small, skeptical laugh. "We just want to make it back alive," he said. "We're not looking for fancy."

Prudence set her jaw, then reached for the brown with gold threads, running her fingers along its edge. "This is for your journey," she said. "It's tough, and warm, and it will hold up against anything the road can throw at you. But it's not enough just to survive. If you're going to start a new life, you need to look the part. You need to believe it, even if no one else does."

She laid the blue on top of the brown, letting the color catch the sun. "This isn't just decoration. It's a reminder. When you put this on, you'll remember what you're fighting for. That you're worth the effort."

Shem's brow furrowed. "You really think a bit of color makes that much difference?"

Prudence didn't hesitate. "I know it does." She let her voice rise, just a little. "Every day in Holderdown, I wore black because it was safer. Because it was what I was told. But I never forgot the feel of blue. Or yellow, or anything that made me feel seen." She stared at the fabric, and for a moment, her own hands trembled. "People think clothes don't matter, but they're wrong. They're how you tell the world you're still here. Even if you're only hanging on by a thread."

There was a long silence. The brothers looked at each other, then back at the array of color on the table. Bryant inched closer, then closer still, until he was almost within reach of the new fabrics.

Lew spoke first. "We only need one set," he said, almost apologetically. "If you could just patch the old ones—"

"No," Prudence said, sharp enough to startle them all. "I'm not patching anything today." She looked at them both, daring them to argue. "You're getting three sets each. One for the mountain, one for the mill, and one for when you're running the place and people have to call you 'sir.'"

Shem snorted at that, but the sound was almost grateful.

Prudence moved around the table, her steps brisk, her hands already sorting and measuring again. She pointed at the blue, then the gold, then the brown. "We'll start with these. I'll fit the first set tonight, and if you don't like it, you can burn the rest for all I care. But you'll leave here prepared."

She gestured for them to sit, and the brothers complied, folding themselves onto the bench with a wariness that was quickly losing its edge. Bryant finally dared to reach for the blue, pinching a tiny piece between his thumb and forefinger before looking up at his mother for approval. She smiled, a real one, and nodded.

Lew cleared his throat. "No one's ever made me new clothes," he said. "Not even when we were kids. My ma used to take the old ones and turn the sleeves backward, so it looked like they were different. But they never really were."

Prudence set a hand on the table, palm flat against the wood. "They will be, this time."

For a while, there was no sound but the click of scissors, the whisper of fabric, and the gentle ticking of the clock in the corner. Prudence moved with a confidence she'd never felt before, each cut and fold informed by something larger than the day or the work or the past that clung to her. The colors on the table made their own kind of music, the blue and gold and brown singing out against the gray of the morning.

At one point, Shem spoke up. "You're different than I expected," he said, but didn't elaborate.

Prudence just shrugged. "So are you."

Bryant, who had been tracing patterns in the blue velvet, looked up. "Are you going to wear color now?" he asked.

Prudence thought about it, then said, "Maybe, when the time is right." She met Bryant's gaze, and he grinned, satisfied.

Lew leaned back, letting his head rest against the wall. "Thank you," he said, the words so quiet they barely reached across the table.

Prudence gave a curt nod, already lost in the work. "You're welcome," she said, and meant it.

As the morning wore on, the brothers relaxed. Shem offered to help with cutting, but Prudence waved him off, content to handle the work herself. Lew watched her for a long time, then started talking about the kind of mill he'd like to run—how it would be clean, how it would pay its workers in coin and not just in trade, how he would never make anyone beg for a meal if there was enough to go around.

Shem chimed in now and then, mostly to mock Lew's idealism, but Prudence could tell that he liked the sound of the dream, even if he'd never admit it. Bryant grew bolder, helping himself to the scraps of blue and gold and making a pile of them on the floor, as if he could keep a piece of the promise for himself.

When the clock struck noon, Prudence straightened, wiped her hands on her apron, and regarded the table. Three stacks of cut fabric, each with its own distinct personality, waited for her needle. The blue shone brightest of all.

She looked at the brothers, then at Bryant, and felt for the first time in years a flicker of real hope. It was not about the clothes, not exactly. It was about the future—about the idea that you could build one, if you just started small and didn't let the old rules hold you down.

She smiled, then, and this time it was wide enough to catch the sun.

"Let's see what we can make of you," she said, and the day seemed to agree.

Once the fabric was stacked and the numbers were settled, Prudence wasted no time. She pointed Lew and Shem to the bench near the front window, set Bryant up with his box of blocks, and cleared the main worktable with a single sweep of her arm. The day was barely started, but she felt the press of urgency—a need to move before she lost her courage, before the doubts could catch up.

She set scissors to the first length of brown, the sturdy stuff with just enough give to make a good travel jacket. The steel blades bit through the fabric with a hiss, and Prudence smiled at how little effort it took. She arranged the pieces in a grid, checked the fit against her patterns, then started on the next color.

At first, the only sounds were the mechanical snick of shears and the tap-tap of Bryant's wooden blocks. The brothers watched with open skepticism, whispering from time to time about the price of flour or whether it would snow again before the sennight was out. Their voices faded as Prudence moved, her hands a blur of motion, her eyes fixed on the work. After a 'mark, the sewing machine's old rhythm filled the shop: the click of the treadle, the low growl of the gear, the steady, pulsing hum that seemed to quicken with every new seam.

When she had the first pieces basted, Prudence called to Bryant, "Come hold this edge for me." He scampered over, solemn with importance, and pressed his finger to the fabric as she had taught him. Lew and Shem exchanged a look—half amusement, half disbelief—but made no move to object.

As she pinned the next layer, Prudence found herself humming. The melody was the one her mother used to sing while darning in the evenings: a lullaby, but quickened by the pace of her work, the rhythm rising and falling with the needle's leap. She realized she was telling the story without thinking, the words coming out in fragments between each stitch.

"It was a hard year, colder than most," she said. "The village had run through every sack of flour and was down to the last bowl of dried peas. That was when the brothers—"

She let the thread snap through, a bright, clear note. Lew raised his head, curious despite himself. "What brothers?"

"The ones who left," Prudence answered, measuring out a new piece of blue for the trim. "They wanted something better, but their father said it was hopeless. He locked the door behind them. But they went anyway."

Shem leaned forward, elbows on knees. "What did they find?"

"A mill," Bryant whispered, already knowing the tale. "One that could grind anything."

Prudence nodded, pleased. "It was supposed to be a myth. But the brothers found it, and when they did, they took turns feeding it rocks, acorns, whatever they could find. And out came flour, white as moonlight, enough to feed the whole valley."

She moved to the machine, guided the brown and blue through its hungry mouth, and watched as the first sleeve took shape beneath her hands. The story grew with the seam: the famine broken, the brothers returning as heroes, the father forced to welcome them back.

"But it wasn't the flour that made them heroes," Prudence said, voice growing stronger with each word. "It was that they came back. That they didn't let the mountain—or the old rules—tell them what they could be."

The shop changed around her. She felt it first in the ease of the thread, which unspooled with no tangles or knots; then in the way the needle found its own path through the thickest parts of the cloth, never splitting or snapping. The air, usually so dry and heavy with lint, grew charged, as if a summer storm were gathering in the rafters. She kept working, but now her skin prickled, and the hairs on her arms stood up straight. The magic was awake, and it was watching.

Bryant abandoned his blocks entirely, standing close enough to see the seam glowing faintly in the sunlight as his mother stitched it. "Is that supposed to happen?" he whispered.

Prudence glanced up, startled, and saw that he was right: the blue thread left a line of light behind it, the color almost electric against the brown. She thought about hiding it, but instead kept going, faster, letting the light trail from the machine in a straight, perfect line.

The brothers had noticed, too. Shem stood, came closer, and stared openly at the work. "That's not normal," he said, but there was wonder in his voice.

Prudence answered without looking up. "It is today."

The day ran forward, each 'mark commemorated by another stack of completed pieces. She worked through lunch, through the bell, through the slow dimming of the shop as afternoon shadows crept across the floor. The sewing never faltered. When one needle snapped, another was waiting; when a spool ran out, the next was already at hand. At times, Prudence felt as though she had four arms, each moving on its own, each following the exact line the fabric wanted to take.

She finished the questing jackets first—brown, with blue at the collar and cuffs, lined in gold that would catch the sunlight or candle-light, depending on where the road took them. She tried them on Lew and Shem, who stood silent and stiff as mannequins. They fit perfectly, and when Lew flexed his arms, he smiled despite himself.

"These will last," he said, almost in awe.

"That's the idea," Prudence replied.

Next came the apprentice sets: clean white shirts with subtle blue piping at the collar, new trousers in charcoal gray, and sturdy boots patched at the heel with a strip of gold. When Shem tried his on, he said nothing, but Prudence saw the way his posture changed, the way he kept glancing at his own reflection in the shop's old, cloudy mirror.

Last were the miller's clothes—stiff, dignified, with a stripe of blue running along the edge of the vest, and a white handkerchief for formal occasions. Prudence finished the last set as dusk closed in, the gold thread shining even in the dying light.

When it was done, she stacked the clothes on the bench, lined up in threes. She stood back, wiped her hands, and looked at the brothers, then at Bryant, then at her own pale reflection in the window.

She felt drained, but not empty. The magic that had filled the room now rested, curled around her ankles like a satisfied cat. She saw in the brothers' eyes the same disbelief and hope that had lived in her own bones for years.

"Try them on," she said. "See if they fit."

Lew and Shem hesitated, then stripped off their old shirts and stepped into the new. The blue glimmered at the throat, the brown sat snug across their shoulders, the gold flashed at the seams when they turned in the light. The clothes fit better than a second skin.

Bryant clapped, unable to help himself. "You look like real heroes," he said, and it was true.

Prudence leaned against the table, exhausted but alive. She looked at the brothers, then at Bryant, and for a moment, she saw him grown—standing tall, wearing color, unafraid. She blinked, and the vision faded, but the hope remained.

She cleared her throat. "The world doesn't have to stay the way it is," she said. "You just have to start somewhere."

Shem grinned, and for once, there was no mockery in it. "You've started plenty, ma'am."

Prudence nodded, then turned back to the machine, already thinking about what she would make next.

The night crept in slow, and for once, it brought only peace.

———

The next day dawned clear, the sun a pale disk behind the winter haze, and by the time Prudence raised the shop's shutters, the brothers were already waiting. They stood side by side on the stoop, awkward in their old clothes, their faces raw with wind but scrubbed clean. Lew gave a sheepish wave; Shem shoved his hands deep into his pockets, but his eyes darted to the window, hungry for a glimpse of what waited inside.

Bryant was still in his nightshirt, sitting on the counter and swinging his heels, half-awake and content to watch. The room glowed with that particular light found only in the moments before dusk, gold and thin and almost forgiving. Prudence moved quietly, arranging the three piles of finished clothes on the bench, the brightest blue on top.

She beckoned them in, and the brothers crossed the threshold like men entering a church, hats in hand, their boots leaving careful, clean prints on the floor. They lingered near the door, staring at the stacks of fabric as if afraid to touch.

"Come closer," Prudence said. "You'll want to see for yourselves."

Shem obliged, his bravado crumbling as he reached for the top jacket, fingers trembling just a little. He held it up to the window, turning the sleeves so the blue trim caught the fading light. "This is…" he started, but could not finish.

Lew picked up the next piece—a shirt, pale but strong, lined at the collar with the same blue. He looked at Prudence, then back to the garment. "You did all this in a night?"

Prudence shrugged, feigning indifference. "It wasn't just me."

Bryant grinned from the counter, his face round and full of mischief. "It was magic," he said, and for a moment, no one thought to disagree.

One by one, the brothers changed into their new questing clothes, casting their old shirts and trousers into a heap by the door. The fit was uncanny: the seams fell just so, the colors made their eyes seem brighter, and the cut gave both men a posture they'd never worn before. Shem's jacket hugged his shoulders; Lew's shirt looked like it had grown there.

They moved to the mirror, uncertain, then stood silent, stunned by the reflection. Shem grinned, rolling his shoulders, admiring the way the blue flashed when he moved. Lew looked taller, more composed; he ran a hand down his sleeve, then let it rest at his side as if claiming the moment for himself.

Prudence stood back, arms folded, letting them take it in. "You'll want to keep those clean as long as you can," she said, "but don't be afraid to wear them hard. That's what they're for."

Shem turned, incredulous. "We'll stand out, you know. Everyone will know we're not from around here."

"You were never going to blend in," Prudence said, her tone gentle. "It's better to be noticed for the right reasons."

Bryant, emboldened, hopped from the counter and circled the brothers, inspecting the blue and brown and gold. "You look like heroes," he pronounced, then ducked away to play.

Lew smiled, the expression new and unfamiliar on his face. "Thank you, Prudence. I don't know how we'll ever pay you back."

Prudence shook her head. "You already have."

She reached behind the bench and brought out two carefully wrapped bundles—one for each brother, tied with a twist of blue thread. "For later," she said, pushing them across the table. "When you're ready. You can open them then."

Shem reached for his, but Lew caught his hand. "We'll wait," Lew said, and Prudence saw that he meant it.

The mood grew quiet, comfortable, the kind of hush that follows a great meal or a long-needed laugh. For a time, the three of them just stood there, breathing in the future.

It was Shem who broke the silence. "We still don't know how we'll get the rest of what we need for the road. Provisions, a map. But…" He trailed off, then grinned. "Somehow, I feel like it'll work out now."

Prudence nodded, smiling. "That's how it starts."

Bryant reappeared at her side, arms full of blue and gold scraps. "Can we keep these?" he asked.

"Of course," Prudence said. "Make something of them."

He grinned, then sat cross-legged by the hearth, already sorting the pieces into patterns only he could see.

The brothers pulled on their new coats, tucked the bundles under their arms, and moved toward the door. At the threshold, Shem looked back, the blue at his collar blazing in the slanting sun.

"We'll make you proud," he said.

"You already have," Prudence replied.

They left, the late light catching the blue and scattering it down the street in flashes of sky and river and morning. Prudence watched until they turned the corner, their voices rising in a tangle of hope and laughter.

She closed the door, gathered Bryant into her arms, and sank into the nearest chair, hands still tingling with the memory of work well done.

The world outside was the same as ever, but in this room, for a moment, everything felt remade. Bryant curled against her side, soft and warm, and Prudence let herself drift.

Later, she would unroll a new bolt of blue, ready for whatever came next. For now, she let the last light linger, gold and gentle, and thought of the future, bright as a promise.

nineteen

. . .

THE SHOP WAS a different animal in the new morning. Prudence could hardly believe it herself. Once, the workroom had been a narrow burrow, designed to swallow mistakes and keep her, and her boy, invisible behind the square's regular commerce. Today, it was light—unrepentant, showy light—spilling in through both windows, bright enough that even the dust in the air looked less like a flaw and more like a deliberate accent.

She had left the shutters open, top and bottom, and the sun threw long bands across the newly rearranged shelves, picking out colors she'd never dared to display before. The old bolts of brown and gray and unadorned black were still there—she would never be rid of them —but now they were flanked by ochre, pine green, and three separate shades of blue, none of which matched anything she'd ever seen in Holderdown. She had spent the evening after the brothers left stacking the new fabrics by hue, then by pattern, then by whim, until the whole of it looked less like a store and more like a painter's arsenal.

She was proud, and a little terrified.

At present, she was not alone. Bartram had visited that morning, bringing with him a commission—though, as ever, he tried to make it sound like a favor. He perched on a stool near the worktable, boots crossed at the ankle, his bald head shining in the stripe of sun that had managed to find him. In his hands he held a battered ledger, open to a page filled with little sketches, each annotated in the cobbler's looping, optimistic script.

"We need to make a woodsman," he declared, tapping a finger at the page. "Not just a man who cuts wood, but a proper ranger. Someone who looks like he could walk into the Mistral foothills and not come back for a year."

Prudence arched a brow. "You want a uniform?"

"No, no, that's the old way," Bartram said, waving her off. "We need something… ah, what's the word? Signature. But it must hold up to the real work. This is for a man who is not delicate."

Prudence considered the sketch—a long, belted coat, reinforced at the elbows and cuffs, with a standing collar that would turn wind but not look showy. She knew the kind: it was the sort of thing worn by men who spent half their life in the deep woods, half in the tavern, and who needed to look the part in both places. "Color?"

"That's what I wanted to discuss." Bartram leaned forward, his face alive with possibility. "You have that dark green, yes? But maybe —" and here he turned the page, revealing a swatch of something brighter— "with a little of this for trim. Something to catch the light, but not too much."

Prudence let herself smile, just a little. "That's not for camouflage, Bartram."

"Who wants to blend in?" he replied, almost gleeful. "Not in this town, anyway."

They both laughed, and for a moment the space between them felt as easy and natural as air.

The bell on the shop door rattled then, and a customer entered, hunched in a coat that was already two winters past its death. He was a traveler, this was clear: his boots were dusted with old snow, and his face had the pale, raw look of someone who'd only recently discovered the concept of indoor heating. His eyes scanned the shelves, then came to rest on Prudence and Bartram.

"Sorry," the man said. "Is this a bad time?"

"Never," Bartram called, already half out of his seat. "Come in, come in. You are early for the fortnights' trade, yes?"

The traveler looked at Prudence, uncertain, and she gave a quick, practiced nod. "We're open. What brings you in?"

He hesitated, then glanced over his shoulder, as if someone might be listening from the stoop. "I heard there was a… solution here. For travelers. A way to make the journey north less—" He searched for a word, found none, and settled on, "miserable."

Bartram grinned, but Prudence noticed the way the man's hands trembled, not from cold but from nerves. "You've been to the salesman's wagon?" she asked, keeping her tone neutral.

The traveler snorted. "His stuff's a joke. I bought a bottle, and all it did was make me see my mother's face in the firelight. Nice, but not… helpful."

Prudence understood. "You're looking for something real."

The man nodded, a little embarrassed. "Something that keeps out the weather. The real weather. And doesn't fall apart if you take a tumble down a ravine."

Bartram winked at Prudence, then gestured at the sketch on the page. "You are the perfect test case. Pru, I think you should do the measuring."

She approached the man, measuring tape already in hand, and he shrugged off the ruined coat, revealing a set of clothes even less suited to survival. The shirt was thin and patched, the trousers bagged at the knees, and the boots—Bartram winced, seeing them—were down to the nail.

"Arms out," Prudence said, and the traveler obeyed. She worked quickly, reading off the numbers to herself and making notes with a pencil tucked behind her ear. The man smelled of old sweat and something more wild, a tang of pine resin and river mud that reminded her of the banks outside Holderdown, and for a moment she was almost sorry for him.

As she measured, the traveler's eyes wandered the shop, landing on each new color with a mix of awe and suspicion. "Are those all for sale?" he asked, nodding toward a shelf lined with fabrics in patterns and hues the lowlands would have called frivolous.

Prudence nodded. "Nothing in here isn't meant to be used. Even the bright ones."

The traveler looked unconvinced, but Bartram clapped him on the shoulder. "Sometimes, a bit of color is all that stands between you and madness. If you stare at nothing but gray for a moon, you'll start seeing ghosts."

Prudence finished the measuring, then stepped back. "I can have it ready by tomorrow evening," she said. "Do you want a hood, or just the collar?"

The traveler considered. "Both. But the hood needs to be big enough to go over a pack."

She nodded, already turning to the racks. She picked out the new green—deep, with just enough blue in it to make it look richer than forest—and paired it, as Bartram suggested, with a strip of coppery orange for the trim. She cut a piece of each, laid them side by side, and let the two men debate the merits. Bartram was enthusiastic, the traveler skeptical, but in the end, the color won. It always did, if you let it.

With the fabric selected, Prudence moved to the worktable and began to lay out the pattern. The light was better than ever, and she found her hands working almost ahead of her mind, the scissors gliding along the lines as if they'd been drawn by instinct. Bartram hovered, offering the occasional tip—"Reinforce the cuffs, he'll be splitting logs by the end of the sennight"—but mostly he just watched, nodding along as each piece came together.

The traveler waited, arms folded, but Prudence could see the change in him. Already, he looked less tired. It was as if the act of being measured—of being seen—had stitched together something inside him.

She cut and shaped, then pinned the sleeves in place, the rhythm of her work so sure and smooth that even the doubting traveler relaxed. As she stitched, she told them the story of the forest guardians—spirits of the old woods who protected travelers by giving them cloaks of green so perfect that even the wind respected them. "They say," Prudence said, "that the best coat will keep you invisible, but only if you know what you're hiding from."

Bartram chuckled. "I'm hiding from boredom, mostly."

The traveler didn't laugh, but he did smile. "I just want to stay alive," he said.

Prudence nodded, understanding more than she wanted to admit. "That's a good enough reason."

The sun moved through the windows, turning the green richer, the copper brighter, and soon the whole coat was laid out, ready to be sewn. She worked the pedal of the old treadle machine, the needle moving so fast it was almost invisible, and for a moment Prudence lost herself in the motion. She thought of Bryant, and the future she'd promised him. She thought of Lew and Shem, of how their faces had changed when they first saw themselves in new color. She thought of herself, and wondered what she would look like in a dress that wasn't black.

When the coat was finished, Prudence held it up to the light, inspecting every seam, every accent. She brushed off the stray threads and turned to the traveler. "Try it on," she said.

He did, slipping into the coat with a care that suggested reverence. The fit was perfect—snug at the shoulders, roomy at the chest, the sleeves ending just above the wrist as if tailored by magic. The copper trim caught the morning sun, sending a line of fire down each arm. The traveler flexed, then pulled the hood over his head. It covered everything, but did not weigh him down.

He looked at himself in the mirror, not quite believing. "It feels… right," he said, and his voice was small but sure.

Bartram grinned, and Prudence smiled wider than she had all sennight. The traveler looked up, meeting their gaze in the glass, and for the first time, he didn't look tired or wary. He looked ready.

Prudence watched as he buttoned the coat, pulled the belt tight, and turned once, then twice, testing the range of motion. "I don't need the salesman's potions," he said, almost to himself. "I just needed to know I could do it the hard way."

Prudence nodded. "The hard way is the only way that lasts."

The traveler thanked them both, paid in coin that smelled faintly of salt and fish, and promised to spread word of the shop as far as the lakeshore. He left with his old coat under his arm, but already Prudence could tell he would never wear it again.

Bartram lingered, his eyes tracing the new arrangement of fabric on the shelves. "You're changing things, you know," he said, softly.

Prudence shrugged, but it was a shrug born of pride, not modesty. "Maybe. Or maybe I'm just catching up."

Bartram smiled, then left her to the silence and the sunlight.

When the door closed behind him, Prudence stood at the window, watching the traveler cross the green in his new coat. The copper flashed once in the morning light, and Prudence felt, for a moment, as though she had sent a small piece of herself out into the world.

She liked the feeling. She wanted more of it.

So she went back to her work, humming the song her mother had once sung, and let the magic do its work.

———

The next day's first customer came well before the shops were meant to open. The sky was still rinsed in pearl, the sun barely lifting the chill from the flagstones. Prudence was tidying the main room when the knock came—a quick, sharp rhythm, precise as a clockmaker.

She opened the door to find a young woman, bundled in a traveling cloak, the edge of a leather portfolio clutched in one hand. The woman looked out of breath, but not from running; hers was the air of someone who had planned every minute of the morning and resented anything that threatened to undo it.

"Is this the tailor?" she asked, already half-stepping inside.

Prudence smiled and swept her arm toward the worktable. "If it isn't, I've been lied to for years."

The woman did not smile back. She took in the shop in a single, hungry glance, eyes snagging on the colors—arranged now in a spectrum that started at the window and spiraled toward the back, all the new bolts interleaved with scraps and ribbons and bias tape. Prudence watched as the woman's gaze paused on the brightest blue, then darted away, as if embarrassed by the attention.

"I'm bound for the South," the woman said. "A caravan leaves in three days. They told me I'd best get desert-proofed, or else stay behind and starve." She set the portfolio down and withdrew a letter, sliding it across the table. "My references. I'm meant to keep the trade records."

Prudence accepted the letter but did not read it. "What's your name?"

The woman hesitated, caught off guard by the question. "Sera," she said, and then, with a hint of apology, "Sera Benadine. I'm not… I've never had bespoke clothes before."

"That's half the point," Prudence said. "If you already knew what you wanted, there'd be no need for me."

Sera's cheeks flushed, but she squared her shoulders. "They said to come here if I wanted to be seen," she admitted. "But—" Her eyes flicked to the indigo on the high shelf, and then away. "I don't think I'm a color person. Not really."

Prudence stepped around the table, hands on hips. "What is it you need, exactly? Sand-proof? Sun-proof? Or just something that lets people know you're not to be messed with?"

Sera considered, then surprised herself by saying, "All three."

Prudence grinned, already enjoying this. "Follow me." She led Sera to the new display, where the blues had been reclassified: ultramarine for the bold, steel blue for the wary, indigo for the ones who wanted to be bold but weren't ready yet.

Sera pointed, reluctantly, at the indigo. "That one," she said. "It reminds me of the sky at dusk, before the stars come out."

Prudence nodded, and reached for it without hesitation. "And for trim?"

Sera frowned. "Is trim really necessary?"

"Not necessary," Prudence admitted, "but you'd be surprised what a line of gold can do. Especially if you want people to remember your face after a long day's ride."

There was a pause, and then Sera said, "All right. A little gold."

The moment the fabric hit the worktable, something in the room changed. The color—deep and almost liquid—soaked up the morning sun, and Prudence felt the softest hum at the base of her skull, like a bee trapped in a jar. She drew the indigo out, laid it next to the gold, and began to cut, the scissors making quick, precise snicks that seemed to echo louder than before.

As she worked, Prudence asked, "You ever been South?"

Sera shook her head. "Never left the region, actually. The furthest I've gone was Evendiam's south shore, for a math competition."

Prudence smiled at the memory of her own first trip—how small and large the world could be, all at once. "You'll need a scarf, then," she said, "for the dust. And a headwrap. And at least three pockets—one hidden."

Sera watched, hands folded so tight her knuckles went pale. "You work fast," she said, almost accusingly.

Prudence shrugged. "There's a lot to do."

She measured Sera's arms and shoulders, noting the way the young woman held herself—upright, but always bracing for a blow. When it came time to measure the waist, Sera flinched.

"Sorry," she mumbled.

Prudence's voice was gentle, but not patronizing. "Don't apologize. Clothes are supposed to fit you, not the other way around."

The next part was the patterning, and here the magic—or whatever it was—took over. Prudence found her hands moving almost of their own accord, drawing curves and darts she'd never seen in any reference, but which made perfect, intuitive sense. The workroom itself joined in: spools of thread unspooled themselves, swatches of fabric landed where she needed them, even the old pin-cushion rolled obligingly down the table when she reached for it.

As she cut, Prudence told a story, not unlike the one she'd told the woodsman, but this time about desert travelers—how they'd once sewn little stars into the hems of their robes, and how the gold thread would catch the moonlight, letting them find their way back to their tents no matter how lost they became.

Sera listened in silence, but her breathing eased as the story went on. When Prudence finished cutting the main pieces, she looked up to find the woman actually smiling, the lines of tension in her face softer now.

"Will it really help me find my way?" Sera asked, half in jest, half in hope.

Prudence winked. "Only if you look up now and then."

She set to sewing, and the machine sang under her hands, the thread moving so fast it left a faint blur in the air. The indigo seemed to shift color with the angle, blue one moment, purple the next, and the gold trim flashed bright every time it caught the light. When the last seam was done, Prudence held up the robe, the scarf, the matching headwrap, and stood back.

Sera regarded them for a long moment, then slipped off her cloak and tried on the robe. It settled perfectly on her shoulders, the fit so good it made her shiver. She tied the sash, then examined herself in the little mirror by the door.

Prudence watched her from across the room, hiding her own pride behind a careful poker face.

Sera turned, then turned again, and then laughed—a real, honest sound. "It's… I've never looked like this before. I don't look like a scribe at all."

"You don't have to," Prudence said. "You're not just a scribe anymore. You're a traveler. A survivor."

Sera ran her hand down the sleeve, feeling the seam. "I thought I needed magic in a bottle," she said, "but this is the real thing, isn't it?"

Prudence stepped forward and adjusted the collar, tucking the edge just so. "Sometimes you have to do the work yourself," she said. "The journey is half of it."

Sera nodded, and this time she looked straight at Prudence. "Thank you," she said, and it carried more weight than all the references in the world.

She paid, tucked the new outfit into her pack, and left with the same careful, measured step she'd entered with—but now, Prudence noticed, she held her head higher, and the sun caught the gold at her throat as she crossed the square.

The workroom was quiet again, the only sound the slow tick of the clock and the faint hum of thread settling back onto its spool.

Prudence ran her hand across the indigo scrap left on the table, and thought about how different she herself had become in just a few short days.

Maybe, she thought, it wasn't magic at all. Maybe it was just finally having the courage to use what you'd been given.

She smiled at the thought, and went back to sorting the shelves, wondering who would come through the door next.

———

It was late the next day, nearly at the end of the afternoon bell, when the next pair arrived. Prudence was bent over the worktable, mending a fray in Bryant's best shirt, when she heard the door open and close in quick succession—a double pulse, not the lazy wander of townsfolk but the urgent beat of travelers who'd rather not be seen.

She looked up to find two figures standing just inside, their cloaks still dripping with the wet of the square. They were not from around here; this was obvious at a glance. The shorter one, a woman with shorn hair and a pinched, windburned nose, held her bag like a shield. The taller, a man with the gray skin of a half-elf and arms wrapped in linen up to the elbow, watched the room like he expected it to collapse at any second.

Neither spoke at first, but Prudence was used to that.

She set aside the shirt and folded her hands atop the table. "Good evening. Looking to have something mended?"

The woman started, then forced a smile. "We're not… that is, we heard you might be able to help." She stepped forward, shrugging off her cloak, and revealed the battered remains of a healer's robe beneath —once white, now a ghostly, pocked gray. "We're… chirurgeons. North-bound."

The man came close behind. "Word is your work is special," he said, voice low and graveled. "Special in ways we can't get in the cities. Or from the wagons out there." He jerked his head toward the door, where the faint glow of Cornelius's lantern still cut through the gloom.

Prudence glanced at the robe, then at the two of them. "You need something that won't frighten the children. Or the sick."

The woman grinned, showing a missing tooth. "You could say that."

Prudence gestured to the bench. "Have a seat. I'll bring out some options."

She moved to the shelves, hand hovering over the racks of new colors, then drew down two bolts: one a blue so pale it looked almost silver, the other a green so soft it seemed made from moss. She unrolled them on the table, letting the colors play together in the lamp-light.

The man whistled. "Is that silk?"

"Half-silk," Prudence said, proud. "Durable, but doesn't chafe. You'll sweat less in the heat."

The woman touched the green, eyes wide. "It's like a forest in spring," she said, and then, embarrassed, "Is it expensive?"

Prudence shook her head. "Not today." She laid the fabrics out, then took the tape to measure the pair—shoulders, arms, chest, always with a practiced, gentle touch. As she worked, the man said, "We nearly bought a remedy off that Cornelius. The potion man. Said it would make us 'impossible to overlook.'"

Prudence's mouth quirked. "And did you?"

He shrugged, embarrassed. "Smelled like lavender and turpentine. We decided to try the real thing first."

Prudence nodded, and began sketching the design. "I can make you matching coats. Lots of pockets. Room for the things you carry. And I can reinforce the shoulders so you can haul a patient if needed." She looked up. "Sound right?"

They both nodded, the woman's face brightening with every word.

As she began cutting, Prudence told them the story of the legendary healers of the Mistral coast—how one had saved an entire village by boiling seawater and wringing the salt into a powder for wounds, how another had made a poultice from the petals of a night-blooming flower that grew only in graveyards. "None of them," she said, "ever looked the part, until someone gave them a coat that did."

The man leaned in. "Did the coat make the healer?"

Prudence smiled. "Not at all. But it helped the village trust him. And sometimes that's enough."

The magic was different now, more obvious than ever. The blue thread glimmered as it drew through the fabric, leaving a line of light that faded only when she pressed it flat with the iron. The moss-green lining slipped into place as if magnetized. When she called for the pocket fabric, the bolt unrolled itself, then stopped, waiting for her hand. Even the old pin-cushion spun obligingly toward her, offering up just the right size every time.

She embroidered a small sprig of lavender—real, not just a symbol—onto each sleeve, and for the woman, she added a tiny leaf to the cuff. "For luck," she said, and the woman blinked back tears she did not bother to explain.

They tried the coats on together. The man flexed his arms and looked amazed at how nothing pinched or pulled. The woman turned twice, then laughed, the sound clear and quick. "I feel like someone," she said, unable to say more.

The pair studied each other in the mirror, a silence passing between them like a wordless vow.

"These clothes," the man said at last, "make me feel like the healer I always wanted to be."

Prudence stepped back, arms folded. "Then you'll be one."

They paid, not with coin, but with a pair of small vials—one blue, one yellow. "Cure for sleeplessness," the woman said, "and cure for pain." She pressed them into Prudence's hand, and for the first time in a long while, she accepted the gift.

The healers left together, their new coats flashing pale blue and moss green in the lamplight. Neither looked back at the square. Neither so much as glanced at Cornelius's wagon, though his lamp still burned.

Prudence watched them through the window until they vanished into the evening.

She rolled the last of the thread back onto its spool, the blue glowing faintly until it was covered.

The shop felt alive, more than ever. It was, she realized, exactly what she had wanted it to become.

And as she swept the last shreds of fabric from the floor, she wondered—not with worry, but with genuine curiosity—what she might make next.

———

By the time the final bell of the following day sounded, Prudence was alone again—Bryant already home, the shop swept and shuttered, the last traces of fabric dust swept into the corners. She was tidying the spools by color, arranging them on the shelf in a spectrum that pleased her, when the familiar scrape of boots sounded outside.

The door rattled. Prudence had barely turned when Jen barged in, helmet tucked under her arm and a look of absolute satisfaction on her face.

"Evening, Pru," Jen said, sliding into the room like she owned it. "Hope I'm not interrupting."

"Never," Prudence replied. She waited as the constable did a circuit of the main table, picking up a bit of blue, then a length of sturdy brown, before leaning against the wall and crossing her arms.

Jen's grin was feral. "You'll be happy to know your competitor out there is dying on the vine. Haven't seen a customer at his wagon since yesterday at second bell." She shook her head, her voice rich with pleasure. "Word's gotten around."

Prudence finished sorting the reds, letting her fingers trail through the different shades. "It's not really a competition," she said. "He's selling dreams in a bottle. I'm just giving people what they can use."

Jen shrugged, unconvinced. "Same thing, if you ask me. But you're winning."

She picked up a stray bolt—a red so deep it bordered on purple—and examined it in the window light. "You've got a knack for this, you know. Every traveler who's passed through in the last two days has left looking like a different person. Even the ones who didn't buy anything." She shot a sly look at Prudence. "The healers said you told them a story about the salt-village miracle."

Prudence laughed, just once. "Sometimes a story helps the medicine go down."

Jen set the fabric aside, then drew herself up, all business again. "Not sure how long the salesman's going to last. Saw him counting his coins on the green this morning. Didn't look happy."

Prudence felt a flicker of something—pity, perhaps, or a vestige of her old fear of being seen as unkind. But mostly, she felt relief. "Maybe he'll move on," she said.

"Maybe," Jen said. "Or maybe he'll take a page from your book and start selling scarves." She eyed a finished robe on the rack and smirked. "Doubt he'd have your touch, though."

They stood together for a moment, the only sound the faint tick of the wall clock and the wind beyond the window. Jen seemed at ease for the first time in days.

"I'll keep steering the travelers your way," she said. "It's better for the town if they leave in one piece."

Prudence nodded. "Thank you, Jen."

The constable hesitated, then picked up the crimson fabric again, running her fingers along its edge. "You ever think about making something for yourself?" she asked, not meeting Prudence's eyes.

"Maybe," Prudence said. "One of these days."

Jen smiled, a slow, rare thing, and let the fabric drop back onto the table. "Let me know when you do."

She left as quickly as she'd come, the door swinging shut behind her. Prudence listened to her footsteps fade down the lane, then looked around at the shop—the shelves in their new order, the patterns taped up on the back wall, the little piles of color waiting to become something more.

She took a breath and felt, for the first time since arriving in North Pointe, that she had staked out a space in the world that was all her own.

The dusk outside was gray and soft, but in the shop, the colors were brighter than ever.

She smiled, and locked up for the night.

———

Three nights later, as Prudence swept the last remnants of the day's work into the hearth bin, the quiet was broken by the clatter of boots and a sudden, exuberant knocking. The bell above the door didn't even have time to ring before Lew and Shem barreled into the shop, faces windburned and eyes wild with joy.

"Prudence!" Lew called, breathless. "We did it! We did everything you said we would!"

Shem was right behind, his sleeve torn and mended with a patch of new blue—her blue, unmistakable in the lamplight. "You wouldn't believe it, ma'am," he said, "but I think we actually scared the skraeling."

Prudence set her broom aside and leaned on the worktable, more amused than surprised. "Is that so?" she asked, folding her arms. "I thought the skraeling were made of sterner stuff."

Shem grinned, showing off a freshly chipped tooth. "Turns out, they don't like gold trim. Or maybe just don't like us."

Lew was already tugging at his jacket, showing where the reinforced cuff had kept his arm from being split by a falling branch. "We made it to the mountain," he said, "and the Enchantress herself met us at the gate. She looked us over, said—" He caught himself, flushed, and tried to compose his face into something more serious. "She said we were properly outfitted for our destiny."

Prudence couldn't help it—she laughed. "Did she, now?"

Lew's smile was shy but proud. "She did. She sent us to the well at the top of the keep, and there was a test, and then this—" He reached into his pouch and produced a tiny sack. When he poured it out, a dozen gold coins clinked onto the table, each stamped with a strange, shifting rune.

Shem leaned close and whispered, "They're bespelled. Can only be spent on our apprenticeship. That's what she told us."

Prudence picked up one of the coins, felt the faint tickle of magic in the metal. It shimmered, catching the workroom light in ways no real coin ever could. "Where will you go?" she asked, quietly.

Lew's eyes shone. "Thornvale. There's a man—Master Miller Eastwick—she said he'd take us both, if we could show the right credentials. She sent a letter ahead, with magic. He already answered."

Shem nodded, more solemn. "He even asked if we had proper shirts. Said it was a matter of pride."

Prudence looked at the patched sleeve, then at the pair of them standing together in their old-new clothes, and her chest ached with something close to joy.

Lew scooped the coins back into the pouch. "We have to hurry," he said. "Tyran's got our next set ready, but he said he wouldn't hold it past the sennight unless we showed up in person."

Shem grinned. "We sort of pawned the apprentice clothes for a map and some gear. Didn't want to lose the way, you know?"

Prudence nodded, smiling despite herself. "Then what are you waiting for?" she said. "Get to Tyran's before he changes his mind."

They dashed out, the door swinging wide behind them, then slamming shut as if to mark the end of a chapter.

Prudence stood for a moment in the center of the room, listening to the fading sound of their voices echo down the street. The shop felt strange without them, almost too quiet—but it was a good quiet, a fulfilled quiet.

She looked at the table, where the gold coin still shimmered in her palm, and set it down in the place of honor above the sewing machine.

For a long moment, she simply stood and looked around, at the colors and the light and the memory of two boys who'd left her shop changed.

Then, with a contented sigh, she swept up the last of the fabric scraps and locked the door behind her, the light of the shop spilling onto the street long after she'd gone.

twenty

. . .

BEFORE THE FIRST pale brush of sun on the rooftops, Prudence was awake, and for once it did not feel like being caught in the sudden teeth of an unseen trap. She lay still beneath the scratchy blanket, hands folded neatly across her chest, listening to the quiet hush of the apartment as it stretched and settled around her. Bryant slept at her side, a gentle, curled warmth that still seemed miraculous after all these months. His breathing was the only sound, soft and regular, more trustworthy than any clock.

She let herself rest there, unmoving, watching the slow fade of the night as it worked itself through the cracks around the window. It was the same window that had overlooked every dawn since they'd come north, but the way the light crept through it felt different this morning —less like a warning, more like a promise.

When the first bell sounded far off in the square, Prudence slipped carefully from the bed, tucking the blanket back around Bryant so the chill would not wake him. She padded across the narrow boards to the stove, struck a match, and coaxed the embers into a sullen, waking glow. She moved with a slowness that was almost deliberate; today, for the first time in years, there was no need to hurry. The work was done. The world would wait.

She prepared breakfast as she always did—bread cut thick, slices of cheese, a small dish of preserves—but even this ritual had changed. She found herself humming as she worked, not the old hymns from childhood but something brighter, tuneless, barely remembered from the common room at the inn. She spooned out an extra portion of honey for Bryant, and when she paused to taste it, she did not chide herself for the indulgence.

Bryant woke just as the kettle began to sing, rubbing his eyes and peering out from the blanket with the solemnity of a child three times his age. "Is it a work day?" he asked, his voice still sticky with sleep.

"Always a work day," Prudence replied, but she said it without bitterness.

He climbed onto his chair, setting Moss the owlcat beside him. The beast yawned extravagantly and then curled back into itself, tail twitching. Bryant regarded the breakfast spread with satisfaction, then set about arranging his wooden figures around the edge of his plate, marshaling them for the day's adventures.

They ate in companionable quiet. Prudence watched Bryant as he ate, saw the new color in his cheeks and the way his hair fell, unruly and light, across his brow. For so long, she had measured his health in tiny increments—counted the ribs, checked the clarity of his skin, monitored every cough and sniffle with a vigilance that bordered on the religious. But today, he simply looked alive. She let herself enjoy it.

After breakfast, she swept the crumbs into a tidy pile and set the dishes in the basin. Bryant wandered off to the far corner, where a small patch of sun had pooled onto the floorboards. He sat with his back against the wall, the wooden figures marching and wheeling before him, their painted faces bright with imagined purpose.

Prudence lingered in the kitchen, but her eyes kept drifting to the stairs that led down to the shop. The idea of it—of what waited there —made her fingers itch. She wiped her hands on her apron, checked on Bryant one last time, then slipped quietly down the stairs.

The shop was silent, but it was not the silence of abandonment or neglect. It was the charged, anticipatory quiet of a stage before the curtain rose, or the hush in a field just before the first snowfall. The sun, still low, fired in through the broad front windows, slanting long golden lines across the floor and catching on the shelves where the new bolts of fabric waited in their bright array.

Prudence paused just inside the door, letting her eyes adjust to the fullness of the light. She saw, with something like pride, the order she had imposed on the chaos—the rainbow rows of fabric, the neat stacks of finished work, the patterns pinned with precision to the corkboard above the table. It was a new world, one she had built thread by thread.

She crossed to the far end of the workbench, where the leftover scraps from her last project were heaped in a loose, multicolored tumble. Among the earth tones and muted grays, a length of ribbon shone: blue, but not the blue of mourning or of twilight. It was bright, almost electric, with a sheen that caught the light and threw it back in little sparks.

She stared at it for a moment, then reached out and let it slide through her fingers. The texture was smooth, almost silken, the color pure and unrepentant. She held it up to the morning light, twisting it this way and that, watching how it shifted from navy to azure to the palest, near-white at its edge.

It was nothing like what she had ever allowed herself before.

Without thinking, Prudence took the scissors from the jar and snipped a length from the bolt. She rolled it between her fingers, then looped it twice, forming a small, perfect bow. It was a child's trick—she remembered her sisters doing it, once, in the back fields of Holderdown—but it felt different now. She pressed the bow flat, then reached up and pinned it to the throat of her plain black dress.

The effect was immediate. She caught her reflection in the glass of the shop door and was startled by the transformation. The black dress was still severe, still the uniform of someone who expected to be overlooked, but the blue ribbon broke it—split the darkness like a vein of something wild, a stripe of sky against a storm.

She stood for a long time, staring at her reflection. In Holderdown, this would have been a scandal. Here, it was only a surprise.

She adjusted the ribbon, making sure the ends hung evenly, then turned and surveyed the shop. The colors on the shelves seemed brighter now, more awake. The sun had climbed higher, and with it, the world outside the windows began to stir—shadows moving across the green, a child running toward the bakery, the faint outline of a wagon at the far edge of the square.

Prudence squared her shoulders. She took a long breath, letting the air fill her all the way to her fingertips, then let it out slow.

She turned once in place, letting the skirt of her dress flare around her legs, then faced the customer mirror. In the glass, she saw herself as she was: not hiding, not waiting, but ready.

She nodded once, a small, decisive gesture.

"It's time," she said, her voice carrying in the empty shop, clear and true.

And for the first time, she believed it.

———

The cold bit sharply at her face, but she barely felt it. The square was mostly empty at first, only a handful of early risers sweeping stoops or ferrying baskets to the bakery. But as she strode down the steps, each one deliberate and noiseless, a current of attention began to build behind her. People noticed the blue at her collar before they noticed her; it was so bright it made her look like a stranger, or a new version of someone they thought they knew.

She ignored the stares. The ground was hard beneath her boots, the grass of the green silvered with frost and edged in gold where the sunlight lapped at it. She set her course directly for the east gate, where she knew—without question, without hope of doubt—that Cornelius would be waiting, his wagon parked in the patch of bare dirt reserved for hawkers and those who had not yet earned the trust of the town.

As she passed the first shops, a subtle hush fell. Dardrad, already out front with his cleaver and a tray of newly cut links, paused mid-sharpening to follow her progress. Darby, his hair still singed from some mishap the day before—stood in the door of the bakery, wiping his hands on a rag and blinking as if not quite sure whether Prudence was a vision or an omen. The bakery windows steamed over with warmth and sugar, and for a moment Prudence thought she saw

Makota's face pressed to the glass, eyes wide and focused, tail a question mark behind her.

Halfway across the green, the town began to wake in earnest. Doors opened, shutters slammed back. Someone called her name—she couldn't tell who, and didn't look back. She marched straight on, head high, heart thudding with a new, steady rhythm. She could feel the word spreading ahead of her, the story of what was about to happen, or maybe just the inevitability of it.

Near the corner of the green, the tea shop's door opened, and Galhani stepped out, her hair still a little wild from sleep, hands wrapped around a cup. She watched Prudence for a long moment, then offered a tiny, almost imperceptible nod—acknowledgment, or benediction, or maybe just the gesture of someone who knew a reckoning when she saw it.

At the edge of the green, Prudence saw Jen emerge from the constable's office. The older woman wore her uniform: black coat buttoned to the chin, the silver badge dull in the morning light, boots shined to a mirror. She leaned on the post for a minute, watching, then fell in behind Prudence, keeping a measured distance. It was not an escort—Jen was not the escorting type—but a silent witness, equal parts readiness and restraint.

Down the lane, the Claw's door was ajar, and Sam stood in the gap, arms folded, shoulder pressed against the weathered wood as if holding the whole building upright by sheer will. She did not smile, but her eyes followed Prudence's path, tracking her like a hawk might track a mouse on a field.

Prudence reached the east gate at the same moment a delivery cart trundled through, the driver slack-jawed at the sudden crowd gathering at the threshold. Bartram was there, too, standing beside the gate post with a length of cord and a sheaf of papers, pretending to inspect the hinge while sneaking glances at the proceedings. He caught Prudence's eye and grinned, then tipped an imaginary hat.

At the smithy, Warren stood like a boulder, arms crossed, one foot propped against the wheel of an ancient plough. He nodded as Prudence passed, the gesture barely more than the lowering of an eyelid, but it radiated approval.

On the stoop of the Weary Head, Minnie and Trevor had stationed themselves side by side, Trevor in an apron too large for him, Minnie with her hair tucked under a cap. They watched Prudence with open, unfiltered attention, like spectators at a parade. Minnie clapped once, quietly, as Prudence drew even with them; Trevor only smiled, his hands lost in the folds of his mother's skirt.

Makota, ever the clever one, had scurried to a spot just outside the bakery where she could see both the gate and the wagon. She stood with a basket slung over her arm, the top lined with a cloth that did nothing to hide the small mountain of pastries beneath. She caught Prudence's eye and raised the basket, as if to say: I'll be here if you need me.

None of them said a word. None needed to. It was enough to be seen, and to know that she was not crossing the green alone.

The last obstacle was the wagon itself. Cornelius had set up his table already, the surface covered with a checkered cloth and a precise array of bottles, each more brightly colored than the last. He stood behind it, hands clasped together, his entire body a study in nervous energy. He wore a coat that had once been fine, but was now faded and patched at the elbows; his mustache drooped, and his eyes darted from Prudence to the gathering crowd and back again.

He saw her coming, and for a second, he looked as if he might turn and run. But there was nowhere to go, and the rules of the road—unspoken but ironclad—dictated that he had to stay, had to face whatever was coming. He straightened, forced a smile, and rested his hands on the table's edge, the knuckles blanching with effort.

Prudence came to a stop two paces from the table, her boots leaving a pair of damp marks in the frost. She met Cornelius's gaze and held it, her own face utterly calm, almost gentle.

Behind her, the square was silent. Every window was filled, every doorway crowded with faces. The air was so still she could hear the faint pop of the frost melting under her heel.

Cornelius cleared his throat, the sound sharp in the quiet. "Good morning, ma'am," he said, voice pitched halfway between deference and dread. "You're out early. I wasn't expecting—"

He trailed off, seeing the ribbon at her collar.

The blue was brighter than any bottle on his table. It caught the morning light, flared, and seemed to draw every eye in the square. Cornelius swallowed, his Adam's apple bobbing once, twice.

Prudence did not respond. She waited, letting the silence stretch, letting him feel the weight of the town's attention.

Then he saw her. Truly *saw* her.

"It's you," he breathed.

"You're not wanted here, you know," she said firmly.

"I didn't know you were here."

"You weren't meant to. This town is *different*. Do you understand me?"

"I've… noticed. Small things."

"And you're preventing it from doing what it's meant to do. What we're meant to do, all of us who live here."

He looked puzzled.

"We help people on their *true* quests. We help them find who they're meant to be, find what they're meant to find. You're distracting them." Her lip curled as she jerked her chin at his tray of wares. "With your false hope. Just like you did in Holderdown."

"I—"

"It's time for you to go."

The man deflated before her eyes. tears began streaming down his cheeks. "I stopped selling the remedies," he said, his throat tight. "I knew… people needed real medicine. But I thought… I mean, people just think it's some fun, a game, like the fortune telling or—"

"They do not. People seek shortcuts, and you offered it to them. Two young men almost died, because they believed in your potions. You are a sickness. You must go. And you must *stop* this." Prudence heard her mother's stern voice come out in her own, and for a moment she almost stopped. *No. It is time.* She squared her shoulders. "You must find something else to do. Something honorable."

"I have no skills," Cornelius sobbed. "My parents threw me out when I was young, nobody would take me as an apprentice… this is all I know." His face was flushed now, his breaths coming in great gulps.

Prudence blinked.

"I was so foolish, back then. In Holderdown. I thought…"

"You thought to take me as your wife," she snapped.

He shook his head, sobbing harder now. "I wanted to rescue you." He wiped his nose and inhaled sharply, struggling to bring his emotions under control. "There was something in you, Prudence." He blinked hard to clear his eyes, perhaps seeing her fully for the first time. "There was color in you. There was *this* in you."

Prudence found herself at a loss for words. "You… could have told me."

"I know, I know. I said I was stupid. Your parents wouldn't let me near you, though. But I know, we should have made a plan." He sniffed again, hard, and then offered a small, watery smile. "I'm glad you're okay."

"It took me a year to find my way here. It was hard."

"I know. I'm glad you did."

The two stared at each other for a long while, while the trade road itself, the entire town, seemed to hold its breath.

"That's a ridiculous outfit," Prudence said at last.

"I know, you don't like the bright colors. I just—"

"I happen to love bright colors," Produce corrected him, although her ton had softened. "What your'e wearing is the suit of a charlatan."

Cornelius looked down at himself. "I know. That's what I am."

"It's not what you *could* be."

twenty-one

. . .

THE WORDS HUNG BETWEEN THEM, visible as breath in the morning cold. For a moment, the two simply regarded each other—Prudence, steady as winter, and Cornelius, trembling in the aftermath of his own undoing. The crowd at the edge of the green had begun to dissolve, the spell of spectacle broken, but the sense of audience lingered: every window, every doorstep, held a watcher, and the trade road's travelers had paused their carts and conversations to see what might come next.

Prudence made her choice. She stepped forward, out of the ruts of expectation, and took Cornelius by the arm. He flinched—then, seeing her expression, allowed it. His sleeve was threadbare, the cuff stained with something blue and sticky. She held on anyway, gripping him above the elbow with the same surety she used for holding unruly fabric at the cutting table.

"Come," she said, and turned him back toward the square.

They walked in silence, the kind that gathered its own gravity as they moved through the thinning ranks of townsfolk. Prudence set a deliberate pace: not a march, not a parade, but a walk of consequence. She kept her head high and her eyes fixed ahead. The blue ribbon at her throat felt newly heavy, as if it had gained an extra dimension since she'd put it on that morning.

Cornelius tried, twice, to speak. Both times, she squeezed his arm and the words retreated, swallowed by the hush. They passed the bakery, where Makota's kits watched from the window, flour dusted on their noses like war paint. They passed the Broken Claw, where Sam leaned in the doorway with her arms crossed and an expression of deep, feline satisfaction. At every stoop, at every open window, people stood and stared—some curious, some openly gloating, a few even sympathetic. Prudence felt it all but let none of it change her stride.

As they neared the inner square, the familiar landscape took on an altered aspect. The grass was still silvered with frost, but now it gleamed, bright and sharp, under the gathering sun. The neat rows of shops—tailor, cobbler, butcher, and more—stood like the teeth of a new world, waiting to see if she would bite back.

She glanced down at herself as they walked. Her dress, though clean and well-kept, looked dim beside the shock of the blue ribbon. The brown wool was the color of resignation, a hue that had suited her in Holderdown, where standing out was a form of self-harm. Here, in the clear air and rising light, it felt like a shroud she had outgrown overnight. The blue at her throat was alive, defiant, a line drawn in the air for everyone to see.

Minnie had said that Prudence would wear through her "old self" soon enough. At the time, it had seemed a gentle taunt, but now she saw it for what it was: a prophecy disguised as small talk.

Cornelius stumbled on the uneven stone outside the tea shop, and Prudence caught him, steadying him with a hand at his back. His coat was thin, barely more than a costume, and as she gripped the fabric she thought she felt, underneath, the flutter of his heart against his ribs.

She did not let go.

They reached the shop in silence. Prudence paused at the threshold, taking in the new arrangement of her window display. The blues and golds caught the light, casting dappled color across the glass. Inside, the space was already lit—Bryant, ever the early riser, had opened the shutters and was perched at the counter, a small army of carved figures arrayed before him like a review of the town's worthies.

Cornelius looked up at the sign over the door—PRUDENCE SIMONSDOTTER, SEAMSTRESS, in clean, steady lettering—and hesitated. She felt the old instinct to pity him, but resisted it. Instead, she pulled open the door and guided him inside, shutting out the stares and the wind.

The bell above the door sang out, high and hopeful.

She released his arm, then stepped around him, the blue at her collar leading the way. "Sit," she commanded, indicating the worktable. "And do not move."

Cornelius obeyed, folding himself small on the bench, his eyes scanning the riot of fabric on the walls with an expression halfway between hunger and dread. Bryant stared at him, unblinking, and Moss the owlcat lifted its head from its basket, sniffed, and then returned to sleep.

Prudence moved to the shelf behind the table, fingers brushing over bolts of cloth, weighing each one in turn. She did not look at Cornelius as she worked, but she felt the weight of his gaze, the raw, almost animal need to be remade.

It was, she realized, the same need she had woken with this morning.

She let her hands linger on the blue—the new blue, not the mourning shade of her past, but the lively, summer-sky color that had first caught her eye in the last trader's wagon. She pulled it down, then added a length of deep navy, a spool of muted silk for trim, and a row of polished wooden buttons. She set them on the table before Cornelius, then stepped back to assess the raw material of the man before her.

He looked up, eyes red but intent. "You're going to—" he began, but she cut him off with a gesture.

"I'm going to make you something useful," she said. "And honest." She reached for her measuring tape, the one she had used to fit a hundred townsfolk and twice as many travelers. "You will not leave this shop until you look like a person who could be trusted with a life."

He flinched at that—at the weight of it—but did not protest.

Prudence circled the table, tape in hand, and began to take his measure. She worked with brisk efficiency, calling out numbers under her breath, making quick notes in the pad Bryant held out to her. As she worked, she let her mind wander ahead, building the man as he could be, not as he was: the width of the shoulders with a little extra, the length of sleeve that would not fray in a sennight, the cut of collar that would sit high and proud.

As she measured, she noticed the hands—Cornelius's hands, thin and dry, the nails bitten to the quick. But the fingers were quick, too, and nimble, with the marks of old ink and more recent stains from whatever colored his bottles. She made a mental note to reinforce the cuffs, to allow for the kind of work that did not show in a ledger but left its story in the seams.

When she finished, Prudence stepped back and regarded him. He looked up at her, not with the old salesman's smirk, but with the uncertain gratitude of a man who knows he is being given a second, perhaps final, chance.

She saw, in that moment, the possibility. Not just of remaking him, but of remaking herself. Of building, from the scraps of the past, something that could stand in the light and not shrink from it.

She nodded, once, to herself. "It will take a candlemark," she said. "Maybe two."

Cornelius tried to speak, but again she cut him off. "Wait. Watch. And do not touch anything."

She set to work. The scissors hissed through the blue, the needle hummed with the old, steady song, and the room filled with the warmth and sound of something being made new.

As she worked, the plan took fuller shape: not just for Cornelius, but for herself, and for the whole shop, and perhaps for the town as well. She would build the future stitch by stitch, color by color, until the old world no longer recognized itself in the mirror.

And for the first time, she was not afraid of being seen.

The shop felt smaller with Cornelius inside it, though it was not for lack of space. He sat, uncertain, on the edge of the worktable's bench, his hands folded in his lap, eyes drawn again and again to the blue fabric Prudence had chosen. He stared at the way it caught the morning light, the sheen and shadow alive even in stillness. His old coat—if you could call it that—had collapsed around him, the battered shoulders drooping lower with every tick of the wall clock.

Bryant peered out from behind the counter, two fingers pressed to the rim, owlcat perched at his feet. The boy's face was bright with curiosity, but there was a wariness too—a way of watching that measured the stranger as both potential and problem. Moss seemed to share the sentiment, flicking its ears in restless intervals.

Prudence ignored Cornelius for a time, letting him stew in the sense of being outclassed by a room full of thread. She cut the first lengths of the navy wool with a series of crisp, decisive snips. The sound was surgical, unhurried, and it made Cornelius's back straighten as though the scissors might find their way into his own seams.

After a few minutes of this, she set down the fabric and regarded him with a narrow gaze. "You remember my son," she said.

It was not a question. Cornelius looked over, blinking once, twice, before finding Bryant's face across the shop. "He was a baby, last I saw," he managed. "He's grown."

Prudence nodded, her lips tight. "He remembers nothing of Holderdown. Or of you." She let the words settle, then added, "It's better that way."

Bryant did not move from his place at the counter, but his eyes did not leave Cornelius. Prudence caught the boy's gaze and nodded, a silent reassurance. Moss the owlcat chirred, low and uncertain, but relaxed when Bryant reached down to stroke its head.

Cornelius cleared his throat, awkward in the silence. "You could have had me run out," he said. "Or worse."

Prudence shrugged, the motion smooth as folding linen. "Why waste the effort?" She began to measure him, brisk and professional, her tape sliding over his shoulders and around his chest, down the length of each arm and across the small of his back. Her hands never lingered, but the touch was thorough, as if she meant to rebuild him from the inside out.

As she worked, she spoke—not to him, but to Bryant, who listened with a solemnity that made him seem twice his age. "There was once a peddler," she said, her tone even, "who thought he could change the world with quick words and cheap tricks. He wandered from village to village, promising health and happiness to anyone with the coin to spare." She measured Cornelius's waist, then the span from collarbone to navel, the tape whispering over threadbare fabric.

"He became famous for his bottles," Prudence continued, "and for his voice, which could sell wind to a sailor. But wherever he went, he left something behind—disappointment, mostly, but sometimes worse. Sometimes, people believed him too much, and when the lie wore off, they blamed him for the pain." Her hands paused at Cornelius's wrist, where the skin was puckered with old scars, some faded, some fresh.

Bryant leaned forward, mouth slightly open. "What happened to him?" he asked.

Prudence smiled, but it was the smile of someone who'd seen the punchline before the joke was ever told. "He kept running, always ahead of the last angry crowd, until one day he ran out of places that didn't know his face. He tried to sell new tricks, but no one bought them. Eventually, he found himself alone, his only customer the echo of his own voice."

Cornelius said nothing, but his jaw clenched tight, and his eyes flinched away from the boy's.

Prudence finished the measurements, then gathered the cut pieces and began pinning them into shape on the form. "He could have vanished," she said, "but instead, he tried something new. He tried listening, instead of talking. Tried helping, instead of selling. It was hard, and he failed at first, but eventually he found that easing people's suffering—honestly, and with patience—brought more joy than all the quick coin in the world." She glanced up at Cornelius, her eyes hard. "The lesson stuck."

Bryant nodded, digesting this. Moss mewled, unimpressed, but happy to nap on the warm wood of the countertop.

Cornelius shifted in his seat, his hands restless. He stared at the half-assembled jacket, the blue brighter than any coat he'd ever owned. "Is that part of the job?" he asked. "Telling stories while you work?"

Prudence set the form upright, turning it so the unfinished jacket faced the window. "It is," she said. "Stories make the work go faster. They also make the work matter." She set to work on the sleeves, her fingers guiding the needle with unconscious speed.

As she worked, Bryant wandered over, settling himself at the far end of the bench, careful not to cross the invisible line between safe and uncertain. He watched every movement, eyes flicking from the thread to the scissors to the pile of buttons waiting their turn.

Cornelius tried to make himself small, but he could not help the way his eyes lingered on the blue. "I've never had new clothes," he admitted. "Not really. Always just… patched or borrowed."

"Everyone starts somewhere," Prudence replied. "The important thing is where you finish."

The story, it seemed, had more than one lesson.

As the 'marks passed, the shop changed. The light grew stronger, the sun inching higher, casting new patterns through the windows. Prudence worked faster and faster, her hands blurring as she pieced the jacket together, then the trousers, then a vest in the same deep blue with a subtle stripe of gray at the pocket. The pieces came together with improbable speed, the seams so straight and true that even Cornelius—who knew little of clothes, and less of care—could tell this was work above the ordinary.

Bryant watched, wide-eyed, as the fabric seemed to move by itself, the thread spooling out in perfect lengths, the buttons rolling across the table to land exactly where they belonged. Even Moss, awakened by the change in the air, leapt to the floor and watched from below, tail lashing as if hunting a mouse made of light.

As Prudence finished the jacket, she turned it on the form, letting the blue catch every angle of the morning sun. She stepped back, folded her arms, and regarded her work.

Cornelius stared, mouth open. "It's… beautiful," he said, the word strange in his mouth, as if he'd never said it before.

Prudence nodded once, sharply. "It will look better on you. Try it."

He hesitated, then shrugged off the old coat and reached for the new one. His hands shook, but he managed to slip the sleeves over his arms, to fasten the buttons with awkward grace. The fabric settled onto his shoulders as if it belonged there—like armor, but lighter. He looked down at himself, then up at Bryant, who was grinning now, wild and wide.

Prudence fetched the vest and passed it to him, then the new trousers, soft but sturdy, with pockets deep enough to hide a fortune or a secret. She pointed him to the back of the shop, where a changing screen shielded a small mirror.

He changed, and when he re-emerged, the difference was shocking. The blue set off his pale skin, the cut of the coat straightened his posture, made him look taller, braver. The vest hugged his ribs, the sleeves ended exactly at the wrist, the collar framed his jaw in a way that made him seem almost dignified. Even Bryant whistled, and Moss, who had never shown the stranger much respect, came over to sniff at his new shoes.

Cornelius looked at Prudence, eyes damp but clear. "I don't know how to thank you," he said.

Prudence shrugged. "You can start by wearing them with honor. And by not going back to the trade."

He nodded, unable to speak.

Bryant watched the exchange, then looked at his mother with something close to awe. "You made a new man," he said, not a question but a verdict.

Prudence met his gaze, her own eyes gentler now. "We all get a second chance," she said. "If we want it."

The shop was full of light, the blue of the jacket and the ribbon at her own throat almost humming with the promise of something better. For a moment, everything else fell away—the old town, the old rules, the old failures.

Prudence turned back to the workbench, hands already searching for the next project. "We have a call to make," she said, not to Bryant or Cornelius, but to herself. "There's someone who needs to see this." Then she paused. "Hmm."

The suit she'd made for Cornelius was better than anything he'd worn in his life, and it made him look like someone you'd ask for directions or trust with your secret. But she saw, with a tailor's critical eye, the way the shoulders set a little stiff, the armholes just half a finger's width too tight. Good enough for a customer, maybe, but not for the next part of his life.

She reached out and plucked the lapel, tugging Cornelius closer. "Off," she said, with the briskness of a doctor, and he wriggled free of the jacket and vest, laying them on the table with a tenderness usually reserved for objects of worship. Bryant ran his hands over the blue, delighted by its smoothness, its weight.

Prudence turned the jacket inside out. She took up her needle, but as she began to thread it, something in the air changed. The workroom, usually warm and bright, grew warmer, brighter; the colors in the sunlight burned more sharply against the plain stone of the walls. The air shivered with potential.

She did not need to check whether Bryant saw it too—he always did. The boy's eyes grew wide, and he reached out as if he could touch the very light that danced around his mother's hands.

Prudence worked with a speed that would have startled the old women in Holderdown. The needle flashed, the thread unwinding in perfect lines, the scissors snipping stray ends before they even dared to unravel. She stitched new seams, let out the shoulders, ran a double row along the hem of the jacket and the cuffs of the shirt. She added three pockets to the inside, each sized for something specific: a notebook, a glass vial, a bundle of dried herbs. She lined the collar in a slightly different blue—one so close to the original that only a connoisseur would notice, but just enough to set it off from the rest. It was, as Bartram would have said, a coat for a man who meant business.

All the while, she told her story.

"The peddler," she said, "found work in a new town—one where no one recognized him. He took a room above the baker's, and every morning he swept the stoop and helped carry in the flour sacks. He didn't sell anything, at first. Just listened, and watched, and learned."

Cornelius listened, hunched forward, the ghost of a smile lurking at the corner of his mouth. Bryant sat cross-legged on the floor, watching the stitches race around the edge of the jacket.

"Soon enough, someone came to the peddler for help," Prudence continued, her voice a calm counterpoint to the rhythm of the sewing. "An old woman with joints so stiff she couldn't open her hand. She'd been to the doctor and to the priest, but nothing helped. The peddler made her a tea, just dried leaves and a drop of honey, and showed her how to soak her hands in warm water before bed. The pain got better, and after a while she could hold her grandchild again."

She finished the seam and set the jacket aside. She picked up the vest and made quick work of the loose threads, then turned to the trousers. With every new line, she spoke another part of the story.

"The peddler helped a farmer, too, whose son had fallen and cut his leg on a rusty plough. The wound was angry and hot, and everyone said the boy would lose the limb. But the peddler made a poultice—nothing special, just salt and clean cloth, but he changed the bandage every day, and after a sennight the wound was healed, and the boy could walk again."

Bryant, who had never heard this version of the story, leaned closer. "Why didn't he use a potion?" he asked.

Prudence smiled, threading a needle with a new color, this one the color of fresh milk. "Because he learned the potions never worked. Only the care did. Sometimes, it takes failing to know what's real."

She finished the trousers, turned them right side out, and ran her hands over the seams to check for any place that might chafe or catch. She found none.

She stood and beckoned to Cornelius, who approached the work-table with a reverence usually reserved for church or library. She handed him the trousers, then the vest, then the jacket. "Go," she said, jerking her chin toward the changing screen. "Try it all together."

Cornelius disappeared behind the fabric, fumbling with buttons and laces, but when he stepped out a few minutes later, the change was complete. He looked nothing like the man who had arrived at the shop that morning; he looked nothing like the charlatan who once sold his hopes and failures in a bottle. He looked, for the first time in his life, like he belonged in a place where people would remember his name.

The blue of the jacket made his eyes less shifty, more searching. The vest brought out the shape of his torso, and the trousers hung clean and true from hip to ankle. The shoes—Prudence had snagged a pair from Bartram's sale bin—were already broken in, but they shined with a fresh polish that made them seem new. Cornelius stood taller, hands at his sides, head up.

Bryant clapped, a sound so quick and sure it startled the owlcat from its nap. Even Moss seemed impressed, twining between Cornelius's ankles before resuming its post by the hearth.

Prudence allowed herself a moment to admire the transformation, then stepped forward and adjusted the collar of the jacket. She fussed with the set of the shoulder, then brushed a bit of lint from the sleeve. "Not bad," she said, her voice almost fond.

Cornelius looked at her, then at the boy, and something uncoiled in his chest. "Thank you again," he said, the words both heavier and lighter than he expected.

Prudence nodded, her lips thin but no longer pressed so hard together. "You'll need a coat for the road," she said, and handed him the last piece she'd made—a soft overcoat in charcoal gray, lined with blue at the cuffs. "It'll keep you warm, and the pockets won't lose your coin or your pride."

He shrugged it on, and it fit perfectly.

Bryant stepped forward, all solemnity. "Will you go back to selling things?" he asked.

Cornelius shook his head. "No," he said, the answer simple, final. "I think I'd rather help, now. If you'll let me."

Prudence tilted her head, as if she'd expected no less. "We're going to see Galhani," she said, reaching for her own coat and pinning the blue ribbon in place. "She'll know how to put you to use."

Cornelius followed her to the door, but paused on the threshold, looking back at the workroom one last time. It was hard not to feel the magic still thrumming in the walls, in the air, in the very seams of his new self. He thought of the story, the peddler who failed and then found a new way, and he understood, suddenly, that it wasn't just a story at all.

It was a pattern—a promise that even the worst stitch-ups could be remade, given time and the right hands.

Prudence opened the door, and the winter sun shone straight through the blue at her neck, lighting up her face like dawn.

"Let's go," she said, and the three of them stepped out into the street, into the cold, into the waiting world.

Behind them, the shop exhaled, its work for the day done, and settled itself for the next story.

They walked the short distance to the herbalist's shop in silence, the winter air biting sharper in the moments after leaving the warmth of the workroom. Prudence led, the blue at her throat a beacon. Cornelius followed, one hand absently gripping the cuff of his new sleeve, as if to make sure it hadn't vanished. Bryant trailed just behind, eyes full of the possibility that anything—really anything—could happen next.

The herbalist's shop was built into the stone wall of what had once been a granary. Inside, it felt more like a burrow than a business: shelves stacked to the ceiling with jars, bundles of dried stems hanging from the rafters, the air thick with the honeyed, sharp tang of yarrow and thyme. The morning sun managed only a few slivers through the oiled paper in the window, casting everything in a soft, herbal gloom.

Galhani herself stood at the counter, grinding a mortar with both hands, her whole body swaying to the slow rhythm. Her face and wrists were dusted in green, and the streak of yellow powder in her hair suggested she had been at this since before dawn. She did not look up when they entered, but Prudence knew better than to take it for inattention.

Bryant stepped inside first, and the gnome flashed him a quick, toothy smile before returning to her work. She let them stand for a minute, sizing up the whole party with the corner of her eye. Only when the last of the powder was tapped into its little brown jar did she set down the pestle and turn.

"Well, this is a change," Galhani said, voice as dry as the bundles overhead. "You've got a new man, Pru?"

Cornelius blinked, and Prudence caught the faintest flicker of a smile in Galhani's eyes.

"Not new," Prudence said, "but improved."

Galhani hopped down from her stool and padded around the counter, her hands clasped behind her back. She circled Cornelius once, examining the fit of the jacket, the shine of the buttons, the way he kept his hands tucked out of sight. "That's a proper coat," she said, nodding approval. "But is the man worth the cloth?"

Cornelius flushed, but held his ground. "I want to learn," he said, voice firm despite the tremor in it. "I want to help. I want to do it right, this time."

Galhani eyed him up and down, then glanced at Prudence. "You vouch for him?"

Prudence hesitated—long enough for it to count—but then nodded. "He has more to prove than most," she said. "That can be useful."

Galhani turned back to Cornelius, her eyes narrowing. "You ever worked a real cure? Or just sold dreams in a bottle?"

Cornelius opened his mouth, but nothing came out.

Bryant stepped forward, his small voice clear in the hush of the shop. "He knows how to listen," the boy said, and Galhani's gaze snapped to him.

Moss the owlcat, who had followed at Bryant's heels, sniffed the air, then hopped onto the counter and began to nose around a tray of drying roots. Galhani let the animal be, then returned to the matter at hand.

"You want to help?" she said. "Start by cleaning the tools. Then you can restock the shelves. After that, we'll see if you can remember more than two kinds of leaf at a time."

Cornelius nodded, relief and purpose mingling on his face. "Thank you," he said, and Galhani waved him toward the back, where a battered tin basin and a stack of grimy mortars waited for attention.

Prudence watched as Cornelius took up the first mortar and set to scrubbing. His movements were careful, intent, not the hurried motion of someone eager to finish, but the deliberate, patient action of someone who knew he was being tested.

Galhani stood beside Prudence, arms folded. "It's not going to be easy," she said, quiet enough that Bryant wouldn't hear. "He's made a mess of things, hasn't he?"

"We all have," Prudence replied. "But he's trying."

Galhani nodded, her sharp features softening. "I'll watch him. You know I will."

Prudence smiled, and for a long moment the two women watched Cornelius work, each lost in her own thoughts.

Bryant wandered the shop, fingers trailing over jars and bundles, his nose wrinkling at the unfamiliar scents. He found a sprig of dried lavender and held it up to Moss, who sniffed it once and sneezed.

The work of the world continued. Galhani called out instructions, her voice alternately sharp and encouraging, and Cornelius listened with a seriousness that bordered on reverence. He asked questions when he didn't know, and tried again when he got it wrong. The gnome corrected him—sometimes with a laugh, sometimes with a click of her tongue—but each time, Cornelius met the correction with gratitude.

Prudence lingered in the doorway, unwilling to leave just yet. She watched as Cornelius began to sort the freshly cleaned mortars by size, then wiped down the counter and stacked the empty jars in neat rows. Bryant settled at a low stool, drawing lines in the dust and humming a tune under his breath.

After a time, Galhani turned to Prudence and nodded. "He'll do," she said. "For now."

Prudence dipped her head in thanks, then looked at Cornelius, who met her gaze and smiled. It was not the grin of a salesman, or the simper of a man hoping to charm his way out of trouble. It was a true, clean smile—a beginning, not an ending.

She closed the door gently behind her, leaving the warmth and scent of the shop behind. The blue ribbon at her neck fluttered in the breeze, bright as a flag.

On the walk back to her own shop, Prudence felt the world open up: the sky was higher than before, the morning lighter, the square full of quiet possibility.

She thought of the story she had told—of the peddler who learned to listen, and the healer who was born from honest work. She thought of Cornelius, now at the start of something hard and good, and of Bryant, who would never know the old world's narrowness.

She thought, for a moment, of her own mother, and what she might say if she could see her daughter now—alive, in color, at the heart of a place that had needed her as much as she'd needed it.

Prudence smiled, and let herself imagine all the stories yet to be made.

And so, in the gray of the town's morning, with the blue at her collar and the memory of work well done, Prudence Simonsdotter began again.

twenty-two

. . .

PRUDENCE WOKE IN THE HALF-DARK, the world holding its breath just before first bell. It was too early even for Bryant, who curled beneath the quilt in a tangle of limbs and small, private dreams. The apartment, high above the shop and quiet as a church, shivered once when Prudence sat up. The cold had crept in during the night, frosting the panes and silvering the edges of every shadow. She listened a moment, confirming that Bryant was truly asleep, then slid from the bed, feet bracing against the boards with the muscle memory of all her prior mornings.

There was something ceremonial about it, the way she moved through the rooms at this time—so much so that Prudence caught herself humming, low in her throat, the old melody that always came when she was about to do something final. She set the kettle to heat, sliced bread for the day's breakfast, and laid out two plates, though she did not expect the boy to wake before she left.

When the first bell rang, Prudence was already dressed. Not in the old uniform of mourning, nor even the inky, proper black she had brought north. Today she wore a slate gray with a faint, honest blue at the hem, the kind of color that didn't just defy notice but made a virtue of it. She pinned her ribbon at the collar, neat and true, and allowed herself a brief, private smile at the reflection in the window above the sink.

The square outside was empty and icy, the green caught in a web of thin, white grass that would vanish as soon as the sun climbed. She unlocked the shop door with a practiced flick of her wrist, and the hinges, newly oiled, opened without complaint. A frigid blast rushed over her, carrying with it the memory of the last days of winter, and the promise that something better was on its way.

The shop, in this light, looked almost luminous. The bolts of fabric she'd arranged the sennight before—ochre and pine, sea-blue and gold —leaned toward the windows, eager for day. The counter gleamed, its new varnish catching the rising light, and every shelf had been fussed over until it looked as if it had always belonged. Prudence ran her hand over the workbench, feeling the grain and the knots, the little scars from her more desperate repairs. It was all in order.

She took inventory, a ritual as necessary as breathing. Thread, needles, chalk, shears. A roll of ribbon for a commission she meant to finish by noon. Two new pieces pinned on the dummy, waiting only for a sleeve or a final tuck. She found herself standing in the center of the shop, hands at her sides, for a long minute, just listening to the clock on the wall and the faint hiss of the kettle in the apartment above.

It was a world she had made, and for the first time, she was glad to live in it.

The moment stretched, then broke: a sound from the street, the clip of unfamiliar boots. Prudence stepped to the window, peered out through the fogged glass, and saw a wagon at the far end of the green. It was not the battered, painted cart of the old Cornelius—the one that had looked like a dare and a joke all at once. This was different: plainer, but in its plainness, more dignified. The wheels were sound, the canvas taut, and the horse—borrowed, most likely, but well-fed— stamped at the edge of the walk, eager to be on with it.

Cornelius stood beside the wagon, not quite at attention but not slouching either. He wore the new clothes Prudence had made: a deep blue coat, clean and unassuming, trimmed at the cuffs with a bit of pale gray thread that would go unnoticed by all but those who cared to look for such things. His trousers matched, but better still was the lined cloak he wore over it, fastened with a simple wooden clasp. No hat, no gaudy cravat, no trace of the showman she remembered from Holderdown and all the months that followed.

He looked, in the most surprising way, like he might actually be taken seriously.

Prudence did not rush to meet him. She watched from behind the glass, careful not to draw attention. She saw him check the wagon's harness, then the bundles stacked in the bed. There were no colored bottles this time, no mysterious pouches of dust or glittering powders. Only the goods he had been trusted with: bundles of dried herbs, boxes of Galhani's teas, packets of actual, honest remedies. Everything neatly labeled in Cornelius's new, careful hand.

She let him wait, as much to test his patience as her own. Only when the sun had cracked the eastern rooftops did she unlock the door and step out, pulling her shawl close against the lingering cold.

The square had begun to wake. There were more people than she expected: Bartram, stopping in the middle of his walk, boots planted wide, arms crossed and face bright with curiosity; Jen, leaning against the bakery's stoop, arms crossed and a look of calculated boredom hiding something keener; Makota's kits, perched on the bakery steps, their heads cocked as if listening for news. More faces, in windows and behind curtains, watching but pretending not to.

The air held a kind of charge—less than a spectacle, more than routine. It was not every day that you sent a snake-oil salesman on the road with the blessing of the town he'd nearly ruined.

Prudence made her way across the green, her boots crunching through the last of the frost. She stopped just short of Cornelius, who stood straighter as she approached. There was a smile on his face— nervous, but genuine.

"Up early," he said, and then, as if rehearsed, "Thank you for meeting me."

Prudence nodded, allowing herself the smallest concession of a smile. "It's your last day here. Didn't want you to forget anything."

Cornelius looked down, hands twisting at his sides, then gestured to the wagon. "It's all there. Galhani said I could take the lot, provided I send back a proper ledger. I left an extra set of coin at the tea shop for her, in case the first didn't cover it." He looked at her, searching for any sign of doubt. "I mean to do it right, this time."

Prudence considered, then inclined her head. "If you didn't, you'd have Jen chasing you before you made the road bend." She jerked her chin at the constable, who raised an eyebrow and gave a lazy salute.

Cornelius tried to laugh, but it came out as a cough. "I believe that."

Prudence reached into her coat pocket and pulled out a small bundle, tied with a blue string. She held it out, and after a moment Cornelius took it, careful not to break the wrapping. "It's from Galhani," she said. "Extra for the road. Something for fevers, something for sleep, and something for homesickness, which I suspect you'll need more than the rest."

Their hands touched, just for a second. Cornelius's were cold, but steady.

He tucked the bundle away. "Thank you," he said, and the words were so plain, so untouched by the old salesman's varnish, that Prudence felt herself soften.

They stood together a while, not talking, just looking at the wagon and the street beyond. The sun was up now, the green alive with light and the faint, rising chatter of a town waking to good news. The square's drama had never been so subtle, but Prudence saw it in every face: the way Jen let herself smile for real, the way Bartram stood a little taller, the way even the bakery's window steamed a little brighter in the cold.

Cornelius glanced at her, then at the wagon, then back again. "I never thought there'd be dignity in this," he said, voice so low Prudence had to lean in to hear it. "In honesty, I mean."

Prudence regarded him. "It suits you better than you think."

He laughed, not the wild, reckless bark of old, but something smaller, a seed of what might one day become genuine joy.

"I should go," he said, and she nodded.

He climbed onto the wagon with more grace than she expected, took the reins, and set his eyes on the gate. Before he left, he looked back at the green, at the small cluster of townsfolk, and then directly at Prudence.

"Thank you," he said again, and this time she believed it.

He touched the brim of his imaginary hat, then flicked the reins, and the horse started forward. The wagon rolled over the frost, past the bakery, past the tailor's, past the rows of shops where the old world had tried, and failed, to keep its grip.

Prudence watched him all the way to the gate, and even after he'd turned the corner and disappeared, she stayed there, hands in her pockets, face pointed toward the brightening day.

She felt, for the first time since arriving, that the town belonged to her—not as a possession, but as a fact of being. She belonged to it, and it to her, and the space between was something that could be filled with color, and hope, and all the work she had left to do.

She let the thought settle, then turned, making her way back across the green to the shop she had made her own.

The day would be busy, but for now, there was time to savor the change.

After the wagon's shadow slipped from the square, the town seemed to release a long-held breath. The silence was not the cold, brittle hush of winter but something softer, relieved and a little amazed at itself. On the green, the frost had begun to melt in the sunlight, and the people who had watched the departure allowed themselves to linger, as if unsure what to do with the sudden, untroubled day.

Prudence remained at the center of it all, arms folded, eyes on the road as though she expected Cornelius to reverse course at any moment. When, after a full count of sixty, he did not reappear, she turned—just in time to catch the first warm note of laughter from the bakery steps. Makota's kits were already rolling in the grass, a tumble of fur and limbs, while Bartram leaned against a fencepost, his whole body grinning.

Galhani appeared next, materializing from somewhere near the tea shop, two delicate cups cradled in her gnomish hands. She crossed the green with brisk, measured steps and stopped beside Prudence, her head not quite reaching Prudence's elbow.

"I saw you watch him," Galhani said, offering up the cup. "You were the only one who looked sorry to see him go."

Prudence accepted the tea, the heat and scent—chamomile and a curl of something citrusy—doing more to settle her than a night's worth of sleep. "I'm not sorry," she said, but her voice softened around the edges. "Just… surprised. It felt final."

Galhani sipped her own tea, peering up with a shrewdness that made Prudence feel seen, through and through. "It was," the gnome said. "He won't come back. Not the way he was."

They stood in companionable silence, drinking tea and watching as the square repopulated itself. Jen ambled over from the bakery, her stride relaxed and loose, helmet still tucked under one arm. She stopped at a polite distance, then closed it with two steps and a grin.

"Never thought I'd see the day," Jen said, her voice carrying across the green. "A snake shedding its skin for something better."

Prudence considered the image. "Maybe it's the town," she said. "Maybe it makes people change."

Bartram, overhearing, made his way over and joined the little circle. He eyed Prudence's ribbon—now vivid in the sunlight, electric against the subtle blue of her dress—and gave a little bow. "Transformation suits this place," he said, "and you." He reached out, as if to take her hand, then thought better of it and settled for a nod.

Jen's attention flicked to Prudence's neck, then to the gnome's tea, then back. "You're not wearing black," she noted, not quite able to keep the pleasure from her tone.

"It's a work day," Prudence replied. "And there's work to do." She lifted the cup in salute.

Galhani looked between them, then raised her own. "To honest work, and to the end of false magic."

Bartram laughed, the sound as round and rich as the loaves in Makota's window. "Real magic's more fun anyway," he said. "Ask anyone here."

Jen, who had never been much for poetry, said, "The town feels better. Stronger. Like it used to."

Prudence thought of the stories she'd heard about the Icosagon, about how the town always seemed one or two people away from falling apart, or from becoming the place it was meant to be. She looked around: at the way the frost had given way to grass, at the bright spots in every window, at the easy way neighbors now drifted into each other's business.

"There's a pattern to it," Prudence said, half to herself.

Bartram cocked an eyebrow. "You're the expert," he said.

The four of them stood, watching the town come back to itself. Galhani's tea was gone first—she drained her cup with a flourish, then bowed to the group. "I'll see you all tonight," she said, and vanished in the direction of her shop.

Bartram lingered for a word with the kits, who by now had conquered the bakery stoop, and then set off toward the western lane, whistling a tune that trailed behind him like a bright scarf.

Jen stayed a moment longer, her eyes crinkling in the corners. "You know," she said, "I kept my sword loose all morning. Expected trouble."

"And?" Prudence asked.

Jen shrugged, but there was pride in it. "Didn't need it." She eyed the green. "Maybe you were right. Maybe change is what's needed."

She left with a wave, boots crunching through the thawed grass, and Prudence was alone again, though it didn't feel that way.

She wandered back to her shop, letting herself savor the walk. The morning light poured through the windows, and the colors inside seemed twice as bold for having stood witness to the day. She opened the door and stepped in, feeling for the first time that she was entering something of her own making, not just a shelter against the world.

She threw open both windows—letting in the cold, but also the new air—and stood in the patch of sunlight by her bench. She traced her fingers along the bright bolts of fabric, and thought of all the things she could make now, all the days to come.

Bryant came in, shoes muddy, hands sticky with some treat from the bakery. He looked up at Prudence, then at the window, then at the ribbon at her collar.

"Did you see the wagon?" he asked, eyes wide.

"I did," Prudence said. "It's gone now."

Bryant nodded, as if that settled something. He climbed onto the stool, feet swinging, and set about arranging his little wooden figures in a parade along the edge of the table.

Prudence watched him, then lifted him up, holding him to the window. "See that?" she said, pointing down the road where the wagon had disappeared. "That's where people go when they're ready to be better."

Bryant squinted, searching for a trace of blue, then nodded. "Do you think he'll come back?"

Prudence considered. "Maybe. If he does, he'll have something to offer. Something real."

Bryant grinned. "Like you?"

"Like us," Prudence said.

She held him there, in the sunlight, for a long time—watching the green, and the road, and the world beyond, all of it shimmering with the promise of change.

And when the bell on the door finally rang, announcing a new customer, she was ready.

twenty-three

· · ·

AT FIRST BELL, the shop was as silent as a church at midnight. Even the street beyond, usually haunted by children's squabbles and the two-dozen sounds of daily bread, offered only the muted hush of a town catching its breath between seasons. Prudence stood at the window, watching the world shiver in its sleep, the blue-gray of the dawn blurring the line between snow and sky.

She waited until Bryant's sleepy face pressed against her apron, his hair still bent in the peculiar shape it took every night. He looked up, owlcat tucked under one arm, and said, "It's today, isn't it?"

Prudence nodded, not trusting her voice.

Bryant wriggled his way into his boots, then stood, uncertain, in the little entry that divided home from world. Prudence crouched, buttoned his coat, and smoothed the sleeve—knowing as she did that by noon he would have found a way to rip it on a fence or tree or the simple act of running. It was, she supposed, the price of freedom.

Cole's oldest boy waited in the square, his red ears bright against the cold. When Bryant joined him, the pair set off at once, trailed by a cloud of intent: there would be garden work, and perhaps a lesson on apples or potatoes, but mostly there would be the serious business of being out in the world, unchaperoned.

Prudence watched them go. When the last echo of their voices faded, she closed the door, locked it, and turned the sign: OUT, read the front, but the word inside the shop was BEGINNING.

She did not light the lamps. The east window filled the room with a slow, blue-brightening light, and for a long moment she simply stood in it, letting the cold tingle through her fingers. The silence was complete—not even the pop and crackle of the stove, which she'd let burn down on purpose.

The shop looked different in this time of day. The bench and bolts of fabric, the racks of colored thread, the iron and glass of the treadle machine, all were clear and clean, as though waiting for an act of magic or violence.

Prudence moved to the worktable, and from beneath it drew out a length of heavy linen, the color of a lake on a cloudless afternoon. It was the dress she'd worn to Galhani's ceremony, two seasons back, a dress unlike anything she had owned before or since. She had made it in a fit of defiance—blue, with gold thread at the collar, and a skirt that flared just enough to catch the wind. She had worn it that day, endured the compliments, the stares, the way even Jen had whistled approval. Then she'd folded it away and not touched it since.

She spread the dress on the table, smoothing the wrinkles with both hands. In the cold light it seemed almost luminous, the blue so rich it made her fingers ache to work it. She stared at it a long time, then took the scissors and began to cut.

It was not an act of destruction but of translation—taking the thing that had once been a message to others, and making it into something for herself. She cut along the seams, following the paths she had stitched in secrecy. The thread, fine as hair and strong as wire, parted with a sigh, and she laid the pieces out in a pattern of her own invention.

The morning passed in silence, save for the small sounds of work: the hiss of scissors, the low rumble of the machine, the click of pins as she anchored the shapes in place. She worked fast, but not hurried, and as the sun crept higher the blue panels began to shift, becoming less like a dress and more like the raw material of a possibility.

Once, when she looked up, she caught her own reflection in the shop's front window. The light had changed—the sky a hard white now, the edges of the world starker and more honest. She barely recognized herself: the hair loose around her shoulders, the face sharp with focus, the hands alive with purpose. There was a flush in her cheeks she had not seen since before Holderdown.

She set the pieces aside and reached for a bolt of green—deep, new, a color she had been saving without knowing why. She cut a long, slender panel, then fitted it to the blue, letting the two colors find each other at the seam. The effect was immediate: the blue grew deeper, the green brighter, each alive in the other's presence. Prudence found herself smiling, a thin and private thing.

She worked straight through noon, forgetting to eat, stopping only to drink a single cup of tea gone cold before she even noticed it. The sun drifted west, the light in the shop turning from silver to gold to the thin, pink haze that comes just before nightfall.

With every 'mark, the dress—or what would become the dress— grew more itself and less its old self. She added panels of a lighter blue at the hem, then a band of gold at the waist, and finally, when she was almost done, a small circle of embroidery at the throat: needle and thread, intertwined, stitched in white. She had meant it as a secret, something only she would notice, but as she finished it she saw that it was the heart of the whole thing.

The thread she used for the embroidery was strange—it shimmered in the lamplight, and seemed to move of its own accord, looping into perfect circles, never once tangling. She realized, as she worked, that the shop itself was awake, watching her, lending its quiet, persistent energy to every motion. The pins stood ready, the fabrics seemed to fall exactly where she needed them, and even the old machine, which so often caught and stuttered, ran smooth and silent.

She paused, hands in her lap, and listened to the shop breathe. For the first time in months, she did not feel the urge to run, or to hide, or to make herself small. She felt, instead, the rightness of the work, and the way the light and the fabric and her own body all seemed to fit together.

As the shadows lengthened across the floor, Prudence stood and slipped out of her old dress. She stepped into the new one, the blue and green cool and crisp against her skin. She fastened the buttons, smoothed the panels, and turned, once, in the center of the shop.

The skirt flared just so, catching the last of the sunset and sending a ripple of color across the floor. The bodice fit perfectly, the sleeves ending at the exact point where her hands began. The embroidery at the throat was a tiny, shining secret, a promise she had made to herself and kept.

She looked in the window again, and this time she saw not a stranger, but the woman she had always been, waiting for her chance.

The lanterns were lit outside now; the world beyond was cold and dark. Prudence stood in the center of her shop, the blue and green of her dress brighter than any lamp, and felt the day settle around her like a second skin.

She did not know what would come next. But whatever it was, she would be ready.

———

By midmorning, the square had taken note. It was not the usual absence—Prudence had shut herself up before, for daylong commissions or difficult repairs—but this was different. The shades were drawn, the sign hung cockeyed and uncorrected, and the only movement from within was the occasional flicker of color as a sleeve or a scrap of ribbon passed the front window, never attached to a person.

Makota was the first to notice. She stood at the bakery's side table, her arms up to the elbows in dough, and her tail looping a slow question mark behind her. She peered out through the beaded curtain that shielded the kitchen from the main shop. Through the fog of the rising bread and the warmth that made even the coldest mornings bearable, she watched the tailor's window with a steady, speculative focus. The contrast between the frost outside and the blues that sometimes flashed within left her unsettled.

"Is she closed?" her eldest kit asked, perched on a sack of flour.

"Not closed," Makota said, dusting her whiskers with the back of one hand. "Just… busy."

The kit's eyes widened, ears forward. "Magic?"

Makota grinned, kneaded the dough with extra force. "Maybe. Or maybe she's just making something the rest of us haven't got the patience for."

Cole, next door at the grocery, was stacking apples into one of the wide wooden crates he kept for deliveries. The produce had come in fresher than usual, and for once he was proud to display it—crimson skins against the pale, gritty blue of the day. He finished the stack, wiped his palms on the apron, and glanced up at the tailor's window.

Nothing. No movement, no sign, not even the usual shadow of a figure behind the curtain. Cole frowned, absently re-arranging the apples for a better balance of red and green.

He debated whether to check on her. He imagined walking across the square, hands in pockets, whistling something casual, and peering through the glass as if he'd just happened by. But Prudence was not the type to welcome interruptions, and besides, she had left Bryant with his family, so he assumed it was not an emergency.

He settled for watching, every now and again, until his wife called from the back: "You're going to wear a groove in the floor."

Cole smiled, shook his head, and went back to work. But every time he reached for a new piece of fruit, he found himself listening for the sound of a sewing machine, or the clatter of pins on a hard surface. The silence made him uneasy.

From the constable's office, Jen had the best view. Her desk faced the square directly, and her eyes—sharp as winter, bright as cut stone —could catch a lie or a truth at three blocks' distance. She sat with her boots up on the battered sideboard, the old town ledger balanced on her lap, and watched the tailor's shop with the air of a predator in no particular hurry.

She knew Prudence, had known her kind in every town from Holderdown to the river at Lapis. She'd seen what happened when people like that didn't have a way to change, or to make the world fit them for a change. She'd seen worse, too, but rarely better.

She rubbed the edge of the silver bracelet at her wrist—a nervous habit she'd picked up in youth, back before the metal had first curled itself around her arm and named itself Hellsting. The cold of it was grounding.

Midday came and went. The tailor's shop remained silent.

Jen let the day pass, but as dusk approached, she found herself getting up more often than usual. She'd pace to the window, watch for a sign, then return to the ledger as if the interruption hadn't happened. By the time the sun dipped below the roofs, she'd convinced herself there was nothing wrong, but she also left her boots laced, her sword balanced on the chair at hand.

Just in case.

When the bells of evening rang, the usual knot of townsfolk gathered outside Bartram's shop, the warmth of his lamps and the smell of cinnamon bread drawing them together. Makota came with her kits, ears pricked and faces flushed from the bakery's fire. Cole arrived, arms empty but eyes a little worried. Even Jen, who had no fondness for group affairs, appeared just outside the stoop, standing with her arms folded and her mouth set in a line of curiosity.

Bartram opened the door and ushered them in. The room was filled with the golden light of three oil lamps, the workbenches swept clean, and a plate of scones on the main table. He poured mugs of tea with a practiced hand, and though he didn't say so, everyone understood why they were there.

"She's been in since first bell," Makota said, licking a paw to clear flour from her nose. "Hasn't left. Hasn't so much as tapped on the glass."

Cole nodded. "Left the boy with us for the day. Didn't want him underfoot, I guess. But even when she's working hard, she usually comes out for a bite."

Bartram smiled, wide and calming. "Sometimes you need a day. Especially after a hard season."

Jen snorted. "You don't hole up like that unless you're brewing something." Her gaze found Bartram's, and she tipped her chin in silent challenge. "What do you think she's making?"

Bartram considered. "If I had to guess? She's making herself. Properly, this time."

Makota's tail lashed behind her, and one of the kits mimicked the movement, nearly knocking over a cup. She caught it, then fixed her eyes on Bartram. "Should we check on her? Bring something?"

Bartram shook his head. "Give her the night. The kind of work she's doing, you don't want to interrupt. She needs to come out on her own terms."

There was a murmur of assent, reluctant but sincere. The group fell to talking about other things: the early frost, the price of dried fish, how Galhani's new blend of tea was supposedly strong enough to "wake the dead and keep them from napping." But through it all, the eyes of the room returned, again and again, to the square outside, and the single, steady light that now burned in the tailor's front window.

When the meeting broke, Jen lingered in the lamplight just long enough to drain her mug, then made her way back across the square. She paused, as she'd promised herself she wouldn't, outside the tailor's shop. She watched the blue glow from the window, the faint motion of a shadow at work, and allowed herself a private grin.

"Take your time, Pru," she muttered, voice gravelly and kind. "We're not going anywhere."

She patted the hilt of Hellsting, feeling the comfort of steel at her side, then turned her face to the cold and vanished down the lane.

The shop's light burned steady all through the night, and if anyone happened by, they would have seen it: the shape of a woman at her work, tireless, unbowed, and becoming more herself with every stroke of the needle.

———

At dawn, the frost returned—thin and fine, dusting every blade of grass and wood shingle in the square. Prudence woke on the work-room floor, arms folded beneath her head, the dress she'd finished draped over the stool beside her like a flag. The lamp had burned out, but the windows were brightening with the slow, inevitable promise of day.

She rose, stiff at first, then lighter. She shrugged off the old shift, pulled the new dress over her head, and felt the chill of morning seep into the fine fabric. It settled around her like a second skin—familiar, but completely new.

The mirror in the back room was small and slightly warped, but it told enough of the truth. The blue panels fit close at the waist, then spilled into a sweep of green, hemmed in gold. Her hands shook a little as she buttoned the cuffs—there, where she had stitched the white thread in its hidden circle. The collar sat high, and the embroidery caught the morning light. She let her hair fall loose for once, then took a single ribbon—blue—and tied it above her left ear.

She stood a moment longer, adjusting the fall of the skirt, the set of the shoulder. Then she stepped out into the hall, and the world.

The door opened with a sound she had never heard before: not the usual creak, but a soft, welcoming sigh. The square was empty, but she felt the attention of the houses, the shops, the lives inside them—waiting, in some way, for her to arrive.

She walked across the green, the hem of the dress brushing frost from the grass, leaving a line of bright color in her wake. The bakery was already awake; she caught the scent of sugar and yeast, and the faint sound of Makota's voice, sharp and cheerful, over the rumble of the oven.

At Cole's, she saw him through the window, setting up crates for the morning delivery. When he looked up and saw her, his face lit, and he dropped the apples—three, bouncing and rolling across the floor—before hurrying to the door.

"Prudence!" he called, grinning so wide it nearly broke his face. "You look—"

She lifted her chin, smiled with the confidence of someone who knew her own worth. "Like myself?" she said.

Cole laughed, loud and delighted. "That, exactly. A seamstress who outfits people for who they will be, not just who they are." He glanced down at her dress, then shook his head, awed. "You've outdone yourself."

Makota appeared in the doorway next, flour dusting her nose, her kits trailing behind her. She took in the dress with a slow, appreciative look, her tail curling behind her. "It suits you," she said, voice soft for once. "Really."

One of the kits whispered, "She looks like a story," and Makota's ears flicked in silent agreement.

Prudence accepted a basket of apples from Cole, then made her way to the back, where Bryant was waiting, hair wild and eyes wide. He saw her and ran at once, owlcat clinging to his shoulder, and wrapped himself around her waist. "You did it," he said, muffled in the fabric. "You made the best one."

She ruffled his hair. "It's for both of us," she said. "To show we belong here."

On the way back through the square, she saw Jen, leaning in the doorway of the constable's office, arms folded and eyes sharp as ever. The silver at her wrist caught the sun, and she nodded once, a soldier's salute, as Prudence passed.

Bartram stood outside his own shop, one foot up on the stoop, a mug of tea steaming in the chill. He raised it in greeting, his eyes warm and knowing. "You've set a new standard," he said, voice pitched just for her. "People will talk."

"Let them," Prudence replied, and the two shared a rare, companionable smile.

She walked on, Bryant's hand tucked in hers, and everywhere she went people stopped what they were doing: a cartman paused in his loading, a group of children clustered by the fountain. Even the old cat that lived by the butcher's watched her, its yellow eyes bright with curiosity.

Even old Knodalon, at his bench even at this early time, took notice. He sat a little straighter as an errant wind tousled his shock of white hair. A smile played at the corner of his lips, and he gave Prudence a slow, deep nod that warmed something deep in her soul.

She felt all the attention—not as a weight, but as a kind of wind at her back, lifting her, carrying her forward.

By the time she reached her shop again, the square was alive with the start of the day. Neighbors greeted her in passing, and several came to the window to watch as she unlocked the door and swept inside.

She left the dress on for the whole of the day, working at the counter, answering questions, pinning new patterns to the wall. When customers came in, they lingered, touched the sleeve or the edge of the collar, and left with their own ideas of possibility.

As the sun climbed, the colors in the shop shifted and grew—blue deepening, green warming, the gold bright as fire. Bryant played on the floor, his owlcat dozing on the windowsill, and every so often he would look up and watch her, his face open and proud.

Near midday, Jen stopped in for a word, then Makota, then even Bartram, each finding some reason to check on her. The visits were brief, but each brought a gift: a scrap of news, a new idea, or simply a nod that meant, *You did it.*

Prudence took the compliments with a grace that felt new. She watched the shop fill with people, then watched them carry the color out into the square, the streets, the world beyond.

By dusk, she was tired, but not in the old way. She stood in the center of the shop, hands on hips, and let the last light of day settle around her. Bryant came to her side, small fingers finding hers, and together they looked at the work they'd made.

"It's different now," Bryant said, voice low. "Everything."

Prudence nodded, and felt, at last, that she believed it.

The bell over the door chimed as a new customer arrived, and Prudence turned, ready, her dress alive with the promise of all the things still left to make.

twenty-four

. . .

THE BELL over the door chimed, and Prudence lifted her head from the worktable, fingers splayed over a length of raw silk the color of a perfect egg. She waited, but no customer entered. Just the draft, wriggling in from beneath the lintel, carrying a tang of woodsmoke and the sharper edge of spring. She listened, poised, and heard nothing more. Bryant, bent over his figures on the rug, looked up and shrugged as if to say: It's just a bell, mother, not a summons.

But Prudence stood anyway, smoothing her skirt—a swirling wash of blue and green, stitched through at the seams with ribbons of yellow so bright they startled her every time she caught them in the mirror—and wiped her hands on the apron. The fabric shop was not yet open, strictly speaking, but she doubted anyone in North Pointe would fault her for a moment's neglect. Even so, she moved quickly, glancing once at the little clock on the wall, then at the stack of work queued on the cutting bench.

There was an order to her mornings, a precise rhythm she'd trained herself to follow in the months since she'd allowed the color back into her life. First, wake and feed Bryant. Second, check the shop for damage—moths, spilled thread, the inexplicable mischief of the owlcat, which now snoozed in a tight comma by the stove. Third, take inventory of the day's projects. Only then, when the world was in its rightful place, could she allow herself the luxury of uncertainty.

Today, the uncertainty was deliberate.

She climbed the stairs two at a time, skirt flaring with every step, and entered the little attic room that had once served as Bryant's nursery. Now, it was a closet of sorts: packed, wall to wall, with the artifacts of her former life. Black dresses, two dozen at least, pressed into the tiny wardrobe until they warped the doors. Black bonnets, black gloves, black ribbed stockings. All arranged in perfect, grim order, relics from Holderdown and the years spent doing everything exactly as her mother had taught.

Prudence stepped into the room, closing the door behind her. For a moment she did nothing, just let her eyes adjust to the dark. The memory of that old life pressed in on her, heavy and close—a shroud with a hundred fastenings.

She reached for the first dress: wool, dyed a true midnight, with a high collar and darts so severe they could have cut bread. She hesitated, then pulled it from its hanger and laid it, folded, on the narrow cot that lined the far wall. Next, a cotton with black lace at the cuffs. Then a shift, thick and serviceable, meant for winters so cold the air cracked. One by one, she gathered them, arms growing heavy under the accumulation. Each dress surrendered with the tiniest resistance, a final twitch of the shoulder or sleeve before it collapsed in her grip.

When the wardrobe was empty, Prudence paused. She looked down at the bundle in her arms, a crumpled monument to another world, and let herself remember—for just a moment—the reason she had needed so much black in the first place.

Then she squared her shoulders, tucked the pile tighter under her arm, and opened the door.

Bryant was waiting at the bottom of the stairs, one hand resting on the newel post, the other clutching his favorite wooden figure—the one Prudence had carved to look like a hero from the border stories. He tilted his head as she descended, eyes narrowing as he took in the old dresses.

"You're not going to wear those again," he said, voice certain.

Prudence smiled, but not in the patronizing way her own mother would have. "No," she said. "We're saying goodbye to them."

He accepted this. "Forever?"

"Yes," she replied. "Forever."

Bryant nodded, grave as a judge, and padded to the door. Moss the owlcat roused at the sound, blinked once, then tucked its nose back under its tail.

Outside, the square was flooded with morning sun. The grass, impossibly green after so much gray, glittered with last night's dew. Shops were only just waking: the bakery's windows steamed with warmth and promise, the tea shop's signboard propped at a rakish angle. The world smelled of yeast, and loam, and the faint metallic edge of the forge at the east end.

Prudence stepped out into it, the armful of dresses sagging a little under its own weight, and felt the square shift to accommodate her. Several neighbors, mid-errand, turned to look. Makota, brushing the stoop of the bakery, froze mid-sweep. Jen, from the constable's window, tracked her progress with a steady, amused gaze. Even Bartram, always the diplomat, managed a smile as he unloaded boxes of new stock from his cart. The attention was not hostile; it was, rather, the curiosity of a town waiting to see what the future would look like when it finally arrived.

She crossed the square, Bryant at her side, their shadows stretched long and true across the flagstones. The morning was still enough that she could hear her own heart beating, could feel the eyes on her back with every step. She didn't mind it. The blue at her hem caught the sun, flashed it, threw it into the faces of everyone who had ever doubted she would be able to change.

At the far side of the green, the smithy loomed: half-cave, half-castle, the walls as thick as a handspan and streaked with soot from centuries of fires. Inside, the sound of hammer on anvil rang out, rhythmic and sure, underscoring the fact that someone in this world still believed in the making and remaking of things.

She stopped outside the forge, the heat of it radiating through the open doors. Bryant hesitated at the threshold, unwilling to step inside until he was certain the noise would not swallow him whole.

Prudence waited a beat, then called into the smoke and shadows: "Warren? It's Prudence."

The hammer paused, then thudded onto wood. A great green shape emerged from the haze, ducking beneath the low lintel with practiced ease. Warren's hair, white as salt, caught the light in a halo; his eyes, almost golden, glittered with welcome. He wiped his brow, then grinned—a wide, gentle expression that transformed his face from ogre to neighbor in a breath.

"Prudence!" he boomed, then, softer, "And young Master Bryant. What brings you to my den of iniquity?"

She held up the bundle. "I need a favor," she said. "A special kind of fire."

Warren nodded, understanding at once. He stepped aside, gesturing them into the warm, iron-rich air of the smithy. Bryant squeezed her hand tight, but followed, his other hand gripping the figure with white-knuckled determination.

Inside, the world was orange and red and black: coals banked in the great pit, tools hanging from pegs, half-finished works glinting on the benches. Prudence set the pile of dresses on a clean section of the counter, then stood back, letting the heat work its way into her bones.

Warren approached, towering but careful, his hands as big as oven mitts and twice as capable. He looked at the black dresses, then at Prudence, then at Bryant, who watched him with the wary awe reserved for things that might, at any moment, become stories.

"Will you burn them?" she asked, the words almost lost in the crackle of the fire.

Warren considered. "You want them gone?"

"Yes. Not just disposed of. Gone. Like… like a spell."

He smiled, showing the smallest chip in one tusk, the badge of a life lived full. "We can do that," he said. "But we'll have to do it right."

He set to work at once, shoveling fresh coals into the forge, working the bellows until the fire blazed hot and blue at the heart. The noise was tremendous, but Bryant stayed, transfixed, as Warren explained each step: how the heat must be even, how the draft must not waver, how a forge was not just a place to shape steel but a place to unmake it, too.

When the fire was ready, Warren turned to Prudence. "Would you like to do the honors?"

She hesitated, then nodded. With both hands, she lifted the top dress—a simple shift, the one she had worn on her first day in North Pointe—and held it out over the coals. The heat licked at her knuckles, but she did not flinch. Instead, she thought of her mother's voice, sharp as vinegar, and the rules that had governed her life for so long. She thought of the black days and the gray nights, and the way the world had once seemed so narrow, so final.

Then she let go.

The dress caught at once, flame racing up the sleeve and down the hem, swallowing the darkness in an instant. The smoke billowed, fragrant with the memory of a thousand careful washings, and then was gone.

One by one, she fed the dresses to the fire. Each caught, each vanished. Bryant watched, eyes wide, and Warren stood at her side, silent and solid, a witness to the ritual.

When it was done, Prudence felt lighter. Not in the way of a woman shedding weight, but in the way of a woman setting down the last of what she did not need.

She turned to Warren, who nodded, and to Bryant, who smiled—a real, gap-toothed smile, full of relief.

They stood together in the warmth, watching the last of the black curl away to nothing.

Outside, the square had changed. The sun was higher, the grass brighter, the faces of the town less guarded. Prudence led Bryant back out into it, the blue of her dress blazing in the new light.

She knew there would be days when the world tried to make her old again, tried to coax her back into a narrower life. But today, she had done what she came to do.

And tomorrow, she would wear whatever color she liked.

———

The smoke lingered, blue-white and sharp in the cold air, as Prudence gathered herself. She pressed her hand to her sternum, feeling the hammer of her heart, and blinked the sting from her eyes. It was not just the heat or the scent of char—it was the way Warren had stood beside her in silence, the way Bryant had watched with solemn attention, the way the town itself seemed to hold its breath, waiting for her to finish.

She was still standing by the forge, one foot braced on the threshold, when the first of the townsfolk arrived. Galhani, her gnome head barely clearing the windowsill, nudged the smithy door open with her shoulder and entered, both hands wrapped around a squat ceramic pot. The heat of the fire flushed her cheeks pink as she placed the pot on the nearest table.

"I brought tea," she said, by way of greeting, her voice as bright and sharp as her hair. "For after. Or for before. Or for whenever the world seems too much."

Prudence tried to thank her, but the words wouldn't form. She just nodded, accepting the cup Galhani pressed into her hand. The flavor was new: sage and citrus, something herbal beneath it, the sort of taste that could clear the mind and settle the nerves in one sip.

Next came Bartram, grinning even wider than usual, with a loaf of bread cradled in his arms as if it were a baby or a miracle. He took in the scene—the smoldering pile, Prudence's face, the forge's glow—and wordlessly broke the bread in half, offering a still-warm section to Bryant. The boy accepted it, tearing a chunk free and stuffing it into his mouth with a ferocity that would have scandalized his grandmother.

Bartram winked at Prudence, then fanned himself with a spare napkin. "Quite a show," he said. "You always did have a flare for the dramatic, Pru."

She tried to muster a retort, but found herself laughing instead, the sound caught somewhere between surprise and relief. Bryant joined in, bits of bread dusting his chin and shirt, and even Galhani's lips twitched with a private joke.

Jen was the next to arrive, moving with her usual economy—boots silent, coat drawn tight, sword nowhere in sight but never far. She glanced at Prudence, then at the forge, then at the others. After a pause, she dug in her coat pocket and produced a narrow box, wrapped in red paper and tied with a knot of gold cord.

"From the constable's office," she said, with the air of someone explaining the weather. "We usually reserve these for town anniversaries, but today seemed important."

She handed the box to Prudence, who turned it over, mystified. The ribbon fell away with a tug, and inside was a single length of silk, the color of a summer sky, with a gold pin at one end.

"It's for your hair," Jen said, almost sheepish. "Or your collar, if you'd rather."

Prudence touched the silk, feeling its softness, its impossible lightness. The color nearly matched the ribbon she already wore, but brighter, more daring. She smiled at Jen, a real smile, and Jen nodded once, pleased to have been understood.

Makota arrived last, her two kits in tow, each clutching a wild bouquet of something—dandelions and violets and the pale, sharp leaves of the new season's green. She knelt beside Bryant and, with the gentleness of a born mother, wove the flowers into a ring and placed it on his head. Bryant, solemn with the importance of the moment, wore it without protest, and for the first time looked not like a child playing at king, but like a prince at his own coronation.

Prudence watched all of this unfold—the gifts, the laughter, the easy intimacy of people who had chosen each other—and felt the tears finally come, unbidden and impossible to hide.

Warren, seeing her struggle, put a massive hand on her shoulder. "OGRE EAT SADNESS?" he roared, then, in a softer tone: "You've done good, Pru. You've done real good."

Galhani, never one for patience, clapped her hands. "Is it over? The burning?"

Prudence nodded, still blinking.

"Then let's move it along," the gnome said, bustling toward the door. "There's food, and tea, and company enough to start a war—or at least a party."

Warren announced, in his formal smith-voice, "The purification is complete!" His words rang through the smithy, echoing out into the square.

The crowd, small at first, grew as the group made its way from the forge to the green. Word had traveled—quick as rumor, as slow as trust—that something new was happening in North Pointe. By the time Prudence and the others reached the center of the square, tables had already been set: long planks balanced on crates, covered with linens and ringed with benches. The butcher had brought meats, glistening and savory; the bakery's pastries, arranged in spirals and towers, steamed with honey and spice. Even Leota, the town's most enigmatic presence, had come down from her cottage, a tray of tiny glass bottles balanced on one arm.

The morning sun, higher now, painted everything in impossible color.

Bryant dashed to join a knot of children near the fountain, the flower ring bouncing on his head, arms raised as if to gather all the light in the world. Prudence let him go, feeling for the first time that she was not letting go at all, but releasing something that had always belonged to the air.

The townsfolk came forward, each in their own way. Some offered quiet words, some just a nod or a squeeze of her hand. Others, like Bartram, made a show of it—clapping her on the back, extolling her bravery, making jokes about the new uniform of the town's premier seamstress. Even Jen allowed herself a moment of unguarded warmth, holding Prudence's gaze long enough to communicate everything she could not, or would not, say aloud.

Leota approached last, her step measured, her eyes—dark and unguessable—fixed on Prudence's. She held out a bottle of cordial, the liquid inside a deep, improbable blue.

"For courage," Leota said. "Or for memory. Take your pick."

Prudence accepted it, unscrewed the cap, and took a sip. The flavor was bright and dizzying, equal parts summer and night. She coughed once, then grinned, surprised at how much it felt like flying.

"Thank you," she said.

Leota nodded. "You wore through the last of it, didn't you?"

Prudence blinked. "The black?"

Leota's smile was faint, but real. "The fear."

They stood together for a moment, watching the square fill. Bryant and the other children played a game that had no rules, only shouts and laughter and the occasional tumble across the grass. The adults settled at the tables, trading stories, eating, drinking, savoring the rare sense that a battle had been fought, and won, without anyone quite realizing it.

At the height of the feast, Warren stood, wiped his hands on his apron, and raised a mug. The entire square fell silent, as if someone had closed a book in the middle of a sentence.

"A toast," he bellowed, then, gentler: "To Prudence Simonsdotter. For showing us how to burn away what holds us back, and for having the courage to dress herself in what comes next."

Every cup, every plate, every crumb of bread was raised in her honor. The square echoed with the sound, a wave of joy that swept over her, buoyed her, made her feel—truly and deeply—that she belonged.

She stood, a little unsteady, and bowed her head. "Thank you," she said, not just to the crowd, but to the square, the sun, the town itself.

After the fourth bell, as the feast wound down and the tables began to empty, Prudence lingered on the steps of her shop, hands folded in her lap, eyes closed to better hear the world. The sun was warm on her face, the taste of Leota's cordial lingering on her tongue. She listened to the children shriek and dart between the benches, to the hum of conversation, to the quiet, persistent heartbeat of the town she now called her own.

She looked down at her dress—the blue, the green, the gold at the hem—and felt, for the first time, that it was more than just a statement. It was a story, a history, a promise to herself and to Bryant and to everyone who might one day need to remember that change was not just possible, but necessary.

She watched as Bryant, his face alight, led a parade of children around the square, each trailing a ribbon or a scrap of color torn from the leftovers of her shop. They looked, in the afternoon sun, like a flock of impossible birds, each winged with hope and mischief.

Prudence smiled, and let herself imagine what else she might become.

When the fourth bell struck, the square fell briefly silent, the echo holding everyone in a moment of perfect, golden light. Bryant turned to her, arms outstretched, and she met him in the middle of the green, her steps light, her heart lighter.

The celebration carried on into the dusk, and if anyone thought to comment on the strangeness of it—the way a single woman's choice had rippled through every part of the town—they kept it to themselves.

By nightfall, the square was empty save for a few scraps of ribbon, the fading scent of bread, and the memory of laughter.

Prudence closed her shop, tucked Bryant into bed, and sat by the window as the stars came out, one by one. She wore the new ribbon in her hair, and it glowed, faintly, in the lamplight.

She did not know what tomorrow would bring. But tonight, she felt ready for anything.

———

The next morning, Prudence woke with the sun, not because she had to, but because the light found her where she slept, and she saw no reason to fight it. She lay for a while, listening to Bryant's slow, even breaths in the next room, the soft patter of the owlcat's feet as it circled for a warm place to curl. There was no weight in her chest, no sense of old alarms tripping her awake. Only the pale gold of the early light, and the promise of a new day.

She rose, stretched, and padded to the window. The town was still, but not silent; there was a rhythm to the morning—a single wagon creaking up the green, the whistle of a kettle from the bakery, the gentle thud of bread set down on a doorstep. The square, empty of last night's celebration, looked both the same and entirely different.

Prudence dressed without thought, reaching for the blue-and-green, the gold-threaded hem, the new ribbon that still smelled faintly of the cordial Leota had given her. It felt like wearing a story—her own, at last. She gathered her hair, pinned it high, and found that the mirror no longer startled her. The face there was sharp, clear, and at ease.

In the kitchen, Bryant was already awake, perched on a chair with his feet drawn up under him, reading by the light that spilled over the table. He wore his flower crown from the day before, a little wilted but no less glorious. He looked up as Prudence entered and smiled, showing every gap in his teeth.

"Is it a work day?" he asked, just as he had the morning before.

"Every day is," Prudence answered, her voice calm and content.

She set about making breakfast—honey on bread, tea still hot in the pot from last night. The routine was the same, but it felt new. Bryant recited facts about birds and colors and what might happen if you crossed an owlcat with a horse. Prudence listened, answered when she could, and let the rest drift over her like music.

When they finished eating, Bryant darted outside to the green, intent on some expedition with the other children. Prudence watched him go, the flower crown bobbing behind him, and felt no fear—only gratitude.

She cleaned up the kitchen, then opened the door to her shop. The bell chimed, not the brittle tinkle of obligation, but the clear, honest note of invitation. She stood for a while behind the counter, looking at the shelves: blues and golds, pinks and greens, the ghosts of the old black and gray now fully banished. The fabric caught the light, shimmered, beckoned.

She spent the morning finishing a commission for Makota's youngest, a dress in purple and yellow that defied every rule of her upbringing. She worked fast and true, hands steady, the machine purring along as if it, too, had shed some secret heaviness.

Midmorning brought the first visitor: Bartram, with a pair of boots that needed mending. He eyed her dress, then her smile, and grinned as if seeing a secret confirmed. They exchanged pleasantries; he left with a story about the best-dressed woman in town.

Other neighbors followed: Cole with an order for tablecloths, Jen with a joke and a request for a new scarf, Galhani with a pouch of tea and a wink that said everything. Even Leota stopped by, this time with nothing to sell and no riddles to trade—just a nod and a brief, "You look well."

At noon, Prudence paused. She set her tools aside, stepped into the sunlight, and looked out over the green. Bryant was there, at the center of a game, his voice rising above the rest. Prudence listened, then smiled, and let the joy of the day fill her up, warm and sweet.

She went back inside, tidied her space, and set the next project on the table. As she worked, she sang—not the hymns of her childhood, but something lighter, borrowed from the market or the bakery or the lullabies she'd made up for Bryant when he was small.

It was late afternoon when Bryant returned, cheeks flushed, flower crown askew. He barreled into the shop, arms wide, and hugged Prudence around the waist.

"I won," he said, breathless.

"Of course you did," Prudence replied, and tousled his hair.

They locked the door together at dusk, the day's work done, the world at peace. Prudence lit the lamps, watched the colors come alive, and felt, at last, that she was fully herself.

She drew Bryant into her lap, held him as the sun slipped behind the roofs, and let herself dream of what tomorrow might bring. The shop glowed in the dusk, and outside, the town square waited—quiet, bright, and filled with possibility.

epilogue

. . .

THE NEXT MORNING arrived with all the subtlety of a marching band, and for once, Prudence let it. She stood in her shop with the door flung wide to the green, sun spooling out across the lintel, pouring over the floorboards and scattering itself across every inch of cloth and table and unfinished order. The air was crisp but warm, a promise of spring, and Prudence wore it like a new shawl—draped, deliberate, open.

The view from the threshold was different now: where once the heavy door had acted as a fortress, now it was a bridge. The green outside was lively with neighbors and travelers, the bakery already humming, children weaving their way between carts and benches. Prudence saw it all as she worked, her eye flicking up now and again to catch the movement on the square, the flash of a familiar silhouette, or a gust that blew the bright pennants of her window display out into the breeze.

The shop itself had transformed. The racks, which she'd built with her own hands from the remnants of old shelving and the skeleton of a prior owner's armoire, now lined the walls in neat, riotous order. Every color she had ever denied herself was represented there, from the piercing indigoes to the lush, wet greens, to the buttery yellows that had, for so long, seemed forbidden. Prudence let her hands pass over them as she moved, fingers brushing each with a kind of greeting, a daily reminder of the freedom she'd claimed.

There was a customer at the counter—a traveler, judging by the hard lines of his coat and the dust at his cuffs. He stood awkwardly, not sure if he was permitted to touch, but his eyes drank in the color as if he'd crossed a desert to reach it.

Prudence finished a seam, clipped the thread, and laid the shirt flat on the table before stepping up to the front. "You said you wanted something for the road," she said, her voice neither shy nor hard, but clean and sure as the thread in her needle. "Will you be northbound, or east?"

He hesitated. "East, ma'am. All the way to the coast, if I can make it."

She studied him a moment, sizing him up—not just for fit, but for story. "The wind off the lake is colder than it looks," she said. "You'll need a collar that keeps the weather out, but not so tight you can't breathe."

The traveler nodded, grateful for the guidance. "I'm not used to… all this." He gestured to the racks, and Prudence saw the flicker of embarrassment in his face. "The last place I bought a shirt, it was just gray, or gray with a stripe if you had money."

She smiled, quick and real. "You'll find the world's less gray here. I'd recommend the blue—makes a man look honest, even when he's not."

He grinned, and the line of his shoulders softened.

Prudence reached for the bolt in question, but the fabric had already slid forward on the rack, as if eager to be chosen. She didn't question it; the shop had always had its small, helpful magic, but lately it had grown bolder, more willing to show its hand. She cut a length, laid it beside the traveler's arm, and watched as the color made the sallow of his skin look healthier, the tiredness of his eyes less desperate.

"Excellent," she said, and her hands moved without hesitation, measuring, marking, pinning. The pin-cushion on the table rotated, presenting exactly the right size and length every time she reached for it. The scissors, when she set them down, never rolled or clattered—always exactly where she needed them.

She worked as the man watched, talking as she went: "You'll want the cuffs a little loose, for layering. The back needs a vent, or you'll sweat through it before noon. And a hidden pocket here, yes? For a map or coin." Each word was matched by a motion, and the fabric seemed to respond—stiffening or relaxing under her touch, aligning itself to her will.

He laughed, amazed. "You make it look easy."

Prudence shrugged, smoothing the new seam. "It's easier now, somehow. The shop knows what to do, if I let it."

He caught the statement, blinked, then nodded in solemn understanding. "You're like the baker in Valisport, aren't you? My mother said she could tell your whole future in a pie, if you let her pick the filling."

Prudence pressed the collar, then added two lines of golden thread at the edge—just enough to catch the light. "Maybe so," she replied. "But I promise, whatever your future is, it'll look better in this."

She had the shirt finished before the bell for second breakfast, a feat that once would have left her breathless and strained, but now felt like merely the natural unfolding of the day. She fitted it to the traveler's shoulders, adjusted the buttons, then stepped back, arms folded, waiting.

He stood taller. The blue made his eyes sharper, the gold at the collar gave him an air of confidence, maybe even purpose. He paid, not just with coin, but with a grateful handshake, the kind given between equals.

Prudence watched him go, the blue of the shirt trailing a comet-tail of approval from every window he passed.

She turned back to her workbench, where the rest of the day's projects waited: a coat for the constable's new apprentice, a dress for one of Makota's kits, a dozen repairs and re-dyeings for the town's growing population. The bench was neat, the machine clean and oiled, the spools of thread lined up like a chorus. As she sat, her posture was different now—no longer hunched or guarded, but upright, relaxed, a woman who had made her peace with being seen.

Outside, the square was alive with light and motion, but inside, it was all order and clarity. Prudence let herself enjoy it, just for a moment, before setting her needle to work again.

The day went on, and the door stayed open, and the shop—her shop—welcomed every moment of it.

———

The morning wore on, and with it came the rise and fall of voices from the green outside—a living chorus that pulled at Prudence's attention, even as her needle danced through the latest hem. She heard Bryant before she saw him, his laugh carrying above the others, bright and sharp as the cry of a jay. It was a sound she had, for so long, guarded against—waiting for it to turn to wailing, or for it to be silenced by an older, louder world. Now it just existed, unburdened, a song with no shadow.

She stepped to the door, the shop's warmth trailing after her like a friendly hand. On the green, Bryant was locked in a tug-of-war over a wooden wheelbarrow, flanked by three other children: one with a mop of red hair and a smudge of soot on his cheek, one so pale and fine-boned she might have been made of spun sugar, and one—this, Prudence still found charming—whose ears and tail flicked with every change in mood.

Bryant gave no sign of noticing the differences. He laughed with the red-haired boy, argued strategy with the girl, and tried—unsuccessfully—to outwit the Felis kit, whose sly grin suggested she had planned the whole ambush. They played without regard for time or season, just a tumble of limbs and color and noise.

Prudence watched, her hands at rest for once. She noticed the flush of Bryant's cheeks, the healthy pink at his knuckles, the way his hair had grown in thicker since the winter. The town's slow-magic—its gentle undoing of illness and hunger, its way of making children shine —was doing its work. It showed in the straightness of Bryant's back, in the ease with which he ran, in the confidence with which he faced down his adversaries, no matter their species or size.

The game shifted—now they were building, not battling. The

wheelbarrow became a wagon, the sticks and stones a fortress, and Bryant, somehow, had become the captain. He knelt in the center of the construction, directing the others with a series of hand gestures and rapid-fire instructions. The Felis kit saluted; the red-haired boy rolled his eyes but complied; the girl found the best rocks and stacked them, careful and proud.

A year ago, Prudence would have worried. She would have wondered if Bryant knew he was different, if he felt the press of expectations, the invisible walls of what her own mother had called "propriety." She would have watched for the moment when the other children closed ranks, or when Bryant's own voice faltered in the face of their difference.

But there was none of that here. Only the joy of play, and the equality of children who had, in their own ways, been made new by this place.

Prudence felt a pang—not sorrow, but a kind of sweet ache. She remembered her own childhood, the careful lines drawn between families, between races, between the hundred categories that had once governed every relationship. She remembered the warnings, the rules, the way color had been something to hide or to tolerate, but never to seek out.

She watched as Bryant offered a hand to the Felis kit, helping her balance a particularly heavy stick atop their fortress. The gesture was easy, unthinking. She watched as the other children accepted him, not as an outsider, but as a necessary part of the game.

It struck her then, with the force of a bell: Bryant would never have to unlearn what she had spent half a lifetime unlearning. He would not carry her mother's voice in his head. He would not look at the world and see only the borders.

The gratitude was overwhelming. Prudence felt it in her fingertips, in her lungs, in the warmth that spread through her chest as she watched her son kneel in the center of his new world, a world she had made for him but could never have fully imagined.

The game ended in a collapse—sticks tumbling, children shrieking, laughter rolling out in waves that reached even the farthest stoops of the square. Bryant dusted himself off, looked up, and caught his mother's eye. He waved, grinning, and she waved back, not caring who saw.

She turned from the door, feeling lighter than she had in years. The shop waited, full of color and work and promise. The green outside was alive, and so was she.

She let herself stand in the sun for a minute longer, just breathing, before returning to her needle and thread.

The day's rhythm was punctuated by the comings and goings of neighbors—some with purpose, some only with the thin excuse of needing a button or a snippet of ribbon, but all of them drawn to the open shop and the scent of fresh, dyed cloth that drifted out onto the square.

The bell above the door announced the first proper customer after the traveler: Dardrad the butcher, dwarvish face ruddy from the cold, arms loaded down with a linen-wrapped parcel of cured meats and a loaf of dark bread. He entered with his usual economy, stomping the dirt from his boots but wasting no time with further pleasantries.

"Morning, Simonsdotter," he rumbled, setting the parcel down on the counter. "Brought your order. And"—he jerked his chin at the window display—"saw the new jacket you made for that blue-blood from Endicott. Never thought to see a man wear a collar like that and still look fit to lift a barrel."

Prudence grinned, hands still busy at the worktable. "He'll need it, if the weather turns. The old ones wore wool, but this is lined with rabbit and stitched so the wind can't find its way in."

Dardrad eyed her a moment, then nodded, conceding the point. He ran a hand over his beard, then reached for a scrap of jerky sticking from the end of the bundle. "You take care of him better than I do some days."

Prudence set her needle aside, dusted her palms, and came to inspect the meats. She ran her fingers over the packaging, noting the neatness of the tie and the care in the label. "Yours looks better every season, Dardrad. I'll say as much to anyone who asks."

He gave a gruff laugh, then looked over her shoulder at the rows of fabric. "You going to make anything for yourself, this season? Or just for the rest of us?"

Prudence shrugged, but it was a comfortable motion, not a dismissal. "Might try something with the new green. Makota says it's the color of a spring leaf, but I think it's closer to fresh moss."

"Spring's too subtle," Dardrad said, shaking his head. "You should go for gold."

"I'll think about it," Prudence replied, and there was genuine pleasure in her voice. She wrapped the cured meats in a square of the butcher's own waxed paper, then tucked them behind the counter for lunch. "Thanks for bringing it."

He offered a final nod, then turned to the door, his boots heavy on the boards. "You keep the colors coming, Simonsdotter. Makes the square look honest, for once."

Prudence laughed as he left, the door closing behind him with a pleasant thump.

The shop was quiet for all of three minutes before another visitor arrived—Makota, the Felis baker, her fur gleaming in the sun, a basket of pastries balanced perfectly in one arm. She slipped inside, nose twitching at the scent of cloth and spice, and set the basket on the bench with the casual grace of someone used to navigating tight spaces.

"Morning, Prudence!" she called, tail curling in a slow figure eight. "I come bearing bribes." She popped the lid of the basket, revealing a pile of sugar-dusted pastries, still steaming from the oven.

Prudence accepted the treat, biting in without hesitation. The flavor was bright, with a hint of lemon, and she chewed thoughtfully. "That's new."

Makota beamed, whiskers perked. "Thought I'd try something to go with the blue you're working on. Next batch will be even better. I added a pinch of poppy this time."

The two stood together, side by side at the table, trading bites and banter. Makota's hands, despite their feline cast, moved with a delicacy that matched Prudence's own, and before long they'd traded half the pastry for a new patch of sky-colored linen that Makota had been coveting since last sennight.

"I hear you outfitted the butcher," Makota said, eyeing the package behind the counter.

"He's got a taste for tradition," Prudence replied, "but I made the collar a little taller. He's vain about the scar on his neck, though he'd never admit it."

Makota's ears flicked, her smile a half-crescent of white. "Everyone's got a vanity. Some hide it better than others."

The bell sounded again. This time it was the traveler, back for his shirt and perhaps another round of admiration. He entered with a careful, tentative step—less hesitant than before, but still aware that he did not quite belong.

"Here for the pickup," he said, then blinked as he saw Makota and Prudence together. "Oh, sorry—should I come back?"

"Nonsense," Makota purred, waving him in. "You're just in time. Prudence was about to model her latest philosophy."

The traveler blinked, puzzled, but then spotted the shirt hanging in the front window. He moved toward it, hand outstretched, as if half-expecting it to vanish. He ran his fingers over the collar, then the golden trim, and held it up to the light. "Never had a shirt this fine," he admitted, turning it in his hands.

Makota sidled up beside him, tail swaying. "You look like a man who needs to make a good impression."

He laughed, but with less embarrassment than before. "Maybe. I think I just want to look like I know where I'm going."

Prudence finished the last stitch on her current project, then joined them. She glanced at the shirt, then at the man. "You'll find people listen to you more, if you dress for what you want instead of what you've always had."

The traveler nodded, rolling up the shirt and tucking it under his arm. "They say clothes make the man. But I never believed it until now."

Prudence shook her head, smiling. "Clothes don't make you. They just tell the story before your mouth can catch up."

Makota made a soft sound of agreement, and for a moment, the three of them stood in companionable silence, watching the light play through the window and over the bright new colors.

The traveler left, promising to send more business from the road. Makota lingered, helping herself to another pastry and surveying the latest bolts of fabric. "You really do belong here," she said at last, her voice softer than Prudence expected. "I don't think you know how much it matters."

Prudence started to reply, but Makota cut her off with a raised hand. "It matters," she repeated, then gathered her basket and glided to the door, leaving the scent of lemon and sugar in her wake.

Alone in the shop, Prudence found herself smiling for no reason at all. She wandered the room, running her fingers over the spools of thread, the finished pieces on the rack, the blue and green and gold that, together, made a new world from the old.

She stepped to the doorway, leaning out into the sun. Bryant was still on the green, now deep in conversation with the Felis kit from earlier. They gestured at the fortress they'd built, each pointing out the features they liked best.

Prudence watched them for a while, then closed her eyes, breathing deep the scent of new fabric and morning air.

When she opened them, she saw not the shop as it once was, but the place she had always hoped to make—a home, a beacon, a story stitched together from all the color the world could offer.

She stood there, in the doorway, and for the first time, felt no need to hide from it.

afterword

I'm very, very proud of this novel—perhaps more than most of the other books in the series, except maybe for *Pubs & Pegasi*. You see, Pru's backstory turned out to be mildly autobiographical: I grew up in a fairly quiet, withdrawn family. There were no contracted marriages, of course, but I very much grew up in a shell. Breaking out of that— exploring the brighter colors in the world—was pretty momentous for me. In fact, a friend once said, "you seem like the kind who eventually breaks out of his shell, and once you do, it'll shatter into a million pieces. No going back." They were right.

So I hope you've enjoyed Pru's story, and that you're looking forward to seeing her again in future novels. I'm off to work on Jen's story next, an equally momentous character for me, as she's deeply inspired by a friend from my distant past, one who pulled few verbal punches but always managed to land exactly where I needed at the time. *Laws & Leprechauns* should offer a bit more humor and a bit less melancholy than this novel did, but I think the story will have a pretty big heart as well.

And with that, I'd like to make you an offer or two, and a request or two:

First, please reach out and let me know what you think. You can email me at don (at) DonJones (dot) com, or contact me on my Facebook page, Facebook.com/donjoneswrites. I'd truly love to hear from you, and I promise I'll reply!

Second, would YOU like to visit North Pointe Common Towne for a novel? I love putting readers into my stories—the antagonist of *Anvils & Avatars* is a cousin who asked for a role. If so, reach out! We can work out who your character is and what they'll do in the next tale!

And the first request: Please leave a review of this novel on your favorite book store website. You might not know it, but their algorithms will bury a book like this, and the rest of the *Tales from the Broken Claw series*, unless honest reviews keep trickling in.

And if you've done that, why not "follow" me on their website as well? I have buttons on the home page of DonJones.com where you can follow me, and that'll let your favorite book website notify you when I have a new release. I mean, you could also join my newsletter —it's on the "Freebies" page of DonJones.com—but you do whatever you're most comfortable with. And thank you for doing so!

And I invite you to consider some of my other books, all listed at DonJones.com. While the others have a bit more conflict than this "cozy" story, I wouldn't categorize any of them as especially dark or dire. And they've got some truly wonderful people in them—ones I think you'll grow to love.

FINALLY… did you know the Broken Claw has a theme song? YUP. If you'd like to hear it, hit me up and I'll send you an MP3 file— it's original music and you're welcome to spread it far and wide.

All right, time to get back to work.

Don Jones

Nov 10th, 2025 • Duck Creek Village, UT

award-winning fiction

Daniel Scratch: a story of witchkind

- Kirkus Starred Review
- Winner, American Fiction Awards—Best Fantasy (2023)
- Finalist, American Legacy Book Awards—Best Fantasy (2024)

———

Clara Thorn, the witch that was found

- Winner, American Fiction Awards—Best Young Adult (2023)
- Runner-Up, American Fiction Awards—Best Fantasy (2023)
- Finalist, American Legacy Book Awards—Best Fantasy (2024)
- Finalist, American Legacy Book Awards—Best Young Adult (2024)

———

Find these books and more at DonJones.com

about the author

Don Jones spent two decades writing tech books before he finally penned his first sci-fi novella, *A History of the Galactic War*. His well-reviewed and award-winning novels span fantasy and science fiction, with a focus on world building and relatable characters.

Connect, get free novels and short stories, and learn about upcoming releases by visiting Don's author website at DonJones.com.

also by don jones

Find more at DonJones.com, including a free fantasy trilogy, a free superhero duology, two collections of short stories, and even more short stories and flash fiction.

Sign up for the author's newsletter at DonJones.com (click the "Freebies" link) for notifications of new novels, and ample opportunities to get free ebooks by becoming a beta reader!

www.ingramcontent.com/pod-product-compliance
Lightning Source LLC
Chambersburg PA
CBHW071209210726
48293CB00002B/356